P9-DZP-080

JOY FROM ASHES

JOY FROM ASHES

AL LACY

With the exception of recognized historical figures, the characters in this novel
are fictional. Any resemblance to actual persons, living or dead,
is purely coincidental.

JOY FROM ASHES

© 1995 by Lew A. Lacy

published by Multnomah Books
a part of the Questar publishing family

Edited by Rodney L. Morris
Cover design by David Uttley
Cover illustration by Sergio Martínez

International Standard Book Number: 0-88070-720-8

Printed in the United States of America.

ALL RIGHTS RESERVED

No part of this publication may be reproduced, stored in a retrieval system, or
transmitted in any form or by any means—electronic, mechanical, photocopy-
ing, recording, or otherwise—without prior written permission.

For information:
Questar Publishers, Inc.
Post Office Box 1720
Sisters, Oregon 97759

95 96 97 98 99 00 01 02 — 10 9 8 7 6 5 4 3 2 1

For April, Chris, Andy, Anna Laura, Sundi, and B.J.—
the GREATEST grandchildren in the
WHOLE WORLD!
What a joy to know that each of you has opened
your heart to Jesus!
Thank you for being such bright spots in my life.
I love all of you more than you will ever know.

✳

PROLOGUE

✦

When the controversy over States' Rights exploded into civil war on April 12, 1861 and the call for volunteers was sounded across the land, enlistment fever ran high. Yankees and Rebels alike feared that the war would end before they got a chance to fight. They had been charged by emotional oratory to expect a rush to the battlefield, a few days of excitement while killing men in the opposing army, and a triumphant, flag-waving return home.

Instead, the Civil War dragged on for weeks. The weeks turned into months, and the months into years. For every day they spent in actual battle, the soldiers of North and South passed weeks and sometimes months fighting such dull and unimaginative enemies as heat, cold, rain, snow, mud, dust, loneliness, homesickness, and irksome monotony. As one Yankee soldier put it, "War—except for the thrill of battle—is an organized bore."

Most of the men who volunteered for service did not seek to become professional soldiers. They were civilians who had temporarily answered the call to fight for their country. Few thought they might be killed in the fight. Their plan was to get the conflict over with and return to their normal lives. Yet over 600,000 of them would never see their homes again. Their bodies would lie in cold graves before the last shot in the awful, bloody war was fired. Hundreds of thousands would return home maimed, scarred, blinded, and missing limbs. What was supposed to be an exciting adventure altered their minds and bodies for the rest of their lives.

The recruits who answered the call of flag and country were no better prepared for the wearisome, everyday realities of military life than they were for the soul-shattering shock of mortal combat. Few of them had ever tasted army camp food or slept under the stars or in a thin canvas tent for months on end.

Neither were they prepared for the harsh realities of the crude medical treatment that awaited the sick and wounded, for the horrid task of burying their comrades, sometimes by the hundreds, in common graves, nor for the grim, rat-infested, disease-ridden prisons that would hold the prisoners-of-war. (The story that unfolds in this novel will take you into one of those horrendous prisons.)

On July 21, 1861, the Confederates routed the Union army under Brigadier General Irvin McDowell, causing great shame and embarrassment to President Abraham Lincoln. The Yankee stragglers from the Bull Run battlefield had hardly caught up with their regiments when Lincoln ordered Major General George B. McClellan to Washington.

McClellan, who had studied engineering at West Point and had served on the staff of General Winfield Scott in the Mexican War, seemed to be a military leader of great promise. He had gained the attention of the War Department and President Lincoln early in the Civil War when he led in routing the Confederates at Beverly, Philippi, Romney, Middle Creek, Laurel Hill, and Rich Mountain in western Virginia in June and early July. The thirty-five-year-old general of the Department of the Ohio had helped build a strong rampart of Union support in that area, which ultimately resulted in the formation of the state of West Virginia.

McClellan had an unusual ability to organize men. Under the watchful eyes of President Lincoln and the War Department, he introduced strict military discipline to the regiments of easy-going recruits placed under his command, and soon had them functioning as hard-line soldiers. His men loved and respected him. He was small of stature and slight of build, and was affectionately referred to (out of his hearing) as "Little Mac." His cocksure bearing and self-sufficiency also garnered him the title, "Young Napoleon."

Answering President Lincoln's call, General McClellan arrived in Washington on July 25, 1861, and on July 27 was placed in charge of the army that had been commanded by General McDowell. For the next fourteen months McClellan was to dominate Union military action in the Eastern Theater and to build a large, smooth-working army.

There were two major Union campaigns during General McClellan's tenure as field commander of the Army of the Potomac: the Peninsular campaign in Virginia in the spring of 1862 and the defense of Maryland against General Robert E. Lee's bold invasion in the early fall of that same year.

The first campaign was the result of McClellan's insistence that the best defense of Washington was the destruction of the Confederate army, which occupied the 105-mile space between the two capitals, Washington and Richmond. Though there were some victories won in the Peninsular campaign, it failed to destroy the Confederate forces that stood in the gap. Lincoln and the War Department blamed McClellan because he seemed reluctant to move his army swiftly enough against the Rebels. When the president and the secretary of war ordered McClellan to hasten his attack, they encountered a reluctance they could not comprehend.

The second campaign produced the bloodiest one-day battle of the entire Civil War. The battle at Antietam Creek, near Sharpsburg, Maryland, was a Union victory, but in the eyes of Lincoln fell short of the victory it could have been had McClellan pursued and destroyed the Confederate army. Once again,

McClellan had proven himself reluctant to strike while the iron was hot.

Lincoln's desire throughout McClellan's fourteen-month tenure as field commander was action, for which he often beseeched his commander. There had been a golden opportunity in the aftermath of Antietam (which took place on September 17) for the Federals to shorten the War dramatically by smashing Lee's weakened army. But McClellan had delayed, allowing Lee to escape into the Shenandoah Valley and reorganize and resupply his battered forces.

For some time, Lee had been operating with the nine infantry divisions of his Confederate Army of Northern Virginia unofficially grouped into two corps. These corps were under the command of his most reliable military leaders, James Longstreet and Thomas J. "Stonewall" Jackson. While Lee was regrouping in the Shenandoah Valley, the Confederate Congress approved Lee's corps organization and created the rank of lieutenant general, to which Longstreet and Jackson were immediately promoted.

An increasingly impatient Lincoln imposed a plan on McClellan—chase Lee southward immediately, moving the Union army along the eastern slopes of the Blue Ridge Mountains, remaining astride his supply lines. Press him, fight him, cripple him, then moved to Richmond and take it. Once the Confederate capital was in Union hands, the War would be short-lived.

Once again, however, McClellan moved his troops with slow deliberation. By the time they had inched their way south as far as Warrenton, Lee had positioned Longstreet's corps directly in McClellan's path. They were dug in and ready to fight. Lee's other corps, under Jackson, had remained in the Shenandoah Valley, posing a threat to the Union army's western flank.

A thoroughly disgusted Lincoln then called for his Army of the Potomac to pull back across the Potomac and wait for further orders. The orders arrived on October 6. McClellan was told by Lincoln through General-in-Chief Henry W. Halleck to cross the Potomac, pursue the enemy, give battle, and drive him south. This was to be done immediately before the wet fall weather came and turned the roads to mud.

McClellan sent a message back, informing Halleck that his army was in no condition to pursue and attack the enemy. Did Halleck—and the president, for that matter—not understand that he had requisitioned ammunition, shoes, blankets, and other indispensable articles shortly after the Antietam battle, and still they had not arrived?

While he waited for the needed supplies, McClellan worked on his campaign plan. He would lead his army across the Potomac and move them parallel with the Blue Ridge. They would swing around Gordonsville, then sweep toward Richmond from a westerly angle. With his men dressed and supplied properly, and his ammunition wagons loaded, he would have the troops and the guns necessary to take Richmond.

The needed ammunition and supplies arrived on October 25, and within two days, McClellan led his army across the Potomac toward Warrenton. Once again, his move was slow and deliberate. They reached Warrenton on November 7, and set up camp just outside of town.

Late that night, General McClellan was sitting alone in his tent, writing a letter to his wife by lantern light. There were footfalls outside his tent, followed by a voice asking if McClellan was presentable. Upon his invitation to enter, Brigadier General C. P. Buckingham appeared, followed by Major General Ambrose E. Burnside, both looking very solemn. After a moment of light conversation, Buckingham handed McClellan the order, of which he was bearer:

Headquarters of the Army
Washington, Nov. 5, 1862
General McClellan: On receipt of the order of the President, sent herewith, you will immediately turn over your command to Major General Burnside, and repair to

Trenton, New Jersey, reporting your arrival at that place by telegraph, for further orders.

H. W. Halleck, Gen.-in-Chief

McClellan read the order, then turned to Burnside with a slight smile and said, "Well, General, I hereby turn the command over to you."

When the Washington newspapers carried the story of McClellan's removal from command, Lincoln was quoted as saying he had replaced McClellan with Burnside because McClellan had the "slows."

As news of McClellan's dismissal spread amongst the troops, they trembled on the verge of mutiny. There had been great affection for McClellan amongst the men, and they were filled with anger. No other commander had ever so captured his soldiers, ever so entranced his followers. Violent invectives and denunciations were heard from the troops, along with threats of vengeance and mutterings of insurrection. Letters to friends and relatives at home denounced Lincoln's action bitterly.

On November 11, General McClellan was allowed to return to his troops to bid them farewell. A sadder gathering of men could not have been assembled. As McClellan passed in front of them, whole regiments broke and flocked around him. They begged him with tears not to leave them, but to say the word and they would storm Washington, demanding he be returned to their command.

A lesser general who was flanking McClellan shouted that he wished McClellan would put himself at the head of the Union army and throw the infernal scoundrels in Washington—including the president—into the Potomac River. Loud voices lended their agreement.

Government and military officials who stood by observing began to fear mutiny.

But their fears were quickly stifled. McClellan himself took control of the near-mob. With wise words he calmed the tumult and ordered the men back to their colors, reminding them of their duty. He told them they did not serve a man, but their country. They should perform as soldiers and follow their new commander, General Burnside. His words had their intended impact, and the men fell back into their places.

A short time later, McClellan met with his officers, telling them good-bye. There was not a dry eye in the assemblage. After grasping each officer's hand, "Little Mac" made a short speech in which he urged all of them to return to their commands and to do their duty to General Burnside as loyally and as faithfully as they had to him.

No military officer in the Civil War so resisted promotion as did Major General Ambrose E. Burnside. Three times in 1862, President Lincoln asked him to assume command of the Army of the Potomac. Burnside and McClellan had fought side-by-side on several occasions, and had been close friends for years. The man whose muttonchop whiskers eventually gave the name "sideburns" to the hair on the sides of a man's face demurred on the grounds that he was not competent to handle so large an army. He insisted that he was content to remain a subordinate under McClellan.

However, when Lincoln tendered his third offer, Burnside thought it over. The president was dead-set on removing McClellan as field commander. If Burnside did not accept the position, the command would go to a man he detested and distrusted—Major General Joseph Hooker.

Reluctantly, Burnside took command of the Army of the Potomac on the night of November 7, 1862, replacing his longtime friend. On the heels of his promotion came orders from General-in-Chief Halleck: "Report the position of your troops, and what you propose doing with them."

The dread with which Burnside faced his new responsibilities deepened with that order. He knew less than any other corps commander of the condition of his troops...and there was no time for him to learn. Lincoln wanted action, and he wanted it immediately. Delay had caused McClellan's downfall. Burnside found himself almost wishing he had let Lincoln give Joe Hooker the job.

President Lincoln had pondered his choices when seeking a replacement for McClellan, and faced the fact he had few men to choose from. The other eligible corps commanders all had disqualifying flaws.

Edwin V. Sumner, at sixty-five, was too old. William B. Franklin seemed too much embued with the same problem McClellan had. Lincoln's only other choice was Joseph Hooker, who was troublesome, cantankerous, and immoral. It was Hooker who brought prostitutes to his men to keep up their morale, and from this the women of that low profession garnered the name *hookers*.

Burnside, however, at the age of thirty-eight, was young and had proven his courage and valor on the battlefield. Though Lincoln wished Burnside had more self-assurance, he was the best available to replace McClellan. As often happened in the Civil War, Lincoln was forced to choose not the ideal man for the command, but the one who presented the fewest apparent liabilities.

Though handicapped with lack of self-assurance to meet the task before him, Ambrose E. Burnside attacked his problems vigorously. Within two days after taking command, he forwarded to Washington a bold new strategy for the capture of the Confederate capital. Instead of making a westward swing as proposed by his friend McClellan, Burnside would move his army rapidly southeastward from Warrenton to Fredericksburg, on the Rappahannock River.

Located forty-eight miles slightly southwest of Washington and fifty-seven miles due north of Richmond, Fredericksburg was considered by Burnside to be the doorway for his campaign to capture Richmond. In his message to Lincoln and Halleck, Burnside explained that by shifting toward the east, his army would stay closer to Washington and its base of supplies. It would also be on a more direct route to Richmond, for Fredericksburg stood on the main road midway between the two capitals. His plan was to outflank

Lee's army, strategically placing his 130,000-man army between Lee's 78,000 troops and Richmond.

The key to Burnside's scheme was to have pontoon bridging equipment available when he arrived opposite Fredericksburg. With the floating bridges in place, Burnside's massive army could quickly cross the deep Rappahannock, take Fredericksburg before Lee could block them, then move south and seize Richmond.

Burnside knew that everything depended on speed. To streamline his operations, he proposed to reorganize his command by creating three "grand divisions" as he labeled them, each containing two corps, and each with its own staff. To command the grand divisions, he named three major generals: Sumner, Franklin, and Hooker.

The rest of Burnside's message dealt with the problems of supplying his enormous army. He requested thirty barges be loaded with goods and sent down the Potomac to a new supply base at Belle Plain, some ten miles northeast of Fredericksburg. He asked for additional wagon trains of ammunition and supplies, along with a huge herd of beef cattle, to move overland from Alexandria to the Rappahannock crossing. Most important was his request for enough pontoons to build floating bridges so he could get his army across the river.

Lincoln and Halleck were skeptical of Burnside's plan for capturing Fredericksburg on his way toward Richmond. Lincoln had tried for months to get McClellan to close in and fight the Confederate army, and now the new commander was proposing to skirt that army, seize Fredericksburg, then move on Richmond. Halleck threw up his hands and told Lincoln the decision to approve Burnside's plan was fully on the president's shoulders.

Glad, at least, to have a commander who was willing to put his army in motion, Lincoln approved the plan, adding in his message to Burnside, "It will succeed if you move rapidly; otherwise not."

The campaign was begun immediately. Under General Burnside's orders, Sumner's division led the way, setting off from the

Warrenton camp at dawn on November 15, a day ahead of the other two divisions. Just after dark two days later, Sumner's advance elements marched into Falmouth, a small town situated on the north bank of the Rappahannock, less than two miles upriver from Fredericksburg. Franklin soon reached Stafford Court House, eight miles from Falmouth, and Hooker halted at Hartwood, just seven miles away.

Burnside seemed to be justifying the trust Lincoln had placed in him. In command for less than two weeks, he had concocted a campaign to seize and occupy the enemy capital, and his 130,000 troops now stood poised, ready to move on their first objective. Everything looked good. Fredericksburg and the hills beyond it were guarded by just four small companies of Confederate infantry, a cavalry regiment, and a battery of light artillery, diminutive at best against a force of 130,000. Longstreet's corps was bivouacked thirty miles away, at Culpeper, and Jackson's corps remained near Winchester in the Shenandoah Valley, a distance of sixty miles.

All Burnside had to do was get his army across the Rappahannock River, and the town would fly a Union flag. But there was one problem. The requested pontoons had not arrived. The Rappahannock was running rapid and riding high on its banks because of heavy rains up north. The water was very cold, even showing large chunks of ice. Burnside would be chancing the loss of men if he ordered them to swim across. He must wait for the arrival of the pontoons.

Fredericksburg, December 13, 1862

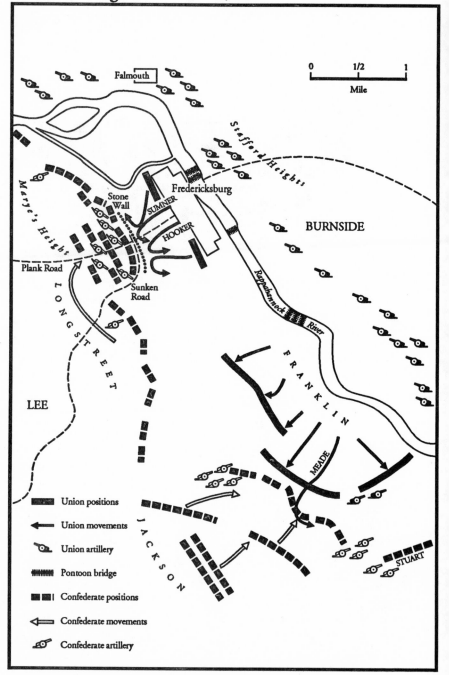

Falmouth

Stafford Heights

Marye's Height

Stone Wall

Fredericksburg

SUMNER

HOOKER

BURNSIDE

Plank Road

Sunken Road

L O N G S T R E E T

Rappahannock River

LEE

F R A N K L I N

MEADE

J A C K S O N

STUART

0   1/2   1
Mile

- **Union positions**
- ← **Union movements**
- **Union artillery**
- **Pontoon bridge**
- **Confederate positions**
- ⇐ **Confederate movements**
- **Confederate artillery**

CHAPTER ONE

★

He stood alone outside his field tent, letting his gaze run the length and breadth of the long rows of tents that sheltered his corps from the weather. The night was cold and crisp, and the harsh, vagrant winds sweeping across the snow-crusted fields around Culpeper, Virginia, made him tighten his campaign hat and pull the lapels of his gray overcoat up around his neck.

The stars twinkled like diamonds above him and a half-moon hung sharp and clear-edged as though—on this night at least—a decorative afterthought of the Creator.

It was Sunday night, November 16, 1862. Lieutenant General James Longstreet watched the campfires along the tent rows winking in their struggle for survival, but shortly the winds would extinguish their flames and reduce them to glowing red embers.

Hands shoved into his overcoat pockets, the general pictured his fifty-eight thousand men asleep in their tents, taking their rest. Soon they would find themselves in combat again. The Federals were coming this way. Longstreet would know more what to expect when General Robert E. Lee arrived on Wednesday.

Longstreet had his own ideas. Abraham Lincoln had his sights set on capturing Richmond, the Confederate capital. But what route would the Federals take as they pressed toward their goal? If they came along the east fringe of the Blue Ridge, they would probably angle southeastward between Culpeper and Charlottesville in a direct line toward Richmond. If, however, they came straight south from Warrenton, they might first seize Fredericksburg, which would stand directly in their path.

Longstreet had made a wager with himself. Lincoln would order his new field commander, General Ambrose E. Burnside, to sweep down and capture Fredericksburg. Lincoln had replaced George B. McClellan as commander of the army of the Potomac because of McClellan's repeated reluctance to move his army quickly when Lincoln ordered action.

Two months earlier, General Lee had led his troops into Maryland, a move Longstreet had openly opposed. Lee and Longstreet were close friends, but the latter had argued against the bold invasion, saying it was foolish to cross into enemy territory when you were vastly outnumbered and outgunned. The Federals would launch a vicious attack simply because Confederate feet were making tracks on Union soil.

Once Lee, backed by President Jefferson Davis, affirmed that the invasion would take place as planned, Longstreet—soldier to the core—ceased to argue. But even as he followed Lee across the Potomac into Maryland on that fateful day in September, Longstreet was silently against it. The foolish scheme stuck in his craw and lay crosswise in his mind.

And now, as he looked back on it, Longstreet knew he had been right. The price paid in lives had not been worth it. The battle at Sharpsburg, Maryland, had left twenty-seven hundred Confederate soldiers dead along the banks of Antietam Creek, not to mention the nine thousand wounded, many of whom died of their wounds during the next three weeks. The Union had also taken six thousand prisoners.

Granted, the Federal forces suffered great losses, too. The Antietam battle had been the bloodiest one-day conflict since the

War began. It would have been worse for the Confederacy, however, if McClellan had gone at the Rebel line as Lincoln had commanded.

The battle was a piecemeal affair. At no time did McClellan launch a concerted assault or even employ his reserves. Instead, he wasted his army's superior strength in a series of fragmentary attacks, using divisions and brigades instead of full corps.

Lincoln's grievance toward McClellan was that when he had the Confederates beaten, he did not follow through and destroy Lee's army. To have done so would, in Lincoln's mind, have spelled the end of the Confederacy. A full-fledged victory by McClellan would have left Richmond vulnerable to imminent capture. The Civil War would have ended.

Instead, Lee's army had escaped into Virginia's Shenandoah Valley and had been left in peace for two months. Lee brought in new recruits to replace those he lost on the banks of Antietam Creek, reorganized, and resupplied his forces.

For some time, Lee had been operating with his nine infantry divisions grouped unofficially into two corps under his top commanders—Thomas J. "Stonewall" Jackson and James Longstreet. In October the Confederate Congress approved Lee's corps organization and created the rank of lieutenant general, to which Jackson and Longstreet were immediately promoted.

In late October the increasingly impatient Lincoln imposed a plan on McClellan: Chase Lee southward, moving along the eastern slopes of the Blue Ridge Mountains and remaining astride his lines of supply. Press him, fight him if an opportunity presents itself...but *beat him to Richmond and capture it.*

Lee learned of Lincoln's orders from Confederate spies and immediately sent Longstreet's fifty-eight-thousand-man corps to Culpeper, placing them strategically in McClellan's path. He left Jackson's corps in the Shenandoah Valley, posing a threat if the Federals came through there on their way to Richmond, rather than from Warrenton. When Lincoln was told by his scouts of Lee's clever move, he knew it had been possible because of McClellan's slow deliberation in marching his army. At this juncture, the Federal president made the decision to relieve McClellan of his command.

Word came to the Confederates on November 8 that on the day before, Major General Ambrose Burnside had been made commander of the Army of the Potomac.

Longstreet raised his eyes toward the star-studded sky and felt the smallness its great expanse always gave him. Though he made no claim to being a Christian, the rugged general was no atheist. God was up there somewhere, all right. He wondered if God cared about the thousands of men who lay sleeping in the fields. He reasoned that if God cared about them, He wouldn't have allowed the War to happen. There had been wars as far back as men have written their history. There always would be. The general had discussed the subject with an army chaplain one time. The chaplain had laid the blame for wars on Satan, the devil, who had inspired Cain to declare war on his brother Abel and shed his blood.

Longstreet wasn't sure what he believed about the devil, but he knew for sure that there was evil in the world.

The general lowered his gaze to the gurgling creek that flowed nearby, the silvery moonlight reflected on its surface. Longstreet drew in a deep breath and let it out with a sigh made visible by the frosty night air. His mind drifted to his wife and children. He knew they were warm and snug in their beds down in Richmond.

James Longstreet loved his family and missed them terribly. He hadn't seen them for over six months. "Maybe one day soon," he said aloud. "Maybe one day soon this war will be over, and we can be together again."

He wheeled about and entered his tent. He laid his hat on the small table that served as a desk and removed his overcoat, then sat down on the straight-backed wooden chair and removed his boots. He blew out the lantern and slid into his bedroll.

✳ ✳ ✳ ✳ ✳

Sunrise the next morning came as no surprise. Longstreet was forty-one years old, and he had never known daylight to fail to come on schedule in all those years. He had recently read Charles Darwin's new book, *On the Origin of the Species by Means of Natural Selection.* Ignoramus. No, God was up there, all right. He made the whole universe and was keeping the earth in its orbit. No accident. Purpose and design in the universe by its Creator and Designer.

Longstreet left his warm bedroll and pulled on his boots. He could hear the activity of the camp as he shouldered into his overcoat and donned his campaign hat. He stepped out into the snappy morning air and filled his lungs. Men who milled about their tents nearby greeted him cheerfully. Though they smiled, he knew that behind those smiles were concerns about when and where the next battle would take place...and whether they would survive it.

Longstreet saw Corporal Ted Landrum hastening toward him from the cook's tent, carrying a tray of steaming food.

"'Mornin', General," grinned Landrum as he drew up. "Your breakfast, sir."

Longstreet smiled, opened the flap, and allowed Landrum to enter the tent ahead of him. Landrum placed the tray on the table and turned his boyish face toward the tall, full-bearded man. "Anything else I can do for you, sir?"

"No. Thank you, corporal. I'll set the tray outside when I'm finished. You can pick it up later."

"Yes, sir. Ah...General, sir...do we have any word yet about which route the Yankees may be taking?"

"Not yet. General Lee will be here day after tomorrow. Maybe he'll have something to tell us by then."

"Yes, sir. It's...it's just the waiting, sir. The men are jittery."

"I am, too," grinned Longstreet. "Guess we'll just have to jitter until the Yankees make their move, eh?"

"Guess so, sir," replied the corporal.

The wind had subsided some since sunrise, but it was still stiff and cold enough to make Longstreet keep his tent flap down. He was just finishing breakfast when he heard footsteps draw up outside, and a sturdy male voice call, "General Longstreet, sir?"

The general grinned to himself. A *familiar* sturdy voice. He picked up the tin cup that held one more swallow of coffee and said, "Come in, Major."

The flap opened and Longstreet looked up to see Major Layne Dalton enter, holding a small bundle of envelopes. "Mail boy at your service, sir."

The general set admiring eyes on the young major and downed the last of the coffee. Layne Dalton, an 1855 graduate of West Point, had served in the regular United States army as a lieutenant until the day after the Civil War began in April 1861, when he resigned from his post near Washington, D.C., and returned to his home at Fredericksburg, Virginia. A week later, he signed up in the Confederate army at Harper's Ferry, Virginia, and was taken in with the rank of lieutenant.

Shortly thereafter, Dalton was assigned to serve under Longstreet, and had served with him in several different divisions ever since. The rugged young officer had been at Longstreet's side in the First and Second Battles of Bull Run, Peninsular Battles, the Seven Days' Battles, and at the Battle of Antietam. He had distinguished himself under fire in every battle and had proven to be an able leader of men. Because of this, Longstreet had seen to it that he had been promoted to captain in July 1862, after the Seven Days' Battles, then had contacted Richmond after Dalton's outstanding valor at Antietam in September, recommending that he be promoted to major.

Longstreet chuckled at Dalton's sly humor and accepted the bundle of envelopes. "Thank you, mail boy. Anything interesting in this stack?"

Dalton grinned. "I believe you will find the one I placed on top to be of interest, sir. It's from Mrs. Longstreet."

The general's eyes sought out the handwriting on the top

envelope. It was written by the hand of the woman he loved, all right. He raised his gaze to the major and smiled. "I'll...ah...read it in private."

"I understand, sir. Sir..."

Longstreet's heavy eyebrows arched. "Yes?"

"Sir, I received a letter from *my* wife in today's mail, too. I..."

"Something wrong? Don't tell me Melody's having a problem in her pregnancy."

"No, sir."

"Thank God for that."

"Yes, sir."

"I can't remember when you first told me about it. How far along is she now?"

"Seven months. Doc Craig says she'll deliver about January 15."

"Well, I can see something's got you upset...something in her letter?"

"Yes, sir. Since we're only thirty miles from Fredericksburg, General, I need to ask your permission to make a quick ride home."

Longstreet's brow furrowed. "You seem a bit reluctant to tell me the content of the letter, Major. If I'm going to grant you time to ride to Fredericksburg, I'll have to know why you need it...and so will General Kershaw, since you're in his division."

Dalton cleared his throat, nodding. "Yes, sir. You see...my father-in-law, Jack Reynolds, is to stand trial for murder at the courthouse in Fredericksburg tomorrow. The family needs me. Especially Melody. She's very close to her father, and if he's convicted, he will hang within a day or two after the trial."

Longstreet's expression froze, eyes unblinking. "Do you know the details?"

"Yes, sir. Melody wrote it all in the letter."

"Let me say right off that you have permission to go. But because of your rank, I'll have to know the details in case some unforeseen complications come up."

"I understand, sir. It's just that...well, a murder trial in the family isn't something a man wants to let out, even though I believe my father-in-law is innocent."

"I can sympathize with that, Major."

"Well, sir, it's sort of a long story, but I'll try to make it as brief as possible."

The general gestured toward a chair in the over-sized tent. "Sit down," he said. "I'll put this tray outside, then we won't be bothered over it, at least."

Once both men were seated, Major Dalton began his story.

The man Dalton's father-in-law was accused of murdering had been a long-time resident of Fredericksburg, Edgar Heglund. There had been bad blood between the Heglunds and the Reynoldses for over forty years—ever since Edgar Heglund, who was fourteen at the time, had shot and killed Jack Reynolds's dog claiming, mistakenly, that it had killed all of the Heglunds' chickens. From that time on, there was continuous trouble between them. When the two young men married and had families, the trouble did not subside.

Edgar and Ethel Heglund had five sons—Steve, Clyde, Everett, Keith, and George. Jack and Frances Reynolds had two children, Jack Jr. and Melody. As the years passed and the offspring of both families were growing up, the Heglund brothers—led by Steve— tormented Jack Jr. and Melody. Neither Edgar nor his wife ever disciplined their sons for their wrongdoing.

When they were in their mid-teens, Jack Jr. happened to run onto Steve without his brothers. Though Steve was somewhat bigger, Jack gave him a royal whipping. Steve ran to his parents and told them Jack Jr. and several of his friends had jumped him and beaten him up.

Edgar went to the Reynolds place with fire in his eyes, demanding that Jack Jr. and his friends be punished. Jack Jr. was there and said he had whipped Steve all by himself. Edgar went into a rage, called Jack Jr. a liar, and swearing, made a hostile move toward him. Jack Sr. stepped in and cold-cocked Edgar, breaking his jaw.

Things only grew worse between the families after that. Another Reynolds dog—this time Melody's—was shot one night, along with four of their horses. The culprits were never caught, but everyone in Fredericksburg knew who had done it. The town constable questioned the Heglund boys and their father, but they said they knew nothing about it. There was no evidence to convict them, so nothing could be done.

The next day, Jack Sr. bought four new horses and locked them up in the barn when evening came. About midnight, he discovered that the barn was on fire. Jack was able to get the horses out of the barn safely, but it burned to the ground. When Jack and the constable confronted Edgar Heglund and his sons, they claimed innocence. Ethel claimed her husband and sons were home with her at the time the fire was set. Jack called them all liars and warned them to leave his family and his property alone.

Several months went by without incident. Then Jack and Frances took their teenage son and daughter on a three-day trip to Richmond. When they returned, their house had been broken into. Cabinets were torn from the walls, the kitchen stove was filled with mud and manure from the corral, dishes had been shattered on the floor, and furniture all over the house had been destroyed. The worst thing of all was the destruction of Melody's piano.

At six years of age, Melody began to show her parents that she was properly named. Her inborn talent for music began to surface. The Reynoldses were poor—Jack was a cobbler—but they wanted their daughter's talent to be developed. They managed to scrape up enough money to pay for piano lessons, and their neighbors were nice enough to allow Melody to use their piano for practice.

They also began to put money away so they could buy their daughter her own piano. It took a long time, but they finally were able to purchase a used upright in Richmond, and presented it to her on her thirteenth birthday. Seven months later, the Heglund brothers destroyed the piano when they broke into the house.

Once again the town constable was called in, and this time he found incriminating evidence—a receipt from Fredericksburg's general store. Steve had made a purchase for the family and was carry-ing a copy of the receipt, which had his signature on it. Somehow while he was tearing up the Reynolds house, it dropped out of his pocket. When the constable confronted Edgar Heglund with the evidence, he had no choice but to call his sons before the constable. The youngest Heglund son, George, had not been in on it, but Steve, Clyde, Everett, and Keith had no choice but to admit their guilt.

The constable severely reprimanded the four brothers, then gave Edgar a choice—pay fully for the damage or have his sons face trial. The money was paid.

The constable warned the Heglunds to stay away from the Reynolds home and not to bother any of them at any time or any place. Another used upright was purchased for Melody, and the Reynoldses went on with their lives.

A couple of years went by with only hard looks between the two families when they met on the streets of Fredericksburg. Then in the spring of 1854, when Jack Jr. was nineteen, he didn't come home one night. His body was found washed up on the bank of the Rappahannock River the next morning. He had been bludgeoned to death with a heavy instrument and his body thrown into the river. Though the constable and the townspeople suspected Steve Heglund and his brothers, there was no hard evidence and no charges were brought against them.

The Reynolds family grieved over their loss, and knew in their hearts that the Heglund brothers murdered Jack Jr., but there was nothing they could do about it.

Footsteps were heard outside the tent, followed by the voice of Colonel Dwight Conley. "General Longstreet, sir...I'm sorry to dis-turb you, but we have a matter of utmost importance that only you can handle. It will only take a few moments."

Rising, the general answered, "Certainly, Colonel. Be right with you." He turned to Dalton and said, "Wait right here, Major. I'll be back shortly."

CHAPTER TWO

✦

Major Layne Dalton was eager to be on his way to Fredericksburg, but there was nothing he could do but wait for the general to return. He would finish his story, then be on his way.

He sat on the chair, thinking about what Melody and her parents must be going through. With Jack Reynolds's life on the line, the waiting had to be excruciating. For several minutes, he dwelt on Jack's predicament, then his mind settled on the baby Melody was carrying.

Layne Dalton was sure his wife was going to give him a boy for their first child. He could feel it in his bones. If he was wrong and Melody was carrying a girl, he would love his little daughter every bit as much as he would love a son. But he desperately wanted a son. His own father had died when Layne was but two years old. The fact that he had never known the sweetness of a father-son relationship fired his desire to have such a relationship with a son of his own.

The major looked toward the tent flap. There was no sound of the general returning. He leaned forward with his elbows on his knees, then sat up straight and sighed. He pulled out the gold pocket watch his mother had given him when he turned thirteen. It had belonged to his father, who was a railroad man. The image of a steam engine was engraved on the back.

Five minutes after seven. The ride would take between two-and-a-half and three hours, if he kept his horse at a steady trot. He had hoped to leave in time to arrive home no later than ten, but he was going to have to settle for later.

Suddenly he heard voices. The voices grew closer, and the major thought he recognized General Longstreet's among them. He rose to his feet as the group of men approached the general's tent. Then they made an abrupt turn, and the volume of their chatter began to diminish. Dalton moved to the tent flap and looked outside. He could see the group of soldiers moving down a long row of tents. They were all enlisted men. The general wasn't among them.

The major went back to the chair and sat down. He thought once again of Jack and the heavy cloud hovering over him. He thought of the baby...and of Melody. How fortunate he was to have Melody Anne as his wife. In his heart, he hallowed the very first time he ever laid eyes on her. Suddenly he was back in Alexandria, Virginia, on that warm night in May 1858.

"Let's sit up front," Lieutenant Layne Dalton said to his best friend as he threaded through the crowd. "There are still some seats in the front row."

Lieutenant Jerry Owens was on Dalton's heels, holding the hand of Linda, who had been his wife for three months. Linda was having a hard time keeping up with her husband, holding onto him with one hand while lifting her long skirt with the other.

Dalton reached the front row of the center section and quickly claimed three seats in line with center stage. Out of breath, Linda sat down and the two men took seats on either side of her.

Jerry laughed as he looked past Linda and said to Layne, "You really like to get close to the action, don't you?"

"I always sit up front. That way I not only can hear everything clearly, but I can also see the expressions on the faces of the musicians and almost feel their heartbeat."

A young boy dressed in a sharp Concert Hall uniform came along in front of them. "Programs, folks? Ten cents."

"Sure," said Layne, reaching in his pocket. "One for each of us."

"Jerry and I can share one, Layne," Linda said. "We don't need two."

Jerry handed the boy two dimes before Layne could get his money out. "We'll take two, son."

As the boy walked away, Jerry handed his friend a program.

"You weren't supposed to do that," Layne said to the man who had been his fellow-classmate at West Point.

"And why not? You bought dinner and the concert tickets. Least I can do is put out a measly dime so you can have a program."

"I bought dinner and the tickets because I did the inviting," countered Layne. "It's your three-month anniversary, and I wanted to share it with you. After all, I was the best man at your wedding, wasn't I? The best man ought to treat the bride and groom on their three-month anniversary."

Jerry grinned. "You're amazing. Simply amazing."

Linda smiled and patted Layne's arm. "Sweet and amazing."

Layne responded with his famous crooked grin. "You just say that because it's true, Mrs. Owens."

Jerry laughed. "Sometimes she lies, Layne. *Amazing* you are...*sweet* you ain't! There were plenty of times at the Point when we bunked together that you were an old grump."

"Is that right? Well, I could tell Linda a thing or two about you."

"Now, boys," interjected Linda, "don't get into a scrap. This is a concert hall, not an arena."

Linda knew how much the young officers cared for each other, and that part of their fun was to make joking little digs.

"A scrap, honey?" chuckled Jerry. "It wouldn't last long enough to be a scrap. Layne couldn't fight his way through a wall of feathers! I'd put him out so fast, he wouldn't know what hit him."

"Hah!" reacted Layne. "If you and I got into it, there'd only be two sounds…me hitting you, and you hitting the ground!"

The tomfoolery ceased as quickly as it had started with the appearance of the orchestra members on stage. They took their places and began preparing their instruments for the concert. Violins, violas, cellos, and a bass viol were carefully tuned to the grand piano that stood to one side of the orchestra.

While the musicians prepared, Linda began reading the program. "Looks like we have several European artists here tonight," she said. "Two solo violinists…one from Germany, the other from Austria. We have a cellist from France, a flutist from Italy, and a singing group from Belgium. And we have talent from New York, Philadelphia, and—well, look here! We have one young lady who's from right here in Virginia."

Jerry leaned close and said, "Really? Let me see."

Layne was interested in who the local lady might be and looked at his program as Jerry read aloud, "Miss Melody Anne Reynolds of Fredericksburg. Piano soloist and songstress. Says she'll be on right after intermission."

"It's good to know we have some high class talent from Virginia," Layne said.

Jerry looked thoughtfully at his friend. "You know, Layne, when Linda and I got married, we agreed that within a month or two you'd be engaged. But you're not even seeing anybody, are you?"

Layne shrugged. "Not really."

"Well, you need to get with it before you end up a confirmed bachelor."

"I'm not worried. I just haven't found the right one yet."

Jerry turned to his wife and said, "Well, honey, looks like you and I are gonna have to get busy and dig up Miss Right for my pal, here. Married life is great, and I hate to see him missing out."

Layne turned mock-dismal eyes on his friend and said, "Did you say *dig* her up? No thanks."

"You and I don't need to play Cupid, honey," Linda told her husband. "A handsome man like Layne won't have any trouble landing Miss Right once she walks into his life."

Jerry shrugged and said, "I guess you're right. But I don't know what you mean by *handsome.*"

At eight o'clock sharp, the maestro appeared from the wings and walked to center stage. The crowd applauded while he took his place at the podium, bowed to them, then turned to face the orchestra and picked up his baton. The concert was under way.

After an hour and a half of delightful instrumentals and vocals, the intermission came. Layne and Jerry stood and stretched while Linda kept her seat.

"Well, it's been good so far," Jerry said. "I hope our little Virginia gal is as good as all those Europeans."

"I hope so too," Layne said.

They chatted about all manner of things for the next fifteen minutes. They were talking about their latest exploits at baseball when once again the maestro emerged from the wings and walked toward center stage. He bowed at the podium and allowed the applause to subside, then introduced the next performer as the Commonwealth of Virginia's own Melody Anne Reynolds. She would play a piano solo followed by a ballad.

Layne Dalton applauded with the rest of the crowd as Miss Reynolds appeared from the wings and moved to the grand piano. She was wearing a long-sleeved, floor-length black dress with a collar of white lace. Her dark-blue eyes glittered from the gas-powered spotlights as she smiled at the crowd.

For the next five minutes, the crowd was mesmerized by the skill, style, and talent of Melody Anne Reynolds. Enthusiastic applause and shouts of "Bravo!" erupted as soon as her lithe fingers brought the piece to a close. Smiling, she rose from the piano bench and bowed to her audience.

Layne was the first to his feet, and within seconds the entire audience was standing, applauding, and shouting their approval of the exceptional performance.

The applause slowly died out and everyone sat down. The orchestra began playing the introduction of the next number, and Melody Anne Reynolds walked gracefully to center stage. As she began singing a touching, sentimental ballad, Jerry stole a quick glance at Layne and smiled to himself.

Layne Dalton had never laid eyes on a woman who so stirred his senses. As she sang, Melody's gaze fell on Layne, who was sitting barely a dozen feet from her. For a fleeting moment their eyes met, and she smiled at him. Layne smiled back. Her warmth and tenderness swept like fire through him. He had never known such feelings before.

As Melody finished the last line of the song, her eyes fell on young Dalton again. She did not smile this time, but she did allow her gaze to lock with his a second or two longer than before.

Layne once again jumped up, applauding for all he was worth, and the whole crowd stood and applauded with him. Smiling, Melody bowed and walked off the stage. The applause continued, with voices shouting their approval of the outstanding performance. Melody came back on stage, took another bow, and disappeared once more. The maestro returned to the podium and the concert continued.

Jerry leaned past Linda and said, "You kinda like her, don't you."

Layne was staring toward the wings where he had last seen Melody and did not hear his friend.

"Layne!" pressed Jerry. "Hey, remember me?"

People around them were scowling at Jerry.

"Sh-h-h!" hissed Linda. "You're making too much noise."

Lowering his voice to a whisper now that he had Layne's attention, Jerry said, "You really like her, don't you."

"She's a very talented young lady," Layne whispered.

"And very beautiful, right?"

Layne met his gaze evenly. "Can't argue with that."

"How about if I introduce you to Melody Reynolds after the concert?"

Both Layne and Linda looked at Jerry wide-eyed.

"You know her?" Layne asked.

"How do you know her?" Linda queried.

"Please, folks," spoke up a man directly behind them. "If you want to talk, go out to the lobby."

"Sorry, sir," Jerry said. Then leaning past Linda, he said, "I'll introduce you to her after the concert."

Layne's heart seemed on fire. He nodded and smiled.

They settled down to enjoy the rest of the concert, and no more was said. As far as Layne was concerned, however, every instrument in the orchestra could have been playing a different tune. He was thinking only of Melody Reynolds.

Finally the last number was played and the audience gave its final enthusiastic round of applause. The maestro bid them all good night. Being down front meant that Layne and his friends would be the last to reach the lobby. Jerry and Linda were holding hands and walking just ahead of Layne as they slowly moved up the aisle.

Layne tapped Jerry on the shoulder and said, "Why'd you wait till Miss Reynolds was off stage before you told me you knew her?"

Jerry waved him off and replied, "Don't worry about it, my friend. Some things in life just have to remain a mystery. You just hold on. In a matter of minutes you and Melody will be acquainted."

Linda tried to get her husband to explain how he knew Melody Reynolds, too, but he avoided giving her a direct answer. Soon they reached the lobby, and Layne's eyes traveled to the greeting line. There was Melody Reynolds amid the European artists, smiling and warming people with her beauty and pleasant personality.

Jerry and Linda were still in front of Layne as they drew near. Layne's heart was drumming his ribs.

Jerry smiled at Melody and said, "That was a stunning performance, Melody. I'd like to introduce you to someone who enjoyed it more than anybody else in the hall."

"Pardon me," Melody said, tilting her head slightly. "Do I know you, Lieutenant?"

"Well, no, you don't. But I would like to introduce you to a young man who was hypnotized by your performance tonight." He motioned for Layne to move closer.

Layne did so, eyeing his friend with suspicion. Jerry laid a hand on Layne's shoulder and avoided Linda's you-conniving-rascal look.

"Miss Melody Anne Reynolds," said Jerry, smiling from ear to ear, "I want you to meet the man who without a doubt is your number one fan. Lieutenant Layne Dalton...Miss Melody Anne Reynolds."

Melody smiled warmly at the man whose dark, expressive eyes she had noticed while singing her ballad. She extended her hand and said, "Lieutenant."

Layne's blood was racing as he took the small hand in his own, did a slight bow, clicked his heels, and lifted it to his lips.

Linda elbowed her husband, saying with her eyes, *Look at that. When did you ever do that with me?*

Layne released Melody's hand and stood to his full height. "Miss Reynolds, this is indeed the greatest pleasure of my life."

"Why thank you, Lieutenant. You honor me."

I more than honor you, he thought. *I think I love you.* Aloud he said, "That was a stunning performance, Miss Reynolds. You truly are blessed with marvelous talent."

"You're very kind," she smiled. Then fixing the audacious Jerry Owens with steady eyes, she said, "Lieutenant Dalton, now that you and I are acquainted, maybe you would like to introduce me to your friend, here, and the charming lady with him."

"Of course," grinned Layne. "May I present Linda Owens and

her brassy husband, Lieutenant Jerry Owens. The lieutenant and I were roommates at West Point, and up until a moment ago, he and I were best friends."

Melody laughed. "Oh, please. Don't let what the lieutenant did destroy your friendship. I'm…ah…I'm sure he meant well."

"I sure did, Miss Reynolds. You see, Layne's been awful lonely of late, and—"

"Jerry," cut in Linda, "why don't you just leave it where it is?"

The four of them laughed together, then Melody looked around and spotted a handsome couple standing nearby. "I'd like for you people to meet my parents."

Jack and Frances Reynolds had been watching and were delighted to meet the Owenses and Lieutenant Dalton. They chatted briefly, then Jack Reynolds turned to his wife and daughter and told them they should be returning to the hotel. As good-byes were being said, Layne moved close to Melody. "I meant what I said, Miss Melody. Meeting you has been the greatest pleasure of my life."

Melody blushed, dipped her chin, then raised her gaze to his. "Thank you, Lieutenant. I really don't understand why you feel that way, but—"

"Would…would it be all right sometime when I can get down to Fredericksburg…if I call on you?"

"Why, of course," she responded with a smile. "That would be nice."

The lieutenant was having a hard time breathing. "Good!" he managed to say. "What is your address?"

It was late in the afternoon two days later when Lieutenant Layne Dalton rode up in front of the Reynolds house in Fredericksburg. It was a warm day, and the windows were open. He could hear the sound of a piano, but could tell it was being played by someone other than Melody.

Layne noticed a buggy coming down the dusty street and recognized Jack Reynolds at the reins. He swung from the saddle, tied his horse's reins to the hitching post, and smiled at Reynolds as he drew up.

"Well, if it isn't Lieutenant Dalton!" exclaimed the cobbler. "Melody said you would be coming to call on her sometime, but I didn't expect it to be so soon."

"Well, I...ah...was able to get a pass from my company commander, sir. I have to report back by sunrise."

"You won't get much sleep, in that case."

"I don't mind, sir. If I can take Miss Melody to dinner and spend a little time with her, it'll be worth it."

Jack Reynolds liked the young lieutenant. He grinned and said, "You two hit it off real good, didn't you?"

"Well, I—"

"All Melody's talked about for two days is *you.*"

"Really?"

"Really. Melody's giving a piano lesson at the moment. Why don't you come on out back with me? I'll park the horse and buggy by the back porch, and you and Melody can use them to go to supper."

"Yes, sir," nodded Dalton, climbing on the buggy.

Reynolds drove the buggy to the rear of the house and hauled up at the porch. Frances was standing at the door, talking to a neighbor.

Frances was also surprised to see the lieutenant, but welcomed him and introduced him to Lizzie Springston, explaining that Lizzie's daughter was taking a piano lesson from Melody. Then Frances said, "Well, Lieutenant, I didn't expect to have this pleasure so soon. Melody's going to be pleased to see you. When the piano lesson's over, Melody and I will start supper. Won't be any trouble at all to put another plate on."

Layne glanced at Jack, then said, "I appreciate the invitation, ma'am, but with your permission, I'd like to take Miss Melody to dinner."

Frances frowned. "*Dinner?* I thought you told us the other night that you're a Virginian. Didn't you say you were born and raised over by Roanoke?"

"Sorry, ma'am. It was always *supper* to me until I entered the Academy. They taught us that army officers have to be refined...and to those Yankee professors the evening meal is *dinner.* I'll have to ask you to pardon my error."

Jack laughed. "Well, we'll pardon you this time, Lieutenant, but don't ever let it happen again!"

Everybody was laughing when suddenly Melody appeared at the kitchen door with twelve-year-old Melba Springston. Melba proceeded onto the porch, but Melody seemed frozen in the door frame, her hands affixed to either side. Her eyes were wide as she held them on the army officer.

Lieutenant Layne Dalton sidestepped Melba, a wide grin across his face, and said, "Hello, Miss Melody."

CHAPTER THREE

★

Melody Anne Reynolds had found her mind and heart fixed on the dashing young lieutenant since meeting him at the concert. She had dreamed of him both nights. She gave him a warm smile and said, "Hello, yourself, Lieutenant Dalton."

There was warmth in her eyes and music in her voice. Layne needed a few seconds to collect himself. "I...ah...I was able to get a pass from my company commander. I'd like to take you to din—to supper if it's all right with you."

"Why, I would be honored, Lieutenant."

"I don't know how well Fredericksburg is fixed for eating establishments, but you can choose your favorite place."

"All right. My favorite place is not very fancy, but it has great food. It's called Mabel's Café."

"Then Mabel's it is," Dalton said, smiling from ear to ear.

"Just hold on, now, Lieutenant," interjected Frances with a look of devilment in her eyes. "You said with *my* permission you would like to take my daughter out."

"Yes, ma'am."

"Well, I just want to make sure about what you're taking her for—dinner or supper."

"Oh, supper for sure, Miz Reynolds," Layne said in an exaggerated Southern accent.

Frances responded in kind. "All right. Y'all be sure you is going for *supper*, and y'all have my permission!"

There was laughter all around.

Layne and Melody arrived at Mabel's Café as twilight was settling over Fredericksburg. Melody found several friends at the café and introduced them to Layne. There were curious eyes and whispering lips all over the place while the happy couple enjoyed their meal and became better acquainted. They both were taken with the other, but discreetly did their best to hide it.

A high moon put a silver wash on the town as Layne drove the buggy through the streets toward the Reynolds home. Melody felt safe and secure with Layne and relished every moment with him. Though he was quite strong, he had treated her like a China doll all evening. Lieutenant Dalton was every inch a gentleman.

Layne pulled up in front of the Reynolds place where his horse was tethered at the hitching post.

"I'll walk you to the front door, Miss Melody," he said quietly. "Then I'll take the horse and buggy around back. Your father will probably want to come out and show me where he wants the buggy parked."

Before Melody could reply, Jack Reynolds came out the front door. "I'll put the horse and buggy away, Lieutenant," he called amiably. "Since its such a nice warm night, maybe you and Melody would like to sit out here on the porch swing for a while."

Melody's father had never made such a suggestion to any other young man she had dated. The gesture was not lost on Layne, either.

"I appreciate that, Mr. Reynolds," he said, smiling. "I won't stay long. I already told Melody I have to be back at camp by sunup."

"Yes," said Melody, "and I told him I feel guilty that he's going to lose a night's sleep just to see me."

"It's only forty miles or so from here to the camp. I just might get back in time to sleep an hour, maybe two. And if not, it's still been worth it."

Jack grinned and said to Melody, "You'd better treat this one real good, honey. He's the kind that'll make some young woman a real good husband!"

"Daddy!"

Jack laughed and said, "If you two'll climb down, I'll put horse and buggy away."

Layne jumped out of the buggy and helped Melody down. Jack led the animal toward the back of the house and said over his shoulder, "Come back anytime you can, son. Only next time, plan to eat here at the house. Between Melody and her mother, they whip up some lip-smacking good meals."

"I'll do that, sir," grinned Layne. "And thank you."

As the couple moved toward the porch, Melody said, "Lieutenant, I'm sorry for Daddy's remark."

"You mean about me making some young woman a good husband?"

"Yes. I don't doubt that you will, but it was inappropriate for him to say it like that. I love him with all my heart, but sometimes…well, his timing is bad."

Layne took Melody's arm to help her up the steps. "Miss Melody," he said, "please don't be embarrassed. His remark didn't bother me in the least. And besides, I hope he's right. I hope I will be a good husband to the woman I marry. I sure plan to, anyway."

Melody didn't know what else to say, so she started asking questions about Layne's childhood. He had already told her at the café that both of his parents were dead, and that he had no siblings.

Layne told her what she wanted to know about his childhood, recounting some humorous incidents. She enjoyed it and laughed repeatedly. The porch lantern and the silver moonlight illumined her features. He loved watching the toss of her head and listening to the melodic run of her voice.

All too soon it was time for him to go. Melody walked him to his horse, and the animal nickered as they drew up to the hitching post. Layne grinned and said, "That's right, ol' boy. She sure is."

Melody looked at the lieutenant quizzically.

"This horse and I talk to each other, Miss Melody."

"Oh? And what did he just say?"

"He said you're the prettiest young lady he's ever seen."

"Lieutenant, you…you overwhelm me. I don't know what to say. I—"

"Miss Melody, it isn't I who overwhelm you, it's the horse. He's the one who made the remark about how pretty you are. I simply agreed with him."

Melody loved Layne's sense of humor and his quick wit. He was the most interesting man she had ever met. She laid a hand on his forearm and said softly, "Well, you tell this fine animal I appreciate his compliment."

The touch of Melody's hand sent tingles through Lieutenant Dalton. "I'll tell him while we head for camp, Miss Melody."

"You can just call me Melody, Lieutenant. The *Miss* isn't necessary."

He gave her a lopsided grin. "All right, Melody. And you can just call me Layne. The *Lieutenant* isn't necessary."

Melody's heart was racing. "Thank you for the supper, Layne. And thank you so much for coming all this way to see me. Please come back again."

"I will."

"Soon."

"I will."

Layne's arms ached to hold her, but he forced himself to turn away. He untied the reins from the hitching post, looped them over his horse's head, and swung into the saddle. Just then the front door came open, and Jack and Frances stepped onto the porch. "Lieutenant," called Jack.

"Yes, sir?"

"Do you think you can get a pass for weekend after next? We're having a family get-together, and there'll be plenty of good food. Frances said she and Melody will cook whatever your favorite meals are for Saturday and Sunday both. And we've got a spare bedroom."

Layne looked down at Melody who was eyeing him with anticipation. "Since it's that far away, sir, I'm pretty sure I can get a pass. I'll be here mid-afternoon a week from Saturday."

"Wonderful!" exclaimed Frances, who was holding onto her husband's arm. "And what are your two favorite meals?"

"Well, ma'am," grinned Dalton, "I'd say one'd be cornbread and beans...and the other would be chicken-and-dumplings with black-eyed peas."

"You can plan on both," Frances assured him. "And you'll stay in our spare room?"

"That'd be fine, ma'am."

"Well, we'll just plan on it then."

"Yes, ma'am. Thank you."

"And I will look forward to it," spoke up Melody.

"So will I," nodded Layne. With that, he touched heels to the horse's flanks and rode away.

Lieutenant Layne Dalton waded his horse across the Rappahannock and headed north toward Alexandria. He visualized Melody's kindly face and sweet smile and let the sound of her voice resound in his mind. Truly she was the most captivating woman he had ever met. He was sure he was falling in love with her.

The anticipated weekend came, and Lieutenant Dalton happily immersed himself in the family gathering, meeting relatives on both sides of Melody's family. Conversation around the table on Saturday evening revealed that Hank Reynolds (Jack's older brother by two years) was taking his family west. Hank had learned of a huge gold strike near Virginia City and was heading out there to get his share of it. While wolfing down cornbread and beans, he tried to persuade Jack and Frances to pack up and go with them. Big money could be made in Nevada. The West was starting to boom, and people were moving out there to build new lives on the frontier. The way Virginia City was growing, Melody would be sure to pick up plenty of music students.

Jack laughed and said he would let Hank do the gold mining. He was a cobbler and would stay and run his cobbler shop.

Later that evening, after the dishes were done and the kitchen cleaned up, Melody gave a concert on her old upright piano, thrilling family members with her talent. But no one was thrilled as much as Layne Dalton.

There was another concert on Sunday night, and afterward Layne and Melody took a short walk together. In their parting moments at the hitching post, he came close to kissing her, but refrained. He knew how he felt toward her; he wasn't sure as yet how strong her feelings were toward him.

Because of planned military maneuvers, Layne was unable to visit Melody for several weeks. The first week of August he obtained a pass, and late on a Thursday afternoon, knocked on the door of the Reynolds house.

There were rapid footsteps on the inside, and when the door swung open, Frances smiled and chirped, "Layne Dalton! How are you? Come in! Come in!" Before Layne could utter a reply, Frances shouted, "Melody! Layne is here!"

From upstairs, Melody's voice called back, "Who's here, Mother?"

"Layne Dalton, honey!"

There was dead silence, then Melody appeared at the top of the stairs. She was in a plain cotton house dress, and touched it at the collar as she looked down at Layne and said, "I'm not dressed for receiving a caller, Layne. I hope you don't mind seeing me like this.

I've been cleaning out some closets, and—"

"You look mighty good to me," he cut in. "Sorry I couldn't let you know any sooner. My commanding officer only granted the pass at supper time last night. I have to be back by sunup, so I rode as fast as I dared."

Melody bounded down the stairs and, to Layne's surprise and delight, into his arms. They held each other tight, then Melody rose up on her tiptoes and planted a tender kiss on his cheek. "It's so good to see you! I appreciate your letters, of course, but it's just not the same. Did you receive my last letter? The one about my picking up four new students all in one week?"

"It came just yesterday. That gives you what...fourteen students now?"

"Mm-hmm. And with the new ones I figure I'll have enough money to buy a new upright by Christmas."

"Christmas present for yourself, eh?" he chuckled.

"Yes! I'm so excited! This old one is really starting to show its age."

"Well, which is it this time, Layne?" Frances asked. "Home cooking or Mabel's?"

"If it's all right with your daughter, it'll be home cooking."

Melody turned to her mother and said, "If it's all right with you, I'll rush upstairs and make myself a bit more presentable, then come help you get supper on."

"You really don't need to make yourself more presentable on my account," Layne said. "You look mighty good just the way you are."

Melody dabbed at her hair. "You sure?"

"Positive."

Jack Reynolds came in just then from the back side of the house. He welcomed Layne with a smile and a handshake and asked how long he could stay. When Layne told him, Jack grinned at his daughter, then looked at Layne and said, "Sure glad you could show up, my boy. Melody's been pining around here, acting like a sick calf. This visit will perk her up for sure."

"Daddy! You shouldn't tell Layne things like that!"

"Why not?" Jack chuckled. "It's the truth."

"You men find a place to sit down," Frances said. "The sick calf and I will whip up some victuals."

"Mother!" said Melody, eyes wide. "You're getting as bad as Daddy!"

"You mean as *good* as Daddy," laughed Jack.

Supper was almost over when a knock came at the front door. Jack excused himself and went to answer it. He returned with a young couple, introducing them to Lieutenant Dalton as Walter and Harriet Smith. Melody got up from the table, embraced Harriet, and explained to Layne that the three of them had gone through school together. Walter had been a couple of grades ahead of them, but Harriet and Melody were in the same graduating class.

Layne shook hands with Walter and did a slight bow to Harriet, who smiled and said to her husband, "I like this man! He knows how to conduct himself in the presence of a lady."

"If I bowed like that every time you came into my presence, I'd have a chronic backache!"

Everyone laughed. Then Harriet said, "We didn't mean to interrupt your supper."

"You didn't, honey," Frances assured her. "We were just finishing up."

"We'll be on our way," Walter said. "We just wanted to come by and remind you that we're having revival services at our church all next week, starting Sunday."

"Oh, yes," said Jack. "You told us about it a couple weeks ago."

"We'd sure love to have you come."

"Well, we'll see about it," replied Jack. "Maybe we can make it on Sunday morning, at least."

"Good," grinned Walter. Then turning to Dalton, he asked, "Are you going to be here on Sunday, Lieutenant?"

"No, sir. I have to be back at camp by sunrise tomorrow morning."

"I see. Well, perhaps we can get you to visit our church some other time."

"Who knows?" chuckled Layne.

When the Smiths were gone, Layne said, "I've never been to a revival meeting. Have any of you?"

"Never have," Jack said.

"I think it might be interesting," said Melody. "I've heard that they usually have some lively music. I'd like to hear it."

"From what I'm told," put in Jack, "the preaching gets pretty lively, too. You know, that hellfire and brimstone stuff."

"I've heard some of that kind of preaching," Layne said. "My grandmother used to take me to a Baptist church in Roanoke when I was little. Scared me."

"Well, maybe a little scaring would be good for us from time to time," Frances said. She sighed, then slapped her hips with the palms of her hands, and said, "Jack, why don't you help me do the dishes and clean up the kitchen so these young people can have a little time together?"

"Okay, I volunteer," laughed Jack.

Layne looked at Melody and asked, "How about a small concert? Then we can take a walk."

Melody took him by the hand and led him into the parlor. She settled on the piano bench, and Layne leaned on the top of the old upright, looking down at her. Melody played three instrumental pieces, then began playing and singing Stephen Foster's "Beautiful Dreamer." Her eyes met Layne's and held them. Layne Dalton was smitten with love. He had to find a way to tell her.

"That was beautiful," Layne said when she finished the song.

Melody blushed, rising from the bench. "Sorry about some of the off-key notes. Some of the strings on this old piano won't hold true anymore."

Layne grinned. "I didn't notice the piano. I was listening to the beautiful voice of the beautiful lady."

"You're very kind, Lieutenant Layne Dalton."

"It's not kindness, Miss Melody Anne Reynolds. It's just factual speaking."

"You ready for that walk?"

He gave her his arm and said, "I'm ready."

They walked around the block four times, then entered the Reynolds's yard, mounted the porch, and sat on the swing. The porch lantern burned a few feet away by the door.

"Nice people, the Smiths," Layne said.

"Yes. Harriet is one of my closest friends. They're very kind and considerate people. Either one of them would go the limit to help someone in need. They're a perfect match."

"I can see that. They were made for each other."

"God does that, don't you think?" Melody said.

"Makes people for each other?"

"Mm-hmm."

"Yes, I suppose He does. Mom used to tell how she looked for her ideal man...you know, the man of her dreams. And Dad said he had done the same thing. They were very happy together."

"I wish I could have known your parents," Melody said.

"You'd have loved them. And they'd have loved you, too. You're easy to love, you know."

Melody wasn't sure how to respond. "Not always," she said quickly. "I can be crabby and mean sometimes."

Layne chuckled. "I can't picture that. But even if you were, I'm sure the man of your dreams would love you anyhow." He let those words settle in her mind, then said, "You do have a man of your dreams, don't you? I mean one you've pictured in your mind since you were a little girl?"

"Oh, of course." Layne was dangerously close to the very thing that had been on Melody's mind ever since they first met. "And you've had a girl of your dreams, I suppose?"

"Definitely."

Melody's throat constricted, but she had to ask. "This girl of your dreams...what does she look like?"

Layne adjusted his position on the swing so as to look Melody in the eye. "Well, she's exactly your height and build."

"Really?"

"Yes. And she has honey-blonde hair, deep-blue eyes, lovely white teeth, and a cute little nose exactly like yours."

"Really?"

"Really."

Melody licked her lips and blinked to clear the mist in her eyes. "May I tell you about the man of my dreams?" she asked.

"Of course."

"Well, if you looked in a full-length mirror, you could see exactly how tall he is, how he is built, what his facial features are like, the color of his hair, and the color of his eyes. And I'll tell you his initials, too, if you'd like to know what they are," she said with a tremor in her voice.

"Would...would they have *Lieutenant* in front of them?"

"Yes," she breathed.

Layne leaned close, and suddenly their lips were together in a soft, velvet kiss. When they parted, Layne embraced her and said in a half-whisper, "I love you, Melody. I fell in love with you the moment you walked out on that stage in Alexandria. I didn't recognize what it was, but it didn't take me long to figure it out. I've only grown to love you more ever since."

Melody reached up and stroked his cheek. "It took me a little longer to fall in love with you. It wasn't until after the performance, when we were so subtly introduced by your friend. And I've only grown to love *you* more ever since."

They kissed again, the fire of their newly confessed love burning between them, joining their hearts in a union of tender emotion.

Layne held Melody close once more. She was quiet within his arms, relishing his love. After a long moment, he said, "I'm afraid I've got to be going."

She pushed back gently so she could look in his eyes. "When will I see you again?"

"I'm not sure. It's liable to be several weeks."

She stroked his cheek once more and whispered, "I'll miss you terribly."

"I'll miss you terribly, too," he said, placing the tips of his fingers under her chin and bending down to kiss her again.

Holding onto his hand, Melody walked with him to the hitching post. His horse bobbed its head and nickered.

"That's right, boy," said Layne. "She sure is."

"Oh, you two!" Melody giggled.

Layne kissed her once more, then mounted. "My letters will keep coming," he said.

"Mine, too," she assured him. "I love you, darling."

"I love you, too. More than you will ever know. I'll let you know when to expect me again, once I know myself."

"I pray it'll be soon."

Layne smiled at her, then turned his horse and rode away into the night.

CHAPTER FOUR

✦

A cool wind whipped across the Rappahannock River on Wednesday, October 6, 1858, as the Reynolds family pulled up to the dock at precisely 1:00 P.M. in their buggy. Neighbor Wiley Price and his three young, husky sons drew alongside them in their wagon.

"I'll be glad when this mystery is solved," Jack Reynolds said to Wiley.

"Me, too," nodded Price. "This young fella must have somethin' pretty big up his sleeve."

"I guess so," Frances said, "since he told Melody in the letter to have four strong men and a wide-bed wagon to meet the boat."

"How do we know who to contact?" asked Richard Price, the eldest son.

Melody held up the letter, which was open in her hand. "Layne says in here just to ask for Captain Elrod Dean. He's the boat's skipper and he'll tell us what item we're to unload."

"Well, here comes the boat right on time," Wiley said. "This mystery will soon be cleared up."

"It sure will," came a resonant voice from behind.

Everyone turned to see the speaker.

"Layne!" exclaimed Melody. "You didn't say *you* would be here!"

Layne dismounted and gave her his famous crooked grin. "I wanted to surprise you."

"Help me down. I want to greet you properly."

Layne stepped to the wagon, took hold of Melody, and eased her down. Melody stood on her tiptoes and kissed his cheek, saying with feeling, "It's so good to see you, darling! I've missed you terribly."

Layne glanced at Jack, who grinned and said, "She's told us all about it, my boy. Seems to me she can call you 'darling' all she wants."

"You're right about that, sir," grinned Dalton, hugging her close.

"All right, Lieutenant Dalton," said Melody, "we have our neighbors, the Prices, here with the wagon as you requested. I think it's time they know what it is they're going to have to load into their wagon."

"Oh, you do, eh?" Layne chuckled. "Well, they'll know shortly. Let's go onto the dock. I'll present a couple of papers to Captain Dean, and we'll soon be on our way."

There were people on the dock ready to meet family and friends as the big boat steamed up and crew members jumped onto the dock to secure it. A gangplank was laid between the boat deck and the dock. While passengers disembarked, Layne hastened across the gangplank, threading his way amongst them, and quickly found Captain Elrod Dean.

Moments later, four crewmen were wheeling a large wooden crate on dollies toward the dock. When Melody saw the crate, she looked at Layne and said, "What on earth?"

"I've arranged to have it unpacked right here," he said quietly. "Once it's out of the crate, it'll be easier to handle. Between the Prices and myself, we should be able to manage it."

When the crate had been wheeled onto the dock, the crewmen

used small crowbars to begin carefully taking it apart. Soon the top of the crate was removed, then the sides were laid flat. Melody's hands went to her mouth and tears welled up in her eyes. Jack was muttering something to himself, and Frances was about to cry.

"Layne!" Melody gasped. "What have you done?"

Layne took her into his arms and said, "We'll take the canvas off once we have it in the house, darling. I figure with a little furniture rearranging, and removal of that old upright, it'll fit fine in the parlor."

Frances moved up to her daughter and Layne, and wiping tears, laid a hand on Layne's arm. "Layne... I hardly know what to say. This is so kind and generous of you."

"Layne, how can we thank you?" Jack said.

"No need to, sir," Layne replied. "I'm in love with your daughter. Presenting her with this instrument is a great pleasure."

"Any idea what it weighs, Lieutenant?" Wiley Price asked.

"I'm not sure," said Dalton, "but the salesman I corresponded with by wire in New York told me five strong men could handle it."

"Well, we're about to find out," Richard chuckled.

A half-hour later, the old upright piano was on the back porch, and under Frances's directions, the men were rearranging some of the furniture in the parlor to make room for the concert grand.

"That should do it," said Frances. "Now you can bring in the piano."

The women looked on as the grunting, puffing men carried the grand into the parlor and positioned it in place. Richard hurried out to the wagon and brought in the canvas-covered bench. He and his father unwrapped the bench while Jack and Layne removed the protective canvas from the piano.

As section by section of the expensive instrument was revealed, Melody "oohed" and "ahhed" at the beauty of its rich, dark wood. Last to be revealed was the keyboard. When she read the make of the piano just above the keys, she squealed, "It's a Steinway! A *Steinway!*"

Jack and Frances were at a loss for words.

Melody leaped at Layne, wrapped her arms around his neck, and planted a quick kiss on his lips. "Oh, Layne, you shouldn't have done it! But I'm glad you did!"

Everybody laughed.

"Congratulations, Melody," Wiley said. "That's the most beautiful piano I've ever seen."

"Thank you...and thank all of you for your help. It is deeply appreciated."

When the Price men were gone, Melody sat on the bench and said, "I know it'll need tuning after coming all the way from New York, but I've just got to hear its tone."

She played a few bars and looked up at Layne. "It's hardly out of tune at all!"

"That's because it's a Steinway, honey," Jack said.

"Oh, I know. Steinway's are marvelous instruments. Ever since I first played one at a concert in Washington a little over a year ago, I've dreamed of owning one. And now I do. Oh, Layne, how can I ever thank you? I love it! I love it! I love it!"

"I'll have Mr. Franks come by and tune it perfectly for you tomorrow, honey," said Jack.

"Thank you, Daddy," she smiled, still running her fingers lightly over the keyboard and smiling at Layne as she played "Beautiful Dreamer." "Mr. Franks won't like it that I now own a Steinway. He was making good money off us, coming by once a month to tune the old upright. Now, we'll only need him once a year...if that often."

"Ah, but you're creating more customers for him by getting more young people interested in playing the piano, my dear," put in Frances. "Mr. Franks is doing all right."

"I guess that's true," Melody nodded. Even though a few of the strings were slightly out of tune, she broke into a concerto and played it all the way through. When she finished, her audience applauded vigorously.

Melody rose from the bench and embraced the man she loved, thanking him one more time.

Jack said, "Well, I've got to get back to the shop. I left a note on the door saying I'd be back at three o'clock. It's almost three, now."

"Would you mind if I ride along with you, sir?" Layne asked. "I need to talk to you for a few minutes."

"You mean in the buggy, or do you mean you'll ride your horse alongside?"

"I'll just ride in the buggy, sir, if it's all right. I can walk back."

Melody and Frances had no idea what was going on, but listened quietly as Jack said, "You're quite welcome to ride with me, Layne. Let's go."

That evening after supper, Layne and Melody were in the parlor alone, sitting on a love seat. Two lanterns burned in the room, both turned low. In the soft light, Melody held his hand and said, "Darling, I don't mean to wear you out with it, but I want to thank you again for my wonderful piano. There are really no words to describe what it means to me. I'll never be able to—"

"Hush, my love," whispered Layne, putting the tip of his fingers to her lips. "You have thanked me quite sufficiently. In fact, just to see the look in your eyes at the dock when you realized it was a grand piano was thanks enough. I'm glad you're happy with it, and I hope it'll give you years and years of pleasure."

Melody stroked the side of his head and said, "You wonderful, wonderful man. I love you so much."

"And I love you, Melody Anne Reynolds," he responded, reaching into a shirt pocket. "In fact, I love you so much, I want your name to be Melody Anne Dalton." Melody saw the diamond engagement ring between his fingers as he added, "Will you marry me?"

Tears filmed her eyes, and as they spilled down her cheeks, she choked out the words, "Yes! Yes, I'll marry you!"

Layne slipped the ring on her finger, held it there, and said with emotion, "I now pronounce me the most blessed and fortunate man on earth."

They kissed, then embraced.

After a moment, Melody eased back to look into his eyes. "Oh, I think I'll just explode! My beautiful Steinway…and now this," she said, holding up the hand that wore the ring. "It's almost too much!"

"I figure an eight-month engagement would be proper," Layne said. "What do you think?"

Melody silently counted on her fingers and replied, "That would make it a June wedding. Yes, that would be very proper."

"I checked the calendar. June 11 is a Saturday. How about June 11?"

"Sounds great to me." Melody paused a moment, then said thoughtfully, "I suppose since we're doing things properly, you should ask Daddy for my hand in marriage."

Layne grinned. "I already did. That's what I wanted to talk to him about when I rode downtown with him."

Melody looked at her engagement ring again. "Well, I guess he didn't object."

"Not in the least. He said he'd be glad to get rid of you."

Melody met his gaze and saw the look of devilment in his eyes. She cuffed his jaw playfully. "Layne Dalton, you scoundrel! Daddy did not say that!"

The happy couple laughed together, enjoyed another kiss, then Layne said, "Well, darling, I'd better be heading north. Sunrise must find me back in camp."

Neither the Reynolds nor the Dalton families had been church-goers, but on Saturday June 11, 1859, Layne and Melody had a military wedding at the Fredericksburg Community Church, where Walter and Harriet Smith were members. An army chaplain conducted the ceremony. Jerry Owens was best man, and Harriet Smith was Melody's matron of honor.

· Layne had a sizable inheritance left him by his deceased parents, and used most of it to purchase a large two-story house next door to the Smith's.

There was no time for a honeymoon. Layne was given a three-day pass for his wedding and was due to report back at camp on Tuesday. On Monday, Wiley Price and his three sons were on hand to help move Melody's Steinway from the Reynolds house to the Dalton house six blocks away.

Layne, Jack, and the Price men loaded the piano onto the Price wagon, then Layne and Jack followed the wagon in the buggy through the streets of Fredericksburg.

Melody, her mother, and Harriet Smith were waiting on the front porch of the newly purchased house for the piano to arrive. When they saw the wagon coming down the street, they left the porch and met them as they drew to a stop in front of the house.

Layne wanted Melody to have a special music room in her new home. On the second floor near the top of the stairs was a large spare bedroom, and Layne had hired a carpenter to install double doors to the room to accommodate the Steinway. In front of the room was a wide landing that dovetailed into the hallway that led to two other bedrooms and the master bedroom.

Layne had told the Prices that he would need their help in moving a large bookcase in the new music room before they carried the piano inside and up the stairs. The women volunteered to stay outside with the piano while the men moved the bookcase.

"Melody," Harriet said, "aren't you afraid to have them try to carry your piano all the way up those stairs? I'd think you'd have chosen a downstairs location for your music room."

"I did," smiled Melody, "but that husband of mine said I needed a larger room than anything that's available downstairs. He wouldn't take no for an answer."

"I think maybe the man you married is going to spoil you rotten," put in Frances. "Your father spoiled you, too, but I think Layne's going to outdo him."

Melody laughed and started to reply when she saw five men on horseback coming along the dusty street. Frances saw her daughter's eyes grow cold and looked to see what Melody was glaring at. Her own eyes narrowed as Steve Heglund and his four brothers reined in at the wagon.

All five Heglunds had a churlish look about them, but the four younger ones together could not match the look in Steve's wide-set, thick-lidded eyes. There was a fixed snarl on his lip, and no one—not even Steve Heglund—could tell you the last time he had ever smiled. He carried a calloused spirit about him, and there was a hostile quality in his voice that always made him sound irritated. It was as though God knew beforehand how ugly the man would choose to be on the inside, so He gave him a face to match.

None of the Heglunds were large men, but they were muscular and known for provoking fights just for the fun of a good scrap. Of course, they only provoked fights when they outnumbered their opponents and felt sure they would come out the victors.

From his saddle, Steve looked at Melody and grunted, "I hear you're a new bride, blondie."

"Yeah," chuckled Clyde Heglund. "Word is you married some fancy-pants army officer."

"He's a lieutenant, yes, but he's no fancy-pants," Melody responded coolly. "Believe me, you don't want to get on his wrong side."

"He's inside the house right now," put in Frances, wanting to keep them at bay. "He'll be back out in a moment. It would be best that you boys move along."

Steve eyed the grand piano and ejected a low whistle. "So that's the ritzy piano he bought ya, huh? Must be true what I heard about your fancy-pants lieutenant. Lotsa money in the bank, eh? Pianos like this'n don't come cheap. Married yourself some money, didn't you, blondie?"

"My name is not blondie, and it's none of your business who I married."

"I ain't got much money, blondie, but if you'd tied the knot with me, you'd know what it was like to be married to a real man."

"I wouldn't marry you, Steve Heglund, if you were the last man on earth!"

Layne Dalton was just coming out the front door with the other men on his heels. His ears picked up the anger in Melody's voice and the name *Steve Heglund*. He concluded the five riders must be the Heglund brothers.

Wiley Price was first behind Layne, and when he saw the familiar faces, he half-whispered, "Trouble, Layne. It's the Heglunds."

"Yeah," Layne said. "Trouble for *them* if they're not careful."

Steve was not yet aware of the men emerging through the front door. He leered at Melody and blared, "You'd be better off married to me than to that fancy-pants lieutenant, honey!"

Layne was off the porch in a hurry. He rushed past the women and rounded the wagon. Before Steve could react, steel-like fingers had him by the shirt, yanking him from the saddle.

Steve hit the ground hard and the wind was knocked out of him. Layne stood over him, fists clenched, jaw set.

Clyde Heglund looked as if he was about to dismount. Wiley pointed at him and snarled, "You stay put!"

Clyde knew that Wiley meant it. He froze where he sat, eyes roving to his three brothers. Everett, Keith, and George were of no mind to tangle with Wiley Price and his muscular sons.

Steve struggled to his feet, gasping for breath and rubbing his left shoulder. There was murder in his eyes. "You just started somethin' I'm gonna finish, soldier!"

"You're not to call my wife *honey!* You got that?"

A devil's temper stirred behind the smoky color of Steve Heglund's eyes and changed the slant of his mouth as he said,

"You're a newcomer here, soldier boy. Do you know who you're talkin' to?"

"I know exactly who I'm talking to! And if you think your name scares me, you'd better think again."

Keith Heglund feared what might happen if his oldest brother tied into Melody's husband. The Price brothers and their father might decide to take on the Heglunds, and make a free-for-all of it. The Prices were too tough to handle. Keith wanted no part of them.

"You're going to apologize to my wife for the way you were talking to her, and you're going to apologize to me for calling her *honey*," Layne said, "or I'm going to pound you into the dirt! Let's hear it!"

In spite of the pain in his shoulder, Steve clenched his fists and was about to go after the lieutenant. Keith, who was the most level-headed of the clan, realized Steve hadn't noticed the Prices standing by. "Steve!" he shouted. "It ain't worth it! Look around you!"

There were five Heglunds and five men to face, even if Jack Reynolds stayed out of it, which he probably would not. Jack was getting on in age, but he was not the kind to back away from a fight. Steve knew the Prices were a tough bunch, and Melody's new husband looked like he could handle himself. Smart thing would be to eat humble pie and back off. There would be another day when he could catch this army man without the Prices around, then he and his brothers would pummel him good.

Steve looked at Keith, then at Clyde, Everett, and George. It was in their faces. They were not eager to get into a fight. He would use his hurting shoulder as an excuse to back out. He rubbed it again and said to Keith, "You're right, little brother. It ain't worth it. Especially since this soldier boy took me by surprise and injured my shoulder."

Steve turned to Layne and said, "You took advantage of me, pal, jerkin' me outta the saddle like you did. But next time—"

"My wife has an apology coming, Heglund!" roared Layne.

"Let's hear it!"

Steve fixed him with a hard look, then turned to Melody and said, "I'm sorry for talkin' to you like I did."

Melody loved seeing Steve Heglund in this position. She held her mouth in a grim line as she nodded her acceptance.

"Now me," Layne said.

Steve Heglund regarded him dismally and ground his reluctant apology between his teeth. "I'm sorry for callin' your wife *honey.*"

"Fine. Now, get on your horse and ride," Layne said.

Hatred for the army man churned inside Steve Heglund as he stepped in the stirrup and swung into the saddle. Barely moving his lips, he hissed, "There'll be another day, soldier boy."

"I didn't mean to take so long."

Layne Dalton was snapped back to the present. General James Longstreet had entered the tent and was sitting down at his table.

"What's that, sir?" Dalton asked.

"I said I'm sorry to keep you waiting. I didn't mean to take so long."

"Oh. That's all right, sir."

"Well, Major, go on with your story. You were telling me about the Heglund brothers getting away with murdering Melody's brother...and what led up to your father-in-law being accused of killing Edgar Heglund."

CHAPTER FIVE

★

M ajor Layne Dalton leaned forward on his chair and said, "Well, sir, when the Civil War broke out, all five of the Heglund brothers decided to join the Union army."

"The *Union* army?"

"Yes, sir. They agreed with Abraham Lincoln that secession was unlawful, and even though they're native Virginians, they would not side with the Rebel 'traitors.'"

The general pulled a cigar from his pocket, held it between his fingers, and said, "I can't understand how anyone could go against their home state. I could no more turn on South Carolina, Major, than I could turn on my mother."

"I feel the same way about Virginia, sir."

Longstreet bit the end off the cigar and said, "I guess you haven't taken up this nasty habit, have you?"

"No, sir."

"I won't offer you one, then."

"That's fine, sir."

The general took a wooden match from another pocket, struck it, and while the flame flared, said, "Proceed, Major." He then touched flame to the cigar and puffed it into life.

Layne Dalton did not like the odor of cigar smoke. He eased back on the chair to escape it as much as possible and went on. "Edgar Heglund was in agreement with his sons and put his blessing on their joining the Union army. There were other Fredericksburg citizens who agreed with the Heglunds, but the majority did not."

"Hurrah for the majority," Longstreet said.

"The Heglund brothers were talking some of Fredericksburg's other young men into joining the Federal side, and one day an argument got started at the town square and almost became violent. Jack Reynolds and Edgar Heglund did get into a fight and had to be pulled apart. Jack screamed at Edgar that he and his sons were the real traitors and that Edgar ought to pack up his wife and move north of the Mason-Dixon line.

"Edgar said that Fredericksburg was his home, and nobody was going to force him out of it. Other Union sympathizers agreed, and one man said it wouldn't be long until the North whipped the South into submission anyway, then the Southern sympathizers would be the ones in trouble.

"Well, the Heglund brothers left Fredericksburg and joined the Union army, as did several other young men from the town. The hard feelings between my father-in-law and Edgar continued to grow worse as time passed and this war grew older."

Dalton coughed and turned his face away as cigar smoke rolled into his face. Longstreet jerked the cigar from his mouth and said, "Sorry, Major. I'll just put this thing out." As he spoke, he ground out the cigar in his ash tray and dropped it in a bucket behind his chair.

"Thank you, sir," Dalton said. "So, to proceed, after the Antietam battle in September, we all got a few days to rest, and I returned home to see Melody. While I was there, I learned that Clyde Heglund had been assigned to serve as a guard in a Union prison camp somewhere. Nobody I talked to knew which one. Steve, Everett, and Keith, I learned, were serving in the Union

Army of the Potomac...I think in General Burnside's division. George Heglund, the youngest, had lost a leg at Malvern Hill and had recently returned home."

Dalton pulled the envelope from his coat pocket once again and unfolded the letter. "In Melody's letter, sir, she says that on November 9, her father and George Heglund met face to face on a side street. Jack's story is that George stood there, balanced on his crutches, and reviled him for being a traitor. Jack lashed back that George's brothers had murdered his son. They had fooled the law, but he knew it was they who did it.

"George bit back, saying he hoped his brothers *had* killed Jack, Jr. My father-in-law went into a rage and shoved George to the ground. As Jack stormed away, George screamed that his father would get even with him."

Longstreet stroked his long, full beard. "So I suppose Edgar went after Jack."

"Yes, sir. That very night Edgar appeared on my father-in-law's doorstep demanding that he come out of the house. Melody says her mother was at our house at the time. Jack stepped out the door and found himself looking down the barrel of a revolver. Jack made a grab for the gun, and suddenly they were in a wrestling match. The gun went off, and Edgar collapsed with a slug in his midsection, and he died four hours later. Neighbors reported hearing the gun shot, but no one actually witnessed the incident."

"Too bad someone didn't see it," Longstreet said, "but since Edgar came onto Jack's property with his gun, I'd think any judge and jury would rule out murder."

"Well, sir, there's a complication. Turns out the revolver is Jack's."

Longstreet's brow furrowed. "I don't understand."

"Well, quite some time after the Heglund brothers tore up the Reynolds house, Jack discovered that his revolver was missing. He reported the missing gun to the town constable, and an investigation followed, but the Heglund brothers denied having stolen it.

Fredericksburg has had two constables since the break-in, and according to what Melody says in her letter, the present constable cannot find any record of Jack's having reported the gun missing."

"So with no record of the report, it looks like Jack is lying."

"Yes, sir. Melody says that four credible witnesses have come forth who saw Jack push George to the ground and stomp away…and they heard George scream that his father would get even with him. Word around town is that the county prosecutor— whom everyone knows was a close friend of Edgar's—is going to say in court that Jack was waiting with his gun for Edgar to show up."

"Major, it doesn't look good for your father-in-law," General Longstreet said. "I hope somehow the truth will come out."

"Thank you, sir."

"I would give you longer," said the general, "but with the Yankees moving this way and another battle in the making, I must insist that you be back here by sundown on Wednesday. General Lee will be here that day, and he no doubt will have information we can act upon. We need to be ready to follow whatever orders he gives, which will, in all probability, see some kind of move on our part on Thursday. I need you here for that, as does General Kershaw."

"I understand, sir."

"I realize this only gives you time to be there for the trial…not for the execution, if it comes to that. But let's pray that Mr. Reynolds will be acquitted, and that there'll be no execution."

"Yes, sir," said the major, rising.

Longstreet took out an official-looking piece of paper with his name printed on it. Dipping pen in ink-well, he wrote out his order, signed it, and handed it to Dalton. "Show this to General Kershaw, then carry it with you."

Dalton saluted and said, "Thank you, sir. I'll be back by sundown on Wednesday."

Longstreet returned the salute and said, "God go with you."

The major smiled and headed for the tent opening. When he reached it, Longstreet said, "Give my best to Melody, Major."

"I will, sir."

Major Dalton headed for Brigadier General Joseph B. Kershaw's tent, which was near the rope corral where the horses were kept. He was moving at a brisk pace when he saw one of his favorite soldiers angling toward him from between two tents. Sergeant Richard Rowland Kirkland, though only nineteen years old, had repeatedly shown his willingness to do anything his superiors asked of him, no matter what inconvenience or danger it might bring upon him.

Kirkland was tall and slender, with dark hair and a thin, hollow-cheeked face. His slim, dark mustache made a sharp contrast with his teeth when he smiled. He was doing just that when he approached Dalton and joined him in his brisk pace.

"Good morning, Major Dalton," Kirkland said. "You seem to be in a hurry, sir. Is there something I can do to help you?"

"And good morning to you, Sergeant. I'm in a hurry because I have to make a hasty ride to Fredericksburg once I show my orders to General Kershaw."

"May I bridle and saddle your horse for you, sir? While you're talking to General Kershaw, I mean. That would speed up your departure once you've finished showing the orders to him."

"Yes, it would," Dalton said. "You know which horse is mine, don't you?"

"Sure do, sir. I'll have him ready to go in no time."

Kirkland veered off toward the corral and the major continued toward Kershaw's tent. The general was just coming out, in conversation with a pair of captains, as Dalton approached.

General Kershaw was a square-jawed, rugged individual, who was all business. He gave Dalton a tight smile and said, "Something I can do for you, Major?"

"Yes, sir," responded Dalton, unfolding the paper and handing it to the general. "General Longstreet said to show you this before I leave. He has given me permission to ride to Fredericksburg imme-diately."

The general, who was in his early fifties but looked ten years older, rubbed his heavy mustache while reading the order. He handed it back to Dalton and said, "Whatever your emergency is, Major, I hope everything will turn out all right. God be with you."

Dalton thanked him and hastened toward the corral to find Sergeant Kirkland leading his horse toward him, saddled and ready to go.

He took the reins from Kirkland and led the bay gelding toward the edge of the camp before mounting. "Thank you, Sergeant. You're a gentleman."

"Just want to be of help, sir," Kirkland replied, keeping pace with him. "Sir?"

"Yes?"

"I don't know if you recall, but you told me about your wife being pregnant right after you found out she was."

"Yes, I remember," nodded Dalton.

"Well, sir…you seem to be somewhat upset. Is…she having a problem with the pregnancy?"

"No. There is an emergency, but it is an entirely different matter."

"I'm glad for that, sir, though I'm sorry about the emergency."

"Thank you."

"Sir, when you told me about the baby, you were sure it's a boy. Do you still feel confident it's a boy?"

"Sure do."

"Have you and Mrs. Dalton picked out a name for him yet?"

"Sure have. Daniel Lee Dalton, after my favorite uncle."

"That's wonderful, sir. I sure hope little Danny will be a strong, healthy baby."

"Thank you, Sergeant," said the major, mounting his horse and settling in the saddle.

✸✸✸✸✸

The November air was nippy as Major Dalton approached Fredericksburg. It was mid-afternoon and the sun was barely peeping from behind some low-hanging, long-fingered clouds.

Dalton greeted the Confederate soldiers on duty at the edge of town and rode straight for his house. People on the streets greeted him along the way. His heart quickened pace when he turned a corner and his house came into view. He hadn't seen Melody for nearly three months.

He wondered how big she would be by now. She had only said in her letters that she was losing her figure and hoped he would still love her. Silly girl.

Layne turned into the yard and rode toward the barn and small corral at the back. Though the windows of the house were closed, he could hear Melody playing her prized concert grand. He removed the saddle and bridle from the horse and made sure it had grain and water, then headed for the back porch. Melody's music could still be heard. He found the back door unlocked, entered the kitchen, and hurried through the dining room. As he approached the staircase, he noted that Melody was playing a hymn. He couldn't identify it, but he had heard it in church services when he was a boy.

The thrill of knowing he was about to see his wife and hold her in his arms had Layne's heart pounding as he bounded up the stairs. He reached the landing and ran his hand along the railing as he moved toward the open double doors of the music room. He adjusted his collar, making sure he was presentable, and stepped into the room.

Melody stopped playing, eyes wide, and breathed, "Layne! Oh, Layne!"

She slowly rose from the piano bench, but before she could take a step, Layne had her in his arms and was kissing her.

Tears touched Melody's cheeks as she awkwardly clung to her husband with the baby between them. They embraced for a long moment, then she eased back from him and brushed away her tears. She looked down at her bulging midsection and said, "I've really lost my figure, haven't I?"

Layne cupped her face in his hands, kissed her again, and said, "You sweet thing. I love you more than ever. You're going to give me a son."

She took hold of his wrists and asked, "You won't throw me away if it turns out be a girl, will you?"

Layne kissed her once more and said, "Silly girl. Of course I won't throw you away. I'll love a daughter as much as I would love a son...but I know it's a boy." He patted her stomach and asked, "You are taking care of yourself and little Danny Lee, aren't you?"

"Of course," she said, taking him by the hand. "Lets' go downstairs. Are you hungry?"

"A little. But I can wait till supper. Why don't we just go to Mabel's?"

"I'll be glad to cook supper for you, darling," she said softly.

"Not tonight, sweetheart. I don't want you working in the kitchen tonight. We'll just go to Mabel's. Okay?"

"Of course, as long as you don't think I'm being lazy."

"That'll be the day...when Melody Anne Dalton becomes lazy. I have to head back Wednesday in time to be at camp by sundown. I'll let you cook supper for me tomorrow."

"Oh, I'm so glad you could be here for the trial. It'll be such a help to all of us."

"I'm glad, too," he replied. "General Longstreet was very understanding. He would have let me stay longer, but General Lee is coming to the camp Wednesday. The Yankees are coming this way, and for sure, there's going to be a big battle. General Longstreet and General Kershaw need me there."

"I wish this awful war was over," Melody said with shaky voice.

"Yes, don't we all," Layne nodded.

They passed from the music room, crossed the landing, and stopped at the rail, looking down to the parlor and reception area below.

"How's your daddy holding up?" Layne asked.

"He's got a good grip on himself. Actually, Mother's the one who's having the hardest time."

"I can understand that. Any further developments since you wrote the letter?"

"No. Daddy's attorney says it doesn't look good, but he's working hard in the records department at the police building. He says if he can just produce evidence that Daddy reported the gun missing, it will put a whole new light on the trial."

"You'd think people in the police business would be more careful with their records, wouldn't you?"

"Yes. Time's running short, but we're trusting the Lord to take care of the matter. Daddy's innocent, and God knows it."

Layne was amazed to hear his wife talk of God in such a familiar way. It caught him off guard, and he could think of nothing to say in response.

They reached the stairs, and he put an arm around her as they began slowly descending the staircase. "I heard you playing a hymn when I came in," he said. "I've never heard you play church music before. I know I heard that hymn as a boy when Grandma used to take me to church, but I can't think of its name."

"'Amazing Grace.' John Newton's most famous hymn."

"Oh, that's right. I knew I'd heard it before."

They reached the bottom of the stairs. Layne released her from his strong arm, and she turned to face him. "Darling, I have something to tell you. I didn't put it into any of my letters because I wanted to tell you in person."

Layne grinned and said, "I know! Doc Craig says you're going to have twins!"

"No! No! Nothing like that," Melody giggled. "It's regarding the hymn I was playing. Come. Let's sit down here in the parlor, and I'll tell you about it."

When they were seated comfortably on a small couch, Melody turned to face Layne and laid a hand on his arm. A strange light danced in her deep-blue eyes as she said, "Darling, I know you remember that night a couple of years ago when Walter and Harriet had us over for supper and talked to us about our need to know Jesus Christ personally, to have salvation and forgiveness of our sins."

"Yes, I remember." A queasy feeling settled in Layne's stomach.

"Well, three weeks ago they had a revival meeting at Harriet's church, and she invited Mother, Daddy, and me to the meeting. And...well, darling, we responded to the preaching and received the Lord Jesus into our hearts. He has forgiven our sins and cleansed us in His blood. We're Christians now."

Layne could tell that Melody was on edge as she spoke, not knowing how he might react. He loved her too much to hurt her in any way. Though the news was a bit disconcerting, he smiled and said, "If this has given you and your parents peace and contentment, honey, I'm glad. Especially in the light of what your dad is facing right now."

"It most definitely has," she told him. "Like I said, we're trusting the Lord to take care of Daddy. Harriet came over and prayed with me last night about it. I just know the Lord will see that justice is done." Melody paused, then said, "My greatest concern now, darling, is that you come to know Jesus, too."

"Well, like I told you when Walter and Harriet talked to us a couple of years ago—my Uncle Dan taught me when I was in my teens that every man has to meet God in his own way. I wouldn't hurt your feelings for anything, but I have to be honest with you. The fanatical approach taken by the Bible-thumpers is just not my way."

Melody started to speak, but Layne took her hand and said, "Honey, I will never stand in the way of your faith, but as for me...I'll leave that part of my life just as it is."

Melody did her best to cover the disappointment in her voice as she said, "I bought myself a new Bible, darling...and I bought one for you, too."

Layne was thrown off balance, but managed to smile and say, "That's fine. Thank you."

"Your Bible is over there on the mantel. I would like for you to carry it with you when you go."

Layne made his way to the mantel and picked up the Bible. Melody had written a note to him on the flyleaf. He read it quickly and was touched by her well-chosen words. She was smiling at him when he looked back at her.

"You're the most wonderful woman in the world, Melody Anne Dalton. Thank you. I will carry this Bible with me everywhere I go."

"I've underlined several passages in the New Testament for you to read. The pages are identified with bookmarks. You'll see them."

"All right," he nodded.

"Darling, when you read those passages, you will see that nobody comes to God in his own way. We must come to Him *His* way. The Scriptures I've underlined make this very clear and will show you the way. You will read them, won't you?"

"Of course," he responded warmly. "I want to make little Danny's mother happy. If my reading this Bible will make you happy, I'm more than glad to do it."

"Thank you," she replied, swallowing a lump in her throat.

After supper that evening, Layne left Melody long enough to go to the Fredericksburg jail and visit his father-in-law. Jack was elated to see him, and in the course of their conversation, told him of his new-found faith. Layne said he was glad for him, and that with the kind of faith Melody seemed to have, it wouldn't surprise him if Jack walked out of the courtroom tomorrow a free man.

By noon the next day the trial was over. The attorney's search in the police records had been rewarded just before midnight the night before. He found papers in an old dusty file cabinet giving proof that Jack had reported his revolver stolen a few months after the Heglund brothers had broken into the Reynolds home.

The jury agreed with Jack's attorney that Jack had no reason for reporting the gun missing if it was not so, and that he could not have foreseen nor premeditated the incident that took place on his porch. The jury believed that the Heglunds had stolen the gun, and that Edgar had carried it to the Reynolds house the night he was killed. Jack was acting in self-defense.

As the Reynoldses, the Daltons, the Wiley Price family, and Harriet Smith stood together in front of the courthouse, some of Fredericksburg's citizens approached Jack, telling him they were glad justice was done. Others, who favored the Heglunds, turned up their noses and walked away.

Frances clung to her husband's arm, elated at how the Lord had answered prayer on Jack's behalf. Suddenly she saw Ethel Heglund coming their direction with George beside her, hobbling along on his crutches. During the trial, both Ethel and her youngest son had glowered at her across the courtroom.

"Ethel and George are coming," Frances whispered to her husband.

All eyes were on mother and son as they drew up. Ethel fixed Jack with hate-filled eyes and rasped, "The jury may have acquitted you, Jack Reynolds, but as far as I'm concerned, you murdered my husband!"

"Edgar carried my stolen gun to my house for one reason, Ethel. He was going to shoot me. You know it, George knows it, and the jury knows it."

"This ain't over, old man!" George railed. "My brothers ain't gonna take it lightly when they find out you murdered Pa! You're gonna be sorry, I'll tell you that!"

Layne moved close to George and said tartly, "Jack didn't murder your father, kid. It was self-defense, and you'd better make sure your brothers understand that."

"My brothers will see it just like me and Ma do…and they'll act accordingly." He made a half-turn on his crutches and said, "Come on, Ma, let's go. It stinks here."

CHAPTER SIX

✦

Layne and Melody Dalton accompanied her parents to their home, and while the four of them were eating a light lunch in the kitchen, Frances said to Jack, "I think we just as well tell the kids right now, don't you?"

"No reason to delay it," he nodded.

"Tell us what?" Melody asked.

"Your mother and I came to an agreement about a week ago," Jack replied. "If I was acquitted—and thank the Lord He brought it to pass—we would pack up and head for Virginia City."

Melody's eyes widened. "Virginia City, *Nevada?*"

"That's right."

"Has Uncle Hank been writing you?"

"Yes, he has," Frances said. "Your daddy hasn't told you this, but his cobbler business has been hurting of late. Uncle Hank has written several times telling us that his gold mining business is prospering magnificently. In his last letter, he asked your daddy to come out and be his partner."

Concern etched itself on Melody's pretty face. She set worried eyes on Layne, then said to her father, "Nevada is a long way from here."

"I know, honey, but this is a once-in-a-lifetime opportunity. The war has hurt my business, with so many men away from Fredericksburg in the army...and with the looks I was getting from some of the townspeople today, it's only going to get worse. Becoming a partner with Hank will set your mother and me up for the rest of our lives. Can you understand that?"

Layne saw Melody's lower lip quiver. He took her hand and said, "When the war's over, honey, we can go visit them in Nevada."

Melody willed herself calm and looked at her mother, then at her father. "I understand. I'm glad for both of you. It's just that I'll miss you both so terribly."

"We'll miss you, too, honey," said Jack. "And we'd sure like to be here when our little grandbaby is born. But if I don't take Hank up on his offer soon, it'll be gone."

"I know, Daddy," Melody said, trying to smile. "We'll just have to pray that the Lord will one day let all of us be together again. Maybe when the war's over, Layne and the baby and I can live out West."

"That could happen," Layne said. "The Indian situation out there is going to warrant a number of forts. It'll take soldiers to man those forts."

"What I'm concerned about, now, honey," said Jack, "is this Heglund threat. They might decide to take out their wrath on you."

"I don't think so, Daddy. It's you they'll want. I doubt they'll bother me."

"Maybe I should move you elsewhere, Melody," Layne said. "I don't want that bunch to have any opportunity to harm you."

Melody patted his arm. "They're not going to harm me, darling. This is my home. I want to stay right here."

"You know them better than I do," Layne said tightly, "but if there's any chance—"

"I'll be fine. I have Harriet right next door, and plenty of other neighbors all around me. The Heglunds aren't going to come around our house, anyway."

"If they even so much as frighten you, this earth isn't big enough to hide them. I'll find them and make them wish they'd never been born."

Jack noted the resolute look in his son-in-law's eyes. "I believe you mean that, Layne."

"With everything that's in me, sir."

The next morning, Harriet Smith had Layne and Melody over for breakfast, knowing Layne would have to leave shortly and ride for the camp near Culpeper.

They discussed the war situation as they were eating. Layne lamented that he might not be able to see Melody again until after the baby was born, since the Union army was making moves toward further aggression against the Confederacy. There might be a whole series of battles before he could get back.

Harriet looked across the table at Layne and said, "I don't want you worrying about when the baby comes. So far, Melody's pregnancy has been quite normal, and we have no reason to believe she's going to have any complications. If for some reason Dr. Craig is not available when the time comes, I've had considerable experience as a midwife. I can deliver the baby."

Layne eased back on the chair and said, "Harriet, you don't know what it means to me for Melody to have such a good friend. My mind will be much more at ease knowing you're here to look out for her."

"It's my pleasure," smiled Harriet.

"And if you should see any of the Heglund brothers slithering around our house, send somebody for the police immediately, will you?"

Harriet laughed. "*Slithering* is a good word for a Heglund. Yes, Layne, I'll keep an eye out for the snakes."

When breakfast was over, Layne and Melody returned to their house for a few private moments before he had to ride out. They went to the music room, where by request, Melody played and sang "Beautiful Dreamer" for her husband.

When she finished, he leaned over and kissed her, and said, "I need to be going, sweetheart."

"Could you stay long enough for me to sing 'Amazing Grace' for you? I'd like for you to have the words ringing in your heart while you ride."

Layne cuffed her chin playfully and said, "If you play and sing it, I guarantee you the words will ring in my heart."

Melody played and sang "Amazing Grace" for her husband, praying in her heart that its message would take hold of him.

When she finished, they walked down the stairs together. Melody waited while Layne bridled and saddled his horse, then met him at the front porch as he led the animal from the barn. They held each other for a long moment, then shared a lingering kiss. Layne mounted to the sound of squeaking leather, then looked down at Melody and said, "Please keep writing me through Richmond, sweetheart. No matter where I am, the War Department will get the letters to me eventually. And send me a lock of little Danny's hair when he's born, okay?"

Melody replied through tears, "Yes. I will, darling. You won't forget to read your Bible?"

"No. I promise. So long, sweetheart. I love you."

"I love you, too," she said, choking out the words.

Melody Anne Dalton watched the man she loved ride away. "Dear Lord," she prayed, "keep him safe. And please bring him to Yourself very soon. I want Layne to be saved more than anything in the world."

Major Dalton rode into the Culpeper camp late in the afternoon on Wednesday, November 19. The shadows were long as he drew rein at the rope corral. When his feet touched ground, Sergeant Kirkland came running up and said, "Major Dalton, sir."

"Yes, Sergeant?" responded Dalton.

"General Longstreet told me to watch for you, sir. He wants you in town at the meeting house immediately. General Lee is there. They are meeting with all the officers in our corps. It's very important."

"All right," grinned Dalton, mounting up again. "I'll get right over there."

"How's Mrs. Dalton, sir?"

"She's doing fine, thank you."

"Things work out okay with the emergency?"

"Splendidly. Everything's fine."

"I'm glad, sir."

"Thank you, Sergeant."

The sun had dipped below the western horizon by the time Layne hauled up in front of the Culpeper Meeting House. He recognized General Lee's horse, Traveler, tied next to General Longstreet's and General Kershaw's animals. Two corporals at the door greeted him. While one opened it so he could enter, the other said, "You're just in time, Major Dalton. They're about to start."

Dalton moved inside and saw Lee and Longstreet standing before the other officers who were seated on backless benches at the front of the building. When Longstreet saw Dalton, he smiled and said, "Ah, Major Dalton. Glad you're here. We were just about to begin our meeting."

Robert Edward Lee knew Dalton. As the major drew up and saluted, Lee smiled and said, "Good to see you, Major."

"Thank you, sir. It's good to see you, too."

Layne admired the Confederate army leader. Lee's full head of silver hair and his ruler-straight military stance highlighted his air of dignity. The general looked tired. There were dark, pronounced circles under his eyes. Though he was only fifty-six years of age, he looked much older. Layne knew it was the price a military leader paid in war time.

Dalton spoke to the other officers and sat down among them. Some asked in hushed voices about his hurried trip home, but before he could explain, General Longstreet interrupted with a loud voice, "All right, gentlemen, your attention, please. General Lee and I have been in discussion since he arrived here this morning. He has information for us, and wishes to address you at this time."

The officers all stood at attention and saluted their beloved leader.

Lee saluted in return, smiled, and said, "Be seated, gentlemen."

General Longstreet remained on his feet, standing a little behind and to the side of Lee as the silver-haired leader spoke in his slow, southern accent. "As you gentlemen know, on November 7, just twelve days ago, Abe Lincoln relieved George McClellan as commander of the Army of the Potomac and replaced him with Ambrose Burnside. I understand that for the first few days, there was almost mutiny amongst the Federal ranks because of it. Too bad it didn't happen." The officers laughed.

"I'm sorry about McClellan's departure. My years as a military leader have developed some kind of sixth sense within me that has helped me to divine an opposing commander's intentions. I found General McClellan to be extremely predictable, as you gentlemen know from some of our previous conflicts.

"I have feared that Lincoln would one day make a change and put in charge a man I did not understand. It is beginning to look like he's done it. General Burnside has me a bit confused. I have learned that in the past few days, he has formed his army into what he calls his three 'grand divisions.' Each division contains two corps, each of those with its own staff. Three major generals command the divisions…Edwin Sumner, William Franklin, and Joe Hooker.

"I learned day before yesterday from my intelligence people that General Sumner and his grand division departed from their camp near Warrenton on November 15, and are headed south. I have no word as yet on any movement by the other two Yankee divisions."

Major General Lafayette McLaws raised a hand.

"Yes, General McLaws," nodded Lee.

"What is your thinking about this move, sir? Are we looking at the beginnings of the thing we've feared most...Lincoln's move to capture Richmond?"

"I'm not sure, General. From the way Sumner's headed, I'm thinking that possibly General Burnside is intending to take his army to Alexandria, put it aboard ships, sail it to North Carolina, and begin an offensive there."

At that moment the door opened and one of the corporals said, "Pardon me, General Lee, but there's a courier here from Confederate intelligence. Says he has important news. Shall I send him in?"

"By all means," nodded Lee.

The courier hastened through the door, half-ran to General Lee, and handed him a sealed envelope, saying, "I brought this as fast as I could, sir."

"Good job, Corporal," smiled Lee. "Thank you."

Lee waited until the courier was gone and the door was shut, then removed a folded sheet of paper from the envelope and read it silently. He looked first at Longstreet, then at the group of officers and said, "Gentlemen, this throws a whole new light on the subject. I think, General McLaws, you were right. This just may be Lincoln's long-awaited drive toward our capital city. General Sumner has bypassed Alexandria, and late today marched his grand division into Falmouth."

General Lee set his tired eyes on Dalton. "Major Dalton, your home is in Fredericksburg. I'm correct, am I not? Falmouth is little more than a mile upriver from Fredericksburg."

"Exactly a mile-and-a-half, sir," responded Dalton, a cold ball of ice forming in his stomach.

Lee nodded, looked at the paper in his hand once more, then said to the group, "Intelligence also says that Franklin and Hooker are leading their divisions southward about a day's march behind Sumner. I can only interpret these moves in one way: the Union army is launching its campaign to move on Richmond! It *could* be a feint, but I'm inclined to believe they've set their Yankee minds on our capital city. Well, I can tell them this much—they're going to have a fight on their hands. The Army of Northern Virginia will be in battle position before they get a glimpse of Richmond's rooftops!"

There was a rousing cheer from the officers.

Lee turned to Longstreet and said, "General, I presume you have a map of Virginia in your tent?"

"Yes, sir," replied Longstreet, stepping closer.

"You and I will burn some midnight oil and meet back here with these men at sunrise."

When the meeting was dismissed and the officers were leaving the building, Layne Dalton approached Lee and said, "General Lee, sir, do you think Burnside will try to capture Fredericksburg on his march toward Richmond?"

"I don't know what to think, Major. If it were McClellan, I could tell you for sure he would want to capture Fredericksburg. But Burnside is untested. I just don't know what might be in his mind. He might bypass Fredericksburg, figuring he'll own it anyway if they capture Richmond. I know you're asking because your wife is there, and I certainly understand your concern. So let me say this…I am definitely going to prepare to defend Fredericksburg. I really wouldn't want to fight the enemy there, but we'll be prepared to do so if we have to."

"Yes, sir."

Lee noted the worried look in Dalton's eyes and said, "Let me add something here, Major."

"Yes, sir?"

"If we see that we have to defend your town, we'll evacuate every civilian to a safe place. Mrs. Dalton will be in no danger."

"Thank you, General. I appreciate your understanding my apprehension."

Lee smiled. "I have a wife, too, son."

General Longstreet was still standing close. Before Dalton turned to leave, Longstreet said, "General Lee, if this is indeed the

Union's move to take Richmond, shouldn't you get General Jackson and his troops over here?"

"I can't afford to move Jackson's corps out of the Shenandoah Valley. At least not the better part of it. I fear that if I did, Burnside might turn some of his army that direction and we'd lose the Valley."

Longstreet did not always agree with General Lee's military strategy. To him, the Shenandoah Valley was in no immediate danger. Were the choice his, he would concentrate the entire Army of Northern Virginia between Burnside's Army of the Potomac and the Confederate capital. If Richmond fell, the Federals would have the Valley anyway.

Longstreet, however, would not argue with his superior, but said tactfully, "I'm glad you intimated, sir, that you might bring at least some of General Jackson's corps over here. Wouldn't it be wise to shift at least a few of his divisions east of the Blue Ridge so they would be closer at hand?"

Lee regarded his subordinate with careful eyes, and nodded slowly. "That might be a good move, General."

Having gained ground, Longstreet was feeling bolder. "And may I suggest, sir, that you bring General Jeb Stuart's cavalry brigade all the way over here? If Burnside is doing what we think, we're going to need more cavalry."

Lee pulled absently at an ear. "I'm sure General Jackson wouldn't mind sending us General Stuart. Let me think on it."

After a long night of study, pouring over the Virginia map with Longstreet at his side, Lee was ready to move his army. The two men slept barely over an hour and were up at dawn.

The officers grabbed a quick breakfast and gathered in the Culpeper Meeting House just as the eastern sky was turning a pinkish-yellow.

Lee wasted no time getting down to business. He laid out his orders to the officers, explaining that after a night of studying the situation, he felt General Burnside would probably try to capture Fredericksburg on his way to Richmond, since it lay directly in his path. Therefore, as much as he would rather fight the Federals some twenty-five miles farther south of Fredericksburg along the North Anna River, he would prepare to take his stand at Fredericksburg.

Two divisions would be sent out immediately from the Culpeper camp. One, under Brigadier General Robert Ransom, would move south along the Orange & Alexandria Railroad to a point just south of Fredericksburg. Dug in there, Ransom would be in a position to defend the town in case the Yankees decided to swing around and come in from the south.

The other division, under Major General Lafayette McLaws, would march directly to Fredericksburg, accompanied by Joseph B. Kershaw's brigade, William H. F. Lee's cavalry brigade, and James H. Lane's artillery. They would take defensive positions around Fredericksburg on the east, north, and west as directed by McLaws.

Lee explained that he was wiring General Stonewall Jackson to move a few of his divisions east of the Blue Ridge in order to have them closer to Fredericksburg if needed. He also would order Major General Jeb Stuart's cavalry to move down from the Shenandoah Valley and scout the enemy's movements along the Rappahannock River.

General Longstreet smiled to himself while Lee explained his strategy.

A cold wind came up as the assigned units moved out of the Culpeper camp, scudding heavy clouds across the sky that soon covered the rising sun. General Lee promptly sent his wire to Stonewall Jackson in the Shenandoah Valley and waited for confirmation that the orders had been received. In less than an hour, Jackson wired back that the designated divisions were preparing to move out, and that Jeb Stuart's cavalry would be headed toward the Rappahannock by 10:00 A.M.

The Confederate troops arrived at Fredericksburg in the middle of the afternoon on November 20. While they were setting up their artillery on the hills to the south and west of the town, and the cavalry and infantry were getting into position, Major Dalton stationed his infantry unit in the trees on top of Marye's Heights. Named for the family whose mansion nestled like a fairy castle in the woods near the crest of the main hill, Marye's Heights was the highest point on the hills that made a semi-circle around Fredericksburg.

Dalton's five hundred men were positioned alternately in small groups between the big guns and howitzers of the artillery. He was checking with Brigadier General James H. Lane to be sure Lane was satisfied with the protection his troops would offer his artillerymen when he saw Sergeant Kirkland coming toward him.

Lane eyed the way Dalton's men were positioned, pulled his overcoat collar up against the cold wind, and said, "Major, you've done a magnificent job. My men will appreciate the protection you're providing, especially if the Yankees come storming up these hills.

"We're here to do our job, sir," grinned Dalton. "We'll guard you like watchdogs."

"I don't doubt it," Lane nodded. "I've already thanked General Kershaw for giving you to us."

Sergeant Kirkland drew up, saluted both men, then said to Dalton, "General Kershaw asked me to come and tell you, Major, that you don't have to check with him again before going into town. He said when you're satisfied that your men know their positions, you can go ahead. He said to remind you that you can only be gone for an hour."

"Thank you, Sergeant," nodded Dalton.

As Kirkland hurried away, General Lane said, "I understand the people in town are pretty upset at the prospect of a battle taking place here."

"I'm not surprised," replied Dalton. "Even though they'll be evacuated before any shooting starts, they don't want their homes destroyed."

"You know someone who lives here?"

"Yes, sir. My wife."

"Oh? So Fredericksburg's your home."

"Yes, sir. My prime concern is for my wife's safety, but I'm also worried about my house. I asked General Kershaw earlier for permission to go into town and spend a little time with Melody. She's expecting our first child, and I want to comfort her as much as I can."

The general smiled. "Then be on your way, my friend. Don't let me delay you."

Melody was seated at the kitchen table with Harriet. They were kneading dough together and discussing the sudden occupation of the surrounding area by the Confederate army. Both women feared what a battle in their town would do to it.

There was a knock at the front door. Melody started to get up, but Harriet was quickly on her feet, saying, "You stay put, honey. I'll see who it is."

Harriet could make out Layne Dalton's tall, wide-shouldered form through the sheer curtains before she opened the door. Turning the key, she swung the door open, and said with a smile, "Hello, soldier. Melody was just saying if you were amongst the troops gathering here, you'd find a way to come and see her."

"I'd wade through a herd of wild elephants to see her," grinned Layne. "How are you, Harriet?"

"Just fine," she replied, closing the door behind him. "She's in the kitchen."

Layne laid his campaign hat on a table in the parlor, draped his overcoat over the back of an overstuffed chair, and headed down the hallway that led to the kitchen.

Harriet called after him, "I'll give you two a few minutes alone together."

Layne looked back and smiled, acknowledging her words, then stepped into the kitchen to find Melody standing by the table, arms open to receive him.

"Hello, darling," she sighed.

He took her in his arms, and they held each other for a long moment, then kissed warmly. He hugged her again, then sat her down at the table and eased onto a chair beside her.

"Oh, Layne, I've been so upset," Melody said. "There's going to be a battle right here, isn't there?"

"It's possible, honey," Layne said, taking both of her hands in his. "It looks like the Federals are beelining for Richmond, and as you know, Fredericksburg is right in their path. General Lee is watching them carefully. He'll see to it that the town is evacuated before any fighting breaks out."

"That's what everyone is telling me," she said, drawing a shuddering breath, "but what about our home? I've heard what those Yankees do when they capture a town. If they don't burn all the houses to the ground, they destroy everything in them and steal what they don't destroy. Layne, what are we going to do?"

"Our soldiers are rooting down all around here, sweetheart. We're going to do everything we can to keep anything like that from happening."

"Harriet and I have been praying together about it...but I have to admit that my faith is a bit weak right now."

"I appreciate Harriet looking after you. She's a gem."

"That she is," Melody agreed. "Where...where do they have you and your men?"

"We're up on Marye's Heights. Sort of bodyguarding an artillery unit. We'll have a real advantage from up there if the battle comes. High ground is always an advantage."

"Is the Marye family still in the mansion?"

"Yes. General Kershaw talked to them. They want to stay, even if the rest of the town evacuates. John Marye said if the high ground is an advantage for the army, it's an advantage for them, so they'll not leave."

"I'm glad you're on high ground," she said with strain in her voice. "Oh, Layne, I couldn't stand it if anything happened to you. I'll be so glad when this horrid war is over."

"Won't we all," he sighed.

Melody met his gaze with a tender look. "Darling, have you read any of the Bible passages I marked?"

"Only a few. I've been pretty busy. But I will as time allows."

They talked for a few minutes about Jack and Frances, wondering how far west they might be by now. Then Layne talked about the baby and how he was looking forward to the day he could hold little Danny in his arms.

The clock on the wall showed Layne he had ten minutes to report back to General Kershaw. He held Melody tight, kissed her, and said, "I'll see you again as soon as I can."

They spoke their love for each other, and as Layne was about to leave the kitchen, Harriet came in. Layne thanked her once again for the way she was taking care of Melody, and hurried away.

CHAPTER SEVEN

★

Rain began to fall from a heavy sky on the afternoon of November 20. At Culpeper, General Robert E. Lee received word that all three of Burnside's grand divisions were closing in on Fredericksburg. It was evident that he was going to have to fight them there.

Lee ordered General Longstreet to march the remainder of the troops to Fredericksburg and make ready for battle. The Rebels trudged through a heavy downpour and the deplorable mud that went with it. General Lee rode Traveler alongside General Longstreet in the lead, his head bent against the wind-driven rain.

When they arrived at Fredericksburg just before dark, the two generals had their tents set up atop Marye's Heights where they could enjoy a commanding view of the town, the river, and the surrounding terrain. Lee was jolted to look across the Rappahannock and behold a massive army. At the same time, a messenger arrived from Major General Jeb Stuart's cavalry brigade, which was moving southward along the Rappahannock. Stuart's message was that the Federals were setting up camp on the hills above the east bank of the Rappahannock at Fredericksburg. Stuart had learned that there were 130,000 of them.

Lee was upset over Confederate intelligence. Reports he had received within the past few days indicated that Burnside's three divisions might total as many as 75,000, but Stuart's figure had to be accurate, for the huge gathering of Union forces Lee could see across the river were much more than 75,000. His heart sank. He would have somewhat under 59,000 troops when Stuart's cavalry arrived.

Longstreet saw the look on Lee's face and said cautiously, "General, sir, shouldn't you send for General Jackson's corps?"

Lee's gaze was riveted on the Union army across the river. When he did not answer, Longstreet said, "General, sir?"

"I heard you, General," Lee drawled, still focusing on the enemy troops, who were fading from view in the gathering darkness. "I can't bring myself to leave the Valley vulnerable as yet."

Longstreet wanted to yell at him. Why couldn't Lee see that the Shenandoah Valley would be a lost cause if the Federals were not halted in their drive to Richmond? They needed Stonewall Jackson's remaining 19,000 troops desperately. But Longstreet knew better than to argue with his venerable leader.

The rain continued to come down in torrents all the next day. Lee stood outside his tent in the downpour and wondered why Burnside did not attack. It could not be the rain. Many battles had been fought in rainstorms. Why wasn't Burnside sending his massive army against the opponent they so greatly outnumbered?

Major General Ambrose E. Burnside paced like a caged lion in his tent just outside of Falmouth, Virginia, a mile-and-a-half upriver from Fredericksburg. Major Generals Edwin V. Sumner, Joseph Hooker, and William B. Franklin stood shoulder-to-shoulder, eyeing their upset and nervous leader. The rain pounded the tent, and water dripped from some of the worn seams along one side.

Few of the Army of the Potomac's officers had full confidence in their newly appointed leader. The three who stood in the tent and observed Burnside's feverish state of mind were wishing General McClellan was still in command.

Hooker and Burnside had never gotten along. They did not like each other, and everyone knew it. Beyond Hooker, however, there was no dislike for Burnside. Whatever his fellow officers and subordinates thought of Burnside's abilities, nearly all of them agreed that he had a captivating personality. Not only had he shown extreme courage, such as in the Battle of Antietam, but there was a certain brigandish air about him. The thirty-eight-year-old major general wore heavy muttonchop whiskers, a broad-brimmed hat atop his balding head, and carried his holstered revolver low on his hip.

The man chosen to replace McClellan smiled frequently, remembered names well, looked after the welfare of his troops, won friends with ease, and took orders in a gracious, submissive manner from his superiors. Hence, he accepted the commission as commander of the Army of the Potomac even though he did not feel qualified.

Burnside's new responsibilities had made him ill the first two days, but he attacked his problems vigorously, nevertheless, and on November 9 he forwarded to President Lincoln a bold new strategy for the capture of Richmond. He proposed concentrating his forces along the route southwest toward Gordonsville to convince Lee that the Federals intended to continue their drive in that direction.

Then Burnside would make a quick pivot and move his army rapidly southeastward from Warrenton to Fredericksburg, on the Rappahannock River. Burnside explained to Lincoln that by veering eastward while maintaining a southerly route, his army would stay closer to Washington and its base of supplies. It would also be on a more direct route to Richmond because Fredericksburg was on the main road midway between the two capitals. Burnside's plan was to cross the Rappahannock and capture Fredericksburg before Lee could amass enough men to stop him, then move south, seize Richmond, and bring an end to the bloody war.

Along with his daring scheme, Burnside requested of Lincoln

that thirty canal boats and barges loaded with needed goods be sent down the Potomac to a new supply base at Belle Plain, ten miles northeast of Fredericksburg. In addition, he wanted a wagon train of ammunition and food to move overland from Alexandria to the bank of the Rappahannock where he would gather his army, across the river from Fredericksburg. And most important, Burnside requested enough pontoons to build several floating bridges across the Rappahannock, which was now swollen and rising due to heavy rains up north. Without the floating bridges, he could not get his troops across the river to attack and seize Fredericksburg.

There had been little enthusiasm in Washington for Burnside's plan. Lincoln discussed it with General-in-Chief of the Union Army, Henry W. Halleck, and Halleck did not like it. He argued that the best route was to swing the Army of the Potomac westward to Gordonsville. This would bypass Fredericksburg and give a straight shot to Richmond southeastward, and avoid the need of pontoons and lumber to build floating bridges.

Wires had gone back and forth between Burnside and Lincoln, but in spite of Halleck's objections, Burnside held firm, insisting his plan was best. It would throw Lee off balance by making him think the Federals were going to take the Gordonsville route. Fredericksburg could be in Union hands and the Federal troops on their way to Richmond before Lee could raise a blockade.

Lincoln had been skeptical of Burnside's scheme, also. He had tried for months to get McClellan to meet the Confederate Army of Northern Virginia head-on, and now his new commander was proposing to skirt that army and simply move on the Confederate capital. However, Lincoln was so pleased to finally have a commander who was willing to put his army in motion that he approved the plan on November 14. His last words in the wire of approval were: "Your plan will succeed if you move very rapidly; otherwise not."

Burnside paced and fumed in front of his three division commanders, cursing the name of Brigadier General Daniel P. Woodbury, who was responsible for delivering the pontoons and bridge-building materials. General Sumner said, "Sir, I'm sure it's the rain that's holding General Woodbury up. It's just one of those things that nobody can control."

Face red with anger, Burnside said, "General Sumner, it's November 25! I ordered those pontoons on November 14, the same day I ordered the wagonloads of food, supplies, and ammunition. The wagons got here four days ago. They had to go through rain and mud, too. No, there's some bungling going on in this army, and somebody's head is going to roll!"

The sixty-five-year-old Sumner held his voice steady and said, "General Burnside, sir, experience has taught me not to speak out against fellow officers until I know the circumstances."

Burnside's face reddened the more. "May I remind you, sir, that the president and General Halleck will hold one man responsible for how this campaign goes? *Me!* If those pontoons had arrived when they should have, we could have made an easy thing of capturing Fredericksburg. Not now! Lee's got his forces dug in too well. I'll take it on the chin for it, but General Woodbury's going to be sorry he fiddled around getting those pontoons here!"

General Hooker, who had never covered his dislike for Burnside, snapped, "Seems to me, *sir*, you ought to take some advice from General Sumner, who was in a fighting uniform before you got out of diapers! You should hold your caustic comments until you learn why General Woodbury's late."

Burnside was about to lash back when a voice called from outside the tent, "General Burnside! Good news! The pontoons are here!"

Burnside moved to the flap, jerked it open, and set dark eyes on a sergeant who stood dripping in the rain. "Is the entire wagon train here?"

"Yes, sir."

"General Woodbury?"

"Yes, sir."

"You go tell him I want him at my tent immediately!"

"Yes, sir," saluted the sergeant, and hurried away.

Franklin, who was a few years older than Burnside, said, "Sir, I mean no disrespect, but you should at least hear General Woodbury out before you take any action."

"General Franklin, it's easy for you to stand there and tell me what I ought to do. But the responsibility for what happens here rests on my shoulders."

"I know that, sir," Franklin replied, clearing his throat, "but if you fly off the handle before you give General Woodbury a chance to explain, you could do yourself some real harm. You need the respect of your men."

"He's giving you sage advice, sir," Sumner said. "I know this delay has dragged wickedly across your nerves, but you must gain control of yourself and meet General Woodbury with conduct that becomes an officer of the Union army...especially the commander of the entire Army of the Potomac."

Burnside took a deep breath, ran both palms over his face, and willed his nerves calm. Then in a half-whisper, he said, "You're right, General. You're right."

"General Burnside!" came the sergeant's voice above the roar of the rain.

"General Franklin, will you open the flap and invite General Woodbury in, please?" Burnside said.

Franklin pulled back the flap and saw Brigadier General Daniel P. Woodbury leaning close to the tent beside the sergeant. Water was dripping off the brim of his campaign hat. "General Burnside asked me to invite you in, sir. Please enter."

Franklin thanked the sergeant and sent him away as Woodbury, a stately man in his mid-fifties, moved inside.

Woodbury saluted Burnside, acknowledged the presence of the other officers, then removed his dripping hat and said, "General Burnside, sir, I'm sure you're fit to be tied with the delay of the pontoons and the building material, but we got a late start, and the mud has been atrocious."

"I know about the mud, sir," said Burnside, "but what is this about a late start?"

"Well, sir, I did not receive the request for the pontoons and material from General Halleck until the eighteenth. I found out while we were loading the wagons that you had actually put in the order in a wire to President Lincoln on the fourteenth. I'm sorry, sir, but we got here as quickly as we could."

Burnside had no reason to doubt Woodbury's word. For some unknown reason, Halleck had delayed turning in the order. Was it because Halleck disagreed with his plan and deliberately held off turning in the order? Halleck was a proud bird. Maybe this was his way of getting back at Burnside for persuading the president to adopt his plan instead of Halleck's. Burnside would never know. There was nothing he could do about it.

"You're right, General," Burnside said. "I have been quite upset at the delay. It has allowed Lee to fortify himself on all the high places and in every nook and cranny of Fredericksburg. The delay is going to result in more Yankee blood being shed than would have been otherwise. However, it is apparently no fault of yours."

Burnside glanced at Sumner and Franklin, thanking them with his eyes for calming him down. He would not look at Hooker.

"Well, sir," said Woodbury, "if you're through with me, I need to get back to the wagons. We'll begin building the bridges immediately. I assume you plan to float them down the river to Fredericksburg for the actual crossing."

"Correct," nodded Burnside. "When can I plan to do so?"

"Well, sir, we should have the bridges built and ready for service in four or five days."

Burnside had hoped the work could be done quicker, but since the construction of floating bridges was beyond his experience or knowledge, he said, "Do your best to make it four, will you?"

"Yes, sir," Woodbury said. He saluted, spoke briefly to Sumner, Franklin, and Hooker, and was gone.

✳✳✳✳✳

At nightfall on November 25, General Robert E. Lee learned of the arrival of the pontoons at Falmouth. Now Lee knew why Burnside had not attacked before. He called his commanders together and informed them that General Burnside was going to float his army across the Rappahannock. Lee admitted that he should have sent for General Stonewall Jackson and his troops earlier, and he wired Jackson while his commanders watched. Longstreet heaved a sigh of relief, hoping within himself that Jackson would arrive before the floating bridges were ready for use.

In the meantime, Jeb Stuart and his cavalry of a thousand had arrived. When Jackson's corps got there, the Confederates would have almost seventy-eight thousand men, leaving them still heavily outnumbered by the Federals.

General Burnside's army faced more problems and more delay. Southern civilians took refuge in old abandoned buildings across the river at Falmouth and began firing on the men building the floating bridges. The bridge-builders were unarmed and refused to work with bullets buzzing at them from across the river.

Burnside dared not pull large numbers of men from the camp across from Fredericksburg for fear that the Confederates might take advantage of the smaller force and make their own attack. Eager to get the bridge-builders back to work, Burnside had a few infantrymen fire at the civilians in the old buildings. The civilians were great in number, and for the most part were skilled marksmen. Though the return fire from the Yankee infantrymen limited their shooting, they continued to take their toll of Yankee lives, making progress on the bridge-building slow. Burnside was strung tight because of the further delay.

The weather turned colder as the days passed, and snow replaced the rain.

Stonewall Jackson had set a grueling pace for his troops, and they arrived at Fredericksburg in a heavy snowstorm late in the afternoon on November 29. The corps of more than nineteen thousand men was a welcome sight to the troops already at Fredericksburg. Lee quickly deployed Jackson's troops, sending Brigadier General Jubal Early's division to Skinker's Neck, some twelve miles down river, Major General Daniel H. Hill's division four miles farther down river to Port Royal. The division of Major General Ambrose P. Hill was deployed at a spot six miles southeast of Fredericksburg, and that of Brigadier General William B. Taliafero at a location four miles south of town. These four commands were to guard against any attempt by Burnside to cross downstream and outflank the Confederates. At the same time, Lee ordered Stuart's cavalry to fill in along the lines and on the semicircle of hills at Fredericksburg, strengthening the ranks.

On December 8 the sky was cloudy, but no snow was falling. Lee, Longstreet, Kershaw, and Layne Dalton stood together, hats pulled low and heads turtled into their coat collars against the icy wind that whipped over Marye's Heights.

Lee set his gaze on the four-hundred-foot-wide Rappahannock below and said, "Word is that Burnside's almost got his floating bridges done."

"When do you plan to call for evacuation of the town, sir?" Dalton asked.

"When I know the blue-bellies are ready to make their move," replied Lee. "Most of the people down there have nowhere to go except the fields and the woods. I don't want to send them out there until I have to. This cold weather could be the death of a number of them if they have to stay away for long. This was one of the reasons I didn't want to fight the Federals here." Lee paused, then asked, "What about your wife, Major? Does she have some place to go? I'd sure hate to see her have to camp in the woods, carrying that baby and all."

"Yes, sir," Dalton nodded. "A widow in the church lives about three miles west of town. She's offered to let my wife and our neighbor stay with her until they can return home again."

"Good," said Lee. "I'm glad she has a place to go."

General Kershaw smiled at Dalton. "Sergeant Kirkland tells me you're pulling for a boy, Major."

"Yes, sir, I am. I'll love her if it's a girl, of course, but down deep, I just know it's a boy."

"I guess that's natural. Most men want a son for their first child. Of course, girls are mighty special, Major. Speaking from experience, I can tell you that a father and his daughter can develop a wonderful relationship. I've got two precious daughters, and I wouldn't trade what we've got between us for anything in this world."

The attention of all four men was drawn to a formidable figure lumbering toward them along the edge of the trees. As he walked, his eyes were fixed on the massive army camped on the hills across the Rappahannock.

"Good morning, General Jackson," Dalton said as the tall man drew near.

Jackson returned the greeting, then moved up beside Lee and once again gazed on the Federal forces across the river.

Thomas Jonathan Jackson, at thirty-eight, was one of the best-known generals in the Confederate army. He had been dubbed "Stonewall" for his extreme courage under fire at Bull Run, and led a corps of rough and rugged soldiers who would follow him anywhere.

"We'll have our hands full when they come across the river, General," Lee said.

Jackson pulled his collar up tight around his neck and nodded. "That we will, sir. We may not be as large as the Yankee force, but we'll see that those blue-bellies have their hands full, too."

"No doubt about it," Longstreet said.

Jackson looked down at Fredericksburg, shaking his head. "What a scene," he said. "Two mighty machines of destruction…and huddled between them the forlorn little town."

"War is a terrible thing," put in Kershaw. "Especially on civilians."

"When are you going to evacuate the town, General?" Jackson asked Lee.

"When I'm sure Burnside is ready to attack. As I was telling the others here, for the most part, those poor people down there have nowhere to go but the fields and the woods. I don't want to push them out of their homes until it's absolutely necessary."

"Certainly," nodded Jackson. "Not with snow on the ground, and as cold as the nights have been."

"Exactly. General Stuart has some men watching the progress of the bridge-building at Falmouth, and when they tell me that the bridges are on the water, I'll advise Mayor Tillman to move the people out."

"How long do you think it'll be?"

"From what I'm told by Stuart's spies, I'd say three days…four at the most."

Jackson rubbed his bearded chin and shook his head. "I hope the people of Fredericksburg have homes to come back to when this ordeal is over."

Dalton excused himself and made his way amongst the trees, speaking to his own men and artillerymen as he walked. He found a private spot a few yards from the gate of the Marye mansion, knelt beside a naked-limbed oak tree, and removed his hat. "Lord," he said, "I'm…not very good at this praying business, but I'm awfully worried about what's going to take place here shortly. Please…please let Melody and little Danny get out of town before those Yankees come. And I'd appreciate it too if You'd protect the house. With Melody's parents gone, she and little Danny wouldn't have anyplace else to live. I know I don't deserve for You to answer this prayer, but…would You for my family's sake? Please?"

CHAPTER EIGHT

✦

A light snow began to fall during supper on the evening of December 8. After the meal, General Burnside crowded all of his generals and colonels into his spacious field tent and stood before them by lantern light.

"Gentlemen," he said with a tone of authority in his voice, "I've gathered you here to announce that the pontoon bridges will be ready for use in two days. I am setting the attack for Thursday morning, the eleventh. We'll float the bridges down the river under cover of darkness on the night of the tenth, and bring the troops across the Rappahannock and move on Fredericksburg at dawn."

Colonel Joshua L. Chamberlain, commander of the Twentieth Maine Infantry Regiment, raised a hand for recognition. Chamberlain, the thirty-three-year-old preacher-turned-soldier, was tall, handsome, and extremely bright. He was Phi Beta Kappa, Bowdoin College, Brunswick, Maine, and could speak seven languages fluently.

"Yes, Colonel," nodded Burnside.

"Do I understand correctly, sir, that you plan to send the whole force across the river, directly against Fredericksburg?"

"That's the plan."

"I don't mean to be argumentative nor disrespectful, sir," Chamberlain said cautiously, "but it is my understanding that you talked to your generals about crossing at other places on the river, spreading our troops out so as to make a wide sweep on the town and all those Rebel fortifications. Is this so?"

"Yes, Colonel. But I've changed my mind. Lee has spread his troops along the river southward and inland. By this I know he expects me to do just as I had planned earlier. I'm going to surprise General Lee by bringing the entire force—except for some reserves—head-on into Fredericksburg."

General Hooker's features registered his disagreement, and he spoke up without asking to be recognized. "Have you notified General Halleck of this change in plans?"

"Just this afternoon," Burnside nodded, fixing Hooker with a level stare.

"And have you heard back from him?"

"Not as yet."

"What if he doesn't reply?"

"Then I'll proceed as planned."

"I protest the idea! Have you seen the way Lee's got the whole area fortified? He's got the high ground on Marye's Heights, and it's loaded with artillery. They'll chew us to pieces if we try to cross the river into the teeth of those cannons. This is preposterous! You're out of your mind!"

Burnside fought to control his rage. "General Hooker, may I remind you that if the pontoons had arrived when they were supposed to, taking Fredericksburg would have been a snap! And may I also remind you that I didn't ask for this command. In fact, as you and these other men know, I tried desperately to avoid it."

"That's no excuse for sending troops into the teeth of those cannons and howitzers!" blared Hooker. "We need to attack from every direction!"

"You're forgetting something, General...and possibly you are too, Colonel Chamberlain. We have our own cannons and howitzers well deployed on Stafford Heights and the ridges below the heights. Our artillery will give cover as the troops cross those bridges."

"I haven't forgotten a thing," retorted Hooker. "But I am wondering if you wouldn't change your tactic if *you* had to cross on one of those bridges while the enemy is blasting them to bits!"

"May I remind you, sir," Burnside said through clenched teeth, "that I am commander of this army by order of the president of the United States of America? Your insolence is both an insult to Mr. Lincoln and unbecoming that of a major general of this army! You will hereby refrain from any more such outbursts, or I will have you put under arrest!"

Hooker cast a furtive glance at General Sumner, who gave him a solemn look and slowly shook his head.

When Burnside saw that Joe Hooker was silenced, he looked at Colonel Chamberlain and asked, "Since we have our own artillery on high ground on the east side of the river, Colonel, do you feel differently about my plan now?"

"Without seeming insolent, sir, may I speak my mind?"

"That's what I want you to do," Burnside nodded. "I ask only that you speak with the proper degree of respect, and not in the manner displayed here by General Hooker."

"Yes, sir. With all due respect, General Burnside, I feel that your logic in this matter is seriously flawed."

Burnside blinked. "Go on."

"Well, sir, General Lee apparently has not anticipated a direct attack on Fredericksburg because, as you have pointed out, he has spread his troops along the river southward and even inland. However, the exceptionally advantageous position his artillery and infantry occupy on the high points behind the town are probably the most formidable he could ever hope to find in any war anywhere. He has distributed his troops intelligently, taking care—in my estimation, at least—to provide for rapid lateral movement to counter any maneuver we might undertake. I believe we should cross the river elsewhere with our troops, let our artillery exchange fire with theirs, and spread our men out for the attack."

General Sumner, who stood flanking Burnside, moved closer to him and said, "What Colonel Chamberlain says, sir, makes sense. Besides, I have some other reservations about your plan."

"And, what are those reservations, General?"

"Well, sir, once we get the pontoon bridges floated down to Fredericksburg, we've got to link them together. That's going to take time. It can't be done in pitch-black darkness, so whether we have moonlight to work by or do it in broad daylight, Lee will have his sharpshooters blasting away at us. Our men will be sitting ducks."

"May I say something, sir?" asked Major General William Franklin.

"Yes," nodded Burnside, his face a grim mask.

"We've got other problems too, sir. I'm sure Lee will evacuate the town before we get there with the bridges. He'll have free access to any and all buildings to place snipers in. When our men move into Fredericksburg, they'll be open prey to them. Not only that, but whenever we show Lee that we're coming across the river with practically the entire Army of the Potomac, the divisions he has spread inland and down the river are within a short march of the town. We outnumber the Confederates, sir, but they've got position advantage all over us. Lee's no fool. He's ready for us. I strongly recommend we spread our men out for the attack as Colonel Chamberlain has suggested, and let them cross the floating bridges somewhere other than right at Fredericksburg."

"You gentlemen still don't see it, do you?" Burnside said, shaking his head. "Lee's outlying divisions can't fly. I still say by sending our entire force across the river at Fredericksburg, we'll surprise Lee, and we can occupy the hills and the town before he can bring anything serious against us. We outnumber them almost two-to-one. With the element of surprise, we can overwhelm them."

Burnside looked at Colonel Rush Hawkins of the Ninth New York and asked, "What do you think, Colonel?"

Hawkins pulled at an ear and was brutally frank. "If you make the attack as contemplated, General Burnside, it will bring upon us the greatest slaughter of the war. There isn't infantry enough in our whole army to take those troops nestled up there in the heights."

Hawkins and Burnside were close friends. Surprised that the colonel had taken this position—and irritated that he had—Burnside looked at Lieutenant Colonel Joseph H. Taylor, another close friend, and asked, "What do you think, Colonel?"

Equally forthright, Taylor responded quickly. "The carrying out of your plan will not be warfare, sir. It will be murder."

"What's going on here?" Burnside said in a rush of angry, biting words. "Am I to be surrounded by men who have forgotten their duty as officers in this army? Where is your sense of loyalty!"

Burnside looked over the faces of the group for some kind of support. All was quiet.

Then Brigadier General William H. French of the Fourth New York said with enthusiasm, "I'm in agreement with General Burnside! With the element of surprise and twice as many men, we'll have the battle won and Fredericksburg in our hands within forty-eight hours!"

The other officers stood silently exchanging furtive glances.

A determined look settled in General Burnside's eyes. He addressed the group of officers with gravel in his voice. "I have the backing and the authority of the president of the United States to lead the Union Army of the Potomac in the way I see fit. Therefore, the final decision lies with me. I realize that with the authority goes the responsibility. I am ready to shoulder both. We will proceed with my plan.

"The attack, therefore, is officially set for Thursday morning, December 11. On Wednesday the men will be issued three days' rations. The infantrymen will be issued sixty rounds of ammunition each. There are wagons positioned on top of Stafford Heights with plenty more food and ammunition if we need it before this battle is won.

"I remind you, gentlemen, that your duty as officers of this army is to back me in my decision and show me total loyalty. You are dismissed."

Mayor Donald Tillman sat on the edge of his bed as he removed his shoes and discussed with his wife the imminent attack by the Federal army. It was half past nine on Wednesday night, December 10.

Mrs. Tillman was sitting at the dresser, brushing her hair. "It can't be much longer till those horrible Yankees storm the town. Don't you think you should issue the evacuation order tomorrow? I'd hate to see the people—and us for that matter—trying to get out of town with cannonballs exploding all around us."

"I've got the townspeople on alert, dear," Tillman said, rising from the bed and carrying his shoes to the closet. "But, like General Lee, I hate to put them out in the elements till it's absolutely necessary. We've got your brother's house for shelter out there in the country, but most of our citizens will only have the sky for a roof."

"I understand," said Sarah Tillman, "but will you be able to move them out fast enough when the Yankees come?"

"I'm sure we'll have ample warning. General Lee said he will send word to commence the evacuation when his spies upriver report that the pontoon bridges are on their way. I've got several of the elderly men in town ready to be criers when the time comes. We should be able to get all eighteen hundred of us out of town in an hour or so."

"I sure hope so," Sarah sighed. "It would be terrible if—" Her words were cut off by a loud knock at the front door. "Who could that be at this late hour?" she said, looking at her husband.

"I'll find out," he replied, putting on his slippers.

Mayor Tillman hurried through the house, carrying a burning lantern, and opened the front door. Two men in gray uniforms stood before him. One was a sergeant, the other a corporal.

"Good evening, Mayor. I'm Sergeant Benson and this is Corporal Manfred. General Robert E. Lee sent us."

Tillman swung the door wide and said, "Come in out of the cold, gentlemen." The soldiers stomped the snow from their shoes and stepped inside.

Tillman gestured toward the parlor. "Would you like to sit down?"

"There really isn't time, sir," replied Benson. "General Lee wanted us to tell you that our spies reported to him about a half-hour ago that the Yankees are floating their pontoon bridges down river right now. Since there's no moon, they'll most likely begin to assemble them at daylight."

"I hope General Lee is ready for them," Tillman said.

"As much as possible, sir. He figures it'll take Burnside's engineers a couple of hours, at least, to assemble the bridge sections together. You should have plenty of time to evacuate the town if you start moving people out at daylight."

"We can handle it," nodded Tillman. "Tell General Lee we'll have the town evacuated by around seven-thirty."

Obscure light broke through a heavily clouded sky at 6:15 on the morning of December 11, 1862, but Fredericksburg and the area around it was shrouded in heavy fog. Ghostly mists danced and swirled on the cold surface of the Rappahannock River, making it extremely difficult for the Union engineers to see what they were doing.

Atop Marye's Heights, General Lee welcomed a messenger from Brigadier General William Barksdale, telling him that sounds coming through the fog on the river indicated that the Yankees were assembling their floating bridges.

At the same time, several of Fredericksburg's elderly men rode through the town, warning the people that the Yankees were coming. Evacuation began almost immediately.

The frightened people bundled up against the cold and began leaving their homes, bearing what food and portable effects they could carry. They made a pitiful procession, trudging through eight-inch-deep snow with nowhere to go but to the fields and the woods out of cannon range. There they would face the cold until the battle was over and they could return to their homes...if there would be any homes left standing.

Little girls carried their dolls and little boys took along one kind of toy or another. Young mothers carried their blanket-wrapped, crying babies in one arm, and food and diapers in the other. Some of the women with older children, or without any children at all, carried plucked chickens, flour sacks, and Bibles.

A handful of nurses from Fredericksburg's small hospital walked alongside horse-drawn wagons, speaking words of comfort to their patients who lay huddled under blankets. Some of the elderly were so feeble, they could carry nothing. They only hobbled and stumbled along in the slippery snow.

The evacuees had to cross a creek swollen with the winter rains and deadly cold. The icy wind sliced through their coats like frozen knives. Some of Jeb Stuart's cavalrymen went to the creek and ferried as many people as possible across on horseback. The line of shivering, dejected people stretched from the snow-laden streets of Fredericksburg to the creek.

At the Dalton house, Melody was upstairs in her bedroom with Harriet Smith, making preparations to leave. Melody's hands were shaking as she stuffed some garments into a small bag, along with a few toiletries and her Bible.

Harriet took hold of her hands and said, "Honey, we've committed our husbands and our homes to the Lord. There's nothing more we can do. Please get a grip on yourself."

"I'm sorry, Harriet. I should be stronger than this. I should be able to trust the Lord better."

"You're a young Christian yet, honey," Harriet said in a tender tone. "It takes spiritual growth to learn better how to lean on the Lord. But may I give you a brief word of encouragement?"

"Yes, of course."

"You trusted God's Word for your salvation, didn't you? I mean, you accepted by faith what the Bible said you had to do to be saved. Right?"

"Right."

"Then what you have to do now is learn to trust the same Book for your walk through this life. God expects you to do that. He says in Hebrews 11:6 that without faith it is impossible to please Him. We're saved by faith, and we walk by faith. Just as we completely trust the Lord Jesus to save us, so we must trust Him in the same way for our daily walk. We must cling to His Word by faith, for instance, when He says, *Be careful for nothing; but in every thing by prayer and supplication with thanksgiving let your requests be made known unto God. And the peace of God, which passeth all understanding, shall keep your hearts and minds through Christ Jesus.*"

Misty-eyed, Melody smiled weakly and said, "Harriet, I'm so glad the Lord gave me a friend like you."

Both women heard a door close downstairs. Harriet headed for the hallway, saying, "You finish up there. I have a hunch it's either your husband or mine."

When Harriet reached the landing, she saw Layne Dalton bounding up the stairs two at a time. "Hello, Harriet. Are you and Melody about to get out of here?"

"Yes. We're almost ready."

Layne moved past her and said, "I talked to Walter yesterday. He said he'd been able to come see you a couple times since he got here."

"Yes, and it sure was good to see him. Is the fog lifting off the river yet?"

"Not yet," Layne said over his shoulder as he preceded Harriet into the bedroom.

Melody was on her feet, arms open wide, as Layne embraced her.

"We were about to leave, darling," she said. "I'm glad you could come before we did."

"So Mrs. Shrewsbury is still expecting you, I assume."

"Yes. I'm so glad we have a place to go."

"So am I. I want you and little Danny to be warm and safe."

"We will be," she replied softly. "The Lord has been so good to give me Bertha Shrewsbury for a friend. She's a wonderful Christian, Layne."

"You told me Charlie Weymouth was going to let you ride his horse while he leads it to the Shrewsbury place. Is that still the plan?"

"Yes."

"Shouldn't he be here by now?"

"He was here a few minutes ago, but we weren't quite ready. He'll be back shortly."

"I want you out of here before that fog starts to lift. Burnside may begin shelling the town once he can see what he's shooting at."

Harriet picked up Melody's small bag and said, "I'll let you two kiss good-bye without an audience. Meet you downstairs."

When Harriet was out of the room, Layne and Melody shared a lingering kiss, embraced, and kissed again.

"I'll walk you down the stairs, honey," Layne said, "then I've got to hightail it back up the hill."

"Oh, Layne, I wish this horrible ordeal was over! I want you back home and in one piece!"

"I'll be fine, sweetheart. Come on."

Melody hesitated. "Layne, have you been reading your Bible...the passages I marked?"

"A little. I've been awfully busy."

Deep lines etched themselves across her brow. "Darling, you're going to face enemy guns out there. I want to know if...if something happens to you, that you'll meet me in heaven."

Layne took her hand and led her out of the room. "I'll be all right, honey. I've got to live through this so I'll be around to provide for both you and little Danny."

Together they descended the stairs. While Harriet stood by, Layne kissed his wife one more time, told her he loved her, and headed out the door. He leaped on his horse, waved at the two women as they stood watching him from the parlor window, and rode away. Within seconds, the house was engulfed in fog and disappeared from his view.

The major trotted his animal out of Fredericksburg and drew near the southern range of hills that skirted that side of town. At the base of the long, gentle slope that led up to Marye's Heights was a stone wall four-feet high. An old road ran along the outside of the wall.

Heavy patches of fog drifted on the wind across the hillsides, partially blocking the view of the Marye mansion high above. The open slope was rough and rugged and dotted with dozens of ancient oak trees. The summit of Marye's Heights was covered with a thick copse of oaks and heavy brush, giving ample protection for the Confederate infantry and artillery that waited there for the battle to begin.

As Dalton headed his horse through one of the wall's few openings and began the ascent, he peered through the mists at what he could see of the two-story mansion that stood like a defiant fortress at the crest. It was made of red brick in colonial style, having a central section with wide porch and four white pillars, and two one-story wings, making it a famous landmark fully visible on a clear day from anywhere in the valley.

On the semi-circle of wooded hills, the Confederates waited behind a continuous line of entrenchments, concealed by the thick underbrush. Most of Longstreet's corps made up the force on Marye's Heights.

The opposite bank of the Rappahannock River was closely lined by a range of commanding hills on which the Union artillery was posted. A greater part of Burnside's big guns, especially those situated on lofty Stafford Heights, bore down on the town, but nearly all of them were in a position to blast the level ground in the valley on the west side of the river.

When Major Dalton reached his post atop Marye's Heights, he saw a figure moving toward him through the drifting mists. It was Sergeant Richard Rowland Kirkland, Dalton's self-appointed adjutant.

"Hello, Major," Kirkland grinned. "Did you get to see Mrs. Dalton before she evacuated?"

"Yes, I did," Dalton responded as he slid from the saddle.

"She doing all right, sir? Carrying the baby, I mean?"

"Yes, everything's fine."

"Well, you can thank the Lord in heaven for that, can't you?"

Layne Dalton was realizing more and more that he owed a great deal to the Lord in heaven. "Yes, I certainly can," he replied. "I certainly can."

Kirkland took the reins of Dalton's horse and said, "I'll take care of him for you, sir."

"Thanks, Sergeant."

Layne turned and looked toward the town below. He could barely make out the rooftops through the fog. Though he could not see the long line of evacuees, he was sure that by now Melody was on her way out of Fredericksburg. His heart was heavy for her. Carrying a baby, with her husband in the army and gone so much, was difficult enough, but now she was having to leave her home, wondering if it would be there whenever she returned.

Major Dalton found himself praying for Melody's safety, and for the baby's safety, too. When he ended his prayer with a sincere "Amen," he smiled to himself and headed toward General Kershaw, who stood talking to some of Dalton's infantrymen.

In a half-whisper, he said to himself, "I do believe Melody's faith is touching you more than you realize."

CHAPTER NINE

★

Harriet turned away from the parlor window while Melody remained to watch Layne ride away into the fog. "Be back in a minute," Harriet said, heading for the kitchen. "I need to make sure the back door is locked."

Lot of good it'll do if the Yankees want in, thought Melody as Layne vanished from view. She turned away from the window and placed one hand to the small of her back, the other to her forehead. With effort, she made her way to the stairs and slowly climbed to the landing. She steadied herself with the banister, then moved down the hall to her bedroom. She sat on the edge of the bed, still holding a hand to her head, and lay down.

"Melody!" came Harriet's voice from downstairs. "Where did you get to?"

"I'm upstairs in my room," Melody called toward the open bedroom door.

Harriet hurried up the stairs and down the hall. "Charlie will be here any minute, Melody." She drew up short when she saw her friend on the bed. "Are...are you all right?"

"Not really. I'm not feeling well. Something's happening inside me."

"What do you mean, *something?*"

"Just…well, pain. Low in the abdomen and in the small of my back. I feel a little lightheaded."

"You think the baby's coming?"

"I don't know. Maybe if I lie here a few minutes, I'll be all right."

"You lie there, all right, honey. I'm going to go get Dr. Craig."

"He may be already gone," Melody said.

"We'll find out. You rest. I'll be back as soon as I can."

Harriet had barely entered the hallway when someone knocked at the front door. She hastened down the stairs and opened the door.

Charlie Weymouth smiled and asked, "You ladies ready, now?"

Harriet's hand was at her throat and her face was pale. "Charlie," she said, "I need your help."

"What's wrong?"

"Melody…she may be going into labor. Would you see if you can find Dr. Craig? I'm an experienced midwife, but I'm not qualified to handle anything out of the ordinary. The baby isn't due for another month."

"I'm on my way," nodded the old man, wheeling and scurrying across the porch.

Harriet dashed up the stairs and into the bedroom. Melody was on her side, doubled up in a fetal position, gritting her teeth and grunting in pain.

"You just hang on, honey," Harriet said, laying a hand on her. "Charlie's on his way to find Dr. Craig right now. Shouldn't take long."

"Unless he's…he's already evacuated," said Melody through clenched teeth.

"Well, if Charlie doesn't find him, and that baby's coming, we'll just have to handle it between the four of us."

Melody looked up at her. "The *four* of us?"

"Mm-hmm. You, me, the baby…and the Lord."

*****

Across the Rappahannock, General Burnside stood with his officers and peered through the fog at the engineers laboring to link the bridge sections together. Burnside had mixed feelings about the fog. It was slowing the progress with the bridges, but so far it had kept the enemy snipers from opening fire on the engineers.

A few yards from where the officers were collected, the Heglund brothers huddled together in the thick mist. They were part of Major General Edwin V. Sumner's division. Steve was a sergeant, and his two younger brothers were corporals. Word had spread among the Union troops that the exodus from Fredericksburg was under way.

Steve turned to his brothers and said, "I gotta make sure Ma and Pa and George get to safety."

"How you gonna do that?" asked Everett. "The bridges haven't been laid across the river yet. Besides, when they *are,* we're goin' to cross 'em into enemy fire. There ain't no way you can check on them."

"I got to," Steve argued. "I wanna see that they get out, and that they got someplace to go."

"They'll prob'ly do like most ever'body else and camp in the woods," Keith said. "What else is there to do?"

"I don't know, but I'm goin' over there right now and see for myself that they get out before our artillery starts to bombard the town."

"How you gonna get across?" asked Everett.

"Float on one of those old dead trees lyin' over there."

"Ain't nobody gonna give you permission to do that," insisted Keith.

"Well, I'm about to find out," said Steve, walking away. "I'll ask Captain Tweed."

Moments later, Steve found Captain Art Tweed standing on the bank of the river with some enlisted men, peering into the fog, trying to make out what kind of progress was being made on the bridges.

Steve saluted and said, "Cap'n, could I talk to you a minute?"

"Sure," nodded Tweed. He excused himself to the other men and walked a few paces with Steve. "What is it, Sergeant?"

Steve Heglund explained the situation to his captain, asking if he could go into Fredericksburg and check on his family.

Tweed looked at him like he had lost his mind. "Sergeant, your life wouldn't be worth a wooden nickel in there right now. That blue uniform would draw Rebel bullets like honey draws flies. And you sure can't swim the river. You'd never make it. You'd freeze up and drown before you got halfway."

"I can float across on one of those old fallen trees, sir," pressed Heglund. "With this fog, ain't no Rebel sharpshooter gonna see me."

"Sorry, Sergeant. Request denied. Every soldier must stay in his place. When this fog begins lifting, General Burnside is going to order us across those bridges in a hurry. Get back to your post."

"But, sir—"

"That's final, Sergeant!" snapped Tweed, and turned away.

Steve Heglund swore under his breath, calling the captain some choice names, and stomped back to his brothers.

"Wouldn't let you, would he?" Everett said.

"No, but I'm goin' anyhow. If anybody should ask where I am, make up somethin' about me havin' to go deeper into the woods for some reason you don't know about."

Steve persuaded his brothers to help him drag one of the logs into the river. Then he scrambled aboard, carrying a thick broken limb to use as a paddle. With much effort and a couple of near mishaps, he finally made it to the other side and onto the bank.

Furtively he made his way through the drifting fog, darting down alleys, cutting through backyards, until he came to the street where he had grown up. Ethel Heglund and her crippled son were just coming out the front door when Steve dashed across the yard.

Mother and son were momentarily startled to see a man hurrying toward them through the mists.

"Ma! George! It's me, Steve! Get back into the house!" Steve said as he bounded onto the porch and urged them back inside.

"Oh, I'm so glad you've come," Ethel said. "We heard that General Sumner's corps was here, so we knew you and your brothers would be over there across the river. Are Everett and Keith all right?"

"Yeah, Ma, they're fine."

"How'd you get across the river? Them bridges in place already?"

"No, not yet. I floated across on a dead tree."

"You did *what?*" Ethel exclaimed.

"Where's Pa?" Steve asked. "Ain't he goin' with you?"

George and his mother exchanged pained glances.

"Your Pa's dead, son," Ethel said.

Steve's mind froze on her words. He shrank back as if she had slapped him across the face with a wet dishrag. *"Dead?"* he gasped. "When? How?"

"A month and two days ago," said Ethel. "On November 9. Jack Reynolds murdered him. Shot him dead."

"Jack Reynolds!" blared Steve, his throat tightening.

"Jack ran into George on the street," Ethel said. "They got to arguin', and Jack got real mad. He took advantage of George and shoved him down real hard. When your pa found out about it, he went over to the Reynolds place and invited Jack outside. He was gonna beat him up good for what he did to George. Jack come out of the house with a gun and shot your pa in the stomach. He died a little while later."

Cold, white fury filled Steve's eyes. "Did they hang him for it?"

George snorted. "Jury acquitted him. Said it was self-defense."

"Self-defense!" exploded Steve. "You mean he's runnin' free?"

"Sure is," George nodded, adjusting his position on the crutches.

"Well, he's a dead man now! Even if he's already evacuated, I'll find him!"

"He ain't here at all," said Ethel. "Jack took Frances and headed for Virginia City, Nevada, over three weeks ago. Joinin' his brother Hank in the gold minin' business."

Steve's eyes pinched back until they seemed almost hidden behind the hooded lids. "When this war's over, I'm goin' after Jack Reynolds."

Steve made sure his mother and brother were out of town and camped as comfortably as possible in the woods, then floated back across the icy Rappahannock and informed his brothers of their father's death. They felt the same fury as Steve and vowed to hunt Reynolds down after the war was over.

Dr. David Craig was packing medicines into a large suitcase when Charlie Weymouth entered his office and told him excitedly that Melody Dalton might be going into labor. Dr. Craig already had his horse hitched to his buggy. Passing the long line of evacuees streaming out of town, he sped to the Dalton house with Charlie riding alongside him.

Charlie waited in the hall outside Melody's bedroom while the doctor examined his patient with Harriet looking on. Harriet had made Melody undress and get in bed before the doctor arrived. As Dr. Craig finished his examination, he drew the blankets up to cover her again and said, "Melody, I believe you are simply experiencing false labor. No doubt it has been brought on by the stress of all that's going on around you. However, I advise you not to travel."

"But Dr. Craig, the Yankees are coming," Melody said.

"I know, and I wish I could tell you it would be safer for you to get out of town. But if you even so much as try to ride in a buggy or a wagon...much less sit in a saddle or even try to walk, you could go into labor quite easily. At this stage in your pregnancy, it could be very dangerous for both you and the baby. The only safe thing right now is complete rest. The pains you are having are warnings that things are not right. Further strain could be disastrous."

Melody's features were chalk-white. There was a desperate note in her voice as she looked at Harriet and said, "You must leave, Harriet. I don't want you vulnerable to whatever is going to happen here."

"Melody, I'm not about to go off and leave you here by yourself," Harriet said.

"But I've heard how vicious the Yankees can be. Who knows what they might do if they found you here?"

"Honey, I can't believe those Union soldiers would harm two helpless women…especially when one of them is about to have her baby, and the other one is there to care for her."

A spasm of pain caused Melody to draw her legs up, clench her teeth, and release a tiny whine.

"Doctor," said Harriet, "isn't there something you can give her for the pain?"

"Not safely. The pains will stop, I'm sure, once she settles down. Look…I'm sorry to make her stay here when she's so frightened, but there really is no choice. I think you're right. No Yankee soldiers are going to hurt two helpless women."

"Doctor," Harriet said, "would it be possible for you to stay here at the house? For the rest of the day, I mean? Just to make sure she settles down and the pains stop?"

"I wish I could, but I've had the town criers telling everyone that I'll be at the Ralph Jones farm in case they need me. I must go there immediately so they'll be able to find me."

"I understand, Doctor. If…if Melody should develop more problems, may I come for you?"

"Of course. Don't you hesitate. But again, I think if she can settle down, the pains will go away. See if you can get her to sleep."

"I'll do my best," Harriet assured him.

Dr. Craig looked down at his patient and said, "Please try to relax, Melody. The sooner you do, the sooner the pains will ease up. However, if they get worse and Harriet decides you need me,

JOY FROM ASHES

1 2 3

have her come and get me, okay?"

"Yes, Doctor. Thank you."

He reached down and squeezed Melody's hand. "You're welcome. It's going to be all right, young lady. It's going to be all right."

With that, Dr. Craig moved to the door and pulled it open. Harriet looked past him and saw Charlie Weymouth standing in the hall with his hat in his hand. "Thank you for bringing Dr. Craig, Charlie," she said. "We both appreciate it."

"Is Melody gonna be all right, Doc?" Charlie asked.

"She'll be fine."

"Well, I gotta be goin' too, Miss Harriet," said the old man. "More people to help before the trouble starts."

"Thank you, Charlie," she said. "And God bless you."

Harriet watched the two men until they disappeared down the stairs, then moved back to the bed and said, "How about I fix you some hot tea, honey? Maybe that would help you to relax, maybe even go to sleep."

"Yes," replied Melody, smiling up at her friend. "Could I get you to rub my back first? It's really hurting."

"Of course. Roll on your side and I'll work on it."

"Doc?" Charlie Weymouth said as the two men passed through the front door of the house and closed it behind them.

"Yes?"

"I could hear pretty much what was being said there in Melody's room. I appreciate what you told them and all, but there's somethin' that's botherin' me."

"And what's that?"

"You didn't mention anything about what they should do if them blue-bellies cut loose with their cannons and start bombardin' the town."

"They won't do that, Charlie. What purpose would it serve? If they want to occupy the town, they sure don't want it in rubble and ruin."

"I don't think they want to occupy it very long, Doc. If they do get in here, they'll steal and plunder and probably do a lot of destruction just for meanness. And if you ask me, they'll also bombard the town just for meanness." Charlie paused a few seconds, then said, "If I'm right, those two sweet gals are in trouble."

"Well, let's hope you're not, Charlie," said Dr. Craig, climbing into his buggy. "Melody is in no condition to travel. Not even a little distance. She must stay in that bed and rest, or I'm afraid she'll lose the baby."

The fog began to lift about ten o'clock that morning. General Burnside was elated. He stood on the river bank and shouted encouragement to his engineers, who had already linked bridge sections more than halfway across the river.

Working unarmed, the Union engineers positioned the pontoons one at a time, moored them securely to each other, and laid the large sections of planking in place, lashing them firmly to the pontoons with heavy lengths of rope. Infantry and cavalry both must use the bridges to cross the river.

On the Confederate side of the Rappahannock, Brigadier General William Barksdale rode uneasily up and down the bank, inspecting his pickets and listening to the sounds of the Union engineers at work. From time to time, he could hear the engineers talking in undertones as they pieced their assault bridges together in the fog.

General Lee had ordered Barksdale's troops—the Thirteenth, Seventeenth, and Twenty-first Mississippi Regiments, three companies of the Eighteenth Mississippi, and a battalion of the Eighth Florida—to open fire on the bridge-builders once they could make them out through the fog. Barksdale had posted his sharpshooters in rifle pits and behind walls all along the river front. They were to stay in their positions and harass the Federal crossing until General Barksdale saw that it was too dangerous to remain there. They would then withdraw to the main Confederate lines.

At last Barksdale's vigilance was rewarded. The fog began to lift. He checked his pocket watch. Ten o'clock. He hurried along the bank, alerting his sharpshooters and telling them to open fire as soon as they had clear targets.

Barksdale stationed himself close to the bank in a stand of trees and waited. By 10:20 the fog was thin enough to make out figures moving on the floating bridge sections. He trotted his horse toward his line of men and shouted, "Open up on 'em, men! Give it to 'em!"

Barksdale fired the first shot as a signal for those along the line who could not hear his voice. There followed a roar of musketry. Men in dark uniforms fell into the icy water while others flattened themselves on top of the bridge sections, attempting to avoid the heavy fire.

On the heels of Barksdale's commencement of fire, General Longstreet, atop Marye's Heights, commanded his artillery to open up, sending a barrage of cannonballs amid the bridge builders.

On the Union side of the river, General Burnside swore and sent a command to his artillery atop Stafford Heights and along the flanking ridges. In reply, 150 Federal cannons opened their iron mouths with a thunderous roar, hurling a tempest into the sharpshooter lines along the west bank of the river.

Barksdale's men, however, were well protected. The general himself took shelter behind a large warehouse near the docks. Though a few of the sharpshooters were hit, most of them were untouched. To counter the Union artillery attack, Longstreet turned all his big guns on Stafford Heights. Soon it was an all-out artillery battle.

While the artilleries pounded each other, the Union engineers went back to work. Once more Barksdale's sharpshooters sent them scrambling for cover.

General Burnside stood amid the sheltering trees on the east side of the Rappahannock and ordered thirty-six guns brought to the river bank to blaze away at the Confederate sharpshooters. This drove Barksdale's troops back into hiding. Longstreet saw the Federal engineers working once again, so he directed several of his big guns on the bridge builders.

By now it was almost 1:00 P.M. A frustrated Burnside decided to retaliate by doing the thing he knew the Confederates feared most. He brought one hundred big guns to bear on the town itself.

As the heavy bombardment of Fredericksburg began, General Hooker dashed up beside Burnside and shouted above the roar, "General, what are you doing? It isn't necessary to destroy the town! Nobody's shooting at us from there!"

Burnside marked Hooker with blazing eyes. "You don't seem to understand that this is war, General! I'll do whatever I have to in order to take the town! Now get back to your post!"

"But destroying it won't help you take it! Why not keep all the guns blasting at the river bank and Marye's Heights?"

"Because this will gall their guts!" snapped Burnside.

"But Fredericksburg is a part of our American heritage. Doesn't that mean anything to you?"

"Do the words *court martial* mean anything to you, Joe?"

Hooker set his mouth in a grim line, turned, and stomped away.

The Confederates on the hills looked down with a mixture of grief and wrath at the enemy's violent storm of destruction upon the historic old town. Fredericksburg, except for its church steeples, was still veiled in the misty fog that had left the river but settled in the town and surrounding valley.

The earth trembled at the deafening cannonade. The howling of the solid shot, the bursting of the shells, and the dismal sound of collapsing houses united in a dread concert of doom. Every heart of the thousands of Confederate soldiers yearned for revenge.

Blue-white clouds from the bursting shells appeared above the town, and from its center rose columns of dense black smoke from houses set on fire by the explosions. There was virtually no wind. The smoke rose in great pillars for five or six hundred feet before spreading outward in loathsome black sheets.

Atop Marye's Heights, General Lee stood with Generals Longstreet and Jackson, peering at the scene below through his field glasses. After several minutes, Lee lowered the glasses and said, "I fear there are not enough of us to prevent the Federals from crossing the river."

"It's inevitable, sir," said Jackson. "But we'll give them a fight they won't forget when they get over here."

"That we will," Longstreet said.

"General Jackson," said Lee. "Send word to General Barksdale that when the enemy starts across the river, he and his troops are to withdraw gradually while firing into their ranks. I want them to join your men at the base of this hill. I will leave it to General Barksdale's discretion just when to begin his withdrawal."

"Yes, sir," said Jackson, moving away to find a messenger.

"We'll still whip them, sir," said Longstreet. "We've got the advantage of position."

"You're right," Lee nodded. "General Ambrose E. Burnside is going to get a baptism of fire for his first battle as commander of Mr. Lincoln's army."

Some fifty yards from where Lee and Longstreet stood, Major Layne Dalton waited with three captains and their units of infantry under his command. They would go into action when the Yankees swarmed across the river and headed for Marye's Heights.

Dalton was heartsick over what was happening to his town and the damage that might be done to his house, but he took comfort in one thing: At least his wife and unborn baby were safe.

CHAPTER TEN

✦

arriet Smith sat in an overstuffed chair in a corner of the bedroom where Melody Dalton lay sleeping. Harriet had taken her Bible from a small canvas bag she had packed for her stay with widow Bertha Shrewsberry. She was reading Psalm 91, drawing strength for her own heart. Her eyes kept coming back to verse one and the note she had made next to it in the margin some years ago.

*He that dwelleth in the secret place of the most High
shall abide under the shadow of the Almighty.*

The note in the margin read: "Safety is not the absence of danger, but the presence of God."

Harriet leaned her head back against the softness of the chair and whispered, "Dear Lord, only You know what is going to happen to us. Please help me to be strong for Melody's sake. And please help both of us to remember that Your presence is with us, no matter how great the danger. Please help me to—"

Melody stirred, rolled her head back and forth on the pillow, then went still.

Harriet had rubbed her back for about a half hour after Dr. Craig and Charlie Weymouth left. It had helped to relax her. Then

Harriet had gone down to the kitchen and made some hot tea. After drinking two cups of it, Melody became drowsy and had fallen asleep. She had been asleep, now, for well over an hour. The grandfather clock in the parlor had just struck a quarter to one.

Harriet would not disturb her. Melody needed the rest. They would have some lunch whenever the expectant mother woke up.

Harriet laid her Bible down and went to the window that faced her own house. Their street was deserted, and what she could see of the side street a quarter-block away was also deserted. She figured everyone was out of town by now. She stood there for some time, staring vacantly. Before turning away, Harriet ran her gaze over her house and said, "Lord, hasten the day Walter and I can live a normal life again."

Harriet turned from the window, cast a glance at Melody, and returned to the chair. Just as Harriet sat down, the chimes in the grandfather clock told her it was one o'clock. The pleasant sound had barely died out when there was a strange rumbling, like distant thunder. It came in a series of deep-throated noises—*pum-pum*—followed by shrill whistles and earth-shaking explosions.

Harriet sprang out of the chair and dashed to the same window she had looked out moments before. Beyond her own house, she saw sheets of flame and billows of smoke. The Federals were shelling the town!

The expression of horror that claimed her features looked back at her in a faint reflection from the glass. There were more shrieking shells and more explosions, each one seemingly coming closer.

Suddenly behind her, Melody sat bolt upright in the bed, screaming, "Layne! Layne!"

Harriet rushed to her and wrapped her arms around her, saying, "It's all right, honey! It's all right. I'm here."

"Layne's dead, Harriet!" Melody wailed. "A cannonball blew him to bits! It did! It blew him to bits!" Melody's entire body was quaking, and her skin was like ice.

"No, Melody!" Harriet cried. "You were dreaming. You were only dreaming!"

Melody drew a shuddering breath and looked around her, then at Harriet. "Layne is all right? He wasn't—?"

"No, sweetie," Harriet breathed, tenderly brushing loose strands of hair from her forehead. "It was just a dream."

A whining shell exploded less than a half-block away, followed by two more, shaking the house.

Melody gripped her friend hard. "The Yankees!" she gasped. "They're bombarding us!"

"Yes," Harriet nodded.

Another cannonball exploded, even closer. Melody's body jerked and her fingernails dug into Harriet's arms. Her eyes blazed in a mixture of anger and terror. "Those wicked devils! Why are they destroying the town? They'll kill us, Harriet! They'll kill us!"

Harriet prayed in her heart: *Help me, Lord! I'm scared, too! Please don't let her lose the baby. Give me strength to help Melody.* Suddenly to mind came Psalm 91:1.

"Melody!" Harriet said. "Listen to me! Psalm 91:1 says, *He that dwelleth in the secret place of the most High shall abide under the shadow of the Almighty.* We're under His shadow right now. He is here with us! Do you hear me, Melody? The Lord is here with us!"

"Yes—yes He is. I know He is." Melody took several deep breaths, trying to calm herself. Shells were shrieking and exploding all around them.

"Listen to me, honey," said Harriet, forcing steadiness into her voice. "I wrote something in my Bible years ago, right next to Psalm 91:1. Something our previous pastor said in a sermon: 'Safety is not the absence of danger, but the presence of God.' Think about it. Jesus is here with us right now. We're safer here with the shells exploding all around us than we would be anywhere else without Him. Do you understand?"

"Yes, I…I think so."

"Then we must trust Him to take care of us," Harriet said, squeezing Melody's arms.

Just then two Union cannonballs slammed into the Smith house next door, exploding in a huge fireball. The windows in Melody's bedroom shattered, spraying shards of glass all around.

Harriet let go of Melody and staggered to the window, crunching glass under her shoes. Flames licked around the edges of a huge hole in the roof amid billows of black smoke. Her lips parted to give voice to a heart-rending wail. Melody, trembling all over, threw back the covers and started to get out of bed.

Harriet heard her and pivoted. "No, honey!" she gasped. "Stay in bed!"

"But your house! Your house is on fire!"

"Yes," Harriet said, bursting into tears. As she rushed to Melody and threw her arms around her, another cannonball shrieked overhead. The two women clung to each other, expecting the missile to strike the Dalton house. It passed directly over the roof and struck a tree in the front yard of the house next door to the west. The tree exploded into a thousand pieces, branches and bark scattering every direction.

More shells whistled and whined around them, but were now striking farther west and to the north, across the street.

Tears streamed down Harriet's cheeks as she held Melody tight and said, "They're shooting beyond us, honey. The Lord is with us! He has protected us!"

"But your house will burn to the ground!" Melody sobbed. "Look at it! It's going up in flames!"

Harriet left her and went again to the window. "The front part of the house on the first floor isn't burning yet. Maybe I can still save some of our things!"

Fear filled Melody's eyes. "No, Harriet! Don't go in there!"

"I promise I won't take any chances," Harriet said.

"But if you go inside the house and it collapses, you'll be killed.

No personal items are worth your life."

"I won't do anything foolish. If it doesn't look safe, I won't try it. Don't you worry. I'll be back to take care of you." With that, Harriet was out the door and moving down the hall.

Melody lay back down, pulled her knees up, and ejected a tiny mew of pain. She was hurting again.

For another full hour, General Burnside's artillery bombarded the town and the area just across the river where Barksdale's sharpshooters were positioned. In a full hour-and-a-half, the Federals fired five thousand shells into Fredericksburg. The explosions destroyed hundreds of houses, tore gaping holes in brick buildings, dug craters in streets, yards, and gardens, and toppled a great number of trees. But the vicious bombardment failed to kill or drive off Barksdale's men.

When Burnside gave command for the artillery to cease fire and the engineers to resume their work, the tenacious sharpshooters emerged from their shelters once more and resumed firing. The Yankee engineers were forced to leave off their work again and head for cover.

Burnside was beside himself with rage. Brigadier General Henry J. Hunt, who commanded the Union artillery, approached the angry leader and said, "Sir, those sharpshooters are too well protected. My artillery just can't dislodge them. May I suggest that you forget trying to connect the bridge sections, and instead, float the troops across the river on the sections? If we don't get our men in that town right soon, we may not ever do it."

Burnside was at his wits' end. The idea sounded plausible. It was worth a try.

"Good thinking, General," he said with a shadow of a smile on his lips. "I'll have some of the infantry shoot at the Rebel sharpshooters while the troops float across on the sections. We'll probably lose a few in the crossing, but as you say, if we don't occupy the town pretty soon, we may never do it."

Burnside gave the order to his officers and assigned teams of engineers to row the troops across on the pontoon sections. Volunteers from the Seventh Michigan, the Nineteenth and Twentieth Massachusetts, and Eighty-ninth New York were the first to clamber onto the makeshift assault boats and start across the icy Rappahannock.

It was just after three o'clock in the afternoon when the Federals began their daring crossing. General Barksdale's sharpshooters put them under heavy fire. One Union soldier was killed and several were wounded during the crossing, but all the floating sections made it to the other side.

The men-in-blue leaped ashore and formed ranks under the protection of the riverbank. Then they rushed into Fredericksburg via the nearest street. The swarm of Yankees was so great that before General Barksdale's sharpshooters could begin to withdraw, thirty of them were taken prisoner. Now more Federals were able to land safely, assemble their units, and push on into the town.

Barksdale knew it was time to withdraw his troops and join those of Stonewall Jackson at the bottom of the hills that led up to Marye's Heights. Barksdale led the withdrawal, his men firing at the approaching swarm of Yankees, retiring street by street through the burning town, hotly contesting every inch. Within a stretch of about fifty yards, the advancing Federals lost ninety-seven men, including several officers.

Finally, the Confederates reached the stone wall at the foot of Marye's Heights, where Jackson and his infantry drove back the oncoming Yankees, giving their comrades cover while they vaulted the wall and fell behind it, exhausted. The heavy fire of Jackson's infantry held the Union troops at bay, and as darkness crowded out the light of the dying day, the firing ceased.

General Barksdale's gallant troops had accomplished their mission superbly, holding up the crossing of the Union troops for the better part of the day. Atop Marye's Heights, General Lee stood amongst his officers, artillery, and infantry, and led in a rousing cheer for the sharpshooters.

General Lee removed his hat, ran his fingers through his silver hair, and looked down at the scene below. Flames licked away at houses, barns, sheds, trees, and commercial buildings all over the town. The flames made the billows of smoke an orange-red color, and their blazing light illuminated the low-hanging clouds that covered the cold, pitiless sky.

Lee took a deep breath and said to Longstreet, "General Barksdale and his men did a magnificent job today."

"That they did, sir," agreed Longstreet. "No one could have expected any more of them."

"This battle will probably produce a good many more heroes before it's over," mused Lee. "Our men have all done well, but there's one thing that gnaws at my insides."

"What's that, sir?" Longstreet asked.

Lee's words came grudgingly from his lips. "Fredericksburg is now in Union hands."

There was a deathly silence among the men within the sound of Lee's voice. In the grip of that silence, Major Layne Dalton looked toward the section of town that included his own neighborhood. Fire and smoke reached skyward. He swallowed hard, wondering if Melody would have a house to return to when the conflict was over.

Sergeant Richard Rowland Kirkland moved closer to Dalton and laid a firm hand on his shoulder. "I know what you're thinking, sir, and I'm sorry if your house is the source of one of those fires. But when this horrible war is over, you can rebuild again, like so many others will have to do. At least Mrs. Dalton is safe. She and little Danny are your future...plus however many other children the Lord gives you. It'll be all right, sir."

Dalton turned to look at Kirkland by the light that glowed

from the burning town. "Thank you, my friend. You ought to be a preacher. You seem to have a knack for coming up with the right words at the right time."

"Of course, we don't know that your house *is* on fire, do we, sir? Maybe the Lord in heaven just cupped His hand over it and spared it from those Yankee shells."

At the Dalton house, Melody lay in her bed, watching Harriet sweep up the broken glass by the light of two lanterns that burned in the room.

"I'm sorry you weren't able to salvage anything from your house, Harriet," Melody said with compassion in her voice.

"The heat was just too great for me to even think of trying to go inside," Harriet said, dumping glass into a wooden waste container from a dustpan. There were tears in her eyes as she added, "I know we can rebuild the house, but there's no way on earth we can replace so many things that were destroyed in the fire. Family things...old letters, picture albums, and the like. You know."

"Yes."

Harriet looked into Melody's eyes from across the room. "Any more pain?"

"Not much. Could I come and look out the window? I'd like to see what it looks like."

"The doctor told you to stay in bed. Complete rest. Besides, you don't want to see it. It's horrible."

"Yes, I do. It's my town, too."

"Oh, all right, but let me help you."

Harriet laid down the broom and dustpan and headed toward the bed. "Put your slippers on. There could be some little pieces of glass that I missed. I sure don't want to have to pick them out of your feet."

"Yes, boss ma'am," smiled Melody.

"It's good to see you smile."

"Can you give me one back?" Melody asked.

"How's this?" Harriet said smiling.

"Beautiful."

Together they went to the broken window and looked out on the burning town.

"Oh, how awful, Harriet!"

"I know. Dirty Yankees."

"Do you suppose they'll shell us again tomorrow? If they do—"

"I don't think so," replied Harriet, pointing down to the street. "Look."

Melody's eyes fell on men in dark uniforms moving about on a side street at the end of the block. "Looks like they've moved in," she said.

"Maybe we'd better lower these lamps so if they come down the street, they won't know we're in here."

"I...I think I'd better get back on the bed," Melody said.

After getting Melody situated on the bed, Harriet lowered the lamps, then said she would go downstairs to the kitchen and prepare them some supper. An hour later, Harriet carried a tray of hot food up the stairs and into the bedroom. She set it on the table next to Melody's bed, then returned to the landing and picked up the lantern she had left there. As she did, the ring of light flowed through the open double doors into the music room, and her eyes fell on the beautiful concert grand Melody loved so much. "Lord," she said, "hasten the day when Melody can play her piano again...in peace."

Harriet returned to the bedroom and pulled a chair next to Melody's bed. She gave thanks for the food and for God's protection, then they began to eat their supper.

"The Yankees will plunder the houses that aren't destroyed, won't they?" Melody said.

"I expect they will, unless General Lee fills these streets with troops."

"But from what Layne and Walter told us, our army is so vastly outnumbered that we won't be able to hold them back."

"Well, all we can do now is pray that the Lord will continue to protect us, Melody. He certainly kept those shells from striking this house today."

"That He did."

"God always knows what He's doing," Harriet said. "We don't always understand the way He does things, or even why He allows unpleasant things to happen in Christians' lives, but He never makes mistakes. This is where faith comes in. We must trust Him when things go our way...and when they don't."

Harriet left Melody long enough to go to the kitchen and wash the dishes, then returned to spend the rest of the evening in womanly conversation. Before retiring for the night, they read the Bible together and prayed for their safety and the safety of their husbands.

As dawn came on Friday, December 12, 1862, Generals Lee, Longstreet, and Jackson stood atop Marye's Heights and beheld the vast number of Union soldiers who now occupied Fredericksburg. The generals, believing that the town had been completely evacuated, agreed that in the face of the overwhelming odds, their best plan of action was to defend the high ground. No matter how many troops Burnside had at his disposal to throw at them, the Confederates had position advantage. They were going to make full use of it.

There was some early morning mist on the Rappahannock, but not enough to hinder the completion of the pontoon bridges. The sky cleared by five-thirty, and while the sun was rising, the Federals made ready to push the remainder of their infantry into Fredericksburg.

General Burnside pondered his next move while his troops moved across the wobbly, bouncing bridges a few at a time.

Burnside chose not to send his men in large numbers for fear the Confederate artillery might cut loose on them at any time.

The Rebel bombardment, however, did not come. Burnside figured—and correctly—that Robert E. Lee would wait for the Union army to come against his well-fortified position.

The delay in getting all the Union infantry across the river and into Fredericksburg afforded the Yankees time to indulge in one of the Civil War's most disreputable ventures—wholesale looting. The evacuation of the town's civilians and the withdrawal of General Barksdale's sharpshooters left Fredericksburg wide open.

Though many houses and commercial buildings had been destroyed, and some were still burning, hundreds were intact. The pickings were easy, and what the wild, reckless Federals could not use, they demolished.

They broke into houses, splintering doors and shattering windows. They smashed mirrors, fine china, and alabaster vases. They ripped up bedding, dumped out the contents of dresser drawers, mutilated books, paintings, and draperies, and used axes and hatchets to chop up furniture.

Rosewood pianos and finely sculpted pump organs were dragged from houses and piled in the streets. The organs were burned and the pianos were employed as horse troughs, or wrecked by soldiers who danced on them and kicked the keyboards apart.

While the looting and destruction were going on, the Heglund brothers hurried to see if their house was still intact. When they turned the corner of their block, they saw men-in-blue doing their wicked work to houses across the street and to the one next door. They hurried inside and were relieved to find that nothing had been touched. Then they went back outside to convince their fellow soldiers not to harm it.

"You know what we oughtta do now?" Keith said.

"What's that?" asked Steve.

"Go over to the Reynolds house."

"Why?" asked Everett. "They don't live there no more."

"I know, but I'd like to tear it up anyhow."

"I'll go for that!" Steve said. "C'mon, let's go see what damage we can do!"

Moments later, they turned onto the block where the Reynoldses had lived and found that out of twenty houses that lined both sides of the street, only nine remained standing. The others were in rubble or had been burned to the ground. One of those completely burned was the house where Jack and Frances Reynolds had lived.

"Well, good riddance," Keith said. "I just wish this war was over so we could go to Nevada, find Jack, and make him pay for murderin' Pa."

"His day's comin'," Everett said.

Suddenly a wicked grin twisted Steve's mouth.

"What're you grinnin' about?" Keith asked.

"Speakin' of Jack," said Steve, "since this house he lived in is gone, how about his daughter's house? I think we oughtta see what's left of it. If there *is* anything left, we can finish it off."

Everett laughed. "I can't think of anything I'd rather do. Sure hope it's still standin' so we can have us some fun!"

CHAPTER ELEVEN

★

Melody Dalton was feeling somewhat better. After breakfast and a bath, she was sitting at her dresser in a heavy robe, looking into the mirror and brushing her honey-blonde hair. Harriet was making up Melody's bed, putting on clean sheets and pillow cases. Both were aware of distant shouts and laughter in the town, along with destructive-sounding bangs and crashes. Harriet had hung a blanket over the broken window, but cold air and noise were still getting in.

Melody's hands trembled as she looked at her friend in the mirror and said, "They'll be here sooner or later. Do you really think they'll leave us alone and not harm us or the house?"

"Like I said before, honey, those Yankees are human beings. I don't think they're going to cause any trouble here, especially when they see that you're carrying a baby."

"I hope you have a better understanding of human nature than I do," said Melody. "I've heard, as you have, what those Yankees have done in other Southern towns. They've—"

There was a sudden splintering crash downstairs. Harriet stopped what she was doing and said, "Sounds like we've got visitors. You stay here."

"It's the front door!" gasped Melody in a half-whisper. "They've broken into the house!" She jumped to her feet, dropping the hairbrush on the dresser.

Harriet paused at the door, fingers white against the frame. "Melody, sit down and stay there! I don't want you all doubled up in pain again!"

With that, Harriet hurried toward the staircase. She heard male voices speaking excitedly, and a sound of shattering glass. She peered around the corner.

Harriet's heart seemed to stop. Her skin crawled, and a chill ran through her. It was the Heglund brothers. Inching back, she swallowed hard, fought for breath, and looked again. There were no other Union soldiers with them. The Heglunds had come to the Dalton house alone. One of them had thrown a straight-backed wooden chair through a parlor window.

Steve picked up a vase and hurled it across the parlor. It struck a large full-length mirror, shattering both. Next he yanked a painting off the front wall and smashed it against a bookshelf. "Until I can get to Jack, I'll have to be satisfied tearin' up stuff that belongs to his daughter!"

"Feels good, don't it?" Keith said, grabbing the bookcase and tipping it over. It crashed to the floor, spilling books in three directions.

Everett picked up a chair and threw it against another window. The chair split apart and the window shattered. The curtain rod gave way and the drapes and sheers fell to the floor.

"Too bad Jack ain't here to see what we're doin' to his daughter's stuff!" Keith said, kicking over a small table. The unlit lantern it held crashed to the floor.

"Yeah!" Steve cackled, sounding like a wild man. "And it's Layne Dalton's stuff, too! I hate that smooth-talkin' Reb almost as much as I hate Jack Reynolds. I only wish he was here so I could tear *him* up!" He went to the parlor fireplace, picked up the poker, and moved to the center of the room where a beautiful chandelier hung from the tall ceiling. Swinging with all his might, he repeatedly struck the dangling glass prisms, splintering them into tiny pieces. Candles and candle holders scattered all over the room.

Harriet wheeled and hurried back down the hallway. Melody was at her bedroom door.

"How many of them are there?" she asked.

"Three, but these are no regular Yankee soldiers."

"What do you mean?"

Harriet took Melody by the hand, pulled her into the bedroom, and closed the door. "Come over here and sit down," she said, guiding her to an overstuffed chair in the nearest corner.

"What do you mean, they are no regular Yankee soldiers?" Melody asked as she eased into the soft chair.

"It's the Heglund brothers...Steve, Everett, and Keith!"

The names struck Melody like a triple slap in the face. Her features went dead-white. Her mouth quivered, and she compressed her lips to stop the quivering. The wicked Heglund brothers had murdered her brother. She had no reason to believe they would not murder her—and Harriet—too.

Melody was about to speak her fears when Harriet said, "I heard Keith say your father murdered his father. So they've been told the lie. Steve just said he hates Layne almost as much as he hates your father. It sounds like they're here to do all the damage they can."

Terror was a living thing in Melody Dalton's eyes. "Harriet," she stammered, "you know those three murdered my brother. If they find me here, they'll kill me, too! Maybe both of us!"

There were more crashing sounds downstairs.

"They'll come up here, Harriet!" Melody said, her whole body trembling. "There's no place for us to hide except the closets...and they're likely to look there for something to smash or break!"

"Look," Harriet whispered, "maybe the best thing is for me to put in an appearance before they come up here and find us. I think it'll sit better with them than if they find us hiding."

Melody's voice was hoarse with emotion, choked with the fear that chilled her blood. "Maybe, if Steve wasn't down there. But he's so wicked, I wonder if he isn't half devil!" There were more crashing sounds, followed by coarse laughter.

Harriet hugged herself, tightly gripping her upper arms. "Honey, we don't have any choice but to try. But first, let's get you back into bed."

Harriet helped Melody into the bed and covered her with a blanket. Steeling herself, she took a deep breath and said, "Here goes." Without looking back, she left the room and made her way down the hall, praying under her breath. She could hear two of the Heglund brothers in the back part of the house. The third was still in the parlor, calling to them with glee. She learned the source of his glee when she saw Everett using a bayonet to rip up Melody's over-stuffed couch.

Harriet clenched her fists against the icy dread that fought to claim her, then started down the stairs, her hand gliding shakily along the rail of the banister.

Suddenly Everett caught the movement out of the corner of his eye and stopped with the bayonet buried deep in the back of the couch. A bit stunned to see her, he blinked, then looked toward the kitchen where his brothers were demolishing dishes. "Steve! Keith! C'mere!"

Harriet continued to slowly descend the staircase with her heart drumming her rib cage.

When his brothers did not respond, Everett shouted, "Steve! Keith! Come in here!"

The noise stopped abruptly and Steve's voice filled the house, "Whattya want?"

"Come in here!" Everett repeated.

"What is it?"

"Come and see!"

Heavy footsteps were heard as Steve and Keith moved down the hall that led from the kitchen to the parlor. When they entered the parlor, they saw Everett looking toward the staircase with a wicked grin on his face.

"Well, what is it?" Steve snapped, turning to follow his brother's line of sight. When his eyes fell on Harriet, he halted in his tracks.

"Well, lookee here!" Steve sneered. "If it ain't ol' lady Smith! What're you doin' here? Don't you know ever'body's s'posed to be outta town?"

Harriet was four steps from the bottom. She stopped, and for a second or two remained immobile, holding her breath. Steeling herself again, she looked Steve square in the eye as he moved toward her, and said with a quiver in her voice, "I...am asking you to leave the house. Please. Right now."

"Why, Mrs. Smith, we can't leave here now. We've got a lot of things to do yet. Besides, why should you care? It ain't your house."

"Steve asked you what you're doin' here, lady," butted in Keith. "Why ain't you evacuated like ever'body else?"

Harriet's hand was still on the railing of the banister. She backed up a step and said, "Mrs. Dalton—Melody—is upstairs. Her baby is due next month, and she's been having some problems. She has been quite ill...and still is. Too ill to leave when everybody else evacuated. Dr. Craig said she would lose the baby if she tried to travel. I'm...staying with her to do all I can to see that she carries her child full term. I ask you again to please leave. She's had it bad enough with all the shelling yesterday. I appeal to your sense of compassion. Melody is very ill. Please don't do any more damage to her belongings."

Steve Heglund grinned wickedly, a demonic look in his eyes. "Now ain't that too bad? The daughter of my pa's murderer is sick. I think I'll have a good cry over ol' lady Dalton."

"Yeah, big brother," Keith said, "maybe we all oughtta shed some tears for her and her kid."

Everett snorted. "So Jack Reynolds's daughter is sick, eh? Well, maybe we can make her sicker! How about we go upstairs and tear up her bedroom!"

"Why, Everett," said Steve, waggling a finger at him, "you're not showin'—how did Mrs. Smith put it?—you're not showin' your sense of compassion. You know, like her old man showed for Pa when he gunned him down in cold blood."

Harriet backed up two steps and said, "Melody's father did not gun your pa down in cold blood. It was your pa who went after Jack…with the gun you three stole when you broke into the Reynolds house years ago. Jack was able to get close enough to wrestle him, and the gun went off, striking your pa in the stomach. The jury acquitted Jack of murder; it was self-defense."

Steve looked around at his brothers. "She ain't tellin' it like Ma and George told it."

"Well, who you gonna believe?" asked Everett. "This ol' biddy's lyin'."

"Sure she's lyin'!" gusted Keith. "She's Melody's friend, so naturally she's gonna lie to protect Jack's name."

"I'm not lying!" snapped Harriet. "Your pa went to Jack's house with the full intent of killing him. It backfired on him. And even if it wasn't so—even if Jack had murdered your pa—that wouldn't be Melody's fault. Why should she suffer at your hands for something she had no control over? Have you no decency at all?"

Again Steve looked around at his brothers. "Everett, you have any of that stuff?" he asked, grinning.

"What's that?"

"Decency."

"Naw. It don't pay to have none of that."

"Keith, you got any decency?"

Keith Heglund threw his head back and roared with laughter. "No, big brother, I ain't got none of that stuff."

Steve turned back to Harriet and noted that she had backed part way up the stairs. "Well, Mrs. Smith, it looks like we ain't got no decency. So I guess it's time we paid a visit to Jack's daughter."

Harriet wheeled and bounded up the stairs, lifting her skirt calf-high. Steve lunged after her, but lost his footing and fell on the stairs. His brothers were on his heels and fell on top of him. All three swore as they unscrambled. When they had gained their feet,

Harriet had already reached the landing and was out of sight.

Harriet plunged into Melody's bedroom to see her frightened friend sitting up with the covers pulled tight around her neck, hollow-eyed and motionless. Harriet swung the door shut and looked for the key. There was none. "Melody, where's the key?" she asked.

"I don't know! There's never been a need to lock the door."

Harriet dashed to the overstuffed chair and began sliding it toward the door. But it was to no avail. The rapid footsteps of the Heglund brothers resounded in the hall, and suddenly the door burst open.

Harriet quickly placed herself between Melody and the three men. Her eyes were full of fire as she hissed, "Don't you dare touch her!"

Steve swore and struck her in the face with an elbow. Harriet stumbled and fell over the chair, landing on the floor.

Steve stood over Melody and said with a sneer, "I hate the name of Jack Reynolds, lady! You hear me? Your old man murdered my pa!"

Melody's insides tightened and she felt the baby move. Even her unborn child could sense the fear that was in her.

"Let me tell you who else I hate, lady. I hate that husband of yours. Since I can't get to *him*, I'll take it out on *you!*"

Harriet was on her feet again, steadying herself against the over-stuffed chair. Melody glanced at her, then back at Steve Heglund as he loomed over her bed. "Get out of my house!" she said.

Steve looked around at his brothers. "Hear that, boys! The little lady with the big belly wants us out of her house!"

Harriet pushed her way between Steve and Melody's bed. "Big brave men, aren't you?" she said. "Oh, sure! You can threaten women! It would be a different story if Walter and Layne were here! You cowards—you'd be running like scared rabbits!"

Steve's mouth pulled down. He reached out and sank his fingers deep into Harriet's hair. He shook her head roughly and growled, "Get this into your skull, lady! I ain't scared of your husband or hers! And neither are my brothers!"

Harriet was doing her best not to let Steve know he was hurting her, but Melody knew he was. Her anger overrode her fear. Face blazing, she railed, "Let go of her, Steve Heglund, and get out of my house!"

Steve swore and threw Harriet to the floor, then slapped Melody's face with a stinging blow, flattening her on the bed.

"Atta boy, Steve!" laughed Keith. "Show 'em who's boss!"

Harriet scrambled to her feet, breathing hard, and pounced on Steve's back as she dug her fingernails into his eyes. Steve howled, but could not shake her loose. "Get her off me!" he screamed to his brothers.

Everett and Keith broke Harriet's hold and threw her to the floor. She went down in a heap.

Melody's voice rang with wild anger. "Leave her alone! Get out of my house!"

Steve slapped her again, flattening her on the bed as before. "Shut up, you!" he blared, rubbing at his stinging eyes.

She sat up again, her cheek bright red from the blows, and screamed, "You'll pay for this! Layne will beat you to a pulp for laying a hand on me!"

Everett and Keith stood by, waiting. They knew better than to make a hostile move before their older brother did. Steve swore at Melody, threw the covers back, and seized her by the arms. She fought him, but his strength was too great. He lifted her up and flung her across the room. Melody slammed into the wall, face-forward, the baby taking the full impact. She slid to the floor, dazed.

Steve stood over her, his teeth bared in rage. "So your fancy-pants husband will beat me to a pulp, will he? Well, let me give him somethin' to make him want me *real* bad!" As he spoke, he drew back his foot to kick her in the midsection.

Everett laid a hand on Steve's shoulder and said, "Wait a

minute, big brother! You really want to get to her? I know somethin' better than kickin' her!"

"Yeah? What?"

Melody was crying in pain, and she could feel the baby squirming inside her. Blood appeared low on the front of her robe and began to spread.

"Remember that expensive piano Layne bought her?"

Steve grinned. "Yeah."

"Well, I noticed it in a room at the top of the stairs. I think it'd be heart-wrenchin' for Jack's daughter, here, to see that piano shoved through the balustrade and fall all the way to the first floor!"

"No-o-o!" Melody wailed. "Don't touch my piano! Ple-e-ase!"

"See, Steve?" Everett laughed. "I was right! It's gettin' to her already!"

"C'mon, Keith," Steve said, moving toward the door. "Let's fix that piano!"

"What about these women?" Keith asked, pausing beside Harriet.

"They ain't goin' nowhere! C'mon. Let's deal Jack's daughter some real misery!"

Melody crawled to her friend. "Harriet!" she wept. "They're going to destroy my piano!" Harriet was still too dazed to respond.

Melody whimpered as she crawled to the bed, gripped the bedstead, and painfully pulled herself to a standing position. She took a deep breath and stumbled to the door. She used the frame to steady herself, then made her way toward the music room, leaning against the wall. She could hear the Heglund brothers puffing and grunting in the room.

Melody was almost to the landing when she saw her prized piano roll through the music room door. Steve saw her bracing against the wall and said, "Watch this, woman!"

The Heglunds rolled the Steinway across the landing. It crashed into the banister, splintering it, and the front leg dropped over the edge, causing the strings to make a sharp, discordant sound. The piano slid slowly forward, then stopped, balancing dangerously.

Screaming at the Heglund brothers to stop, Melody groped her way to the landing and staggered toward Steve. In a mindless frenzy, she began beating on him with her fists. He cursed her and shoved her to the floor, then leaned against the piano. It was enough to tilt it over the edge. With a loud scraping noise, the Steinway slid off the landing and crashed to the floor below.

The Heglunds looked down and laughed.

Melody was on her hands and knees, weeping. Blood ran down her legs as she struggled to her feet and shuffled unsteadily to the edge of the landing. Tears stained her cheeks. For a long moment, she didn't move. She just stood there, staring down at her demolished Steinway with wide, disbelieving eyes. These wicked men had destroyed the most wonderful gift Layne had ever given her. A black wave of anguish surged through her. Releasing a wild, primal scream, she made a dash for Steve, intending to push him over the edge.

Harriet was now at the door of Melody's room, leaning on the frame. In horror, she saw Steve meet Melody's charge and shove her toward the edge of the landing where the piano had crashed through moments before. Melody clawed desperately at the broken banister and grasped a dangling length of railing for a second. Then it broke off in her hand, and she went screaming over the edge.

Melody landed on top of the piano, which stood at an angle. Her head struck the hard wood, knocking her unconscious. Everett and Keith drew up beside their older brother, who stood at the lip of the landing, looking down at Melody.

"Is she dead?" Keith asked.

"Naw, she's still breathin'."

"She's bleedin' pretty bad, though," Everett said.

"That's what she gets for her old man murderin' our pa. C'mon. We've done enough damage. Let's get out of here."

Harriet moved unsteadily down the hall. She reached the staircase and looked down at the horrid sight below. Melody had slid to the floor and lay in a heap beside the Steinway. The lower part of her robe was soaked with blood.

"Oh, dear God, no!" Harriet gasped as she started down the stairs.

When the Heglund brothers reached the street, a lieutenant on horseback came trotting toward them. "General Burnside is calling all the looters back to their posts. You men need to get back there as soon as possible."

"Yes sir, Lieutenant," said Steve, saluting.

The lieutenant nodded and rode away, looking for more looters.

Everett glanced back at the Dalton house. "What if she dies, Steve?"

The elder brother shrugged his shoulders and replied coldly, "So she dies. Pa's also dead, isn't he?"

"Her baby will die, too," Keith said.

Steve spit in the street. "So what? Just one less Dalton in the world. C'mon. We better get back to our posts."

CHAPTER TWELVE

✦

Harriet Smith's head cleared quickly when she knelt beside her unconscious friend. Melody Dalton lay in a limp heap. Her mouth sagged open, and her breathing was shallow and irregular. There was a large bruise on the left side of her forehead that was swelling quickly and turning purple. This, however, was the least of Harriet's worries. The bleeding frightened her most.

There was no choice in the matter. Harriet was going to have to leave Melody and go for Dr. Craig. She straightened Melody out, then placed a pillow from the ripped-up couch under her head. From a linen closet down the hall she picked up several hand towels and used them to stay the flow of blood as much as possible. She then covered Melody with blankets. With shaking hand, she wrote a note telling Melody where she had gone in case she came to and found herself alone and lying on the floor. Then Harriet donned coat and scarf and dashed out the door.

The streets were deserted as Harriet ran westward toward the edge of town, the cold air assaulting her lungs. She glanced up and saw the Confederate artillery on top of Marye's Heights. They were ready for the full-fledged invasion that was coming.

"Oh, dear God," Harriet said, "don't let them start the battle till I can get Dr. Craig. Please, Lord...let her be all right."

Harriet reached the outskirts of Fredericksburg and stopped to catch her breath. Coming toward her were several riders in gray uniforms. When they drew up, the leader touched his hatbrim and said, "Hello, ma'am. I'm Lieutenant Carlin. We're attached to General Jeb Stuart's cavalry. You really shouldn't be going into town. The Yankees have occupied it."

"I'm not going *into* town, Lieutenant," she gasped. "I'm *leaving* town."

Surprise showed on the young officer's face. "You mean you've been staying in town, ma'am?"

"Yes. During the shelling...and the looting."

"But, why, ma'am? Everyone was supposed to evacuate yesterday morning."

"Are you acquainted with Major Layne Dalton, Lieutenant?"

"Yes, ma'am. He's on Marye's Heights under General Kershaw."

"All right, then. Let me explain."

Once Lieutenant Carlin understood, he asked, "Where is Dr. Craig, ma'am?"

"He's at the Ralph Jones farm two miles southwest of town."

"All right. You go back to Mrs. Dalton. I'll send one of my men right now to fetch Dr. Craig. I'll send another up to Major Dalton and let him know what's going on."

Harriet thanked Carlin and headed back into town. She heard the lieutenant barking orders as she ran. Looking over her shoulder, she saw one rider head southwest away from town and another for Marye's Heights.

General Kershaw rubbed his stubbled jaw and said, "I'd like to let you go, Major, but this lull isn't going to last. The Yankees could attack at any minute."

"But, sir," argued Layne Dalton, "from what the sergeant said, my wife could be dying. Put yourself in my place. If it was your wife down there, wouldn't you want to go, no matter what?"

Kershaw nervously pulled at an ear. "Of course I would," he said. "But there are two reasons I'm hesitating. Number one, if the blue-bellies attack while you're en route, you could get killed real quick. Number two, I need you here to lead your men when the battle comes."

"Look at it this way, sir. What would you do if I went down in the midst of battle? You'd replace me with another officer, right?"

"Yes."

"Well, if the Federals launch their attack while I'm gone, put that man in my place. I'll get back here as soon as I can. As for the situation en route...I'll make sure I don't run into the enemy. Please, sir."

Kershaw sighed. "You drive a hard bargain, Major."

"I try, sir."

The general sighed again. "You're a good man, and this army needs you. Just be real careful, okay?"

A tight smile curved Dalton's lips. "Thank you, sir. I will."

Harriet knelt beside Melody, who had just started coming around when she returned to the house. The bleeding had subsided, for which Harriet was thankful. As she gave her friend water from a dipper, she told her that Lieutenant Duane Carlin had sent riders for Dr. Craig and Layne.

Melody looked up at Harriet and said with a tremor in her voice, "My baby's dead. I can't feel any movement."

"Now, honey, that doesn't mean the baby's dead. You're not moving right now, yourself. Both of you took the fall, and you're both a bit numb at the moment."

"I don't know what Layne will do if the baby dies, Harriet."

"Are you afraid he'll turn against God?"

"Yes. And not only that—I'm concerned about what he might try to do to the Heglund brothers. He could get himself killed."

They heard footsteps on the front porch, and the broken door squeaked open. Both women turned to see who it was.

"Layne!" Melody cried out.

Layne dashed across the parlor, knelt beside Melody, and cupped her pallid face in his hands. He kissed her tenderly.

"Doc Craig should be here soon," Harriet said, standing over them.

"I don't want Melody trying to talk," Layne said. "Can you tell me what happened? I can see that the Yankees have been here."

Harriet thought about not telling him it was the Heglund brothers who had been there. But she knew he had a right to know.

Before Harriet could speak, Layne said, "I see she's lost a lot of blood. Did you get the bleeding stopped?"

"As best I could. I don't think she's losing much now."

"And this bruise on her forehead..."

"Not a lot I could do for it. I soaked it with cold water."

"You're a gem, Harriet," he said. Then to Melody: "You and little Danny are going to be okay, honey."

Melody pressed her lips together and blinked her eyes slowly to signify her agreement. In her heart, however, she feared the baby was dead.

Looking back up at Harriet, Layne said, "Go ahead. Tell me what happened. Looks to me like Melody fell from up there."

Harriet told Layne the story as quickly and as accurately as she could, making sure he understood that it was Steve Heglund, not the other two brothers, who threw Melody across the bedroom and pushed her off the landing.

Layne was about to speak when Dr. Craig tapped on the partially open door and said, "All right if I come in?"

"Please do!" Layne exclaimed, rising to his feet.

The doctor gave Melody a quick examination as Harriet again

explained what had happened. Dr. Craig rose to his feet, shaking his head, and said, "I've got to do a much more thorough examination, Layne. We need to get her upstairs on the bed."

"I'll carry her, Doctor," said Layne.

"Be very careful," warned the physician. "Her bleeding has almost stopped. I don't want it to start again. She could have some broken bones, too."

"I will," said Layne, bending over to pick her up.

He cradled Melody in his arms as he would a small child and carried her up the stairs. When Melody was comfortable on the bed, Dr. Craig said, "Layne, I need to ask you to leave the room while I work on Melody. I'll need Harriet to stay and help me."

"I understand, Doc. I'll be downstairs or out in the hall. Just call when you're finished."

Layne closed the door behind him and moved slowly down the hall toward the landing. He was feeling a mixture of emotions—wrath toward the Heglunds and icy fear for Melody and the baby. When he reached the landing, observed the broken banister, and looked down at the destroyed piano, his wrath increased.

Layne descended the stairs and assessed the damage in the rest of the house. His hands trembled with the desire to lay hold of the Heglund brothers, especially the brutal Steve.

Nearly an hour had passed and Layne was in the parlor placing books back in the bookcase. Out of the corner of his eye, he saw movement on the stairs. Dr. David Craig was descending slowly, a gray, dismal look on his face.

Biting his lower lip, the doctor reached the last few stairs, paused, and said solemnly, "I'm sorry, Layne. Melody went into labor right after you left the room. The baby's dead. It was a boy."

Dr. Craig's words were like fists striking Layne Dalton in the chest and stomach, leaving no breath in him. The blood drained from his disbelieving face. His mind was in a wild, maddening spin. He began to shake, every muscle and fiber in his body strung tight.

"It was the Heglund brothers who hurt my wife and killed my

son, Doc," Layne finally managed to say through clenched teeth. "I'm going to—"

"Layne, listen to me!" cut in Dr. Craig. "Right now, Melo—"

"No! You listen to me! I'm going to kill all three of those...those wretched Heglunds, Doc! They're going to pay for what they did here!"

"Layne, listen to me! Right now Melody needs you! That baby was hers, too, and she's bearing the physical *and* emotional pain of its loss. You've got to calm yourself and go up there to her."

Layne drew a deep breath and got a grip on himself. "Okay...okay, Doc. You're right. I'll go up to her. But the day will come when I will make those murderers wish they'd never been born."

Dr. Craig took hold of the major's muscular arm and mounted the stairs with him. As they made their way upward, Craig said, "I'm sure you have to get back to your unit as soon as you can, Layne."

"Yes, sir."

"I'll take care of burying the baby."

"Thank you, Doc. I appreciate it."

When the two men entered the bedroom, Dr. Craig picked up the tiny bundle wrapped in a sheet and hurried out the door, saying he would return in a moment.

Layne eyed the bundle, biting hard on his lips. Then he moved toward the bed, where Harriet sat on the edge, holding Melody's hands.

"I'll leave you two alone," said Harriet, standing to her feet. "You need some privacy in your grief."

When the door closed, Melody set tearful eyes on her husband and said, "Darling, I'm sorry."

Layne stroked her cheek tenderly. "It's not your fault. Are you okay?"

"Yes. Dr. Craig says he can't find any broken bones."

Layne leaned over, wrapped her in his arms, and held her. They wept together for several minutes. When they drew apart, Layne sat on the edge of the bed, looking sadly into her eyes.

"I'll give you another son, darling. You'll still have your little boy," Melody said, drying her tears with the bedsheet.

Layne worked up a wan smile and was about to respond when Dr. Craig tapped on the door and said, "May I come in?"

"Yes, please do," Layne said.

"Sorry to barge in," the physician said, "but I do have to get back to the Jones place so others who need me can find me. As far as I can tell, Melody's all right, Layne. No broken bones. You can both be thankful that the piano came to rest at the angle it did. I believe it was the angle that helped break her fall. If she'd hit it flat, who knows how many bones she might have broken."

"That's something to be thankful for," Layne said.

"We all know there's a bloody battle pending," the doctor continued, "so I recommend you get these two women to Bertha Shrewsberry's place as soon as possible."

Dr. Craig mixed some powders, saying Melody would need something to sedate her and help ease her pain. Then Layne and the doctor left the house together. Layne returned shortly with an army wagon and drove the women to Bertha Shrewsberry's house in the country. Bertha received them gladly, and as Layne carried Melody, she led them to the room that would be Melody's for the duration of their stay.

Melody was a bit groggy from the powders administered by Dr. Craig, but she patted her husband's cheek as he gently laid her on the bed.

"You rest real good, won't you?" he asked.

"Yes," she said. "And I'll be praying for you during the battle."

Melody saw fire leap into her husband's eyes at the mention of prayer. She took his hand and said slowly, "Darling, don't let yourself become embittered toward the Lord. Our little son is in heaven now. He's with the Lord Jesus. There's no better place for him to be."

Layne gripped her hand tightly and looked out the window,

staring vacantly at the setting sun.

"Layne, only those who put their trust in Jesus are going to heaven. If you want to see Danny there, you will have to turn to Jesus for salvation."

Layne Dalton was so filled with grief for his son and with hatred for the Heglunds that he barely heard her.

"Layne? Are you listening to me? Layne…?"

Slowly, Layne lowered his eyes to look at his wife. "One day, sooner or later, I'll have my vengeance on those filthy vermin!"

Harriet saw the fear that settled in Melody's eyes. She moved close to the vengeful man and said, "Layne, you could get yourself killed going after the Heglunds. God will make them pay for what they did."

"It's not up to God. It's up to *me*," Layne said.

Bertha Shrewsberry's house had a Bible in every room. Harriet picked the one up off the small table beside the bed and said, "Layne, let me show you something."

Layne was not interested in what Harriet was about to show him, but his gentlemanly sense of courtesy held him silent.

"Here," said Harriet. "Romans 12:19. The apostle Paul says, *Dearly beloved, avenge not yourselves, but rather give place to wrath: for it is written, Vengeance is mine; I will repay, saith the Lord.* Layne, God is saying that we are not to avenge ourselves…that vengeance is His. *He* will repay the wrongdoers."

Layne Dalton stood like a rock, not giving an inch. "I mean no offense to you, Harriet, but this is one time when vengeance will be *mine!*"

With that, he leaned over and kissed Melody on the forehead, the tip of her nose, and on the lips, and said, "I must get back to my post, sweetheart."

Melody tried to focus on his face as she said, "I'll be praying the Lord will bring you back safely. I love you, darling."

"I love you, too," he said. "Take care of yourself, won't you?"

"Yes."

Layne thanked Harriet and Bertha for their help, then drove away in the army wagon.

Darkness was falling as Layne approached the campfire where General Kershaw stood with several of his officers and enlisted men. Sergeant Kirkland spotted Layne first and dashed to him. "Hello, sir," he said, saluting. "General Kershaw told us about your wife. How is she, sir? And the baby?"

Dalton continued walking toward the campfire, face grim. "Not so good, Sergeant. I'll explain it to General Kershaw and you can listen."

"Ah, Major Dalton!" General Kershaw said as Layne drew up with Kirkland beside him. "I'm relieved that the hostilities didn't begin while you were gone, and I'm glad to see you back. How are Mrs. Dalton and the baby?"

Layne gave Kershaw a solemn look and said, "Melody is all right, but...but the baby...the baby is dead."

"No. What happened?" Kershaw asked.

With tears in his eyes, Layne quickly told what had happened. When he was done, the soldiers gathered close and spoke their condolences. Word was carried to the men of Dalton's unit, and they gathered to him, wishing to share their sympathy with him in his loss. While they were doing so, Generals Lee and Longstreet came along, and General Kershaw told them the story. They also offered Dalton their condolences.

General Kershaw then turned to General Lee in the presence of the men gathered near the fire and said, "What do you think, sir? What has held the Federals back from attacking? Do you think they will attack tomorrow?"

Lee had ridden out in early afternoon with General Stonewall Jackson to reconnoiter the enemy's position and to brace up Jackson's division for the impending attack. Jackson's troops would engage the Federals first, since they were positioned at strategic spots along the Rappahannock and at the stone wall that ran along the base of the hills that made up Marye's Heights.

Standing close to Lee was Major Robert Stiles, of Longstreet's division, a gifted writer who had chosen on his own to keep a log of the events at Fredericksburg. Stiles angled his paper toward the firelight and wrote as Lee spoke.

"The reason General Burnside didn't attack today was because he wasn't ready. However, I feel confident he will be ready by morning. My reconnaissance mission has erased any doubts whatsoever about where Burnside is going to attack us. By the way the Federals are positioned, I am sure they are going to try to turn our right side down there at Hamilton's Crossing with their artillery and cavalry…and come straight at us with the massive infantry they have assembled out there in the fields to the north. I have directed General Jackson to summon Generals Hill and Early and their brigades from their downstream positions. They must bolster the rest of General Jackson's division when the attack comes.

"We must be ready up here on the Heights to cover General Jackson's troops with cannonballs and bullets. I have an idea that stone wall down there is going to get a real blood-soaking before this is over."

Layne Dalton lay in his bedroll under the cold night sky and wrestled with his troubled emotions. He was concerned for Melody, that she recover from losing the baby. He wept for the loss of his little Danny. And his blood boiled with wrath toward Steve Heglund and the two brothers who dared assault his wife and property.

"God," Layne whispered, "I don't know why You let those…those men take the life of my little boy, but You did. I don't understand it. They tell me You're a good God…and I'm not saying You're not. You know every human heart, so I'm not telling You anything You don't already know. I think You should have kept Steve Heglund and his brothers out of my house this morning. But since You didn't, I'm going to get my revenge. *An eye for an eye and a tooth for a tooth,* Your Bible says. No matter how long it takes, I'm going to kill those slithering snakes for taking my son from me."

The cold night breeze blew over Marye's Heights, whining in the trees. It took Major Layne Dalton till nearly 3:00 A.M. to fall asleep.

CHAPTER THIRTEEN

★

Dawn came on Saturday morning, December 13, 1862, with a heavy fog hanging low on the Rappahannock River and on the battered, deserted town.

When Major Layne Dalton awakened amid the trees on Marye's Heights, he found Sergeant Kirkland sitting on the cold ground next to him. "How long have you been sitting there?" Dalton asked.

"Only about a half-hour, sir. I just wanted to make sure you were all right. Did you sleep okay?"

"Not too good," replied the major, sitting up and stretching his arms. "Took me quite a while to get to sleep to begin with, then I kept waking up."

"I can't say that I understand, sir, because I've never been a father, and I've never had a child die. But I want you to know that I sorrow with you in your grief."

Dalton stood and picked up his campaign hat, which lay close by. Like everyone else atop Marye's Heights, he slept in his uniform without removing his boots. He placed his hat on his head and gave Kirkland a weak smile. "You're quite a friend, Sergeant. I want you to know that I deeply appreciate your kind thoughts."

Both men noticed a small, slight figure in gray coming toward them. They recognized Private Benny Hay, who was in Dalton's unit and, like Kirkland, had taken a special liking to the major. Hailing from South Carolina, Hay was eighteen, small and frail, but he had shown great courage under fire in previous battles.

Hay saluted Dalton and nodded at Kirkland, then said, "Major Dalton, sir, I was on sentry duty last night when you came in, so I didn't know about your loss until after you had retired. I just want to say, sir, that I'm sorry about your little baby."

Dalton managed a slight smile. "Thank you, Private," he said softly. "I appreciate your taking the time to come and say so."

Hay turned and looked at the fog below. "From what I'm told, we'll be fighting the blue-bellies today soon's that fog lifts."

"I don't think there's any doubt about it," replied Dalton. "General Lee says this will be a bloody day."

"Well," spoke up Kirkland, "let's hope it won't be *our* blood."

"No sense worrying about it," said the major. "Worrying won't change a thing. Guess we'd better get our breakfast down. We're going to need all the strength we can muster here in a little while."

At ten o'clock, the sun was burning the last of the fog away, and both armies were set for battle.

Atop Marye's Heights, Major Dalton conferred with Generals Longstreet and Kershaw, then left to have a talk with his captains. As he walked along the edge of the trees, he came upon Major Robert Stiles, paper pad in hand, writing as he stood facing the massive force of the Army of the Potomac in the open fields to the north.

"'Morning, Major," said Stiles.

"'Morning, Major," echoed Dalton. "Writing about what you see, I presume."

"More about what I see in my mind than with my eyes at the moment," Stiles replied.

"May I take a look at it?"

"Certainly," nodded Stiles, and handed him the pad.

Dalton read it aloud. "We are about to enter into the arena of battle. I think of the gladiators of old, entering into the amphitheater in the presence of Caesar. *Morituri te salutamus!* 'We who are about to die salute thee!'"

Stiles looked into Dalton's eyes without a word.

"I'm afraid these graphic words are also portentous, Major," Dalton said. "Like General Lee, I think this is going to be a bloody day."

Before the fog lifted, the Confederates on the lofty hills around Fredericksburg could not see the force assembled in front of them, but they could hear a band playing, the muffled sound of troops in motion, the rumble of cannons and caissons being moved about, and the jingle of harnesses. Nerves were stretched tight.

General Robert E. Lee, as was customary for top military commanders, had retired to a relatively safe spot in the hayloft of the Marye barn. The door of the loft faced the stone wall at the bottom of the hill, giving Lee a perfect view of the town and the potential battle site.

General Jackson was at the lower elevation with his troops, standing near the four-foot-high stone wall. Outside the wall was the sunken road. It was a natural entrenchment and afforded protection for three thousand of Jackson's riflemen, arranged in ranks four-deep behind it. Lee had placed Longstreet's artillery and infantry on the heights above Jackson's infantry so the ground in front of the stone wall would be subjected to a murderous crossfire. Lee thought of what Longstreet's artillery chief had said earlier that morning: "A chicken could not live on that field when we open up on it."

Lee studied the men along the wall with his field glasses, picking out General Jackson. He smiled to himself. *Fitting,* he thought. *Dubbed "Stonewall" at the Bull Run battle, there he stands like a stone wall, preparing his men to fight the enemy at the stone wall!*

Lee let his gaze drift to the woods off to his right. There at the edge of the trees stood Longstreet. The command to commence fire for both artillery and infantry lay on his shoulders. Longstreet's command would set in motion a conflict that would cost many lives. Lee hated the thought, but this was war. Men bleed and die in war.

General James Longstreet felt fully the weight that lay on his shoulders. He knew the Union army would begin its advance soon at the command of General Burnside. Along with the advance of the foot soldiers and cavalry would come the command to open fire with the artillery socketed in the hills across the river.

Longstreet would have to trust his experience and his instincts for the proper moment to tell the men at his number one cannon when to fire the first shot, signaling the entire Confederate force to commence fire. Longstreet was of the "old school." He believed it best to let the advancing enemy get so close "you can see the whites of his eyes" before opening fire.

Longstreet took in the scene below through his binoculars. There were dazzling portions of snow on the surrounding fields. The sun forced its sharp light through the remaining patches of fog and intensified the reflections from fifty thousand bayonets. Interminable columns of infantry stood in ranks in the open fields. Longstreet could make out Union officers in dark-blue uniforms rushing from point to point.

Field artillery was whisked into position like so many children's toys. Rank and file, footmen and horsemen, small arms and field ordnance presented a sight to see.

Suddenly Longstreet heard a Yankee bugle and recognized its message. General Burnside, from his position on the opposite bank of the Rappahannock, had just given the command that would put the giant Army of the Potomac in motion. The dark-blue columns of infantry flowed toward the waiting Confederate lines like the massive waves of a steadily advancing sea.

Longstreet's attention was drawn to General Jackson, who now rode his horse to a small hill within a few hundred yards of Hamilton's Crossing, from where he would command his division. General Lee had ordered him to stay with the bulk of his men at the stone wall until the Federals began their attack. Jackson had a certain charisma about him that instilled in men the courage and the will to fight. The Rebels at the wall would need all the encouragement they could get.

Longstreet could feel the tension come alive in his men all along the lines atop Marye's Heights. They were waiting impatiently for the command to open fire. Too early.

The atmosphere on that cold winter's day was tight and fierce. From his position on the Heights, Longstreet's eyes were glued on the advancing army. It was a military panorama the grandeur of which he had never seen.

On they came, in beautiful rank and order, as if on parade—a marching forest of steel and hundreds of colorful regimental flags, contrasting with the dark blue of the uniforms and the dull russet hue of the wintry fields through which they marched. Somewhere in the midst of it all was a military band, the brass instruments sounding sharp and clear above the rumble of drums.

Suddenly it seemed that a tremendous thunderstorm had burst over Fredericksburg as three hundred Union artillery opened fire from Stafford Heights and its flanking hills across the river.

An instant howling of shot and shell hurled against the Confederate troops along the river and on the semi-circle of hills south and west of Fredericksburg. Scores of missiles crashed through the woods atop Marye's Heights, breaking down trees and scattering branches and splinters in all directions.

General Lee was on his feet, along with his aids, in the open door of the hayloft. The Yankee missiles were overshooting the Confederate artillery and infantry lines, but soon they would find the range. Lee wondered why Longstreet didn't give the command to commence fire.

General Kershaw dashed up to Longstreet, who was still peering through his binoculars at the sea of blue. "Sir!" gasped Kershaw. "Pardon me, but shouldn't we be firing back at those Yankee guns?"

"We will shortly," Longstreet said without removing the field glasses from his eyes. "They're still trying to find the range. We're safe for a few more minutes. I want to let those lines of infantry get a little closer before we start cutting them down, and I want to unleash all our fire power on the whole army of blue-bellies at the same time."

A Yankee shell whistled over their heads and struck in the woods behind them, exploding and felling a slender young oak.

"They're finding the range, sir," said Kershaw.

"Just need to get those blue-bellies down there in the fields a little closer, General," Longstreet said casually.

All along the Marye's Heights line, the men-in-gray hunkered down as missiles zoomed over their heads and exploded behind them. They were coming closer.

The men in Major Dalton's regiment were getting jittery. One of the riflemen called out from his position behind a tree, "Major Dalton! Do you suppose something is wrong with General Longstreet? Why isn't he giving the command to commence fire?"

"There's nothing wrong with him," Dalton shouted back. "He knows what he's doing. Just sit tight, everyone! We'll have more Yankees down in the first rush if we do it General Longstreet's way!"

The same kind of tension was mounting on the lower elevation, where Stonewall Jackson's division of infantry and artillery waited.

On came the men-in-blue, wondering themselves when the

Confederates were going to open up on them. Meanwhile, their artillery across the river continued the cannonade with unabated fury, giving a background of fleecy, blue-white smoke to the animated scene.

General Longstreet, fully aware of the tension among his troops, continued to peer through his field glasses. Jackson's front cannons on the lower level were loaded with canister, and he wanted the Yankees close enough that the first burst of canister fire would take out several hundred.

"Come on! Come on, you blue-bellies!" he said in a half-whisper.

General Kershaw knew the long-awaited moment was upon them. Wheeling, he ran back to his men, saying, "Get ready! He's about to give the command!"

The words were hardly out of Kershaw's mouth when Longstreet shouted the command to the signal cannon to fire.

Thunder rolled along the Confederate lines, sending deadly canister whistling and plowing into the dense columns of oncoming soldiers. The effect was devastating. Men were being blown in every direction, most of them dead before their bodies stopped rolling.

The rattle of musketry from behind the stone wall and atop Marye's Heights punctuated the deep roar of the cannons, filling the valley with an ear-splitting din.

The deadly accuracy of the Rebel artillery, backed by the sudden unleashing of thousands of muskets, seemed to paralyze the Union troops momentarily. Then in terror, they stampeded.

Confusion reigned for several minutes. It was a scene of blood, smoke, fire, and death. Soon, however, several Union batteries moved into position north and west of Marye's Heights. Together they fought back, concentrating tremendous fire on the Confederate positions.

Above the tumult could be heard the wild cheering of the attacking hosts in blue and the defiant, blood-curdling yell of the men-in-gray. The battle of Fredericksburg was under way in full force.

General Burnside had sent some five thousand footmen into the town the night before. He held them back for a while after the battle began, then sent word for them to pour out of Fredericksburg in close ranks and attack the Rebels behind the stone wall.

It was a horrible carnage. The Confederate artillery and musket fire that opened up as the Yankees emerged from the town was frighteningly lethal. Line after line of brave Union soldiers moved forward in strict order. Some leaned into the fearful crossfire as if advancing against a blizzard wind. They fell dead and wounded in droves.

Across the river, General Burnside stood amid a thick stand of huge oak trees and observed the wholesale slaughter of the first blue wave. Flanking him were Colonel Adelbert Ames and Lieutenant Colonel Joshua L. Chamberlain of the Twentieth Maine Regiment, a part of the Fifth Corps held in reserve on the east side of the river.

Colonel Ames, commander of the Twentieth Maine, was unhappy to be kept in reserve. He was a fighter, and he was eager to get himself and his men into the thick of it. Ames had been seriously wounded in the Battle of Bull Run a year-and-a-half earlier, and had received a Presidential Commendation for gallantry in that battle. He had done little fighting since.

Chamberlain, who was second in command of the Twentieth Maine, was likewise eager to get into the fight. His regiment had been held in reserve a few weeks earlier at the battle of Antietam and had seen limited action. The Twentieth Maine was champing at the bit.

Chamberlain turned to Burnside and said, "Sir, you have the entire Fifth Corps in reserve, here. I'm sure Colonel Ames will agree that in view of what's happening over there, our regiment is more than ready to cross the river and get into the fight."

"Whenever you're of a mind to send some of the reserves over there, sir, we'd sure like to be first," Ames concurred.

"I'll keep that in mind, Colonels," Burnside said. "We've just lost a lot of men, but I'm not ready to send any reserves as yet."

The Union troops behind the first charging lines stumbled over the dead under the scorching fire that was coming from behind the stone wall and the top of Marye's Heights. Long waves of men-in-blue pressed forward, firing their muskets. When one line halted to reload, another would move past them, overreaching their comrades' forward positions, trying gallantly to break the enemy line. Their only hope of success was to use their massive numbers to simply overwhelm Robert E. Lee's smaller army.

Huge clouds of smoke drifted over the plains, hills, and town as the firing increased. The roar was deafening. Shot and shell screeched in maddening sounds. The Confederates cannonballs came thicker and faster, dropping with uncanny accuracy into the midst of the tightly packed columns. It seemed that no Yankee could live through such firepower, but the endless waves kept coming.

At about 2:30 in the afternoon, Confederate cannonade set the high winter grass on fire at several points. The flames, quickened by a light breeze that swept down over the valley, spread rapidly in every direction. Agonizing screams and despairing cries came from the unfortunate wounded left lying in the path of the flames. They struggled vainly to flee. All over the burning fields they were crawling, stumbling, falling, overcome by pain and fire and smoke. They begged for help, but no one could help them.

At Bertha Shrewsberry's country house some three miles from the scene of carnage, the widow and Harriet Smith sat beside the bed where Melody Dalton lay. Melody was experiencing pain, but this was minor discomfort compared to the agony of soul she was feeling as the sounds of the distant guns rattled the windows of the house.

The women had spent much time in prayer together, and Bertha had also spoken many words of encouragement to Melody and Harriet concerning the hand of the Lord on their husbands. They discussed Psalm 91:1, and Harriet's note in the margin of her Bible: *Safety is not the absence of danger, but the presence of God.*

"We saw that when those Yankee shells were falling all around us," said Harriet. "Even though our house next door was hit and demolished, the Lord was with us."

"Praise the Lord for His sheltering hand," Bertha said.

Melody looked up from the pillow with tears in her eyes. "Bertha...Harriet..."

"Yes, honey?" said the older woman.

"Could we have another time of prayer right now? I want to ask the Lord not only for Layne's safety...but for Layne to come to Jesus."

The three women joined hands and prayed.

At about three o'clock, General Burnside decided it was time to send some of his reserves into the battle. Several of his units had almost reached the stone wall, but had been turned back. Burnside knew he could never hope to win the battle unless his army got past the wall and up the slopes to the top of Marye's Heights.

Burnside called his Fifth Corps officers to him and ordered that First, Second, and Third Brigades make ready to cross the river. The Twentieth Maine Regiment was part of the Third Brigade. Within minutes the three brigades of cavalry and infantry were lined up at the two pontoon bridges that bobbed in the water at the riverbank. A bugle trilled, and the Union troops started across the floating bridges.

It took Stonewall Jackson's and James Longstreet's artillery only minutes to see what was happening at the river. Quickly, they turned some of their guns on the bridges and opened fire.

They did not have the range at first. Some of the cannonballs fell short, exploding as they hit the river bottom and sending great gushers in every direction. Other cannonballs sailed just above the soldiers' heads. The waves caused by the exploding shells made the pontoons rock and sway. Men and animals struggled to keep their balance. The horses were wild-eyed with fear and fought their bits.

The entire Twentieth Maine was across the river before Lee's artillery began finding the bridges. The troops who had made it across made their way through the streets, their determined faces pointed toward the stone wall and Marye's Heights. When they reached the plains at the edge of Fredericksburg, they could see the terrible toll the Confederate artillery fire had taken—all around them were bodies and parts of bodies.

The fields spread before them were now a melee of mangled men and horses, living and dead, wreathed in powder smoke. Wounded soldiers, with the aid of others, streamed from the fields in search of cover. They yelled words of encouragement and warning to the men who had just come across the river.

The sun went down while what was left of Burnside's three fresh brigades slowly picked their way across the fields toward the stone wall. They leaped over fences, pushed through hedges, avoided the bodies of the dead and living, and joined their comrades on the front lines.

The battle went on briefly until muzzle flames shone in the gathering darkness. And finally the firing on both sides stopped.

CHAPTER FOURTEEN

As darkness fell and the temperature dropped, a mist rose from the Rappahannock and was carried by an icy breeze across the land. The moon was rising, trying to force its silver rays through the mist.

General Robert E. Lee was at the crest of Marye's Heights, assessing the damage from the day's battle. General James Longstreet reported that many Confederate soldiers had been killed and wounded amid the trees atop the hill, and General Thomas J. Jackson reported many casualties among his troops on the lower level. His artillerymen and infantry that flanked the stone wall had suffered more than the riflemen behind the wall, though there were many men at the wall who lay dead and wounded. The cavalry stationed along the river bank had also sustained some casualties.

Major Layne Dalton stood near Lee, along with General Joseph Kershaw. They listened as Jackson described his casualties, and they could hear the moaning and crying of their wounded comrades.

Lee turned to Kershaw and said, "General, have your men carry water to the wounded back there in the trees, and see what they can do to alleviate their suffering."

"They're already doing that, sir," replied Longstreet.

Turning to Jackson, Lee said, "How about down below, General?"

"We're doing what we can, sir," said Jackson, "but we do have a problem. Many of our men fell over the wall after they were hit. We've probably got a couple dozen who are lying there wounded. The Yankees have a line not more than fifty yards from the wall. With what moonlight is filtering through the fog, any men I send over that wall would be perfect targets. I can't sacrifice men in order to give aid to the wounded."

The other officers who stood around could see the concern in Lee's eyes as the cries of the wounded carried up the slopes.

Major Dalton moved close to Lee and said, "Pardon me, General…"

"Yes, Dalton?"

"Sir, I think some of the cries are coming from wounded Yankees out there between the wall and that Federal line. Seems to me the Yankees are probably wanting to get help to their wounded as much as we are to ours. Would you give me permission to go down there and see if I can talk the Yankees into a truce so we can both get to our wounded?"

Lee frowned and said, "Truce, eh? You might get your head shot off while you're trying to talk those blue-bellies into it."

"I really don't think so, sir. I'm sure it's snipers they're worried about right now, too."

Sergeant Richard Rowland Kirkland and Private Benny Hay had brought more wood for the fire and heard Dalton's words to General Lee. They stood looking on as Lee ran his gaze over the faces of Longstreet, Jackson, and Kershaw and asked, "What do you men think?"

Each general agreed that the major should be given permission to proceed.

"All right, Major," Lee said. "Go down there and see if you can work out a truce. But be careful."

"I will, sir," nodded Dalton.

Just then Sergeant Kirkland and Private Hay moved up and Kirkland said to Dalton, "Major, sir…"

"Yes?"

"Private Hay and I would like to volunteer to go with you. Just in case those Yankees decide to take a shot at you."

Dalton grinned. "Sergeant, there are plenty of General Jackson's men down there. If any trouble starts, they'll pitch in."

"I don't doubt that, sir," said Kirkland, "but those are General Jackson's men. Private Hay and I believe there ought to be at least a couple of your own men with you."

Dalton looked at Lee, who smiled his approval.

"All right," said the major. "I'll take you two 'bodyguards' with me."

Moments later, the trio reached the bottom of the hill and approached the Confederate troops who huddled in the cold behind the long curved wall. Brigadier General Thomas Cobb of the Georgia Brigade saw them coming and moved to meet them.

"Is there something I can do for you, Major?" Cobb said, keeping his voice low.

"I'm on a special mission with General Lee's permission, sir. Sergeant Kirkland and Private Hay, here, volunteered to come with me. I'm going to try to talk the Yankees out there into a truce so we can get to our wounded men, and they can get to theirs."

"Jolly good idea," said Cobb, smiling. "I hope it works."

"Well, we're about to find out."

"We'll be ready to move over the wall if you can get 'em to agree to it, Major," Cobb called after him.

As they drew near the wall, Dalton bent low and said, "Keep your heads down. Those blue-bellies might start shooting if they see movement over here."

Dalton stooped down and peered over the wall toward the Federal troops, barely visible across the body-strewn field. The moans and cries of the wounded tore at Dalton's heart.

He cupped his hands to his mouth and shouted, "Hey,

Yankees! Can you hear me?"

Calls for help came from the wounded. Beyond them, across the misty field, a voice answered back, "Yeah! We can hear you, Johnny Reb! You wanting to surrender?"

"Never! But I have a proposition for you. I'd like to talk to your highest ranking officer present. I am Major Layne Dalton, speaking under the authority of General Robert E. Lee."

"Most of our officers are farther back, Major," came the reply. "But if you'll hold on, I'll get the closest one."

"I'll stay right here."

Some three minutes passed, then a different voice came across the field. "Major Dalton...?"

"Yes!"

"I am Lieutenant Colonel Joshua Chamberlain, Twentieth Maine. What's your proposition?"

"I hear many of your wounded crying for help. We have the same thing here close to the wall. How about a truce until dawn to allow us to help our fallen men? Fair enough?"

"Fair enough," came Chamberlain's reply. "Speaking for Major General Burnside, the truce is on until dawn."

"Thank you, Colonel!"

"Thank you, Major! And give my regards to General Lee."

Moments later, Dalton stood before General Lee, announcing the truce agreement. Lee commended him for making it work and commanded Longstreet and Jackson to take advantage of the all-night truce and bury their dead.

Ghostlike figures of Yankee soldiers moved about on the open field in front of the stone wall, caring for their wounded and picking up their dead. The carnage suffered by the Union army was devastating.

Along the front of the wall, wounded Confederates were given water, then hoisted over the wall with caring hands and taken to the top of the hill for further care.

Confederate supply wagons carried picks and shovels to the

Rebels who shivered in the cold night air, and hundreds warmed themselves by digging a common grave along the south side of the hills. The fog grew thicker by the time the long grave was deep enough, and though it was too dark to identify the dead, their gray-clad bodies were sadly placed in the grave and covered over.

The next morning was Sunday, December 14. Dawn came over a land covered with massive patches of fog, and with it, the end of the truce. On both sides, riflemen and cannoneers waited at their posts, and officers stood by to give their battle commands.

The day was only minutes old when the Union left opened up on the Confederate right near Hamilton's Crossing, where General Jackson was situated. The view from the wall and atop Marye's Heights was obstructed by the fog, but it soon began to lift, and the battle was underway in force.

From his perch in the door of the hayloft, General Lee was amazed to see the size of the force coming toward him. The immense army moved like a huge blue serpent about to encompass the Rebel force and crush it in its folds. The lines advanced at double-quick pace, and suddenly they opened fire.

The Union artillery cut loose from both sides of the river at the same time, and the command came from General Longstreet for the Confederate guns to unleash. Flame and smoke fringed Marye's Heights along its forward base, and death's dreadful work had begun once more.

The first wave of blue was repulsed after nearly thirty minutes, and the Union lines retreated, leaving their dead and wounded on the fields. From the stone wall and from the crest of Marye's Heights, the Confederate forces sent volley after volley after the retreating Federals.

Only a few minutes passed, then came a fresh wave of blue. Confederate cannons, canister, and bullets cut great gaps in the

Union lines, but it seemed their supply of new troops was endless. They just kept coming.

Lee studied the battle through his field glasses and scrubbed a shaky hand over his face. How long could his dwindling forces hold up against such overwhelming odds?

The fog soon dissipated completely, and under the cold winter sun, the battle continued in all its horror. As the bloody day wore on, the Union troops made indents on the Confederates that flanked the stone wall. Many Rebel prisoners were taken.

The repeated thrusts of the massive Union waves were slowly thinning Jackson's troops. General Longstreet studied the situation through his binoculars. He was not surprised when General Lee moved up beside him and said, "General, I think it's time to send some of this infantry on the hill down the slopes. One of these times, the Union thrust is going to overtake our men at the wall. They're going to need help."

"I was about to order just that, sir," Longstreet replied.

Lee returned to his hayloft, and within ten minutes, General Longstreet was flanked by Major Generals McLaws, Hood, and Anderson, as well as Brigadier General Kershaw. Together they observed ten thousand men-in-gray as they descended the slopes of Marye's Heights.

The first Rebel wave was within forty yards of the stone wall when the Federals suddenly created a wide breach in the Confederate line and poured over the wall with wild, blood-chilling yells. While many Yankees fell, the majority set their sights on taking the hill and raced up to meet the oncoming Rebels.

Union artillery that had been concentrating on the stone wall and the slopes above it suddenly went silent when they saw their own men scrambling over the wall.

Bayonets flashed and bullets flew when the two infantries met on the slopes. More Federals came from the woods and fields. The battle was fierce at the wall and grew worse up the slope as the

Confederates tried to defend their hill and keep the determined Yankees from taking it.

Marye's grassy slopes were dotted with oak trees. Men on both sides used the trees as shields as they fired, reloaded, and fired again into the melee, cutting down enemy soldiers in the midst of bayonet and hand-to-hand conflict.

Hours passed as the battle continued, the Rebels holding the Yankees at about the halfway point. Suddenly a Union bugle sounded from somewhere outside the stone wall, and the Yankees made a hasty retreat toward the bottom of the hill. Weary, worn, and battered, the Rebels let them go and slowly began ascending the steep slopes toward the crest of Marye's Heights.

Just as the Yankees reached the wall, their artillery began to bombard the exhausted Rebels. Layne Dalton was two-thirds of the way up when suddenly his attention was drawn down the slope where Rebels were being blown into eternity. Even fallen, wounded Yankees were dying in the barrage.

Dalton's line of sight focused on young Private Benny Hay some eighty or ninety yards below, wandering in circles. His hands were outstretched and his face was blackened with powder. He was blind.

Dalton wheeled his mount and raced down the slope toward Benny. He intended to grab Benny's frail body and carry him to safety at the top of the hill. As Dalton drew near, the blinded Rebel soldier was stumbling toward a cluster of naked-limbed oak trees.

On the opposite side of the stone wall, the Union soldiers gleefully observed the rain of fire on the fatigued Confederates struggling to reach the crest of Marye's Heights. Among them were the Heglund brothers, cheering with the others as they watched the Rebels suffering and dying. They had spotted Layne Dalton earlier, and Steve was keeping an eye on him. When the major suddenly put his horse to a gallop and charged down the slope, Steve shouted, "Look, boys! Looks like Dalton's gonna try'n rescue that Rebel up there by those trees!"

Dalton, jaw set with determination, dodged bodies dead and alive, Rebel and Yankee. He was almost to Benny Hay when a Yankee shell exploded at Benny's feet and killed him instantly.

Dalton skidded his mount to a halt beneath the oak trees where Benny met his death. Two more shells came shrieking out of the sky and burst into flames and smoke. One of them was close enough to send a load of shrapnel into the chest, neck, and face of Dalton's horse. The other exploded at the base of one of the large oak trees, toppling it.

The concussion of the dual explosions stunned Dalton. His mind was barely clear enough to react. He tried to avoid being pinned under the horse as it went down, but was unable to clear himself. The oak fell on top of horse and rider, and a limb struck the major's head, knocking him unconscious. He lay with one leg under the dead animal, covered with the branches of the tree.

From behind the wall, the Yankee soldiers prepared for another attack. Abruptly the Union bombardment stopped, and with a wild yell, the Yankees went over the stone wall, guns blazing.

Atop Marye's Heights, Longstreet ordered a fresh unit of Rebels out of the woods and down the slopes to meet the enemy. Within moments there was fierce hand-to-hand fighting once again. The fighting went on for about an hour on Marye's blood-soaked slopes. The Rebels were outnumbered by nearly two-to-one, and for a while it looked like they would be conquered. But they gallantly fought back until they began to drive the Yankees toward the stone wall. The tide was turning for the Confederates.

From a position General Burnside had taken on the second floor of a warehouse at the edge of Fredericksburg, he saw the fierce

Rebel forces driving his army back. He immediately sent word to sound the retreat. He felt sure the Rebels were tired enough that they would draw back for rest. While he allowed his men to rest, he would bring up fresh reserves for a renewed attack. There were about two hours of daylight left. He wanted to hit them one more time before dark.

The lower inclines of Marye's Heights were covered with the wreckage of battle—dead men in blue, dead men in gray. Amid them were the wounded of both North and South, some moaning in pain, others crying out, shell-shocked, bleeding, and begging for water.

The Yankee soldiers implored their officers to do something for the wounded, but were told nothing could be done. If they tried, the Rebel sharpshooters would pick them off. Some argued that they should negotiate another truce, and a request was sent to General Burnside. But the general refused, saying they must hit the Rebel forces on Marye's Heights one more time before dark. As much as he disliked the situation, he could not allow time to help the wounded Yankees.

High above on Marye's Heights, the Rebels prepared for another assault, knowing Burnside was not through. He wanted the victory and would send his massive forces yet again.

Sergeant Richard Rowland Kirkland stood at the edge of the trees, looking down at the wounded men sprawled on the slopes. Their cries for water gripped his heart. Unable to stand it any longer, he went to General Kershaw and said, "Sir, I would like permission to take water to those poor men."

Kershaw shook his head and said, "No, Sergeant. I can't let you do that."

"But, sir, listen to them!"

"I hear them, son," Kershaw replied, his voice strained. "But those blue-bellies will come charging up here again shortly. You'd only get caught in a crossfire and be killed. I can't let you do it."

"What if I carried a white flag as a sign of truce?"

"No. They might think the white cloth signified surrender."

Kirkland looked toward the suffering men and said, "Then I'll go without the white cloth and take my chances. I can't stand to hear those pitiful cries and not do something about it."

Kershaw let his eyes roam over the carnage and said, "All right, Sergeant. Go ahead. But the instant those Federals start coming toward that wall, I want you up here on the double! You understand?"

"Yes, sir," Kirkland said, and hurried away.

Kirkland strapped on as many canteens as he could carry and headed down the slope. He was some thirty yards below the crest, drawing near the first line of wounded men, when Union rifles from below began to bark. Bullets chewed sod all around him. Ignoring them for the cries of the wounded, he dropped beside the first man he came to, which happened to be a Yankee. He could hear General Kershaw shouting at him from above, commanding him to return immediately. The bullets continued to whiz past his head, but paying them no mind, he said, "Here, my friend. Let me give you some water."

The Yankee ran his gaze over Kirkland's gray uniform and smiled grimly. Rolling his tongue in a dry mouth, he choked, "Th-thank you, Sergeant."

The sun was dropping low in the sky. Down on the plain, the Yankee officer who had commanded his men to commence fire saw what Kirkland was doing and gave a loud, sharp command for the firing to cease. The Federals looked on with amazement, realizing that the man-in-gray was giving water to one of their comrades.

"Well, God bless 'im!" someone said.

"Amen!" said another.

General Burnside's adjutant hastened up and asked the officer what was going on. Without a word, he simply pointed to the scene halfway up the hill.

Troops on both sides looked on in awe as Sergeant Kirkland moved from man to man—whatever the color of his uniform—giving him water to help relieve his suffering.

On Marye's Heights, General Lee stood amongst his officers and smiled as he beheld Kirkland through his binoculars. "What courage!" exclaimed Lee. "He ignored those Yankee bullets as if they were no more than common houseflies buzzing around him."

Lee lowered the binoculars and turned to Major Robert Stiles, who was furiously writing notes on his paper pad. "Major Stiles."

"Yes, sir?"

"While you're writing about this tremendous deed, I want you to dub Kirkland, 'The Angel of Marye's Heights.'"

Stiles grinned broadly, nodding. "Yes, sir. I like that. The Angel of Marye's Heights." As he spoke, he wrote the words in large capital letters.

On the opposite side of the stone wall, General Burnside, curiosity aroused, appeared among his men and looked on the touching scene before him. At that moment, Kirkland was kneeling beside a Union lieutenant.

"I've never seen the like," Burnside said. "That young sergeant is some kind of man."

"The man's an angel, sir," a nearby corporal said.

"I hope he lives through this battle," said Burnside. "I hope he lives through the war. Somebody ought to write a story about him...call it 'The Angel of Marye's Heights.'"

CHAPTER FIFTEEN

★

Down slope in Sergeant Richard Rowland Kirkland's path, a mortally wounded Rebel private named Ewan Simms was sprawled on the brown winter grass a few feet from where Major Layne Dalton lay unconscious. Dalton's lower body was under the horse's shoulder, and the dead animal's head rested on his chest. The horse's blood was on his face and neck.

Simms had seen Dalton race down the hill to rescue Benny Hay, and had watched the cannonballs kill Hay and bury Dalton beneath the horse and fallen tree. Simms's midsection had been badly torn by shrapnel, and he knew he was bleeding to death. His strength was gone. He could barely move his head. Concerned for Dalton, he turned his face toward him and called in a hoarse, weakened voice, "Major! Major!" When the unconscious major did not respond, Simms assumed he was dead.

Moments later, Sergeant Kirkland knelt beside Simms, took one look at the gaping wound, and realized the man was not long for this world. They knew each other well. "Hello, Ewan," he said softly. "I have some water for you." Simms gritted his teeth in a spasm of pain, then opened his mouth and drank.

While pressing the canteen to the dying man's lips, Kirkland looked around to locate the man he would visit next. The fallen oak with the dead horse beneath it caught his eye. His heart leaped in his breast when he peered through the branches and recognized the bloody face of Layne Dalton. "Major Dalton!" he gasped.

"The major's dead, Richard," Simms said. "I saw him go down."

Kirkland was stunned. Leaving Simms for a moment, he moved to the spot and stared down at Dalton beneath the horse and tree limbs. He began to weep as he returned to Simms, feeling a deep sense of loss. He had loved the major very much. He would miss him.

When Simms had his fill of water, he thanked Kirkland, and the sergeant moved on. Wiping tears, Kirkland went to another fallen comrade a few steps away, then moved on to a Yankee corporal some fifty feet or so from where Simms lay.

Simms was praying silently when suddenly he heard a weak moan from under the fallen oak. His vision was clouding, but he could see Dalton's head rolling slowly back and forth. Simms twisted himself with effort until he could see Sergeant Kirkland kneeling beside the Yankee corporal. He tried to call out, but his voice was too weak to be heard. He rolled onto his stomach, wincing with pain, and began crawling toward Kirkland, whose back was toward him. When he had inched his way about six feet, he saw Kirkland rise and go to another wounded Yankee farther down the slope. He tried desperately to call out, but could hardly make a sound.

Simms crawled on, ignoring the pain and using every ounce of his remaining strength to reach Kirkland. He made it another ten or twelve feet, but could go no further.

"Richard, the major is still alive!" he gasped in a hoarse whisper...and died.

Layne Dalton almost came to consciousness, then slipped back under and lay still.

✴ ✴ ✴ ✴ ✴

From their position some fifty yards on the other side of the stone wall, the Heglund brothers looked on and assumed Dalton was dead when they saw the Rebel sergeant turn away without trying to give him water.

"I'm glad he's dead," Steve said. "The only thing I'm sad about is it wasn't me who killed him."

Everett and Keith looked at him and caught sight of their older brother's inordinate cruelty, an insidious and fleeting manifestation. It flitted over his face like some shadowy creature from its lair, revealing itself in its subtle wickedness.

Heavy clouds were gathering in the sky, covering the sun as it went down, while Sergeant Kirkland finished giving water to his final sufferer.

General Burnside sighed as he tore his gaze from Kirkland and looked at Generals Franklin, Sumner, and Hooker, whose curiosity had also brought them to the unusual scene on the slopes of Marye's Heights. "No time for another attack, now," he said. "Best thing for us to do is negotiate another truce and bring down our dead and wounded. We'll attack again in the morning."

When Sergeant Kirkland arrived at the top of the hill, he received a rousing cheer from his comrades. Generals Lee, Longstreet, and Kershaw met him, shook his hand, and commended him for a job well done. Then Lee asked, "Sergeant, we saw Major Dalton go down under that oak out there. Are we to assume that he is...dead?"

Kirkland's eyes filmed up as he nodded and replied solemnly, "Yes, sir. He's dead. His horse is dead, and he's lying underneath it.

What I could see of him was awfully bloody. The shrapnel must have torn him up real bad."

Hundreds of Rebel soldiers gathered around Kirkland to express their appreciation for his heroic deed. Those who had seen Major Dalton's attempt to rescue Benny Hay talked about it in Kirkland's presence, expressing their deep sorrow at the loss of the major.

The Federals called for a truce, and it was agreed upon by the Confederates. The truce—as on the previous night—would end at dawn.

As darkness fell under a cloudy sky, both armies began carrying their dead and wounded from the battlefield. The Federals dug a common grave in the open field north of the stone wall, and the Confederates merely extended the one they had dug the night before.

As Steve Heglund and his brothers went over the wall to do their part in picking up Union dead and wounded, Steve said, "You know, it's so dark out here, we could get Dalton's body, and the stinkin' Rebels would be none the wiser. If we hurry, that is."

"What would we want with Dalton's body?" asked Keith. "You wanna stuff it?"

Steve peered at Keith in the dim light. "Not a bad idea, but what I really want is the privilege of dumpin' him in the ground. What's the matter with buryin' him in a Union grave?"

"Nothin' as far as I'm concerned," replied Keith. "Just so he's buried."

"C'mon," whispered Steve. "Let's go!"

Men of both armies were busy all over the hill, picking up the wounded first and carrying them where they could get at least a measure of medical attention. They would pick up the dead later.

The Heglund brothers reached the fallen oak, and together, rolled it off horse and rider. They were about to pick up Dalton when they saw him roll his head and heard him moan.

"Steve! He's alive!" Keith said in a hoarse whisper.

"Sh-h-h-h!" hissed Steve, looking around to see if anyone had heard. None of the soldiers nearby showed any sign of having heard Keith's outburst.

Everett bent low over Dalton and said, "I think he's semi-conscious. I don't think he knows what's goin' on, though."

"Fate is with me!" Steve said, whispering excitedly. "Now I get the privilege of killin' the dirty skunk myself!"

"You can't shoot him right here," Keith said.

"You ever hear of strangulation?" Steve hissed.

"That man alive?" The Heglund brothers were startled by the voice of Union Captain Eldridge Bonebraker.

Steve was trying to think of how to answer when Dalton moved his head and ejected a low moan.

"Yes, sir," replied Steve. "He's…uh…he's a Rebel major, sir. Don't you think we ought to take him prisoner?"

"Not if he's hurt bad. We don't need to use up our medical supplies on enemy officers."

"What if he's not hurt bad, sir?"

"Then take him prisoner," said Bonebraker, walking away. "But you better find out real quick, or his pals will be on your back."

The Heglunds worked Dalton free from the weight of the dead horse and went over him quickly. When they could find no wounds, except for a bad bruise on his head, they picked him up and carried him toward Burnside's warehouse headquarters where many Rebels were being kept as prisoners.

"I heard General Burnside say that all prisoners from this battle will be taken to the Federal prison at Point Lookout," Steve said.

"Yeah?" said Everett, surprised. "You mean Dalton is gonna be in the prison where Clyde is servin' as guard?"

"I'd like to kill him here and now," Steve growled, "but since Captain Bonebraker might be checkin' on him, guess I'll have to let Clyde find a way to work out an 'accident' for him at the prison."

Point Lookout, Maryland, was some sixty miles southeast of Fredericksburg on Maryland's southern tip, and had been chosen by General Henry W. Halleck as the prison where Burnside would deliver the Rebels he captured in the present campaign. The unconscious Confederate major was laid out in the warehouse, along with some two hundred other prisoners.

Because of his exhaustion, Sergeant Kirkland was not part of the "pickup" party on the Marye hillsides. No one in the Confederate Army of Northern Virginia was aware that Major Layne Dalton's body had not been picked up nor buried by men in gray. Generals Lee, Longstreet, and Kershaw assumed he was buried along with all the other dead Rebel soldiers.

At eight o'clock that night, General Burnside met with his three commanding generals and ordered them to get as accurate a count as possible on the number of dead and wounded. When they came back two hours later, they stunned Burnside with the figures.

The Federals had buried nearly thirteen hundred men, but in addition to over nine thousand who were wounded—many of whom would eventually die—they as yet could not account for another seventeen hundred men. By the yellow light of the two lanterns that glowed in Burnside's makeshift warehouse office, Sumner, Franklin, and Hooker noted the sickly look that etched itself on their commander's face.

Burnside swallowed with difficulty, ran trembling fingers over his balding head, and said weakly, "Gentlemen, this is a sad situation."

"I think *debacle* is a better word than *situation*, General," Hooker said dryly. "But I sure agree it's sad. You and your tactics have cut a massive hole in the Union Army of the Potomac. Why don't you just admit it? You're bullheaded pride has cost us better than twelve thousand casualties!"

"Because this is a time of battle and great strain on all of us, General Hooker, I will not act as I would otherwise on your insolence." There was fury behind Burnside's shadowed eyes.

"Act however you want, sir," Hooker countered, "but if you'd listened to these two gentlemen and me, there would be thousands of men going back to wives, sweethearts, and parents from this encounter who now will never see them again."

Burnside saw the same attitude in the eyes of Franklin and Sumner, who remained silent. Drawing a short, sharp breath, he ran his gaze over their solemn faces and said, "That will be all for tonight, gentlemen."

"What about tomorrow?" pressed Hooker, rising to his feet.

"We will attack again," Burnside replied tartly.

Joe Hooker shook his head and walked away. Sumner and Franklin exchanged puzzled glances and followed Hooker, not looking back.

Monday morning, December 15, 1862, came with heavy clouds and a driving storm of sleet, snow, and freezing rain. Soldiers on both sides endured the elements, but there was no fighting.

Sumner, Franklin, and Hooker appeared at Burnside's makeshift office and asked to meet with him. Burnside, who looked as if he had not slept, welcomed them and sat down with them, asking what they wanted to see him about. All three said emphatically that the Union army should pull out before the weather cleared, and go back to Washington.

"Sir, it isn't just the three of us," General Hooker said. "We hear the men talking everywhere. Officers and enlisted men alike are blaming you for what has happened to us here, saying that General Lee has outsmarted you. The men are demoralized, and you will kill thousands more if you send them into battle when this storm clears."

Burnside shook his head and said, "You gentlemen and the men of this army are correct. This debacle is my fault. I laid awake all night thinking about your stinging words, General Hooker. I had them coming. I am telling you gentlemen now, I will tell the entire Army of the Potomac shortly…and I will admit it to General Halleck and President Lincoln. History will lay the blame for this awful beating at my feet…and that is where it belongs." He drew a deep breath, let it out slowly, and added, "We will wait until dark this evening and withdraw."

General Hooker left his chair and moved toward Burnside, extending his right hand. Burnside rose, met it, and gripped the hand firmly.

"Sir," Hooker said with feeling, "I admire a man who has the courage to face his mistakes and admit them. I may not like you, but I admire you."

"We'll leave it at that, sir," nodded Burnside stonily. "Now, let's make plans for our graceful withdrawal."

The storm continued all day, and the freezing rain became sleet late in the afternoon. After dark, the dispirited Union troops began their evacuation, crossing the Rappahannock on hastily repaired pontoon bridges that had been covered with mud and straw to muffle the sound of feet and hooves.

Major Layne Dalton, fully conscious and, except for a bad headache, unhurt, was put in a train of wagons and headed east. The prisoners would be ferried across the Potomac River to Point Lookout, Maryland, and locked up in the Federal prison.

Layne's mind went to the wife he loved and adored. He wondered how long it would be before he would hold Melody in his arms again...if ever. He knew that prisoners died by the hundreds in prison camps—Northern and Southern. Filth and disease took their toll.

Dalton was unaware that the Heglund brothers had captured him. Neither did he know that Steve Heglund had persuaded his division commander to let him and his brothers go along as guards on the prison-bound wagon train.

The weather cleared during the night, and the Confederates awoke on Tuesday morning expecting the Union forces to attack, their minds set on squashing the smaller army and taking Marye's

Heights. To their surprise, they found that Burnside's entire Army of the Potomac was gone.

An elated Robert E. Lee spoke to his troops, commending them for whipping the Federals in spite of the overwhelming odds. Then waving to thousands of cheering soldiers, he rode off the hill with a cavalry escort and headed for Richmond.

The remaining generals met on the porch of the Marye house to make plans for getting their four thousand wounded to hospitals. Sergeant Richard Rowland Kirkland made his way up to the steps, and when General Longstreet saw him, he paused in what he was saying to the others and asked, "What is it, Sergeant?"

"Pardon me, sir," Kirkland said, saluting, "but it is important that I speak to General Kershaw."

"Of course," Longstreet said, swerving his gaze to Kershaw. "We'll excuse you for a few moments, General."

Kershaw nodded and descended the steps. "What is it, Sergeant?" he asked.

Kirkland's features were serious. "Sir, Major Dalton—God bless his memory—told me where his wife is staying. I would like your permission to go and tell her of the major's heroism and death on the battlefield."

"Of course, son," the general said. "It's very thoughtful of you. I know you and Major Dalton were close friends."

"Yes, sir."

"Tell you what—would you give me a couple minutes to write her a message?"

"Certainly, sir."

The slender young sergeant, now known as "The Angel of Marye's Heights," waited while Kershaw produced a small note pad from an overcoat pocket and used a pencil stub to hastily offer his sympathy to Melody Dalton. He used a second page to eloquently word his feelings about the major's gallantry and courage in dying to save a fellow-soldier's life.

When Kershaw finished, he folded the two pages and placed

them in Kirkland's hand. "Tell her my love and prayers are with her, Sergeant."

"Yes, sir," said Kirkland.

Bertha Shrewsberry and Harriet Smith were working at the kitchen table, making a new dress for Melody Dalton. It was just after nine o'clock, and the morning sun was slanting through the east kitchen window.

The two women were discussing the fact that they had not heard the sounds of war since Sunday. They wondered if the battle was over.

Tears were in Harriet's eyes as she said, "Oh, Bertha...how much longer can this war go on? I do so long to have a normal life again."

"I know, dear," said Bertha, reaching across the table to give Harriet's hand a motherly pat. "I'll be so glad when this awful bloodshed and killing is over...and our men can come home again."

Harriet was about to say something else when a knock at the front door stole her words. "I'll get it," she said to Bertha, who had started to get up.

Harriet hurried to the door. When she opened it, her eyes took in the horse tied to the hitching post at the porch, then she looked into the face of the youthful soldier whose silhouette stood out sharply against the sunlit snow on the ground behind him. "Yes, Sergeant?"

"I believe this is the home of Mrs. Shrewsberry," said the tall, slender man.

"Yes, it is."

"And Mrs. Dalton is staying here, right?"

"That's right," replied Harriet, a cold feeling capturing her stomach. The sergeant's eyes told her there was bad news.

"Ma'am, my name is Richard Kirkland. I was in the battle at Fredericksburg."

"Do you mean the battle is over?"

"Yes, ma'am."

Harriet's heart was thudding. "I'm Harriet Smith, Sergeant. My husband, Walter, is in General Jackson's division. Do you know him?"

"No, ma'am, I don't. I can understand your anxiety, though. For your encouragement, all I can tell you is that we did not suffer near the casualties that the Union did. I...I certainly hope your husband is all right."

"Thank you," Harriet said, then swallowed hard. There was a quavery edge to her voice. "Please don't tell me you're here to tell Mrs. Dalton something's happened to Layne."

"Yes, ma'am. I...I was Major Dalton's adjutant, ma'am." Kirkland choked on the words. "He and I were very good friends."

"Is...is he dead, Sergeant?"

"I'm afraid so, ma'am."

"Harriet," came Bertha's voice from behind as the older woman drew up, "why don't you ask the young man in?"

Harriet's hand went to her mouth. "Oh! I'm sorry, Sergeant. It's just that...well, this news—"

"I understand ma'am," said Kirkland.

Harriet stepped to the side, widening the opening of the doorway. "Please come in."

Harriet looked at the widow. "Bertha, did you hear what he told me?"

Bertha's face reddened and moisture gathered in her eyes. "Yes. I heard you say, Sergeant—"

"Kirkland, ma'am. Richard Kirkland."

"I heard you say that you were Major Dalton's adjutant and close friend."

"Yes, ma'am."

"Did...did he suffer?"

"No, ma'am. He was killed instantly by an exploding shell."

A quivering hand went to Bertha's temple. "I'm glad for that, but oh, my. Poor little Melody."

Harriet put an arm around Bertha's shoulder.

"Is Mrs. Dalton here?" Kirkland asked, removing his cap.

"Yes," nodded Harriet, "but she hasn't been feeling well. She lost her baby, and seems to be having some complications."

"I know about the baby, ma'am. Major Dalton told me. If you don't think I should tell her right now, I can come back later."

The two women looked at each other.

"I wish she never had to hear this horrible news," Bertha said, "but it isn't right to withhold it from her, even though she's not feeling well."

Harriet was fighting tears. "You're right. It's going to be an awful blow, but it must not be kept from her."

Kirkland's features were gray. "Since you want me to go ahead, could I do it now? I...I'd like to get it over with. This is going to be the hardest thing I ever did in my life."

"Of course, Sergeant," Bertha replied, touching his arm. "Let Harriet and me go to her room and see if she's awake. If not, we'll awaken her. Is it all right with you if we stay in the room while you tell her?"

"I want you to," said Kirkland.

Sergeant Kirkland laid his cap on a nearby table and took off his overcoat as the women disappeared from the parlor. There was a large mirror on the wall to his right. He looked at his own image. The face looking back at him was edged with a graven somberness. It was a face that had grown considerably older in the last two days. Harriet returned, her features as gray as his, and said, "She's awake. All we told her was that a Sergeant Richard Kirkland is here to see her, and that you are her husband's adjutant. She suspects that something is wrong. I'll have to let you take it from there."

"Yes, ma'am."

Harriet led him down the hall and into Melody's room.

Melody was sitting up in the bed, looking peaked and weak. Cold dread was evident in the lines of her face and in her eyes as she looked at him and waited for him to speak.

Kirkland's heart was racing, pounding so hard he could feel his pulse throb in his temples. "Mrs. Dalton, I'm Richard Kirkland."

"Yes. Harriet told me. You're my husband's adjutant?"

"Yes, ma'am. I've come to tell you…that the major—"

"No!" gusted Melody. "No! Layne's not dead! Please don't tell me he's dead!"

Harriet was standing by the bed on Melody's right, and Bertha was on her left. Both women sat on the edges of the bed and laid their hands on her shoulders and arms.

"Yes, ma'am. He was killed on Sunday, ma'am. But he died a h—"

"No-o-o!" screamed Melody, throwing her head back and forth in disbelief. "No, it can't be! Layne's not dead! Not my baby and my husband, too! No! No! No!"

Harriet wrapped her arms around Melody, holding her tight. Bertha leaned close, stroking her face as Melody broke into uncontrollable sobs.

It took some fifteen minutes for Melody to cry it out and grow calm. While the two women held her, she wept silently for several more minutes, then looked up at Kirkland with red, swollen eyes. "The battle at Fredericksburg is over, Sergeant?"

"Yes, ma'am. The Yankees pulled out last night."

Melody sniffed. "How…how did it happen?"

"It was on the hill at Marye's Heights. The Yankees came in such great numbers that they finally broke through our defenses and started up the hill. There was hand-to-hand fighting for hours. Then suddenly the Yankees pulled back, and their artillery started bombarding us."

Melody broke for a moment, cried a little, then got hold of herself again. "Go on, Sergeant."

"When the bombardment started, ma'am, the major and I were

about two-thirds of the way up the hill. All of a sudden he looked down the hill and saw Benny Hay groping his way blindly amid the exploding shells. The major raced his horse down the hill to rescue him."

Melody closed her eyes, bracing herself for the words that would tell her exactly how her husband had died.

"Just before the major got there, ma'am, a shell exploded in front of Benny. More shells struck a second or two later. One or both of them took the major's life. He…he died a hero, Mrs. Dalton, a real hero. He gave his life trying to save the life of Benny Hay."

Melody took the hands of her two friends in her own and squeezed them hard.

"Dear Jesus," said Bertha, "help her. Give her strength, Lord, as only You can do."

"What about burial, Sergeant?" Melody asked. "Is there someone I should contact?"

"It's already been done, ma'am," Kirkland said softly. "We had to do a mass burial at the south base of Marye's hill."

She nodded silently, biting her lips.

Kirkland pulled the folded slips of paper from his shirt pocket. "I have something from General Kershaw, ma'am. He asked me to give you this and to tell you that his love and prayers are with you."

"Thank you, Sergeant," she said, accepting the papers and managing a faint smile. "You've been so kind to come all the way out here and tell me about my husband. I'll never forget it."

"I will admit, Mrs. Dalton, it's been the hardest thing I've ever done. I loved the major, and because of that, I wanted to be the one to break it to you. God bless you."

When Kirkland was gone, Melody read General Kershaw's note and cried again. Her two friends sat with her, offering every bit of comfort they could give her.

"The hardest part of all this is…that Layne died without the Lord," Melody said shakily.

Harriet squeezed her hand and said, "Honey, we don't always understand God's ways. We don't know why He let Layne be killed...but haven't we prayed that He would bring Layne to Himself?"

"Yes."

"You gave Layne a Bible to read, and you witnessed to him of your own salvation. Perhaps the Holy Spirit dealt in Layne's heart and brought him to Jesus before he was killed."

"Yes, let's hope so," nodded Melody, silent tears streaming down her cheeks. "I do so want to see my darling husband in heaven."

Only a few minutes had passed when Walter Smith showed up on the Shrewsberry doorstep. He and Harriet had a happy reunion, thanking the Lord that Walter had been spared in the battle. Walter had heard that Layne was killed, and offered his sincere sympathy to Melody.

Walter had gone home to find his own house demolished, but reported to Melody that hers was still intact. Melody invited the Smiths to move in with her until the war was over and they could rebuild their own house.

Walter returned to his division under Stonewall Jackson, and Harriet moved in with Melody.

During the next few days, Melody continued to have problems as a result of losing the baby. Dr. David Craig was summoned, and after examining Melody, he told her that she had sustained permanent injuries and would never be able to bear children. Dr. Craig explained that the pain she was having would subside as she healed, and within a couple of months, she would be fine. He expressed his condolences over Layne's death and spoke words of comfort.

By the middle of February, Melody was feeling fine again and announced to Harriet that she was going to move to Virginia City. With Layne gone, she needed to be with her family.

Harriet understood, though she told Melody she would miss her terribly. Melody said the Smiths could live in her house until theirs was rebuilt. By then she would know more what direction her life was going to take, and would decide about selling the house. They would keep in touch by mail.

CHAPTER SIXTEEN

★

No issue during the Civil War stirred such passions or inspired such deep-seated bitterness as the prisons of both sides. When the War began at Fort Sumter in April 1861, neither side made immediate preparation for the incarceration and care of prisoners. Southerners believed they would wear down the Yankee resistance to their secession in a very short time, and the hostilities would be over. Northerners expected to subdue the Rebels easily within three months, and return to their normal course of life.

Neither side expected to hold great numbers of prisoners. So unprepared were they that there was no coherent policy for the handling of prisoners. There was not a single military prison above or below the Mason-Dixon line capable of holding more than a handful of men.

Fortunately for both sides, there was little action—therefore comparatively few prisoners taken—during the remainder of 1861. In the East, the only battle with significant numbers of prisoners taken was in July at Manassas, which yielded some thirteen hundred Federal prisoners and only a handful of Confederates. In the West, the only major action was at Wilson's Creek in Missouri, where the tally of prisoners taken by both sides was barely over three hundred.

These were manageable numbers, and neither side as yet felt pushed to develop extensive prison systems. Most of the captives were held in a few tent camps. The thirteen hundred Federals taken at Manassas were spread all over the South, giving little if any problem to the Confederacy.

As the War dragged on, however, and bigger battles produced thousands of prisoners on both sides, Presidents Lincoln and Davis began to push government leaders to make room for them.

Prison camps were hastily developed and immediately jammed with captives. It soon became apparent that they were insufficient to handle the legions of prisoners being brought in. In prisons both North and South, meager rations, bad water, poor sanitation, and drafty tents or buildings brought on scurvy, dysentery, pneumonia, a host of other diseases…and death.

The unsanitary conditions also drew rats by the thousands. With food so scarce and the absence of adequate protein, prison rats were staple fare.

No matter what they ate, prisoners learned to gobble their food for fear it might be seized by other hungry inmates. Vicious and sometimes deadly brawls exploded over a few morsels of spoiled meat or vermin-infested rice.

In late 1862 the worst Confederate prisons were Castle Pinckney at Charleston Harbor, South Carolina, and prisons at Danville and Belle Isle, Virginia. The three most disreputable Federal prisons were at Johnson's Island, Ohio, Camp Douglas, Illinois, and Point Lookout, Maryland.

Point Lookout Prison consisted of several poorly built barracks to house noncommissioned men, and a few better-built barracks to house Confederate officers. The officers' barracks were also kept cleaner, and the officers were given better food and boiled water. The prison was situated on a barren, swampy bit of land at the mouth of the Potomac River where it emptied into Chesapeake Bay.

The sixty-mile trip from Fredericksburg to Point Lookout took three days. The wagon train of prisoners and guards was led by Captain Eldridge Bonebraker. On the morning of the first day—December 16—Major Layne Dalton sat in a rear corner of a wagon bed, facing forward. His head was still aching, and his thoughts were fastened on Melody. Would she know he was taken as prisoner, or would she think he was dead?

Captain Bonebraker and two lieutenants were the only ones in the train on horseback. There were three sergeants, five corporals, and twenty-four privates to drive and guard seventeen wagons, holding a total of 221 prisoners. The Heglund brothers avoided Dalton during the night, not wanting him to know they were in the train.

The sky was clear and the air was cold. As the wagons moved slowly eastward toward the Potomac, the Confederate prisoners rode in silence, each man absorbed in his private thoughts.

Layne Dalton huddled against the cold in his overcoat, thinking about Melody and his little son. A Union private was walking alongside the wagon, rifle-in-hand. Their eyes happened to meet, and the youthful private said, "Major, I saw what you did on Sunday...riding hard to rescue that soldier who had been blinded. I know we're enemies, but I recognize courage when I see it. That was a commendable thing for you to do."

A voice familiar to Dalton came from behind: "Private, are you fraternizing with the enemy?"

The private and Dalton turned to see Steve Heglund. "No, Sergeant," the private replied. "I was just commending him for his courage."

"Well, let's not be commendin' lowdown Rebel scum for nothin'. You hear me?"

"I hear you, sir."

"Just move on up to the next wagon," clipped Heglund. "I'll walk beside this one for a while."

When the private obeyed, Steve kept pace with the wagon,

leaned close, and said, "You know who captured you, Dalton? It was me! Everett and Keith and me found you sleepin' like a baby under that dead horse and those tree limbs."

"Congratulations," Dalton said dryly. "You're a big brave soldier."

Heglund leaned even closer and dropped his menacing voice to a whisper so no one else could hear it. "You're a dead man, Dalton! My brother Clyde is a guard at Point Lookout. He'll get you, one way or another. I'd take care of you right now, but Captain Bonebraker frowns on murder. But you get this in your craw—Clyde'll get you, and you'll be just as dead!"

Seconds later, Everett and Keith drew up beside their older brother and sneered at Dalton. Steve called the private back, and the Heglund brothers moved out of Dalton's sight.

When the wagon train arrived at Point Lookout late in the day on December 18, the sky was spitting snow, and a cold, biting wind was coming off the bay. The Confederates from the Fredericksburg battle learned that there were already some six thousand prisoners housed on the Point. The enlisted men were ushered to their barracks, and the officers were taken to the small cabin that was the office of the prison commandant, Major Allen Brady.

Dalton was the highest-ranking officer amongst seven captured at Fredericksburg. Brady, a coarse and hard-faced man, stood them before him and explained that they had better quarters and would receive better food and water than the enlisted men. He then went over the prison's rules, and made sure they understood that any man who tried to escape would be shot. They were then ushered to one of the officers' barracks and placed in their cells.

Dalton was placed in a small cubicle with two bunks, but had no cell mate. The next morning, the officers in his barracks ate their breakfast together, then were sent back to their cells. They were told that they could not go outdoors until they had been there a week.

At breakfast, Dalton had learned that the prison camp covered some twenty-eight acres. Except for about a hundred yards of beach at the very tip of the Point, the camp was enclosed by an eight-foot-high stockade fence. The prisoners knew that any man who tried to swim in those icy waters would drown before he could ever reach land. In warmer weather, guards were posted at the water line to make sure no prisoner tried to swim for it.

Eight feet inside the perimeter wall and the one-hundred-yard stretch of beach was a built-in deterrent to escape—an ominous cordon called the "dead line." It consisted of short wooden posts topped with a single rail. The frail structure was no physical barrier, but the prisoners were forewarned of the consequences of venturing beyond it. Guards were instructed to call out a warning to a prisoner who approached the line. If he stepped over it, he would die in a hail of bullets.

Dalton learned that some fifty men had been shot to death beyond the "dead line." In all, some fifteen hundred prisoners at Point Lookout had died from wounds, dysentery, scurvy, pneumonia, typhoid, cholera, consumption, or being shot down in escape attempts.

Dalton also learned that Clyde Heglund was Sergeant of the Guard under Major Brady. Layne knew that as head guard, Clyde would be in a good position to carry out Steve's threat and have him killed. He would have to stay alert at all times.

When it came time for Steve, Everett, and Keith Heglund to leave the Point and head for Washington to report to General Burnside, Clyde told them he had an idea. He had three guards who had been wanting to return to active duty. He would go to Major Brady and suggest that he let those guards have their wish, and put his three brothers in their place. Not only would it keep all four brothers in one place, but it would put them in a position to work together to kill Layne Dalton.

Clyde Heglund presented his proposal to Brady. The prison commandant liked the way Clyde led the guards and handled the prisoners. He was sure Clyde's brothers would fit in nicely. He wired Washington immediately, and the exchange was approved within a day.

As the days passed, Layne Dalton wondered how the enlisted men stayed alive. The food he was eating was horrible, and what he was getting was better than what they were getting. Many of the officers had bad colds because there was little or no heat in the barracks. Dalton knew it had to be worse in the enlisted men's barracks. Every day he heard of men who were dying of pneumonia and from various other causes.

On Dalton's sixth day in the camp, Steve Heglund visited him and told him of the appointment he and his brothers had received as guards. He did all he could to intimidate the Confederate major and warned him to stay on guard. One day soon, Steve would have the joy of killing him.

On day seven, Layne was allowed to go outside after breakfast and mingle with the other Confederate officers near their barracks. He was talking to some of the men who had been with him at Fredericksburg when he happened to glance across the compound at another group of Confederate officers and saw his old friend Jerry Owens. Layne had lost track of Jerry when he had been assigned to the Trans-Mississippi Department of the Confederacy in late 1861. Layne excused himself and headed toward the other officers.

A guard stepped in front of him and asked curtly, "Where are you going, Major?"

"I just spotted an old friend of mine over there," Layne replied, pointing. "Any harm in my talking to him?"

"I guess not," the guard conceded. "The officers in both barracks often talk to each other."

"Thanks," nodded Layne, and broke into a run.

Jerry saw him coming and hurried to meet him. They came together and embraced. Then, as they gripped each other by the shoulders, Jerry said, "I'm sure sorry to see you in here, Layne, but I sure am glad to see you!"

"No more glad than I am to see you!" said Layne. "So you're a captain now."

"And you're a major!"

"That's what they tell me. How long you been here?"

Jerry explained that he had fought under General Van Dorn in the battle at Pea Ridge, Arkansas, on March 7 and 8. He was captured, and at first had been taken to Johnson's Island Prison in Ohio. The prison was filling up beyond capacity, so the Yankees transported him and four hundred other prisoners to Point Lookout.

The presence of his old friend lifted Layne Dalton's spirits. He asked about Linda and learned that she and their eight-month-old daughter were living with her parents.

"And how's Melody?" asked Jerry. "You got any younguns yet?" Jerry saw the sadness flit across Layne's face. "Layne, is something wrong?"

"You remember the Heglunds."

"Yeah. How could I forget? Especially since I have to look at Clyde every day. I guess you know we've got all four of them here now."

"I'm afraid so."

"So tell me what's happened."

Layne explained how the three Heglund brothers had forced their way into his house during the looting of Fredericksburg, and what Steve had done to Melody, which resulted in the stillborn child. Layne told him of taking Melody to Bertha Shrewsberry's house for safety, and that as far as he knew, she was doing fine.

"It's gotta be hard for you, not being able to go to her," Jerry said.

Layne nodded. "If I can just survive this place," he said glumly. "I know I haven't seen the worst of it, but what I've already seen is pretty disheartening. And even if I don't die of some disease, the Heglund brothers have a grave planned for me—threatened to kill me."

"They're fully capable of it, too," Jerry warned. "There was a young lieutenant in here named Hyman Stanton. Clyde got it in for him, and he ended up dead. Murdered. Made it look like some of the other prisoners did it, but everybody in here knows it was Clyde."

Layne shook his head. "Those Heglunds never seem to get caught. What about Brady? I detect that he's a hardhead, but is he for murdering prisoners?"

"You're right about him being a hardhead, but he won't put up with the guards killing prisoners unless they're trying to escape. Last spring one of the guards killed a Confederate captain just because he didn't like him. Brady executed him."

"Really?"

"Yeah. He doesn't mind giving prisoners a good beating, but that's where he draws the line. He seems to have a special feeling toward officers. That's why we have it better here than the enlisted men."

"Isn't right," mumbled Dalton, "but there's nothing I can do about it."

"I feel the same way." Jerry ran his gaze to the officers in Layne's barracks and asked, "Who's your cell mate?"

"Don't have one."

"Oh? Neither do I."

"No? Any possibility Brady might let us share the same cell?"

"Maybe. We could ask for an appointment with him, but the best way is to do it through a chaplain in my barracks."

Dalton's eyebrows arched. "They've even taken a chaplain prisoner?"

"Name's Captain Michael Young. He's from Roanoke. Brady likes him. I think Captain Young could talk him into letting us bunk together. Come on. He's in the barracks. Let's go talk to him."

The two friends found Chaplain Young in his cell reading his Bible. He was in his late thirties and had been a pastor in Roanoke before the War. He and Layne took a liking to each other immediately. Young was sympathetic to their idea and went to Major Brady with their request. Brady granted it, and within the hour Layne had moved into Jerry's cell.

Young stood in the doorway of the cell while Layne adjusted his cot. Jerry took advantage of the moment to tell the chaplain about the Heglunds causing the death of the Daltons' unborn child and of their threat to kill Layne.

Young was touched by the story. He stepped into the cell as Layne was taking note of the Bible on Jerry's cot and said, "Major, let's sit down and talk for a moment."

"Certainly," Layne said.

The chaplain sat beside Jerry and looked across the small cubicle at Layne. "Do you understand, Major, that your little son is in heaven?"

"Yes, sir. Melody told me that. She's...well, she's a regular church attender. She believes in God and knows a lot about the Bible."

"I'm very happy to hear that." After a brief pause, he said, "From what I just heard about your being captured, it sounds like Melody must believe you're dead."

"It would seem that way to me, sir," said Layne. "If I'm not on the dead list, I'm sure on the missing list."

"Poor girl. This has to be hard on her, especially after losing the baby."

"Yes, sir."

"These Yankees won't let us get word to anybody on the outside, Major, so there's no way she can learn that you're alive. There's one thing we can do, though. We can ask the Lord to comfort her and give her strength in His own wonderful way until such time as this horrible war is over, and you can go home to her. Could we pray together for her?"

Layne Dalton, battle hero and leader of soldiers, was thrown off balance by the chaplain's request. "Uh...sure," he replied. "I...I appreciate that."

When Chaplain Young brought his prayer to a close, Layne was surprised to hear Jerry add an "Amen." He thought about the Bible lying on Jerry's cot, and wondered if his old friend had done the same thing Melody had.

Young smiled at Dalton and said, "You told me about Melody's faith in the Lord, Major, but you didn't tell me about your own. Are you a Christian?"

Layne felt his face heat up. He hoped it wasn't showing. "Well, I, uh…I was taught by my favorite uncle as a child that every man has to find God in his own way."

"No offense to your uncle," said Young, "but we have to come to God *His* way, not ours."

Layne remembered someone saying that to him before. Was it Melody?

"Seems my wife said something like that to me, sir. She also gave me a Bible and underlined several passages for me to read, but it was in my saddlebags when those Yankee shells put my horse and me down."

"The Yankees have provided me with several Bibles," Young said. "Would you like to have one?"

"Why, uh…yes. That would be nice. I appreciate that, Chaplain."

Young hurried back to his cell and returned with a Bible. He gave it to Layne, saying he had previously marked some passages and urged Layne to read them.

When Young was gone, Jerry told his old friend that only two weeks before, the chaplain had led him to Christ. Jerry then opened Layne's Bible and read aloud some of the passages the chaplain had marked. When he had read to him for some ten minutes, Jerry urged Layne to turn to the Lord, also.

Layne was nursing a deep-seated grudge toward God, but kept it to himself. He told Jerry he would think about it.

Each cell in the officers' barracks was allowed a kerosene lantern. That night, as they sat on their cots by the yellow glow of their lantern, Layne followed in his Bible as Jerry read Matthew's account of the crucifixion. Jerry saw that his friend was deeply touched by it, and decided to read the Mark, Luke, and John accounts, also. Jerry would let the Word of God do its work in Layne's heart. He closed his Bible and did not comment.

Later, when the guards had checked to make sure all cell doors were locked and all lanterns were out, Jerry lay in the dark and said, "Layne, now that the guards are out of the building and no one can hear us, there's something I want to tell you—I'm working on an escape."

"You are? By yourself?"

"Yep. Have to. The escape is going to be from this very cell."

"What do you mean?"

"Under my cot you will find the floorboards loosened in a section large enough to crawl through. I've been digging a tunnel for the past seven months. The back wall of the barracks, which is the back wall of our cell, stands just twelve feet from the fence. Did you notice the barracks was that close to the fence?"

"No, I didn't."

"It's slow-going, but by working a few hours almost every night these past seven months, I've dug back about ten feet. I figure that in another three months, I'll be out of here. Now, of course, *both* of us will be going."

"How are you digging? With your fingernails?"

Jerry chuckled. "I found a chisel that was probably used when this barracks was built. It was in the dirt near the side wall. So, using the chisel, I've chipped away a little at a time. I stuff the loose dirt in my pants pockets and throw it down the holes in the privies each morning."

"Owens, you're a genius."

"I know."

"You haven't told any of the other officers?"

"Wouldn't do any good. The door's always locked at night, and that's when the escape will have to be made. I couldn't take anyone but a cell mate with me. I don't see any reason to tell the others."

"So you crawl down in there, light the lantern, and dig away, eh?"

"That's it."

"Well, if you'll show me how you've been doing it, I'll take a turn at it right now."

The new year came, and the two cell mates continued to make progress on the escape tunnel.

Some time during each day, Jerry led in Bible reading. He had finally figured out that his friend was bitter toward God over the death of his son. Layne often talked about Danny and what it would have been like if the boy had lived. Though Layne did not let on to Jerry, the Bible reading was doing something in his heart.

On January 27, two Confederate corporals and three privates tried to escape from the prison, and were shot and killed.

The next day, Steve and Clyde Heglund approached Layne Dalton when he was alone outside the barracks. "Unusual for you to be alone, Dalton," Clyde said. "Where's your buddy, Owens?"

"Inside," said Dalton, fixing him with hard eyes. "He's got a cold. Thought it best not to come out in this frigid air."

"You know what I wish, fancy-pants Major?" Steve said.

"I don't really care," Layne replied levelly.

"Well, I wish *you* would try an escape like those boys did yesterday. I'd love to shoot you down like a mangy dog!"

Dalton eyed him steadily. "And nothing on this earth would make me feel so good as to wring the neck of the coward who beat up my wife and killed my unborn baby!"

Steve was about to retaliate when Clyde said in a quick whisper, "Look out! Brady's comin'!"

Steve looked across the compound and saw the commandant moving their way. Scowling at Dalton, he hissed through his teeth, "I'll get you, fancy-pants! I'll get you!"

With that, Steve and Clyde strolled away, leaving Dalton with a fiery-red face. Layne wheeled and entered the barracks before Major

Brady drew near. His wrath was hot and his breathing erratic. He imagined how good it would feel to get Steve Heglund's throat in his hands. *An eye for an eye...*

As he was gaining control of his emotions, the Bible words Harriet Smith had quoted to him came to mind: *Vengeance is mine; I will repay, saith the Lord.* He headed down the corridor for the cell he shared with his best friend. "But the vengeance should be *mine!*" Layne whispered. "It was *my* son he killed!"

The weeks passed and Layne Dalton continued to be appalled at the atrocities of the prison. Men died almost every day because of the squalor and lack of sanitation. When he discussed it with Michael Young, the chaplain could only say that the Southern prison camps were worse.

Time and again, all four Heglund brothers dealt Dalton misery whenever Major Brady was out of sight, hoping he would retaliate and they could kill him and claim self-defense. Fortunately, each time Jerry was with him and restrained him from making a fatal mistake.

Near the end of February, Steve Heglund drew up to Dalton when Owens was elsewhere and made a ribald remark about Melody. Dalton struck him, knocking him down, and had to be pulled off him by other guards. Unbeknownst to Heglund, Major Brady happened to be near and witnessed the whole thing. Dalton was confined to his cell for a week for striking Heglund, but Heglund was reprimanded severely by Brady for inciting the trouble.

On March 1, Dalton was in his cell alone during the afternoon, lying on his cot and wishing he could be working in the tunnel. Footsteps sounded in the corridor, and Steve Heglund's face appeared at the little window in the cell door.

Layne looked up, saw him, and said, "On your way, baby-murderer. There's nothing going on in here that's any of your business."

Steve looked up and down the corridor to make sure no one

was in sight, then pressed his face close to the opening and said, "You know what, Dalton? I'm glad I knocked your ol' lady off that landin'…and it made me real happy to find out that your kid died. One less Dalton in the world! Somebody oughtta pin a medal on me!"

The stinging words were too much. Dalton thrust his right hand through the opening and grabbed the man's throat. Heglund made a gagging noise and tried to break the hold with both hands, but the angry major's thumb and fingers were like spring steel.

Heglund struggled to free himself, but Dalton held on with wild determination. Heglund was turning blue and his eyes were rolling back in his head when suddenly two guards entered the corridor.

"Hey!" blared one as they both ran down the corridor.

It took both men to break Dalton's hold and save Heglund's life.

A quarter-hour after the guards had carried Steve Heglund out of the barracks to revive him, Dalton heard footsteps again. This time he looked up from the cot to see Major Allen Brady at the door.

"Major Dalton," Brady said tightly, "I must reprimand you for what you just did. I could have you flogged to within an inch of your life. You understand that?"

Dalton rose from the cot and moved up to the door. "I know that," he replied, looking Brady square in the eye.

"But I'm not going to, Major Dalton, because I've observed how Mr. Heglund has badgered you. Some kind of grudge between you two?"

"Yes, sir. He beat up my wife in the Fredericksburg occupation. She was eight months pregnant, and the baby died. That's murder in my book."

Brady held Dalton's hard gaze, blinked, and said, "I'm sorry. There's nothing I can do about that. But I will order the sergeant to stay away from you."

"Well, keep his brothers away too, Major. There's trouble between me and the whole family."

"I'll talk to them, but you understand I can't keep them from their duties, only from speaking to you unnecessarily or doing anything else to rile you."

"Fine. Just so they leave me alone."

CHAPTER SEVENTEEN

✦

On March 4, 1863, one of the officers in the cell next to Layne Dalton and Jerry Owens died of pneumonia. He also had a severe case of diarrhea. Colonel Byron Merrick, the surviving officer in that cell, was sick with a bad cold, and it appeared he might also be coming down with pneumonia.

The camp physician lived and had his practice at Lexington Park, Maryland, some twenty miles north of the Point. Dr. Alex Campbell came once every couple of weeks to do what he could for the sick and dying prisoners, but they were still dying an average of one per day.

Each of the officers' barracks had an eating area at one end. Meals, which were cooked in a shack nearby, were brought in by the guards. At breakfast on the morning of March 5, Steve Heglund was among the guards who delivered the meals to Layne Dalton's barracks, which housed some sixty officers.

Jerry Owens sat across the long table from Layne Dalton as Heglund laid a crude wooden tray before each of them and said, "I was sure sorry to hear about your neighbor dyin' yesterday, fellas. That's the way it goes in this place. Men are dyin' just about every day. Never know who'll be next, do we?" Heglund grinned wickedly and walked away.

During the day, Layne and Jerry talked about their tunnel. As best as they could figure, they were about six inches past the stockade fence. Just two more feet, and they would be free men.

At supper that night, Steve Heglund made sure he was the guard to carry the trays to Dalton and Owens. He said nothing when he set them down, just grinned maliciously and went on delivering trays with the other guards. The barracks door was closed and locked as the guards moved on, and the officers were about to begin eating when a large rat skittered under a table.

"Rat!" yelled one of the men, and jumped to his feet.

Within seconds, all the officers were up. Layne grabbed a broom that stood in one corner and, with grim determination, set out to corner the rat and kill it. One officer kicked at the rat as it ran toward him, then reversed directions. Finally, Layne cornered the rat and killed it with a few strokes of the broom handle.

Dalton and Owens disposed of the rat, then returned to their table and sat down to their meals. Without thinking, Jerry sat down where Layne was moments before. Layne eased down on the bench opposite him, grinned, and said, "I think we're sitting in each other's places, but I guess it doesn't make any difference. It's the same slop on that tray as this one."

"Guess so," Jerry chuckled, picking up the fork from the tray.

The meal was about halfway through when Jerry suddenly laid down his fork, clenched his teeth, and gripped his midsection.

"What's the matter?" asked Layne.

"Cramps," Jerry grunted, his face losing color. "Kind of dizzy, too."

Layne stood up, went around the table, and took hold of his friend by the shoulders. "Come on, I'll help you to the cell. You need to lie down."

"Yeah," Jerry nodded, struggling to rise while clutching his stomach. "This isn't good. I...I really am sick."

Layne spoke to the other officers at the table. "Better call the guards. Dr. Campbell should still be on the grounds. I heard somebody say he was staying to eat supper with Major Brady."

While two men banged on the door, shouting for the guards, Jerry Owens went from white to deathly gray and collapsed on the floor.

Layne knelt beside him and said, "Hang on, Jerry. We'll get help for you."

Jerry spasmed violently, thrashed about on the floor for fifteen or twenty seconds, then lay still. He closed his eyes, expelled one tremulous breath...and died.

Two guards came through the door and stood over Layne Dalton as he knelt beside his dead friend. Chaplain Michael Young knelt on the other side.

Young looked up and said to the guards, "He's dead. But I want Dr. Campbell to check the body. From what I saw, I think Captain Owens got some kind of poison."

While one guard was running after the doctor, the chaplain moved to the table and began to pick through the food on Jerry's plate. "Seems to me the captain must have gotten the poison from this food. He was perfectly fine until he had eaten about half of it." His eyes widened. "Major Dalton, come here, please."

Layne bent over the plate, and Young used the fork to separate out a number of tiny yellowish-brown seeds. "What do you make of these?" Young asked.

"Looks like the stuff they put out in those little tins to kill the rats."

"Rat poison. Put in there rather hastily, I'd say. Whoever did it didn't have time to make sure all the seeds were completely mixed into the rice and gravy."

Some of the other officers closed in, wanting to see for themselves. Dalton stood back, his mind in a whirl, and knelt once again beside the body.

Major Brady entered the room, followed by Dr. Campbell.

Layne stood over his dead friend while Campbell examined the body and asked questions.

When Layne finished his description of Jerry's agonizing death, he said, "We believe he was poisoned, Doctor. Wouldn't you say so?"

"Sure sounds like it," nodded Campbell. "We'll have to check with the cooks. Something poisonous got into his food, all right." He looked around and asked, "Anyone else having similar symptoms?" The men shook their heads.

"Doctor, Chaplain Young has something to show you," Layne said.

Young was still standing at the table, keeping guard over Jerry's plate. He made eye contact with the physician, then said, "Tell us what you see here, Dr. Campbell."

Campbell bent low and examined the diminutive seeds Michael Young had separated from the rice and gravy. "Mm-hmm," he said, standing to his full height and setting his gaze on Major Brady. "The captain was poisoned on purpose, Major. These are *nux vomica* seeds."

"What's that?" Brady asked, moving close and looking down at them.

"You use rat poison here in the camp, I believe."

"Yes. We put it in tins in all the barracks and other buildings. This place has quite a population of rats."

I could name you the biggest one, Layne thought. He knew exactly what had happened.

"*Nux vomica* is the poisonous seed of an East Indian tree, Major," said Campbell. "*Strychnos nuxvomica.*"

Brady's eyes widened. "Strychnine?"

"Yes. As used in rat poison. In a very short time, it kills anything or anybody that eats it. Somebody purposely put rat poison in the captain's food."

Brady wiped a shaky hand over his face. "I'll have to talk to the cooks. Somebody in this place has some answering to do."

"I can tell you who that somebody is, Major," Layne Dalton said.

Brady swung his gaze to him and raised his eyebrows. "Now, Major, you must be careful with any accusations. I—"

"It's really quite simple, sir. Everybody here knows that Steve Heglund hates me with a passion...and I haven't tried to hide the fact that it's mutual."

"Now, Major—"

"Ask these men who were sitting at this table. It was Steve Heglund who delivered our trays to us. The poison was meant for me."

Brady started to speak again, but Layne cut him off. "Before any of us had taken a bite, a big rat came in here. We were all running around, trying to corner it and kill it. When the rat was dead, we sat down again to eat. Jerry unwittingly sat in my place, so I sat down in his."

"I'll question Sergeant Heglund," the commandant said evenly.

Layne shook his head. "Won't do any good. He'll deny it. Unless some honest guard testifies that he saw him put the poison in, he's going to get away with it."

Major Layne Dalton was right. When questioned, Steve Heglund denied putting the rat poison in the food. Since no one would testify they had seen him do it, the matter was dropped.

The next day, before Dalton was let out of his cell for breakfast, Dr. Campbell entered the barracks to check on Byron Merrick in the next cell. Merrick seemed to be doing better, but Campbell left him some medicine for his cold.

When the doctor was gone, Dalton and Merrick conversed through the wall for a few minutes, then the major looked up to see Steve Heglund peering at him through the small window in the cell door.

"So they're gonna bury your partner this mornin', huh?" Heglund said, keeping his voice low.

Layne left the wall and moved to the door. A dark stain of red started low on his neck and crawled up into his scowling face. "You'll get yours one day, Heglund!"

"Yeah? Well, it won't be *you* who gives it to me, fancy-pants!"

"Well, if it isn't, maybe it'll be God Himself!"

Heglund pursed his lips and huffed, spraying saliva. "There ain't no God, Reverend Dalton. Don't preach to me!"

"You'll find out when you take your last breath."

"Well, let me tell you this, darlin'...you'll draw your last breath a long time before I take mine. I'm gonna see to that!" His voice was still a sibilant whisper as he added, "Missed you last night with the rat poison, but sooner or later I'll put you in your grave." With that, he walked away and left the building.

Layne skipped breakfast. His grief over Jerry's horrid death had stolen his appetite. While the others were eating, Chaplain Young came to the cell, sat down with Dalton, and said, "Major, I know you're hurting inside because your friend died the death that was meant to be yours."

"Yes, you're right. And I'm hurting because his murderer is getting away with it."

"Well, let me say first that he *won't* get away with it. The Bible says vengeance belongs to the Lord. Sometimes God's wheels turn slow, my friend, but they do turn. Let Him deal with Steve Heglund."

Layne wanted to object, but he knew it would accomplish nothing.

"What I came by for," continued Young, "was to comfort you with one fact."

"Yes, sir?"

"Jerry was a Christian, Major. His faith was in the Lord Jesus Christ for his salvation. Jerry's in heaven, and I'm sure by now he's even met your little Danny. They're both in the sweet presence of Jesus. Don't wish either one of them back. To come back to this earth after one glimpse of the wonderful, shining face of Jesus would make this old world seem mighty dark."

"Yes, sir," Layne nodded, biting his lower lip

"You about ready to let the Lord into *your* heart, Layne?"

The biggest thing in Layne Dalton's life, other than his love for Melody, was his hatred of Steve Heglund. His meager knowledge of Scripture and his observance of Christians combined to tell him that if he received Christ into his heart, he would need to lay aside his desire to seek revenge. Layne Dalton did not want to stop hating Steve Heglund; his entire being longed for revenge.

"Not yet," he replied, meeting Young's steady gaze. "I'm still thinking about it, and I'm still reading my Bible."

"Well, just don't wait too long. If you die like you are, you'll never see Jerry or Danny again."

Every night, Layne Dalton worked on his tunnel. His desire to see Melody was stronger than his desire to get even with Steve Heglund. That could come sometime later. His arms ached to hold the woman he loved, and he longed to see her face. Besides, he wanted her to know he was alive and well. What a surprise she would have when he showed up!

As the weeks passed, Byron Merrick took a turn for the worse. He spent most of his time in his cell, lying on the cot. He could be heard coughing and wheezing all through the long hours of the night. Dr. Campbell visited him and gave him what medicine he could, but Merrick grew steadily worse.

On the night of April 2, Layne Dalton was working in his tunnel by lantern light. It was about 10:30. He would work till midnight, which he figured would put him inches from freedom. Tomorrow night he would break through the six to eight inches of sod above the roof of the tunnel, and head for home.

Colonel Merrick lay on his cot, getting sicker by the minute. His lungs were hurting, and he was feeling dizzy. He needed to take some of the powders Dr. Campbell had left him.

Merrick sat up on the cot and fumbled in the pitch-black darkness for a match on his small table. Finding the match, he groped for the lantern and removed the glass chimney. He struck the match and touched the flame to the wick, then raised it high enough to get enough light and blew out the match. He stood up to go for the powders, which were on the chair near the door.

When Merrick got to his feet, a coughing spasm came over him. He staggered, bumping the table. It rocked, and the burning lantern wobbled dangerously, scooted a few inches, and fell to the floor. Merrick's head went into a spin, and he passed out, falling on the cot.

Kerosene spilled in a wide pool across the wooden floor, and the flame quickly followed its path. The old wood used to construct the barracks was tinder-dry. In no time at all, the flames swept across the floor in a fiery sheet and began climbing the walls and the door.

The intense heat awakened Byron Merrick. He ejected a wild scream and began beating at the flames. Merrick's scream was heard throughout the barracks, and within minutes the place was filled with guards. The flames had spread from Merrick's cell to those on either side, and were licking up the walls and spreading to the doors.

Major Brady was on the scene, shouting for the guards to get the prisoners out of their cells and away from the building. Brady knew the old wood would go up in a hurry. All he could do was get the Confederate officers out before they burned to death.

By the time the guards reached Merrick's cell, he was writhing in flames on the floor. The door was ablaze. There was no way to get him out. The two men in the adjacent cell were yelling for help as the guards struggled against the intense heat to get the door open.

Layne Dalton was at the extreme end of his tunnel when the fire broke out, and at first he was unaware of it. But when he heard Merrick's screams and the shouting of the guards, he backed his way out of the tunnel and pushed his head through the opening under his cot. The cell was filled with smoke, and he could hear Steve Heglund saying, "I don't see him in there, Clyde!"

"He's gotta be in there! You just can't see him for the smoke!"

"Well, why ain't he screamin' to get out?"

"Maybe the smoke's overcome him."

"Well, in any case…he's stayin' in there!" Steve growled.

Layne decided to let the Heglund brothers think he was trapped. He coughed loudly and rolled on the floor from under the cot, crying, "Help me! Let me out!"

The flames had worked their way around the corner and were licking at the door frame. Layne looked through the smoke at Steve and Clyde and screamed, "Hurry! Open the door!"

The Heglund brothers laughed above the shouting of guards and prisoners and the roar of the fire. Everyone was too busy to pay any attention to them.

Steve pushed his face close to the small window in the door and said, "Well, darlin', I told you I'd get you! *Too bad we couldn't get to Major Dalton, Major Brady. Tch. Tch. We're sure sorry that nice Rebel officer had to die because his door was on fire and we couldn't get it open.*"

"Please!" Layne wailed. "Please don't leave me to burn to death! Let me out!"

Steve sneered at him and said, "Tell you what, fancy-pants major—I'll lie for you and make it sound to your sweet little wife that you died a brave man."

"No!" coughed Layne. "Please! Let me out!"

"Good-bye, ol' pal," Steve said. "Tell the devil hello for me!"

As the Heglunds turned away, Dalton cried, "You dirty rats! I'll come back from the dead and get you!"

Steve and Clyde laughed and disappeared. Dalton dived into the tunnel.

Guards were working frantically to get all the Confederate officers out of the barracks. As the two Heglund brothers left Dalton and headed down the corridor, they came upon Chaplain Michael Young, who was at his door, waiting for someone to let him out.

"Ah," said Young as the Heglunds drew up, "I knew someone would come pretty soon."

The corridor was thick with smoke. Steve and Clyde coughed and looked at each other. A guard came running down the corridor. He paused, blinked at the smoke that smarted his eyes, and said to Clyde, "We've got them all out of the west end, Sergeant."

"Good," nodded Clyde. "Keep at it."

"Will do," said the guard, and hurried on.

The sounds of shouting men and roaring fire were all around them. Steve moved through the smoke and put his face close to the opening in the chaplain's door. "You look a little worried, Reverend," he said. "Gettin' warm in there?"

"Come on, open the door!" Young replied.

Steve laughed. "Well, now, whaddya know! The man of God is scared of the fire! I think Clyde an' I will do to you what we just did to your friend, Dalton. We'll just find it impossible to get the door open."

"You left Major Dalton in his cell to burn?"

"Yeah. And now it's your turn, man of God." He laughed. "Where's your God now? Seems to me if He exists, he'd be here to rescue you. Too bad. Hope you toast up real nice. *We're real sorry, Major Brady. Just like with Major Dalton, we couldn't get Chaplain Young's door open. It was just too hot to handle!*"

Clyde was laughing, too.

"You'll never get away with it!" Young shouted. "Other guards will come along before the fire reaches me!"

"You forget, holy man," Clyde said. "I'm the Sergeant of the Guard. As long as I'm standin' here actin' like I'm tryin' to get you out, I can keep the guards runnin' elsewhere. Nobody'll know the difference. Like Steve said, where's your God right now?"

"The chaplain won't need Him this time!" came the loud voice of Major Brady from behind them.

The Heglund brothers wheeled about to see the smoke-wreathed forms of the commandant and four guards whose rifles were aimed at them, hammers cocked. The two sergeants were quickly disarmed, and Young's door was opened.

"You're under arrest!" Brady said in an angry voice. "We heard every word! From your own mouths, you've condemned yourselves. Major Dalton's cell is an inferno now, and you'll face the firing squad for murdering him and for what you were about to do to Chaplain Young!"

Brady told two of the guards to take the Heglunds and lock them up in one of the shacks. While the rest of the building was being cleared, the guards moved Steve and Clyde across the fire-lit compound at gunpoint. Everett and Keith were together outside the blazing building, watching several guards throw water on the adjacent barracks to keep it from catching fire, and saw their brothers come out of the building with two guards holding guns on them.

"What's going on here?" Keith said to Everett.

"I don't know, but whatever it is, we gotta stop it," Everett said, cocking his rifle. "C'mon."

As the two guards ushered Steve and Clyde up to the door of one of the shacks, the other two Heglund brothers came up behind them, guns leveled, and Everett said, "Hold it right there!"

Surprised, the guards looked around to find ominous black muzzles pointing at them.

"Don't interfere!" said one of the guards. "Your brothers are under arrest."

"For what?" demanded Keith.

"Murder, and attempted murder."

"Drop those guns!" Everett said.

The guards complied, and the Heglund brothers locked them in the shack. Then they dashed to the corral, stole four horses, and rode away into the night, laughing because they had succeeded in killing Layne Dalton. They laughed even more when Steve told how Layne had said he would come back from the dead and get them.

Once they were a safe distance up the bank of the Potomac, the brothers agreed that they must wait until the war was over to return home. Steve thought of Jack Reynolds and felt a renewed desire to go after him for killing their father. He knew where Reynolds was, and he knew they needed to put plenty of distance between themselves and the Union army. He suggested to his brothers that they head west to Virginia City, Nevada, and kill Jack Reynolds.

CHAPTER EIGHTEEN

$\bigstar$

Major Layne Dalton worked his way northward through the back woods of Union territory for two days and was able to find a secluded spot on the bank of the Potomac River across from Coles Point, Virginia. By night, he floated across the river on a dead tree and quickly passed through Coles Point.

Outside of town the next morning he approached a farmer, told him his story, and was given a good horse and saddle. He headed northeastward for Fredericksburg, taking the back trails. After he had seen Melody and spent a few days with her, he would report in at Richmond and advise the Confederate army that he had been taken captive at Marye's Heights. His heart thrilled at the thought of holding Melody in his arms.

Dalton also thought of Steve Heglund and his brothers. Some day, he told himself, I'll find those four and make them pay. As he made the promise, Harriet Smith's voice resounded in his head, and Chaplain Michael Young's voice seemed to blend with it: *Vengeance is mine; I will repay, saith the Lord.* But God was too slow with His vengeance. Steve Heglund should have already received his just due for killing Danny.

Fredericksburg was still in a shambles as the major rode into town about nine o'clock at night. What few people were on the streets only saw a gray-clad rider by the dim street lamps, but no one recognized him or paid him any mind.

His heart drummed his ribs as he mounted his own front porch and knocked on the battered door. He heard footsteps inside and braced himself. When the door opened, he was looking into the wide eyes and gaping mouth of Harriet Smith. He knew the Smith house was in ruins, and seeing Harriet there did not surprise him. He figured she was living with Melody and happened to be nearest the door when he knocked.

He removed his hat, smiled and said, "Hello, Harriet."

It took Harriet several seconds to find her voice. "Layne! We thought you were dead!"

Layne stepped inside and closed the door behind him. "I figured that's what you and Melody would have been told. Where is she? How's she feeling?"

"She...she's not here, Layne. But the last time I saw her, she was feeling quite well."

"Not here?" he said, surprised. "Where then?"

"Well, when she was told that you were killed, she went into deep mourning. It was really rough on her, especially with the problems she had after losing the baby."

"Harriet, where is she?"

"She's in Nevada with her parents. Virginia City."

A hollow feeling settled over Layne. Melody was over two thousand miles away. He scrubbed a hand over his eyes and said, "Of course. With me dead, she would want to be with her parents."

"Yes."

"You spoke of problems after losing the baby. You mean something in addition to what she was experiencing the last time I saw her?"

"Well, it was all related. She finally got better, but Dr. Craig told her that she'd never bear any more children."

"She...she can't ever have children?"

Harriet's hand went to her mouth. "Oh, Layne, I'm sorry! You shouldn't have learned that from me."

Layne's heart felt as though it were made of cold lead. Steve Heglund had not only murdered his unborn son, he had made Melody incapable of ever giving him another one.

"I'm going west," Layne said. "But what if she finds and marries another man before I get there?"

Harriet shook her head and patted Layne's arm. "Not the way she was grieving over you. She told me she would never marry again. You have nothing to worry about there."

"I hope you're right."

"You haven't told me where you've been, Layne. Prison camp?"

"Yes. Point Lookout, Maryland. Rotten place. Long story on how I escaped. Don't have time to tell it. What about the house?"

"Melody said Walter and I could live in it until we get ours rebuilt. Said we'd keep in touch by mail, and she'd make up her mind about selling it later."

"Guess we'll leave it at that for now. I'll head for Nevada tomorrow. Just keep it to yourself that you saw me, okay? As long as the Confederate army thinks I'm dead, I'll leave it that way till I can get to Melody. She has a right to know I'm alive and to see me. After that, I'll come back, surprise General Lee, and get back into the War."

"I think you're doing the right thing," agreed Harriet. "I won't breathe a word to anybody."

"Thanks. Walter all right?"

"Yes. Thank the Lord he made it through the battle here without a scratch. He's in Richmond."

"Tell him hello for me. You'll hear from us once I get to Virginia City."

"Will do. You want to stay here tonight? I can go down the street to Susanne Eckley's."

"I'll just sleep out in the barn," he replied. "Got a horse outside.

He and I will do fine in the barn. That way you won't have to go to all that trouble."

"You're very kind. How about a nice hot breakfast in the morning?"

"Sounds good to me!"

Layne had some money stashed in a secret place in the house. He took the money and rode westward out of town, wearing civilian clothes and a pair of western-style boots he had owned for a couple years.

He made his first stop at a small town on the east side of the Blue Ridge Mountains, where he bought a rifle, a revolver, holster and gunbelt, ammunition, bedroll, and a small supply of food. He also bought a map, and in a hotel room that night, mapped out his route.

Dalton would travel west through Cincinnati, Ohio, on to Springfield, Illinois, then to St. Joseph, Missouri. From there he would cross the Missouri River into Kansas and head straight west for Denver. He would cross the Rocky Mountains, pass through Provo City, Utah Territory, and ride across the great desert of Nevada into Virginia City, which was only a few miles from the California border.

The Heglund brothers had chosen almost the same route to Nevada. After stealing guns, ammunition, civilian clothes, bedrolls, and food in Virginia, they headed west through Columbus, Ohio, and from there across Indiana to Springfield, Illinois. They arrived at St. Joseph, Missouri, on April 30, unaware that the man they believed to have perished in the fire at Point Lookout Prison was only a day behind them.

✳ ✳ ✳ ✳ ✳

Traveling by horse and buggy, railroad, commercial wagon train, and stagecoaches, Melody Dalton arrived in Virginia City, Nevada, on April 9, 1863. Her parents were shocked to see her, and were saddened to hear that their son-in-law had been killed and that Melody had lost her baby.

Jack Reynolds had done well in his partnership with his brother and had built a large two-story house. Melody would have an upstairs bedroom at the front, overlooking the wide street that also gave her a view of the towering Sierra Nevada Range to the west.

Melody immediately began looking for a job. Jack told her she did not need to work, that he would provide for her, but Melody said she wanted to pay her own way and that she needed to stay busy. A job would help keep her mind off of Layne.

Within a week, a waitress job opened up at a local café, and Melody took it. Her father warned her that many of the miners who frequented the café were obnoxious and foul-mouthed and would be hard to deal with. But Melody was determined to make her own living and to pay her room and board, so she told him she would deal with them the best she could.

And deal with them she did.

It wasn't long until every miner in town knew he was to keep his distance from the beautiful young Civil War widow. She was chained to the memory of her husband, and aimed to stay that way. Soon they also learned that she was a Christian, and came to respect her. Melody enjoyed her job and seldom had to fight off advances from unruly men.

Her worst times were when she lay in her bed alone at night. Memories of her life with Layne came like a flood, and though she treasured them, they made her miss him more and long to be in his arms. A night did not pass without tears soaking her pillow.

Often Melody dreamed of Layne and awakened in the middle of the night with her heart breaking for want of him. Sometimes ugly thoughts would stab her mind, as if Satan were trying to tell her that Layne had died lost. She would begin praying, and with it came peace about Layne's spiritual condition when he died.

On the night of April 30, Melody dreamt that Layne was alive, and they were together with Danny. The War was over, and they were frolicking in the yard of their home in Fredericksburg. Little Danny looked just like his father, with the same dark, curly hair and chocolate-brown eyes.

In the dream, Layne was on all fours and Danny was laughing, riding on his daddy's back. Layne was whinnying like a horse and acting as if he was trying to buck his little son off his back. When the ride was over, Layne lifted Danny up and hugged him, then stood him down and took Melody in his arms. Their lips came together in a magic kiss—

Suddenly Melody was awake and sat bolt upright in bed. She heard a heart-wrenching wail echoing in the room, then realized it had come from her. The bedroom door flew open, and both parents entered. Jack was carrying a lighted lantern.

Melody began to weep.

Frances moved to the bed and wrapped her arms around her daughter. "Another one of those vivid dreams, honey?"

Melody clung tight to her mother. "Yes. Oh, Mother, it was so real! Layne and Danny were playing together, then Layne took me in his arms and—oh, it hurts so much to know I'll never see Layne and little Danny this side of heaven. I miss them so much!"

"I know, sweetie. I know," said Frances, embracing her and patting her back.

Jack set the lantern on the bedstand and said, "Let's pray. I want to ask the Lord to ease the pain in your heart, darlin', so you can get back to sleep."

On the evening of May 6, 1863, Major Layne Dalton rode into Marysville, Kansas, and boarded his horse with the local hostler. He ate supper at a small café, then entered the lobby of the Jayhawker Hotel and approached the desk. "Got a room for a tired man?" he asked the middle-aged clerk. "Been on the trail all day."

Layne noticed that the man's face was battered and swollen, and his lips were split.

The clerk tried to smile past the stitches in his lips. "Sure do, mister. Have a nice clean room just waiting for you. Please sign the register there. How long will you be with us?"

"Just one night. Have to move on tomorrow morning."

As he was signing the register, Layne heard the lobby door open and close, followed by footsteps.

"Howdy, Les," came a friendly male voice. "What in the world happened to you?"

Layne laid the pen down and turned the register back to the clerk.

Les Cummings set friendly eyes on the newcomer and said, "I got beat up last night, Avery."

Layne waited patiently while Cummings told of four men who had registered at the desk the night before. They checked in about suppertime, then left the hotel. When they returned around ten-thirty, they were drunk. There were two ladies in the lobby at the time, and the four drunks began talking to them in a ribald way and using foul language. Cummings had reprimanded them, and one of the men went behind the desk and beat him into uncon-sciousness. When he came to, the four men were gone. The two women and the town marshal were there, looking down on him as the doctor worked on his battered face. The four men had left town in a hurry.

Three times in telling Avery his story, the clerk had used the name *Steve* for the man who beat him up. As he mounted the stairs and entered his room, Layne wondered if brutality just went with the name *Steve*. His mind, of course, went to the man he hated so passionately, who was probably finding some other poor Rebel offi-cer to pick on at the prison by now.

After traveling steadily for two more days, Layne rode into Smith Centre, Kansas. Hardly had he turned his horse onto Main Street when he picked up that everybody in the town was talking about the bank robbery that had taken place there that morning.

Layne listened to a conversation at an adjacent table while he ate his supper and learned from a man who had been in the Smith Centre Bank that there were four robbers. They were ugly, filthy-mouthed men, and the one who seemed to be their leader had pistol-whipped the bank president.

Layne suspected that the four men who robbed the bank were no doubt the same four men who had caused the trouble at the Marysville Hotel. He told himself that the leader who pistol-whipped the bank president was no doubt the Steve who had beat up Les Cummings.

Steve. The name made his stomach go sour. He pictured the repulsive face of Steve Heglund and renewed his vow to make him feel every ounce of his smoldering revenge.

On May 10, Dalton was riding into Oberlin, Kansas, at sunset, and his attention was drawn to a dozen or more riders coming toward him from the west end of town. They hauled up in front of the marshal's office and were met by a host of townspeople, who were all asking the same thing: Had they caught the bank robbers?

Layne's ears perked up as he guided his horse to the hitch rail close by and dismounted. He saw by the sign over the office that the marshal's name was Jed Rice.

Rice had left his horse and was standing on the edge of the boardwalk as he raised his hands and shouted for silence, "Everybody quiet! I'll explain if you'll get quiet!"

The rest of the posse stayed in their saddles as the babble of voices settled down.

"No, we didn't catch 'em," Rice said. "They gave us the slip."

"You mean you're gonna just let 'em go?" came a voice from the crowd. "They not only cleaned out the bank, but they killed Mack Henelt!"

"We did all we could," Rice said, "but we can't follow 'em forever. These men have jobs to work and businesses to run. I don't dare be out of town very long. That would leave Oberlin with no law at all. You don't want that, do you?"

The people began to talk among themselves. None of them wanted their marshal gone from town for any length of time. There were no government lawmen to pursue the robbers, and there was no militia. All army men were occupied with hostile Indians or fighting in the Civil War.

"We understand, Marshal," spoke up an elderly man. "At least we got one of those dirty killers. If he lives, we'll have the satisfaction of hangin' him!"

"You mean he's still alive?" Rice asked, eyebrows arched in surprise. "Doc told me before we rode out he'd prob'ly be dead time we got back."

"Just barely hangin' on, from what I'm told, Marshal," spoke up another man.

"I'd swear those four are brothers," said Rice, running his gaze over the faces of the crowd. "Anybody know if Doc's got a name outta the wounded one?"

"His name's Keith somethin', Jed," put in a portly man standing near him on the boardwalk. "Leastwise I heard one of 'em call him that when he took Mack Henelt's bullet."

Layne Dalton could not believe his ears. There were four robbers. They appeared to be brothers. The meanest one was named Steve. One of them had been shot during the bank robbery, and his name was Keith. The coincidence was too much.

Layne's scalp tingled. Could it really be the Heglund brothers? But they were at the Point Lookout Prison. Or were they? If this really was not coincidence, what were the Heglunds doing in Kansas? Where were they headed?

There was only one way to settle this. Marshal Rice was saying something about going to the doctor's office to check on the wounded robber. Layne would follow him.

The posse dispersed to put away their horses, and the crowd broke up. Just as Marshal Rice was approaching the door of Dr. Efram Pennock's office, Dalton called from behind him, "Marshal Rice!"

The marshal halted, looked over his shoulder, and said, "Yes, sir? Do I know you?"

"No, you don't, but I need to talk to you before you go in there."

Rice was congenial and allowed the stranger to explain why he needed to take a look at the wounded bank robber. Layne held nothing back. As briefly as possible, he told Rice the whole story.

The marshal, a stout man in his late fifties, said, "Well, Major, I don't blame you for wantin' to see that Steve Heglund pay for what he did. His brothers, either, for that matter. But on the other hand, I don't like to see you takin' the law into your own hands."

"Marshal, I heard you say that you and the posse couldn't spend any more time chasing these outlaws. There isn't any other law west of the wide Missouri who's going to bring them to justice. So what's wrong with me going after them?"

Rice saw the stubborn set to Dalton's jaw and the dogged look in his eyes. "Well, let's go in here and see if this Keith fella is the one you've got in mind."

Dr. Pennock's nurse, secretary, and receptionist was his wife, Erline. She looked up from the desk and smiled as they entered. "Hello, Marshal. I imagine you're here to see about the wounded outlaw. Who's your friend?"

"Name's Layne Dalton," Rice said. "Mr. Dalton, this is Erline Pennock, Doc's wife."

"Glad to meet you, ma'am," Dalton smiled, touching his hat.

"Is he still alive?" asked Rice.

"Yes. My husband's with him now. I don't think he'll make it through the night, though."

"It's important that we both see him. May we go in?"

"Let me ask the doctor," Erline said, rising from the desk.

While Erline was out of the room, Layne asked for the details of the robbery and shooting. Rice told him that while all four robbers were inside the bank, a teller named Mack Henelt had pulled a gun from a drawer in his cage and shot the one who now lay in the clinic. The others gunned Henelt down, ran to their horses, and galloped away. Rice added, "I think they left him because the bullet was in the center of his chest. No way they could take him with them. They figured he was done for."

Erline returned and told the two men they could go in. As Rice and Dalton moved through the door, they saw the wounded man on the examining table, and Dr. Pennock standing over him. Pennock motioned with his head for them to come to the table. It was Keith Heglund!

Keith's languid eyes focused on Dalton and went suddenly clear. His already pale features turned flour white, and his mouth flew open.

The doctor saw the reaction. He was about to speak to Dalton when Keith gasped weakly, "No, it can't be! Doctor, it's a ghost! Help me!"

"I told Steve and Clyde I'd come back and get them, Keith," Dalton said. "Where are they headed?"

The dying man's whole body shook violently as his eyes bulged with terror. "D-Doctor, do something! I'm...I'm dyin'! I know it! I'm lookin' at a dead man!"

"Jed, what's this all about?" Pennock asked.

"I'll tell you later," Rice replied. Turning to Dalton, he said, "Looks like he's your man, all right."

The major nodded, then set piercing eyes on Keith. He leaned closer and said, "Some brothers, eh, Keith? Ran like scared rabbits and left you to hang. They need to pay for deserting you, Keith."

Keith Heglund could do nothing but stare in terror at the man he thought had burned to death in the barracks at Point Lookout.

"Keith," Dr. Pennock said, "you aren't going to live long enough to hang. That bullet is touching your heart. It's a miracle you're not dead already. But if I try to take it out, you'll die instantly. You're losing blood, and there's nothing I can do to stop it. You will die before morning. If you can help these men stop your brothers from killing others, you ought to do it."

"The man's making sense, Keith," Layne said. "Where are they headed?"

Keith licked his lips, still wary of Dalton's presence, not knowing what to believe about him. "Could...could I have some water?"

Dr. Pennock gave him a drink. After he had taken his fill, Keith ran his frightened gaze to Dalton and licked his lips again. "They're headed to...to Virginia City."

A cold hand clutched Layne's heart. "To kill Jack Reynolds." It was a statement, not a question.

Keith nodded.

Rice turned to Dalton. "You told me your wife is in Virginia City with her parents. Is Jack Reynolds her father?"

"Yes, and I've got to catch up to them before they get there. They'll kill Jack, and probably my wife and my mother-in-law!"

Keith coughed in a strained, choking manner. "Layne...I...I'm sorry about...the baby." His eyes rolled back in their sockets. He coughed weakly again, and his chest went still.

"He's gone," said Pennock, feeling for a pulse in the sides of Keith's neck and finding none.

"Well, at least you got an apology from one of them," said Rice.

"I'll get more than that from the others," Layne said.

The three brothers rode hard into the night. When they were a safe distance from Oberlin, they found a wooded area next to a small stream and made camp. With the camp fire throwing flickering shadows on their faces, they ate pork and beans and drank whiskey.

"Too bad we had to leave him there," lamented Everett.

"Yeah," agreed Clyde.

"No choice," said Steve. "We'd have been caught and hanged if we'd stayed around tryin' to take him with us. When I saw that big hole in his chest, I knew he wouldn't make it. No doubt he died right away. Ain't nobody can live with a .45 slug in his ticker."

"Well, at least we showed that posse how stupid they are," Clyde said.

"Yeah," Steve laughed. "Only bad thing was we didn't get to blow none of their heads off."

"Stupid as they was," Everett said, "they're almost as bad off now as they'd've been if they'd got their heads shot off."

The Heglunds had a good laugh, finished their meal, and turned in early. They wanted to make sure they had a good head start just in case the Oberlin posse tried a second time to catch them.

Layne Dalton rode out of Oberlin at the crack of dawn. He grinned to himself. Jed Rice had not said another word to him about not taking the law into his own hands.

"Well, God," he said as the Kansas prairie stretched out before him to the west, "You got ahead of me with Keith. He did taste of Your vengeance, didn't he? But I'll take care of the other three myself."

CHAPTER NINETEEN

✦

The Heglund brothers were finding that robbing banks was quite lucrative. They had done it at first merely to fill up their empty pockets as they rode west. Though they lost Keith, it did not deter their avaricious appetites.

They crossed the border into Colorado Territory on May 12, and on May 14 robbed the bank in Byers, killing two bank employees. As they galloped away from Byers on the rolling plains toward Denver, Everett's horse stepped in a gopher hole and went down with a broken leg. Everett was thrown hard, but was only bruised. He climbed up behind Clyde, and they continued on toward Denver.

The sun was almost touching the western horizon when they spotted a small herd of cattle grazing in a pasture near a shaded house, barn, and outbuildings. In the corral were several saddle horses, along with a few head of cattle.

"Well, boys, think I can find me a good animal in there?" Everett said.

"If you don't, it's because you're blind," chuckled Clyde.

"Ranch looks small enough there shouldn't be any ranch hands to contend with," said Steve. "Looks like the rancher and his wife there on the porch."

"Should be easy pickin's," Clyde said.

The Heglunds turned into the yard, riding through the long shadows of the tall cottonwoods that surrounded the buildings. The rancher said something to his wife and rose from the bench where they were sitting. His wife remained seated.

The rancher was a tall, slender man. He tilted his straw hat to the back of his balding head, smiled, and said, "Howdy, gents. Somethin' I can do for you?"

"Yeah," Steve nodded, pulling his horse a little closer to the porch. "My brother Everett here lost a good horse back the trail a ways. Stepped in a hole and broke a leg. Had to shoot it. We noticed some nice-lookin' horses there in your corral. We'd like to let Everett pick out the one he likes."

The rancher shook his head, grinning innocently. "Sorry, gents. None of those horses are for sale."

"What's your name, mister?" Steve said.

"Cashman. Floyd Cashman."

"Now Mr. Cashman, I guess you don't hear too good. Who said anything about buyin' 'em?" As he spoke, Steve pulled his revolver, cocked it, and leveled it on Cashman's chest.

"N-now, wait a minute!" the rancher gasped. "What's going on here?"

Mrs. Cashman rose from the bench and gripped her husband's arm. "Floyd, don't argue with them! If they want a horse, let them have it."

"Now there's some real sound advice, Mr. Cashman," Steve said. "Better listen."

"Do you know the penalty for horse stealing in these parts, mister?" Cashman boomed.

Steve aimed his gun at the rancher's face and roared, "Do you know the penalty for givin' me trouble?"

"Floyd, please," begged his wife. "Let them have a horse. He's going to kill you if you don't!"

"All right," Cashman sighed. "You can have the gray roan gelding."

Steve shook his head. "Everett'll take the one that suits his fancy, along with the bridle and saddle of his choosing. Now you two just mosey over there and sit down on that bench. Be real nice and quiet, and you'll be rid of us before the sun's all the way down."

Everett slid off Clyde's horse and made his way to the corral. Steve and Clyde sat their horses and trained their weapons on the Cashmans.

Everett opened the corral gate and moved in behind the split-rail fence. The cattle and horses stared at him and began stirring about. He was a strange body with a strange smell. Some of the animals moved around the back corner of the barn to a part of the corral Everett couldn't see. He was unaware that around that corner was an ill-tempered, long-horned bull.

Everett could see six horses—three stallions, two mares, and a gelding. The gelding was a bay with bald face and four perfect white stockings. He decided he would take the bay unless he found something he liked better around the corner.

The horses and cattle moved away from him as he headed for the back corner of the barn. When he reached it, he saw more cattle and horses, but the bull was blocked from his view by two black stallions. Everett liked the look of the stallions and began moving toward them.

"C'mere, boys," he said, holding out his hand. "Easy. I just want to take a look at you."

The stallions parted and dashed around him. Suddenly Everett was standing face-to-face with the bull. It gave him a menacing look, snorted, and shook its head.

Everett's blood ran cold. There was fifty feet of open space between him and the bull. Could he make it to the fence, about the same distance away, before the beast got him? Everett wanted to call out to his brothers, but he feared the sound might cause the bull to charge.

He felt riveted to the spot, as though he were standing in two feet of solid ice. He had to get away from the bull, but he would have to move very slowly.

He tried to slide one foot, but it barely moved. His body responded to his will only grudgingly. Icy sweat was trickling down his back.

The bull snorted, shook its head again, and pawed dirt.

Everett's heart was pounding like a mad thing in his chest. Ever so carefully, he moved a few inches to his right. The massive beast shook its head again, throwing a string of white saliva on the ground. Its eyes shone like angry coals. This strange man had dared enter its domain. It grunted, and Everett was sure it was about to charge. He glanced at the fence. It seemed no closer than before.

The bull lifted its head and bellowed. It was now or never. Everett sprang to his right, stumbled, caught himself, and bolted for the fence.

But he was too slow.

The bull roared and charged. As if in a nightmare, Everett's legs would not respond to the panic driving his mind. He let out a whimper of terror as he strained toward the safety of the fence. He knew he would not reach it in time. His knees gave way. As he struggled to right himself, the maddened bull hit him full force.

At the house, Steve and Clyde had heard the bull's snorting and bellowing, but only sent casual glances in that direction. When a wild scream pierced the air from the other side of the barn, they exchanged startled glances, wheeled their horses about, and galloped toward the corral.

Both brothers vaulted the fence and ran toward the back corner of the barn. When they reached it, the sight before their eyes startled and sickened them.

The bull—horns crimson with blood—had just dumped Everett on the ground and was about to spear him again. As Steve and Clyde opened fire on the massive beast, it lifted Everett over its head, shook him violently, and tossed him aside. Everett's lifeless form landed hard and rolled several feet, arms and legs flailing like a rag doll.

The pain from the bullets intensified the bull's rage. It turned with fiery eyes toward the source of its affliction and charged.

"The head!" shouted Steve. "The head!"

Both men fired as fast as they could, emptying their guns at the charging beast. Finally the bull's knees buckled, and it went down no more than a dozen feet from the backtracking brothers. They made sure the bull was dead, then darted to the spot where Everett's body lay in a crumpled heap.

"Man, what an awful way to die," said Steve, shaking his head. "Come on. Let's get him outta here."

Together, Steve and Clyde carried Everett's body from the corral. As they passed through the gate, they saw that the Cashmans were nowhere in sight. Movement down the road caught Steve's eye. Several ranchers had heard the gunfire and were coming to investigate.

"We gotta get outta here!" Steve gasped.

"What about Everett?" Clyde said, focusing on the oncoming riders.

"Leave him! Let the rancher bury him! Let's go!"

On the morning of May 15, Major Layne Dalton rode along the fence that led to the Cashman ranch house and spotted the rancher in a nearby field, standing knee-deep in a rectangular hole. There was a shovel in his hand and the body of a man lying close by.

Layne dismounted, wrapped the reins around the top pole of the fence, and hopped over. The rancher saw him coming and ceased digging, leaning on the shovel. He watched the approach of the stranger carefully, but showed no alarm.

Drawing up, Layne set his eyes on the mangled corpse and

recognized Everett Heglund. "Mornin', sir," he said, nodding at the rancher. "My name's Layne Dalton. I'm trailing a gang of killers through these parts. Brothers named Heglund. I was going to stop and ask if you had seen them, but I don't need to ask now."

"They came in here, put guns on my wife and me, Mr. Dalton. They were going to steal one of my horses. Said this guy's horse had broken a leg farther back on the trail."

"Yeah, main reason I stopped. Yours is the first ranch from the spot I found the dead horse." Layne looked at the corpse. "I'd say Everett here died a pretty violent death."

"He went into the corral to steal a horse, and my bull gored him to death. The other two killed the bull."

"And rode on."

"Yep."

"You and your wife all right?"

"Yes, thank God."

"Well, I'll get back on their trail."

Back in the saddle, Layne pointed the horse's nose west. *Well, God, looks like You got there ahead of me again. But I want Steve and Clyde for myself—especially Steve.*

Layne Dalton trailed Steve and Clyde Heglund through Denver and over the Rockies toward the Utah Territory border, about twelve hours behind them. Layne pushed his horse as hard as he dared and was encouraged to find that he was gaining on them as they neared the Utah line.

On June 3, Dalton rode into Grand Junction, Colorado Territory, just after noon. A crowd of people was gathered in the street in front of the Rocky Mountain Bank. Layne suspected that the Heglunds had been there and robbed the bank. He hauled up at a hitch rail near the bank, slid from the saddle, and approached the crowd, which was formed in a circle in the middle of the broad, dusty street. Layne was tall enough to see over many of the heads. A man with a badge on his chest was lying in the dust.

The town's marshal was down with three bullets in him, and a doctor was kneeling at his side.

"What happened?" Dalton asked a young man who stood beside him.

"Bank robbery. Two gunmen held up the bank. Someone saw them go in with their guns drawn and notified Marshal Walls. He got there just as they were coming out, and they put him down."

The young man's words were barely out of his mouth when a woman's wail sliced through the warm air. Cries of alarm came from the crowd as the doctor stood up, shaking his head. The men in the crowd wanted a posse to go after the robbers, but without the marshal to lead them, none of the men would attempt it. There would be no posse.

"How long ago did this happen?" Layne asked, turning to the young man.

"About twenty, twenty-five minutes."

The major's heart leaped in his breast. They were now less than a half-hour ahead of him!

Dalton hastened to his horse and swung into the saddle. He was glad there would be no posse. He wanted the Heglunds for himself. He trotted the horse to the west end of town, then put it to a gallop.

The Heglund brothers rode hard for the first half-hour out of Grand Junction. Their treasury was growing. They now had two large canvas sacks stuffed full of money, tied to Steve's saddlehorn. They slowed to a walk to give their horses a breather.

"You really don't think they'll send a posse after us?" Clyde asked, looking over his shoulder.

"Nope," Steve said. "We put the marshal down. Town doesn't

seem big enough to need or afford a deputy. Most townsmen won't try to put a posse together on their own. We won't have a problem with anybody from Grand Junction."

After a few minutes of silence between them, Steve glanced at Clyde and said, "Really upset over Everett and Keith, ain'tcha?"

"Yeah, but I been thinking of somethin' else too."

"What's that?"

Clyde paused, ran a finger under his nose, and replied, "Do you suppose somethin's doggin' our tracks because of what you did to Dalton's wife and kid and what we did to Dalton himself…and what we're plannin' to do to Jack Reynolds?"

"Somethin' like what? *God!*"

"Well, there's *somethin'* out there…or up there. I dunno. But it's like somethin' unseen might be followin' us, and is gonna make us pay."

"Melody's old man murdered Pa! The law let him get away with it, but we ain't! He's got it comin'. Don't you be frettin' about some kind of God gonna have retribution on us."

"Well, don't you think it's strange the way Keith and Everett were alive and healthy till we put ourselves on this journey to kill Jack?"

"Hey, Keith got in the way of a bullet! Happens every day."

"I don't think it happens every day. And look how Everett went out—that ain't somethin' that happens every day, Steve, and you know it. I tell you, we've been jinxed or somethin'."

"Aw, c'mon, Clyde, don't go nuts on me now! What happened to our brothers just *happened.* I'm tellin' you there ain't no God out there or *up* there. Ain't no jinx, neither."

"Well, maybe it's Layne Dalton!"

Steve pulled rein, stopping his horse, and glared at his brother. "Don't tell me you believe he's come back from the dead to get us! Those were just words of spite from a dyin' man. Nobody comes back from the dead!"

"Then what're ghosts?"

"Ghosts!" Steve laughed. "You know what ghosts are? Just figments of dumb people's imaginations. I'm tellin' you, nothin' and no one is doggin' us. Now come on, let's move."

The Heglunds were following a wagon trail that led into Utah. Some ten minutes later, they started down a gentle hill and saw a buggy off the side of the road. It was a one-horse vehicle, but there was no horse. As they drew abreast of the buggy, they saw a middle-aged man on the ground near the tongue. An arrow protruded from his left shoulder. He was conscious and holding a bandanna at the base of the arrow to stay the flow of blood.

The Heglunds halted their horses and looked down at the man, who raised his head painfully and said in a weak voice, "Help me...please."

"Sorry, pal, we ain't got time," Steve said. "We're in a hurry."

As they rode away, Clyde said, "Maybe we shoulda helped him. Did you notice the Bible on the seat of the buggy? He was prob'ly a preacher."

"I didn't notice no Bible," grunted Steve. "And if he's a preacher, all the more reason to leave him just the way he is."

Layne Dalton couldn't be sure it was the Heglunds, but he had spotted two riders ahead of him several times after leaving Grand Junction. The hilly country took them from his sight periodically, but the last time he had seen them some five minutes earlier, they had topped a rise, then disappeared on its other side.

Galloping the horse for all it was worth, he soon reached the rise and thundered over its crest. He saw a buggy sitting off the side of the trail, and noted that it had no animal harnessed to it. Seconds later, he spotted the man lying near the buggy's tongue and skidded his mount to a halt.

The arrow protruding from the man's left shoulder caught his eye as he leaped from the saddle. He knelt beside the wounded man, saying, "I didn't realize there were hostile Indians about. I'll take you into Grand Junction. I know they've got a doctor."

"Thank you," the man replied, running his tongue over dry lips.

"Here, let me get you some water."

Layne gave the wounded man water from his canteen, then examined the area where the arrow had entered. "I've never seen an arrow wound, sir, but I've seen lots of bullet wounds in the Civil War. I think you'll be all right. By the way, I guess I should introduce myself. My name's Layne Dalton."

"Pleased to meet you, Mr. Dalton," the wounded man said weakly. "I'm Reverend William Cady. I'm pastor of the Presbyterian church in Grand Junction. I was heading home from a visit to an ailing member of the church when a band of Utes came at me. They shot me and took my horse. Utes have been on the prowl lately."

Layne thought of the Heglunds. He wanted desperately to catch them before they reached Virginia City, but the preacher's life was at stake. There was no choice but to take him to the doctor. He broke the arrow off close to Cady's body, loaded him on his horse, and headed back to Grand Junction.

Night had fallen by the time Reverend Cady was bandaged up and ready to go home. His wife had been summoned to the doctor's office, and when Layne was about to leave and get a hotel for the night, the Cady's invited him home for supper and to stay in their guest room. He gladly accepted.

Supper was eaten in the parlor at the Cady home, where the preacher could lie on a sofa and take his meal. Mrs. Cady and the major sat nearby at a small table.

When the meal was over and Mrs. Cady was washing dishes in the kitchen, Layne sat in a chair next to the sofa and chatted with the preacher. Cady asked Layne where he was going, and Layne decided to tell him the whole story.

"I hope you find your wife and her parents doing well when you get to Virginia City, Major," Cady said, "but I'm concerned that your vindictive spirit toward this Steve Heglund and his brother will dry you up inside. I'm pulling for you to stop them from killing your father-in-law, and all, but I've seen vengeance get down deep into a man's soul and destroy him."

"I'm not going to let that happen, Reverend," Dalton smiled. "But I *am* going to catch up to those two and—"

"Kill them?"

Layne adjusted himself nervously on his chair. "I'm going to save my father-in-law, and perhaps my wife and mother-in-law, from being murdered, sir. There's some vengeance mixed in here, I'll admit, but they've got to be stopped before they reach Virginia City, and there's no one going to do it but me."

Cady studied him for a moment, moving his wounded arm in its sling to a more comfortable position. "There's a whole lot of vengeance in there, son. And since you say there's no one to stop them but you...what if you keep stopping to help people like me? Then who's going to protect your family from the Heglunds?"

Layne's mouth pulled into a thin line. "I just won't be stopping to help anyone else."

Cady grinned. "I can read people, Major. It isn't in you to ignore someone who's in trouble."

"Okay, okay. I know what you're driving at."

"Oh?"

"Yes. You preachers have your way of sneaking up on us. What you're about to say is that God can stop the Heglunds. Right?"

"Well, from what you told me, it wasn't you who took out Keith or Everett."

"No, you're right about that."

"Then who did?"

Layne knew the answer, but chose to skirt it. "Could have been God, but it might just have been circumstances."

"Maybe, but I doubt it. You told me your wife is a Christian, and your in-laws, too."

"Yes."

"So they're God's children. He watches out for His own, Major."

Layne had nothing to say.

"What about you, son?" Cady proceeded. "Since you haven't told me that you're a Christian, I assume you're not."

"Every man has to come to God in his own way," Layne said stubbornly, knowing that philosophy was about to get shot down again.

Cady called for his Bible and explained the gospel to Layne, pointing out that the only way to the Father is Christ Himself. Layne knew that the Lord in heaven was breathing down his neck. Nearly everywhere he went, someone was there to correct his lame philosophy and confront him with the gospel.

Cady took Layne to the cross from a half-dozen different directions, then closed his Bible. "Decision is yours, son. You can go on turning Jesus away, or repent, receive Him, and settle this thing."

Layne wanted desperately to unleash his vengeance on Steve Heglund, and he knew that things would change in his heart if he became a child of God. He held on with the tenacity of a bulldog. "I'm not ready, Preacher," he said, shaking his head. "I have to have more time to think about it."

"Well, let me ask you something? You say you're not ready to turn to Christ...are you ready to die?"

"I really need to get to bed, sir," Layne said, rising to his feet. "I have to ride out of here before dawn."

The Cadys saw to it that Layne Dalton had a hearty breakfast before he rode away from their house and out of their lives. They both thanked him for saving William's life and said they would pray for the safety of Layne's family in Virginia City...and for Layne to turn to the Lord before it was too late.

The major was ten miles west of Grand Junction when dawn's gray light appeared on the horizon behind him. He had to push hard to make up the time he had lost the day before. Worried that he might not catch the Heglunds in time, Layne started to pray, almost without thinking about it.

"God, I'm…in a pickle here. You know I couldn't just leave that poor man lying there with the arrow in him. So I…well, I've got to ask a favor of You. You know what those men are planning to do. Somehow You've got to—"

Layne Dalton gripped the reins till his fingers hurt, shook his head, and said, "What are you doing, Dalton? What right have you to ask your Maker for anything when you continue to turn your back on Him?"

Scolding himself changed nothing except to keep Layne from continuing his prayer. He would have to catch up to the Heglunds and stop their murderous scheme on his own.

By the time Steve and Clyde Heglund reached the town of Duchesne, Utah, near Indian Canyon, their horses gave out. Both were limping badly when they carried their riders into town.

"Let's hope we can find us a couple of good horses real fast," Steve said. "We're gettin' close enough to Nevada that my trigger finger is developin' an itch."

They spotted a sign along the town's main thoroughfare that read: *Jasper's Stable—Horses Bought, Sold, Boarded, Curried.*

"See that?" Steve said. "We'll get rid of these nags and be on our way!"

They dismounted and entered the tumble-down office to find an elderly man sitting at a crude desk made of wooden crates. "What can I do fer ya, gents?" the old man asked.

"We need to buy a couple good horses," said Steve. "We ain't poor, so don't waste time tryin' to sell us some broken-down nags."

"Wish I even had some broken-down nags to sell," the old timer said. "I ain't got a horse of any kind. The Uintahs came into town a couple nights ago and stole everythin' I had. No-good Indians, anyhow!"

"You mean you don't have any horses at all?" Clyde pressed him.

"That's right."

"Now, wait a minute!" said Steve, bending down to the level of the hostler's face. "My brother and I both saw two horses in your corral when we were comin' in here. Don't lie to us!"

"I ain't lyin'. Them's mine and my son's. We had 'em at home when them Indians come into town. I can't sell you those."

Steve whipped out his revolver and cracked the old man on the head with the barrel, sending him to the floor. Steve looked down at him and said, "We weren't wantin' to *buy* your horses, mister. We were just wantin' to make a trade!"

Jasper's son didn't show up while the Heglunds switched saddles and bridles. The old man was just coming around when they rode away, leaving their worn-out horses in the corral.

Layne Dalton rode into Duchesne the next day, his own horse worn out and hardly able to carry him. Entering the stable office, he found Jasper with a bandage on his head. Jasper told him about the Indians stealing the stable's horses a few days earlier and about the two men who yesterday had clobbered him on the head and stolen his horses. Layne knew who the two men were.

It took Layne half a day to locate a good horse he could purchase on a ranch several miles north of Duchesne. Once the deal was made, he was on his way west, headed toward Provo City.

He rode hard, feeling almost as if God was against his saving Jack Reynolds's life. *If not*, he thought, *why all these delays?*

CHAPTER TWENTY

✦

It was a hot day in late June when the Heglund brothers robbed the bank in Stillwater, Nevada Territory, some sixty-five miles east of Virginia City. The saddlehorns of both their horses were laden with canvas bags stuffed with money.

Three days earlier they had robbed the bank in Eureka, Nevada, and the following day the bank in Austin. Steve had not noticed that a bag hanging from his saddlehorn had *Bank of Stillwater* emblazoned on it.

Layne Dalton knew he was once again drawing close to the Heglunds when he arrived in Stillwater just two hours after they had robbed the bank. He watered his horse good, filled his canteen, and pushed on westward.

When night fell he wanted to keep going, but his horse was tiring, and he dare not push it too hard. He stopped beside a small stream and camped for the night.

Just nine miles ahead, the Heglunds camped on another stream about seven or eight miles from Virginia City. They would have their revenge on Jack Reynolds tomorrow, June 30, 1863.

✤ ✤ ✤ ✤ ✤

On the afternoon of Monday, June 29, Hank and Jack Reynolds waved good-bye to their families from the Wells Fargo stagecoach as it pulled away from the stage office in Virginia City. As joint-owners of the Reynolds Mining Company, they were off to Sacramento to negotiate the purchase of a gold mine in the High Sierras. The entire trip would take them a week.

That evening, Frances Reynolds and her daughter had supper together, then spent a couple of hours in Bible study discussing how a good God could allow evil in the world.

Later, lying in bed in the dark, Melody found sleep eluding her. Memories of Layne came to mind, one after another. They were still so fresh and her need for him so great that she began to weep uncontrollably, crying out his name over and over.

Soon there was a knock at her bedroom door. "Yes, Mother?" she said, sniffling, and using the sheet to dab at her wet face in the dark.

The door squeaked open. "Having another one of those bad nights, honey?"

Melody sniffed again. "Yes. I'm sorry I disturbed you."

A lantern burned on a table in the hall. Frances left the door open and sat down beside her daughter on the bed. They embraced, and Melody said, "Oh, Mother, I miss him so much...so terribly, terribly much."

"I know, dear," Frances said softly. "I know. I realize I can't fully enter into your grief because I've never lost your father. I shudder to think what it would be like if I did. And if I had the power to ease the pain in your heart, I would."

"I know you would, Mother," sniffed Melody, drawing a shuddering breath. "But we mortals can only go so far, no matter how much we love each other."

"That's right, honey. Jesus is the only one who can really ease your pain."

"Yes, and He does most of the time. Maybe sometimes He lets

the pain come back to my heart so I'll draw closer to Him. I do pretty well with it, but sometimes I just have to have a good cry."

"And this is one of those times."

"I saw a little boy in town today, probably about four years old. He looked so much like Layne must have looked when he was that age—same dark, curly hair and eyes so brown they were almost black. I…I guess laying eyes on that cute little boy, and seeing how much he looked like Layne, made me want my little Danny so bad."

"Where'd you see him?" Frances asked.

"In front of the sheriff's office. You know that new deputy who came to town a week or so ago?"

"I've heard people mention him. His name's Wes something. Can't think of his last name. I haven't seen him yet, as far as I know. What about him?"

"Well, the deputy was talking to Sheriff Wyler, and the little boy was holding onto the deputy's hand. I figure he's probably the deputy's son."

"We'll have to make it a point to find out where they live and pay his wife a call. Maybe take her a meal or something."

"That would be nice. I'm sure it would help her feel welcome. Besides, I'd like to meet that little boy. Maybe even get to hug him." Melody's eyes filmed up.

"Oh, honey," said Frances, taking her in her arms again.

"I'm sorry," Melody said. "It's just that…knowing that even if Layne was alive, I could never have another child—"

Melody's body shook as she broke into heavy sobs.

"Go on, sweetheart," Frances said softly. "Cry it out."

Birds were singing in the trees to welcome the new day. Dawn had come, and the eastern sky was already growing pink.

Clyde Heglund rolled over in his bedroll, glanced at the birds flitting amongst the branches of the cottonwoods that lined the small brook nearby, then looked at his brother.

Steve's sleepy eyes focused on Clyde. "Go on back to sleep," he said. Since we're only an hour's ride or so from Virginia City, let's take it easy this mornin'."

"All right by me. Just so this is the day we give it to Jack Reynolds for killin' Pa."

"We will, little brother. We will."

Layne Dalton awakened to find a slight hint of gray streaking the eastern horizon. According to his map, he was within little more than two hours' ride of Virginia City if he kept his horse at a steady trot.

He downed hardtack and beef jerky with water, then quickly saddled his mount and headed west. He almost implored the God of heaven to let him find the Heglund brothers before they could get to Jack Reynolds, but the guilt he carried on his conscience for the way he had kept the Lord from his heart and life would not let him go to Him for help.

Steve and Clyde Heglund lazily settled into their saddles and trotted away from the stream toward Virginia City. The sun was already giving promise of a hot day. The land about them, though furnished with a few streams, was mostly barren. Cottonwoods grew along the streams, but in the brown maw of the Nevada desert lay sun-bleached rocks and boulders amid patches of catclaw, rabbit-bush, and cacti of various sizes and shapes.

They saw smooth-skinned salamanders sunning themselves on hot rocks, along with their scaly lizard neighbors. There were signs of the desert night creatures in the soft sand, and periodically they noticed a diamondback rattler slithering among the rocks.

Bald, sun-scorched mountains lay on either side of them as they followed that westbound trail through scattered clumps of brush and cactus. Soon they were climbing a steep slope onto a rugged hogback. When they reached the crest, the jagged scars of two canyons stretched their shadowed length before them into the rocky terrain to the north.

The Heglunds found themselves staring at a range of rugged peaks, the sun magnifying the magnificent shapes into which centuries of wind had carved them. They descended the hogback and began to skirt the towering range. After several hours, they were riding once again on level ground among thick patches of scrub oak. Broken boulders, as though thrown down and smashed by some massive giant and his sledgehammer, were strewn about them.

"Look, Steve!" Clyde was pointing due west. "See it?"

"Yeah. Virginia City. Looks to be about five miles or so, wouldn't you say?"

"Yep. I can feel it in my bones. Pa's gonna do a somersault in his grave when we gun down Jack Reynolds!"

Suddenly Clyde's horse began to limp.

"Hold it, Steve," he said, drawing rein.

Steve's mount had already carried him a few yards ahead. "What's wrong?" he asked as he hipped around in the saddle.

"My horse's limpin'. Right foreleg."

"Well, see about it."

Swearing, Clyde dismounted.

"Could just be a rock," Steve said, leaning on his saddlehorn and patting the money-filled bags that hung there.

Clyde leaned over and hoisted the horse's right foreleg. Neither Clyde nor the horse saw the diamondback coiled on a rock shelf inches from his face.

"That's what it is," Clyde said loud enough for his brother to hear. "Got a big ol' stone wedged in between the shoe and the hoof."

Suddenly the snake struck. The horse gave a terrified whinny, shied, and bolted away. Clyde fell to his knees, letting out a blood-curdling scream. There was a look of stark terror in his eyes as he threw a hand to the snakebite on his cheek.

Steve was frozen to his saddle, gaping, appalled, as his brother screamed like a madman. Clyde's shrill cries evolved into "Steve! Ste-e-ve! Help me! He-e-lp me-e!"

Steve gave a shudder of revulsion. He feared snakes, and the sight of the diamondback slithering away sent waves of horror mixed with nausea through his body.

Clyde fell flat on the sand, still screaming Steve's name and writhing in pain and terror.

Steve finally went into action. He leaped from the saddle, grabbed a long-bladed knife, and dashed to his brother. Dropping to his knees, he seized Clyde's flailing hands and shouted, "Clyde! Clyde! Listen to me! I've got to lance the bite and suck out the venom. Lie still!"

"Steve, don't let me die!" he cried, trembling. "Don't let me die!"

"Hold still!" blared Steve, wielding the knife.

The sting of the sharp knife made Clyde wince and cry out, but he held as still as he could. Blood streamed down his face as Steve bent low and worked feverishly to suck out the venom.

Deputy Sheriff Wes Domire and his four-year-old son were enjoying a few hours together, allotted in kindness by Storey County Sheriff Chuck Wyler. Domire had rented the team and wagon from one of Virginia City's hostlers so that he and his son could see some of the country around their new home.

The boy was on the seat beside his father when Domire spotted a lone horse off the side of the trail. It wore saddle and bridle, which made him wonder what had happened to the rider. Seconds later, he spotted a second riderless horse about a hundred yards farther up the trail near a large boulder. And he saw a man on his knees, bending over a man who lay flat on his back.

If someone was in trouble, Domire wanted to be of help. He also realized there could be danger. "Son, I want you to climb back in the bed of the wagon and lie down flat," he said, patting the boy on the head.

"Why, Daddy?"

"I've got to stop up here and talk to a couple of men. I'm not sure what I'll find, so I want you down and out of sight. Don't even raise your head until I tell you to, okay?"

"Yes, sir," replied the boy, hurrying to obey.

When the child was flat in the bed next to the seat, Domire headed for the two men and said, "Don't make any noise, either, son."

"I won't, Daddy."

"Promise?"

"Promise."

"Good boy."

Steve Heglund glanced over his shoulder at the wagon and team as it came to a halt. At the reins he saw a dark-haired, clean-shaven young man wearing a broad-brimmed hat.

As the man was climbing from the wagon seat, Clyde let out a piteous wail. "Somethin's happenin' to my eyes! I can't see good! Don't let me die, Steve! Don't let me die!"

Steve cast another glance at the wagon and saw its driver moving his direction, then turned his attention back to Clyde. "It'll be all right," he assured him. "It'll be all right."

As Wes Domire strode toward the two men, his eye caught the canvas money bags tied to Steve's saddlehorn. He saw *Bank of Stillwater* on one of the bags and suspected he had come upon a pair of bank robbers. He lowered his hand over the butt of his

Colt .45 and proceeded slowly.

Steve looked back at the approaching man and saw the sun glint off his badge. He didn't know why a lawman would come after them in a wagon, but the moment was too tense for deliberation.

Clyde's whining filled the hot air as Steve—his body turned so that his gun was out of the lawman's sight—slowly drew his gun and cocked the hammer. He noted that the lawman was holding his hand in ready position over his gun butt. The man was almost in point-blank range; there was only one thing to do.

"My brother just got bit by a rattler and—" Steve cut off his own words as he brought the gun to bear and fired, hitting Wes Domire in the midsection.

The deputy's instincts had his weapon out of the holster, but it slipped from his fingers when he jack-knifed from the impact of the .45 slug. His knees buckled, and he went down.

Steve kicked the deputy's revolver out of reach and was about to put a bullet in Domire's head when Clyde began to gag and choke, his face turning deep purple.

Quickly, Steve knelt over him. The venom was assaulting Clyde's brain, throwing him into convulsions. Steve's mind was spinning. There was nothing he could do for his brother. Clyde was going to die. There could be other lawmen in the area who might have heard the shot. He looked down at the deputy, who lay in a heap, barely moving.

Panic set in. Steve had to get out of there. Holstering his gun, he dashed to his horse and swung into the saddle. Without looking back, he galloped to Clyde's horse, relieved it of the money bags that hung from the saddlehorn, and sped away toward Virginia City. He had enough money to live like a king anywhere he chose. Maybe California. He would decide on that later. The main thing now was to have his revenge on Jack Reynolds.

In the wagon, the frightened little boy raised his head over the seat of the wagon. When he saw his father lying on the ground, he cried, "Daddy!" and went over the side.

His father was lying in a fetal position, clutching his mid-section. Blood was running through his fingers.

"Daddy!" cried the boy. "That bad man shot you!"

"Yes," Domire said through his teeth, struggling to rise. "I've got...to get into the wagon...find the doctor."

"Come on, Daddy, I'll help you."

Though the four-year-old's strength was small, Wes Domire was glad for it as he made it to his feet and staggered to the wagon. "You go ahead and get in, son," he said. "I need to lean on the wagon a minute before I...try it."

"I'll help, Daddy," insisted the lad.

"No, son...I'll do it. Just get in so we can move out as soon as I'm in the seat."

While the boy was using the spokes on the left front wheel to climb up to the seat, Domire heard hoofbeats coming from the east. He turned to see a lone rider skidding to a halt. The rider slid from his saddle, glanced at the man on the ground, then hurried to the deputy, whom he could see was shot.

Layne Dalton saw the badge on the wounded man's chest and said, "I heard shots and came as fast as I could. Did the other one get away?"

"Yes," Domire nodded. "I'm sure these men are bank robbers. The other one had a money bag with the Stillwater bank's name on it."

"They're more than bank robbers. They're cold-blooded killers. I've been on their trail for a long time."

"Are...are you a lawman?"

"No. I'll have to explain later. Here, let me help you into the back of the wagon. We'll get you into town as fast as we can."

Layne picked the lawman up like he would a child and carefully lowered him into the wagon bed. When he had made him as comfortable as possible, he looked at the white-faced little boy. "This your daddy, son?"

"Yes, sir," replied the child, his eyes teary and his lips quivering.

Dalton picked him up, held him close, and said, "We'll get your daddy to the doctor."

The child hugged Dalton's neck, then said, "I want to ride back there with Daddy."

"Sure," said Dalton, setting him on the floor of the bed.

"Right in the belly, is it?" he said, looking down at the wounded man.

"Yeah. Went through my belt buckle."

"Can you hold the wound closed?"

"I think so."

"Okay. Let me check on Clyde over there and we'll go. What's the matter with him? I see blood on his face."

"The other one said he'd been bitten by a rattler."

Layne rushed to Clyde, who lay still, barely breathing. When he saw where the snake had bitten him, he knew the man was a goner.

"Clyde…"

The dying man looked up with languid eyes and focused on the speaker. His eyes widened in fear. He found his voice and choked, "It…can't…be!" He grimaced and stopped breathing. His sightless eyes stared at the cloudless sky.

Well, God, Layne said, turning away, *You got ahead of me again. And You've given me another delay. I know I'm a no-good sinner, but I'm asking you anyhow—please don't let Steve get to Jack…or the women.*

"He going to live?" the deputy asked as Layne tied his horse to the rear of the wagon.

"He's dead. I'll leave his body for the buzzards."

Layne noticed that the boy had eyes and hair the same color as his. A sharp pain lanced his heart. Would his little Danny have looked as much like him as this little boy did?

Layne climbed into the seat and took the reins in hand, then looked over his shoulder and said, "I didn't ask your name, Deputy."

"Wesley. Wesley Domire."

"Well, Deputy Domire, I'd like to put these horses to a gallop, but I'm afraid all the hard bouncing would do you more damage than taking a reasonable pace."

"Just go easy," replied Domire. "I'm losing blood, but not as fast as when I was first shot."

"We'll get you there," Dalton said, and put the horses into motion.

As they moved slowly toward Virginia City, Domire asked about Dalton's pursuit of the bank robbers. Since there was time, Layne began his story from the time the Heglund brothers murdered Melody's brother. When he told the part about his unborn son's death, he swallowed hard and said, "We were going to name him Danny."

"Really?"

"Yes, sir."

"Well," said Domire, "Dannys are special boys. I guess I didn't tell you, this little guy's name is Danny."

Layne looked over his shoulder, forced down the lump in his throat, smiled and said to the youngster, "With that name, you *have* to be special." Layne then finished his story, bringing Domire up to the moment.

"I'm sorry about this situation, Major," the deputy said. "If you weren't waylaid by getting me to the doctor, you would be breathing down Steve Heglund's neck by now. I hope something happens to keep him from your father-in-law."

"Me, too." Layne paused a moment, then asked, "Do you and your wife have other children besides Danny?"

The wagon hit a hard bump, and Domire gritted his teeth in reaction to the pain.

"There's only Danny and me, Major," Domire managed to reply. "My wife, Laura, died giving birth to him four years ago."

"Oh. I'm sorry."

"Thank you. Danny and I arrived here just eight days ago from Fresno. Sheriff Wyler is planning to retire at the end of this term, and he contacted me, asking if I'd come and take the job as his deputy. He says that with his recommendation, I'll be voted in as Storey County sheriff, hands down."

"Sounds good," Dalton said over his shoulder. "Main thing right now is to get you to that doctor."

When Layne drove the wagon into Virginia City, Wes Domire had taken a turn for the worse; he was losing blood fast. The deputy directed Layne to the doctor's office.

They pulled up in front of Dr. Jacob Meyer's office, and people on the street watched as Layne helped Danny down, then carried the wounded deputy into the doctor's office with Danny following.

Someone on the street said, "I'll go get the sheriff!"

A crowd began to collect in front of Dr. Meyer's office. Word was spreading fast that the new deputy had been brought in, wounded and bleeding, by a stranger.

Layne was ushered quickly into the examining room and laid Domire on the examining table. Then he stood by, holding little Danny Domire in his arms while the doctor made a hasty examination of the wound.

Wes's pain was growing worse. With teeth clenched, he did his best not to cry out. The small boy looked on, fearful for his father. Layne held him tight, patting him and speaking soft words of encouragement.

Teeth still clenched, Domire looked up at Dr. Meyer. "What do you think, Doctor?"

Meyer glanced at his nurse on the other side of the table, then replied, "You've lost an awful lot of blood, Deputy. An awful lot."

"More than I thought, I guess."

The doctor did not comment.

"Daddy," the boy said, fear written all over his face. "I want you to be all better!"

Layne patted him, squeezing him tighter.

Dr. Meyer raised his eyes to Layne, and he saw the sadness there. Little Danny's father was not going to make it.

CHAPTER TWENTY-ONE

✦

Steve Heglund rode up to the Reynolds Mining Company office and left the reins looped over his saddlehorn. If he found Reynolds in his office, he would make sure the man knew he was killing him for murdering his father, then gun him down. He would bolt for his horse and ride away, knowing he had paid Jack Reynolds in full for murdering his father.

Hard-faced miners were milling about the grounds, some carrying mining tools. As Heglund approached the log building, a miner was headed straight for him.

"Say, could you tell me where I might find Mr. Reynolds?" Steve asked.

"I don't know whether you mean Hank or Jack, but both of 'em are on their way to California. Sacramento."

Heglund's countenance fell. "Oh. Do you know when they're expected back?"

"About a week."

"That long, eh?" said Steve, rubbing the back of his neck.

"Ed Dorrenson is in the office. He's the office manager. I don't know what you need, but he can probably help you."

"Oh, uh…no…I need to see Jack. Thanks."

"You bet," said the miner, and went on his way.

Heglund cursed under his breath. All he could do now was hole up in one of Virginia City's hotels and wait. He would get the most expensive room in town, stash the money in the room, then get himself a good hot meal.

Layne Dalton stood in Dr. Jacob Meyer's office with Danny Domire in his arms. Sheriff Chuck Wyler stood beside him.

The wounded deputy could see it in Meyer's eyes. He was in real trouble. Looking up at him, he said, "Doctor, don't…don't hold back on me. It's bad, isn't it?"

The nurse turned and walked away, knowing there was nothing more that could be done.

The doctor nodded grimly. "It *is* bad. When the slug chewed through your belt buckle, it carried myriad little metal slivers with it. The slug's lodged next to your spine, and it really tore up your insides. I—"

"I'm losing a lot of blood, aren't I?"

Meyer cleared his throat. "Yes. You're hemorrhaging badly."

"There's nothing you can do?"

The physician's features were ashen. He moved his head back and forth slowly and spoke with a dry tongue. "No."

The child in Dalton's arms understood that his father's condition was serious. "Daddy!" he cried, reaching for him. Layne lowered the boy and let him wrap his arms around the deputy's neck.

Wes embraced his son. His voice came out cracked and broken. "Danny. Danny, I love you."

"I love you, too, Daddy. Please be all right."

The dying man held his boy for a long moment. There was blood on the child's shirt and pants as his father eased him back, saying, "Let Major Dalton hold you again, will you, son?"

Danny reached for the man he had come to trust in a very short time.

"I'm sorry, Wes," Sheriff Wyler said. "So sorry."

Wes Domire lifted his gaze to the man who held his son. Danny was clinging to his neck. "Major..."

"Yes?"

"I...I have to ask you a monumental favor."

"You name it," Layne nodded.

Wes licked his lips. "I told you...Danny and I have only been here a little more than a week. I...hardly know anyone in town."

"I understand."

"I have no family anywhere. Since...since your Danny died...would you and your wife take my Danny and raise him as your own son? I...can see that he already loves you and trusts you."

Layne Dalton's mind was awhirl. None of this seemed real. He didn't know what to say.

"He can even have your name...if you wish."

Danny was weeping, not understanding his father's intent. Layne was fighting tears of his own. He thought of Melody. He knew she would love Danny and would be happy to become his mother.

Layne's throat kept constricting on him. He turned to Wyler and asked, "Sheriff, is there some legal process here?"

"No," Wyler replied, shaking his head. "This is the Wild West, Major. If you're of a mind to comply with Wes's request, Doc and I can stand as witnesses to it. We'll even sign a paper to that effect, if you'd like. That way, nobody could ever give you a problem about it. You can make his last name Dalton officially, if you wish."

The child had his face buried against Dalton's neck, soaking it with his tears.

"Maybe we'll make it Daniel Domire Dalton."

"You...will do it then, Major?" asked Wes.

"Yes. Before you and these witnesses, I am adopting this boy in the name of my wife, Melody, and myself. I promise...we'll give him a good home."

Wes Domire smiled, then his face twisted with pain.

Dr. Meyer bent over him, then turned to Layne and whispered, "Take the boy into the waiting room."

As Layne headed for the door with Danny in his arms, the boy extended an arm back over Layne's shoulder, crying, "Daddy! Daddy!"

The nurse stood up from where she was sitting in the waiting area as man and boy entered. "Is he…"

"Not yet, but real soon."

Nurse and major tried to keep Danny's mind occupied by talking to him about things he liked to do, what kind of animals he liked, what his favorite foods were.

Less than five minutes had passed when doctor and sheriff passed through the door, faces glum. Dr. Meyer said quietly, "You have a new son, Major."

Layne picked the boy up. "I need to know how to get to the Reynolds Mining Company office, and how to find Jack Reynolds's house."

"I can direct you to both," Sheriff Wyler said, "but before you go, I want some answers. About all you told me was that a bank robber had shot down my deputy."

"That's right," Layne nodded. "Wes said the one that shot him rode away in a hurry."

"Did he give you a description of him?"

"No."

"Then Wes's killer is going to get away scot-free."

"He'll get his sooner or later, Sheriff."

Shaking his head, Wyler said, "You told me in there that you're Jack Reynolds's son-in-law."

"That's right."

"Melody's your wife?"

"Yes, and I need to go find her, Sheriff. You said you'd tell me how to find the mining company office and Jack's house."

Wyler provided both quickly.

Layne decided to go to the mining company first, and hoped he wasn't too late. The sheriff stayed on his heels as Dalton carried the boy outside. The crowd was still there looking on.

"You go ahead," said Wyler. "I'll tell the crowd about it."

As Layne placed Danny on the wagon seat, the boy said in a frightened voice, "I want to go see my daddy."

"I'm sorry, son. Your daddy had to go far, far away, and he can't ever come back. I'm your new daddy now. And you've got a mommy, too. You're about to meet her. We'll take good care of you, I promise."

Somehow the four-year-old knew he was loved by this man he had only met earlier that day. He didn't understand where his daddy had gone, but he had picked up enough to know it was something that could not be helped. He would miss him. There was a bright spot for Danny, however. He was going to have a mother! The boys and girls he knew in Fresno all had mothers. He had wanted one very much. Now he would.

Layne rolled the wagon onto the Reynolds Mining Company property and hauled up in front of the office. Miners were busily moving about, laughing and talking amongst themselves. Surely if anything serious had happened to Jack, the atmosphere around the place would not be like this.

Layne entered the office, taking Danny with him. He was greeted by a rather chubby man, who winked at the four-year-old and said, "Fine-looking lad you have there, mister. Looks just like you."

"Thank you," Layne grinned, meaning it with all his heart. "I'm looking for Jack Reynolds."

"He's not here right now. I'm Ed Dorrenson, office manager. Is there something I can do for you?"

"Will he be back soon?"

"Be about a week. He and Hank left for Sacramento by Wells Fargo stage yesterday afternoon."

Relief washed over Layne Dalton like a cool, refreshing ocean wave. Jack had left Virginia City while the Heglunds were still on the trail. But where was Steve now? Had he found out where Jack was going? Would he follow him to California to kill him?

"Say, has there been anyone else in here asking about Jack's whereabouts today?"

"Not that I know of, and I'm the guy they'd see to find out. Why?"

"Oh, nothing really. Well, I guess I'll catch Jack when he returns. Thanks."

"May I tell him who was looking for him?"

"Can't let you do that. It's a surprise. I'm from back east. See you again sometime."

"Sure."

"Could you tell me where the Wells Fargo office is?"

"This end of town, right on Main Street. Can't miss it."

"Thanks again."

Ten minutes later the wagon pulled away from the Wells Fargo office and headed into town. According to Sheriff Wyler's directions, the Reynolds house was at the other end of Virginia City. The Fargo agent had added more relief to the major's mind. Steve Heglund had not been there asking any questions about yesterday's Sacramento-bound stage, or about Jack Reynolds himself.

Steve must not be following Jack to California. But where was he? He must be somewhere close by. Somehow, after his reunion with Melody, Layne would find him.

Layne's heart was pounding with anticipation as he drove through the business district on his way to his beloved Melody. He kept an arm around Danny, who sat beside him, and began to pray.

God, I don't understand how You work. But then, I guess I'm not supposed to. Chaplain Young told me once that You hold the keys to death. Nobody can die unless You say so. And when You have a set time for somebody to die, nothing can keep them alive. You allowed Wes Domire to die, and You allowed me to find him and Danny and drive them into town. And now…now I have a little son—named Danny.

You took my unborn son to heaven, but You have given me this one to love and to raise. Thank You. I know Melody will love this little fellow as much as I do already. And God, about my salvation, I—

Suddenly Layne's line of sight fell on a familiar face.

It was Steve Heglund! He was coming out of the plush Sierra Madre Hotel, headed for his horse, which was tied at the hitch rail.

Before checking into the hotel, Heglund had tied the horse in the alley at the rear of the building. Once he had his room key, he used the back stairs to transport the money bags to his room on the second floor. That done, he brought the horse to the street and returned to the room to count his loot.

Heglund was now going to take the horse to a stable down the street, then make a tour of the stores.

The flame of vengeance inside Layne Dalton fanned into full force at the sight of his mortal enemy. He yanked back on the reins, stopping the wagon in the middle of the wide, dusty street. At the same instant, Heglund's gaze settled on the man in the wagon with the small boy at his side.

Steve could not believe his eyes. Was he hallucinating? Layne Dalton was dead, burned to death in that tinder box of a barracks at Point Lookout. Could it be his ghost? No! Steve Heglund didn't believe in ghosts. But how could this be?

Steve's pulse raced. He felt an icy hand against the back of his neck, then it moved over his scalp, making it tingle. His eyes seemed to fill his whole face as Layne quickly lifted Danny over the seat and told him to lie flat on the bed. Steve would get over his shock, and when he did, a shootout was inevitable.

Layne was right.

Heglund's arms and legs had gone leaden upon first sight of the man he thought he had killed. It was Layne Dalton, all right, not some ghost. Steve was about to face off with flesh and blood!

Layne let go of Danny and clawed for the gun on his hip. Heglund went for his, but Layne was ahead of him, rising to his feet in the wagon box. Just as Layne dropped the hammer, one of the horses moved a step, jerking the wagon. The slug hit Heglund in the right shoulder, spinning him around and jarring the gun from his hand.

Layne's shot frightened the team, and they jumped a step, throwing Layne off balance before he could get off a second shot. The brief respite gave Heglund time to grab for the gun with his left hand. Just as his fingers were about to close on the butt, Layne got off another shot, though he was still a little off balance. It plowed a furrow through the crown of Steve's hat, missing his scalp by an inch.

The team lurched forward at the sound of the second shot, again unbalancing the vengeful major.

Suddenly Heglund realized that it was the shoulder on his gun-hand that was hit. He wouldn't stand a chance now, shooting it out with Dalton. People were milling about on the busy street. Dalton would not dare fire at him if he could put people between them.

A surrey was parked by Heglund's horse, and it was loaded with a large family. Heglund hurried to his horse, and though his shoulder was on fire, managed to swing into the saddle.

Dalton stood in the wagon box, steadying himself for another shot, when he saw his prey stagger to the horse and mount up. Layne saw that the family in the surrey—eyes bulging at what they were witnessing—was in his line of fire. Helplessly he watched the man he hated gallop away on a street busy with vehicles and riders.

Within seconds, Steve Heglund had ridden out of sight, southward.

People on the street were gawking wide-eyed as Layne pulled the wagon to an open spot near the boardwalk. He jumped out of the vehicle and grabbed Danny, whose face showed the fear that had him in its grip.

Layne spoke soothing words to the boy, then spied a portly, middle-aged woman standing in the door of Myrtle's Dress Shop, gawking like the rest of the people.

Layne rushed to the woman with Danny in his arms. "Ma'am, do you run this shop?"

"Yes, I own it. I'm Myrtle Roberts."

"Take care of Danny for me, will you? I have to go after that man."

Myrtle took the boy in her arms. Layne assured Danny he would be back shortly, then made a dash for his horse and rode southward like the wind. He had lost nearly five minutes.

Steve Heglund galloped south out of Virginia City, looking back as he pushed the animal beneath him as fast as it could go. Blood ran down his arm from the shoulder wound, which burned like fire. The blazing sun bore down on him, and sweat streamed into his eyes.

Heglund knew Layne Dalton would be coming. He had to throw him off his trail and find a place to hide. He also had to get the wound tied off somehow, so he wouldn't bleed to death.

Layne Dalton. How he hated the name! What kind of man could escape from a blazing inferno? All four Heglund brothers had reined their stolen horses to a halt on the crest of a hill that night and had looked back at the burning barracks just in time to see it collapse and throw up billows of flame and smoke. There was no way a mortal man could have lived through that.

Heglund was unarmed. There was no way to simply haul up and ambush Dalton as he came riding after him. He had no choice but to find a safe place to hide.

Heglund's hasty escape southward was taking him through rugged country, a devil's playground of tall rock formations, jumbled boulders, sandy arroyos, squat cacti, sagebrush, and tumbleweeds. He held the reins with his right hand, gripping the wounded shoulder with his left. The desert sun was a ball of fire and seemed to have picked him out to torture.

The galloping horse carried him down into a low draw, then climbed the sandy slope on the other side. Just as horse and rider topped out, Steve saw a dark opening in the side of a rock-edged knoll. It was a low-ceilinged cave, large enough to contain him, judging by what he could see. The area around the knoll was laden with huge tumbleweeds.

Steve Heglund had his hiding place. If he crawled into the shallow cave and camouflaged the opening with tumbleweeds, Dalton would ride on by and never know he was there. Once the hated Rebel had given up the chase and headed back for Virginia City, Steve could make good his escape.

Steve slid stiffly groundward and took another look toward the north. No sign of Dalton. He would come, all right. No question about that. But he wouldn't find Steve Heglund.

Heglund moved to the horse's back side and gave it a hard slap on the rump. The animal leaped with a start, then galloped down the gentle slope southward.

Steve gathered loose tumbleweeds that the wind had driven against the knoll and dragged them to the small cave. He clutched the prickly weeds and backed into the opening. It was cooler inside, and he liked that. He wriggled further back until the tumbleweeds fit nice and snug and cut out most of the brilliant sunlight.

There was no way Layne Dalton or anyone else was going to find him in here. He was safe. All he had to do was wait. Soon he could emerge from his little hiding place, sneak back into town under cover of darkness, retrieve his money, and go on his way. Once his shoulder was better, he'd come back to Virginia City. He would kill Jack Reynolds, and if Layne Dalton was still around, he'd kill him too. In fact, if Dalton was no longer around, he'd track him down and shoot him in the back.

He needed to give attention to his bleeding shoulder. The bullet had passed on through, for which he was glad. No lead poisoning.

He pulled a large bandanna from his hip pocket and started to wrap it around the wound. His position on his belly was awkward, so he rolled onto his side. As he shifted, he found that there was a little more room further back in the cave.

He was inching his way back when he heard a chorus of hisses, accompanied by the unmistakable buzz of diamondback rattles.

Steve Heglund's blood turned to ice. His heart froze, then thawed and banged his rib cage. His breath was rasping in his ears.

Suddenly countless pairs of deadly fangs were striking flesh, from legs to chest.

He couldn't scream. He tried, but the sound was locked in his throat. He thrashed toward the mouth of the low-ceilinged cave, arms waving wildly in spite of the bullet wound.

The sharp, fiery stings kept coming.

Desperately, Heglund clawed at the tumbleweeds, trying to get out. But his strength was already draining away. He could barely lift a hand. It seemed the snakes would never stop striking.

His brain was fogging up. His throat was getting tighter. He couldn't get a breath. A black curtain was descending over him. A scream tried to wrench itself from his throat, but it wedged there and died.

And the snakes kept striking...striking...striking.

The hot wind seemed to scorch his face as Layne Dalton gouged his horse's sides to get all the speed the animal could give. He kept hoping to catch a glimpse of Steve Heglund off in the distance, but there was nothing but sunlight glaring off rocks, boulders, and sand.

The land was level for a while, then began to undulate. At one point, the galloping steed carried Dalton into a low draw, then sped up the sandy slope to its crest. A dark spot at the bottom of the gentle slope before him caught the major's eye. It was better than a mile away, but he thought it was a horse. Only seconds had passed when he was sure it was a horse. Moments later, he drew up to the riderless horse he had seen Heglund hop on back in town. There were drops of blood on the saddle and on the horse's coat.

Where was Heglund?

Layne rode back slowly, leading Heglund's horse and looking for some sign of the killer's departure from the trail. His eyes darted back and forth, taking in the gullies, rocks, and boulders where the killer could be hiding.

Layne figured if Heglund had been carrying a spare gun in his saddlebags, and was able to use it, he would have tried to ambush him by now. He was most likely down somewhere, unable to function well because of his wound.

Layne was almost to the crest of the long slope when suddenly he saw drops of blood on the stones and sand on the side of the trail. They led to a rock-edged knoll where a pile of tumbleweeds was strangely collected against its side.

Dismounting, gun-in-hand, Dalton moved slowly to the spot where the blood drops stopped. He saw, then, that Heglund had crawled into a small opening and pulled the weeds up to hide himself.

"Heglund!" he called, backing away at an angle with his gun pointed at the cave's mouth. "Come on out of there!"

Nothing.

"Heglund! You're wounded...bleeding! I can out-wait you!"

Nothing.

If the man had a gun, he would have fired it by now.

Layne moved up to the side of the cave and pulled the tumbleweeds away. The sight that he saw turned his stomach.

Steve Heglund's hands were outstretched, his fingers curled. His eyes appeared lidless, bulging from their sockets. His mouth was locked open in a silent scream of death.

Slithering over the dead man's legs and lower body were dozens of diamondback rattlers, their tongues darting silently in and out.

CHAPTER TWENTY-TWO

An empty feeling came over Layne Dalton as he mounted his horse, took the reins of Heglund's animal, and started back toward town at a slow walk.

For months, he had lived for one thing: to unleash the flame of his vengeance on the Heglund brothers, especially Steve. But not one of them had felt even a spark of it.

The God of heaven had kept him from fulfilling that yearning. It had been exactly as Harriet Smith and Chaplain Michael Young had pointed out from Scripture: *Vengeance is mine; I will repay, saith the Lord.*

Layne's mind drifted back to the day they buried Jerry Owens at the prison. "So they're gonna bury your partner this mornin', huh?" Steve Heglund had sneered at him.

"You'll get yours one day, Heglund!" Layne had fired back.

"Yeah? Well, it won't be *you* who gives it to me, fancy-pants!"

Layne's retort came strong from the recesses of his memory: *"Well, if it isn't, maybe it'll be God Himself!"*

As he rode toward Virginia City, Layne's words echoed through his mind over and over: *Maybe it'll be God Himself! God Himself! God Himself!*

Suddenly Layne felt as if his heart had burst into flame. It was a consuming fire, burning to the very depths of his soul.

Hot tears blinded his eyes, but at the same time they were washing away his spiritual blindness. He had caught glimpses of God's hand in his life the past several months, but now he could see clearly. The vengeful flame that had burned in his heart would have made him a murderer if the Lord had not taken control. He knew full well he would have killed any of the Heglund brothers as quickly as he had tried to kill Steve in front of the Sierra Madre Hotel.

Layne understood at that moment that the main reason God had taken control was in answer to Melody's prayers. She wanted him to be saved, and now he could serve his new Master unhindered by the consequences that would have been his to carry the rest of his life.

The rugged soldier and war hero veered the horses off the trail into the shade of a patch of scrub oak, slid from the saddle, and fell to his knees in the sand. He cried out in repentance of his sin to the Christ of Calvary, calling upon Him for salvation.

As he wiped tears, aware of the great relief in his heart, the new man in Christ thanked the Lord for saving him and for the way He had worked in his life. Then, settling in the saddle, he rode toward town.

Layne Dalton would take Danny Domire Dalton to Melody and show her that God's providential hand had allowed Steve Heglund to give them another Danny. Layne would take his wife and son back to Virginia and report to General Robert E. Lee for further duty.

The sun was touching the western horizon as the major drew up in front of Myrtle's Dress Shop and dismounted.

Danny was sitting at a small desk, drawing pictures on paper with a pencil when Layne entered the shop. Myrtle was standing over him, speaking in soft tones.

Both Myrtle and the boy looked up as Layne came in.

Danny jumped off the chair and ran to him with open arms.

Layne picked him up, hugged him, and asked, "Were you a good boy, son?"

"He sure was," Myrtle said. "No problem at all. Did you catch up to that man?"

"Yes, I did. Everything's fine. I want to thank you for taking care of Danny for me. May I pay you for it?"

"Not on your life," Myrtle laughed. "We had a good time, didn't we, Danny? He even helped me make some sales."

"Oh, really?" Dalton said as he moved toward the door with the lad in his arms. "Maybe Danny will share his sales commission with me."

Myrtle laughed, walked them to the door, and told them to come see her again. Layne thanked her once more and headed for the wagon. The door closed behind them.

Layne had already tied both horses to the rear of the wagon. While they drove to the stable by the light of the setting sun, Layne explained that Danny would now have a new home with a mommy to cook meals and wash clothes for him. He also assured Danny that his new mommy would love him very much, even as his new daddy did.

Layne returned the team and wagon to the hostler who had rented them to Wes Domire, and gave Steve Heglund's horse to him.

Back on the street, as the lowering sky was going from orange to deep purple, Layne placed the boy in his saddle and swung up behind him. Danny twisted around to give him a hug.

"Would it be all right if I call you Daddy? I love my other daddy, but he's gone far away and can't come back."

A lump lodged in the major's throat. He swallowed hard and said, "You sure may, son. You sure may."

After another hug, the little boy settled in the saddle, facing forward.

Layne's heart was racing. Next stop, the Reynolds house and a big surprise—no, two surprises—for Melody Anne Dalton.

"Well, Danny, let's go see your new mommy!" Layne said, clucking at the horse to put it in motion.

EPILOGUE

✦

The conflict at Fredericksburg, Virginia, put more men on the field of battle than any other military confrontation in the Civil War. A few days after the battle, the vital figures were released by both sides.

Union losses were: 1,284 killed, 9,600 wounded, 1,769 missing or captured...a total of 12,653 casualties.

Confederate losses were: 595 killed, 4,074 wounded, 653 missing or captured...a total of 5,322 casualties.

These figures were the greatest source of embarrassment to the United States government since their terrible rout by the Confederates at the first battle fought at Bull Run. Most embarrassed was Major General Ambrose E. Burnside. It is reported that on their way back to Washington, the badly whipped Yankees were formed up in a review at the camp near Falmouth, Virginia. Commanding officers rode up and down the ranks, waving their caps and swords in an attempt to rouse a cheer for their chief commander, but all they could elicit were boos and catcalls.

While Southern newspapers praised General Robert E. Lee and his outnumbered Army of Northern Virginia, the Northern newspapers denounced Burnside for his "shameful bungling," and even castigated Abraham Lincoln for firing General George McClellan and replacing him with "Bungler Burnside."

The war correspondent for the *New York Tribune*, A. D. Richardson, talked with General Burnside after the battle and left a record of the interview:

> I was not present at the battle but returned to the army two or three days after. Burnside deported himself with rare fitness and magnanimity. As he spoke to me about the brave men who had fruitlessly fallen, there were tears in his eyes, and his voice broke with emotion. When I asked him if anyone else was responsible for the slaughter, he replied, "No. I understand perfectly well that when the general commanding an army meets with disaster, he alone is responsible, and I will not attempt to shift that responsibility on anyone else."
>
> Burnside was, at least, great in his earnestness, his moral courage, and perfect integrity.
>
> Every Union soldier knew that the Battle of Fredericksburg had been a costly and bloody mistake, and yet I think on the day or the week following it, the soldiers would have gone into battle just as cheerfully and sturdily as before. The more I saw of the Army of the Potomac, the more I wondered at its invincible spirit which no disasters seemed able to destroy.

As we now know, Richardson's words were portentous. Perhaps the "invincible spirit" he wrote of was instilled in the Union army by their commander-in-chief, Abraham Lincoln, who wrote an open letter to the Army of the Potomac immediately after their return to the Washington camps. It read in part:

Although you were not successful, the attempt was not an error, nor the failure other than accident. Condoling with the mourners for the dead, and sympathizing with the severely wounded…I tender to you, officers and soldiers, the thanks of the nation.

The courage with which you, in an open field, maintained the contest against an entrenched foe, and the consummate skill and success with which you crossed and recrossed the river in the face of the enemy, show that you possess all the qualities of a great army which will yet give victory to the cause of the country.

Lincoln's faith in his army proved legitimate, for the victory was the Union's at Appomattox Courthouse, Virginia, on April 9, 1865.

At Marye's Heights during the Fredericksburg battle, thousands of soldiers on both sides looked on in awe as nineteen-year-old Confederate Sergeant Richard Rowland Kirkland carried water to the wounded men of the Union and the Confederacy. Both armies thereafter hailed him as the "Angel of Marye's Heights."

Kirkland was fatally wounded in the Battle of Chicamauga on September 20, 1863, at twenty years of age. His name was remembered in Fredericksburg, and after the War a street in that city was named in his honor.

AN EXCERPT FROM

SHADOWED MEMORIES

★

His first sensation when coming to was that of bitter cold. He could hear the wind wailing about him like a wounded, dying beast, and the ice crystals that stung his face stimulated his senses and tore at the fog that webbed his brain.

The solid surface beneath him seemed to whirl and undulate. Suddenly aware that he was spread-eagled on his back, he slowly raised up on his right elbow and shook his head. A flash of blinding pain stabbed his left temple, and lights glittered before his eyes like a shower of meteors. His head swam and he tried to open his eyes. The right one cooperated, but the left one refused to come open. He caught a glimpse of a frozen landscape of white and shadow just before dizziness claimed him and an inky black curtain descended over his brain.

He stirred to consciousness again. His body was numb with cold. He recalled coming to before, but had no idea how long it had been. With effort he opened his right eye again. Looking directly above him, he saw the full moon hovering in a black, starlit sky. He felt around him and realized he was lying on crusted ice and snow.

Pain lanced his throbbing temple as he forced himself to a sitting position. Though he could see fairly well with his right eye, the left one stubbornly remained shut. He raised his left hand to find out why, and his fingertips touched a mat of clotted blood. He clawed at the clot until it was gone and he could see with both eyes.

He found that he was in a low spot on an open field. There was a stand of trees nearby, their ragged, naked branches resembling skeletal hands in the moonlight.

The pain in his temple caused him to probe with his fingertips till he found a long, slender ridge that burrowed horizontally along his temple and into his scalp. It was sticky with blood.

What could have caused this?

He looked down and discovered that he was clad only in long underwear and socks. No wonder he was so cold! Working against the stiffness of his joints, he forced himself to his knees. The silver moonlight showed him bodies strewn everywhere! Some were prostrate on their faces, some lying face-up, others crumpled. They had all been stripped of their outer clothing—their *uniforms*.

Yes, their uniforms! He was on a battlefield!

Now he knew what had caused the bloody ridge along his temple. A bullet had creased his head. He had narrowly escaped death.

He was on a battlefield, all right, but what battlefield? What war? Wait...the war between the states. The Civil War! Abraham Lincoln. Jefferson Davis. But...but *who am I*?

He could recall the names of Lincoln and Davis, of Lee and Jackson, of McClellan and Grant. But why couldn't he remember his own name? And where he was from? He was a soldier. But which side was he on?

He searched his memory for answers, but found none. He could remember nothing about himself except that he had come to consciousness some time earlier, then passed out again.

He struggled to suppress the fear welling up inside. He tried to calm himself, telling himself that soon he would remember everything.

The wintry wind lashed him with snow and ice. His eyes fell on a pair of boots lying a few feet away. Quickly, he crawled to them, sat on the frozen crust of snow, and pulled the boots on his aching feet. They fit. They were likely his boots.

With extreme effort, he worked his way to his feet and took a deep breath. A gust of wind hit him like a fist, knocking him off balance. Steadying himself, he fought off a wave of dizziness. When it cleared, he looked at the corpses that surrounded him. He moved among the dead soldiers and studied their faces. None were familiar. He couldn't even remember what his own face looked like. Another dizzy spell halted him in his tracks, and he swayed with both hands to his head. His breath puffed out in cones of frost. Crossing his arms over his chest, he tucked his freezing hands into his armpits.

When his head cleared once more, he continued moving amongst the dead. If he could remember the names of Lincoln and Davis, and even recall what they looked like, why couldn't he recognize the men he fought beside? The evidence around him was clear—the battle had been fierce, and there were dead soldiers from both sides. There should be men here that he had known. There had to be. Yet there was not one familiar face.

He groped among the dead, hoping to find one man who had not been stripped so he could don his clothing. Whoever had stripped the bodies must have thought he was dead. Or did they? Maybe they were the enemy, and just left him to die.

Cold! Yes, it's so cold.

This clothing search was getting him nowhere. Every man in sight had been stripped. He must get to a warm place, or he would soon freeze to death.

But where?

He rubbed his arms vigorously and continued walking, though still unsteadily. Try as he might, he could not make any of the white, moon-struck land look familiar. The fear that had been rising within him now threatened to become panic. "Why can't I remember who I am?" he cried out. "Or where I am?"

Directly ahead of him, he saw a wide river, shining like a silver ribbon as it reflected the brilliant moon. Following its trail off to his left, he saw the land rise up and top out at the edge of the river in a complex of square roofs, surrounded by a dark, looming wall.

A fort!

Abruptly he recalled that the war between the states was being fought on Southern soil. Then he was looking at a *Confederate* fort, and it was occupied, for he could make out movement atop the walls. He caught sight of winking campfires farther up the riverbank. It had to be a Union camp. Both sides were no doubt waiting for morning so they could resume the battle.

His heart quickened pace. There would be *warmth* in either the camp or the fort.

But which one was the enemy?

The panic within him surged. With effort, he strove to suppress it while his mind raced. If he went to the wrong place, he could be executed as a spy. Anyone captured in a battle zone out of uniform could very well be taken for a spy. If they believed he was a spy, he would be shot. There was no way he could prove otherwise. And even if they believed he was a soldier, if he didn't know which side he was on, certainly they could not either. They would have no choice but to incarcerate him for the duration of the war.

The truth came home. *Either* place was the wrong place. Yankees or Confederates would have to deal with him the same—shoot him, or put him in a prison camp till the war was over. He could not go to the camp, and he could not go to the fort.

Pain lanced through his head. Dizziness followed, and waves of nausea washed over him. He dropped to his knees and braced his hands against the crusted snow to keep from falling on his face. The wind took his breath. Soon the nausea was gone, and the dizziness eased off. If he could just get to a warm place and rest...

He decided to see if he could find a farm. In a barn or a shed he could get out of the wind. He dare not approach a farmhouse. This was Southern soil, and if the farmer chose to believe he was a Yankee, he could still be shot. A barn or shed would have to do for now, until he could thaw out and decide what to do.

He struggled back to his feet. Rubbing his hands together and whacking his upper torso with his arms, he headed back the way he came. There had to be a farm somewhere near. Threading amongst the dead, he moved as quickly as his legs would carry him. He recognized the stand of trees near the spot where he had first awakened, and another two hundred yards beyond them, he saw the beginnings of a forest. He would cut along the edge of the forest. Surely it would lead him to a farm...and warmth.

As he stumbled toward the woods, he noted for the first time that no weapons were in sight. Whoever stripped the bodies also took whatever guns, bayonets, and knives they could find. He was drawing nearer the edge of the forest when something off to the right caught his eye. He stopped, turning his head in that direction.

Something moved over there, didn't it?

Or was it a trick the wind and the shadows played on his confused mind?

He blinked against the wind, searching for further movement among the scattered corpses.

Then something else halted him. Was that a moan? It was hard to tell with the wind whining about him. He held his breath, straining, listening.

Then they came, both movement and sound at the same time. One of the men on the ground moaned and moved his legs, trying to raise his head.

The amnesiac breathed, "Oh, dear Lord in heaven, he's alive!" Even as he spoke, he stumbled toward the fallen soldier. "Lord, please let him know me! Please!"

He reached the wounded man and saw the broad spread of blood on the long underwear that covered his chest. Gripping the man's shoulder, he said, "Soldier, can you hear me?"

The moan stopped abruptly, the head quit rolling, and the bleeding man opened his eyes. Attempting to focus on the moonlit form above him, he gasped, "Who...who is it?"

"I'm a friend. Can you see me?"

"Yes."

"Do you know me?"

The soldier squinted, licked his lips, and replied shakily, "I...I can't...see you that good." He coughed, winced with pain, then said, "I'm hit bad. Can you...get me to the camp?"

The camp! He's a Yankee.

The amnesiac's thoughts jumbled, then cleared. If he took the wounded man to the camp, it would leave him in the fix he had pondered earlier. But this man was in bad shape. If there was a chance he could save his life, he must do it, no matter the risk to himself.

For a moment, he wondered at his willingness to sacrifice himself for a man he didn't even know, who might even be his enemy. Somehow it was a settled thing in his mind. He would carry the man to the camp.

"Sure, my friend," he breathed. "I'll get you to the camp. I assume there's a doctor there?"

"A medic," came the weak reply. A frown creased his brow. "But if you're a Yankee...you already know that."

No time to explain. He reached underneath the wounded man and surprised himself as he cradled him in his arms and stood up. Where had he gotten the strength to do this? The man had to weigh somewhere around two hundred pounds.

As they headed toward the camp, the wounded man looked at him with half-glazed eyes and said, "You're a Rebel, aren't you?"

"Yeah." No sense wasting breath.

"And you're willing...to carry me into the camp? You know they'll...take you prisoner."

"Yeah."

The wounded man was quiet for a long moment. Then he said weakly, "You're a Christian, aren't you."

"Yes, I am," he replied before he even pondered the question.

"I thought so. Only...only a man who...knows Jesus would do what you're doing."

His mind raced again. He couldn't remember who he was, where he came from, or even what army he belonged to, but he knew what a Christian was, and he knew he was one. His thoughts rushed to Calvary—the cross, the blood, the dying Redeemer with nails through His hands and feet. And he knew that this Jesus lived in his heart. This was not only a source of peace and comfort, it was also encouraging. Maybe his memory was already coming back!

The wounded Yankee coughed and spit up blood as they continued slowly across the battlefield. When he could speak again, he said with a voice that was growing even weaker, "I'm a Christian, too...my brother. I thought about it before we...attacked Fort Donelson. I wondered how many men...in that fort were my Christian brothers. Bad enough...bad enough for blood brothers...to fight each other, but even worse for...men in God's family...to be killing each other."

A sick feeling went through the amnesiac. He couldn't say if that awful thought had ever crossed his mind before, but he figured it was true.

His legs were growing weaker. They had traveled about a hundred and fifty yards when he said, breathing hard, "I'm going to have to put you down and rest a moment."

There was no response as he stopped and carefully lowered the Yankee soldier to the ground. The Yankee's eyes were closed and his mouth was sagging open. A quick check for a pulse revealed none. The man was dead.

There was a sudden piercing pain in his left temple, and with it came a rush of dizziness. His equilibrium gave way, and he found himself on the frozen ground next to the dead Yankee. The earth went into a spin and a black shroud began to overwhelm him. He was almost unconscious, but the sensation of spinning in a tight circle seemed to keep the shroud from blacking him out.

It took about three minutes for the spell to pass. When he felt he could stand once again, he struggled to his feet. The wind was easing some, though it still lashed his face enough to dispose of the sweat that beaded his brow.

He stood still for a moment waiting for his legs to quit shaking. Looking down at the dead man's face, he said softly, "I never asked your name, dear brother, and couldn't have told you mine. Well, now that you're in heaven, you can ask the Lord my name. He knows it, even if I don't."

He looked toward the hulking Confederate fort on the bank of the wide silver stream. "Fort Donelson, eh? Then that must be the Cumberland River." He paused, then said, "I can remember the name of the fort and the name of the river, but there's a fog bank when it comes to my own name."

He felt pain in his hands and looked at his fingers. They were deep purple. He feared frostbite. Breathing on his hands to warm them, he moved on unsteady legs toward the edge of the forest once again.

Turning slightly to follow the wooded rim, he felt another sharp pain in his temple. He staggered a few steps and fell. He clawed at his frozen surroundings, but was soon swallowed by a swirling black vortex.

When he came to, the moon had reached the western sky. He was chilled more than ever. His fingers were numb and so were his toes.

Forcing himself to a sitting position, he pulled off his boots and rubbed his feet until some measure of warmth returned. When his boots were back on, he breathed on his hands and rubbed them together until the stiffness left them.

His knees felt watery as he rose once again, but he forced himself to keep moving. If he didn't get someplace warm soon, he was going to freeze to death. He had been plodding along the edge of the trees for about fifteen minutes, scouring the moonlit landscape for some sign of a farm, when from within the woods, he heard the distinct blow of a horse.

He looked into the deep shadows and listened. Above the rush of the wind through the treetops, he heard the sound again. There was a horse amongst the trees, and not very far away.

He plunged into the shadows, using the solid trunks to steady himself. It took only seconds for him to find the horse, a bay gelding standing beside the crumpled body of its rider.

A few other bodies lay amid the trees, and none of them had been stripped. They were all clad in Rebel gray.

The horse nickered at him as he moved about, studying the dead men. He would take the uniform and coat of the man nearest his own size. He was already anticipating the warmth the clothing would give his shivering body. He finally decided the rider of the horse was closest in size.

The man had been a Confederate captain, and a single slug had plowed into the left side of his forehead, killing him instantly. There was a little blood on his hat, which lay next to him, and a small sprinkling of crimson on the left shoulder of his overcoat.

He hastily removed the outer clothing from the dead officer and put it on. The uniform fit him perfectly, even the hat, which he had to wear cocked to the right side because of the bloody furrow on the left. He touched the furrow and found that it was oozing blood. He must have reopened it when he fell the last time.

Searching the dead captain's pockets, he found a bandanna and tied it around his head. He then picked up the captain's gunbelt and strapped it on. As he was buckling the belt, he noted how natural it felt, even the heft of the revolver's weight against his hip.

Was he an officer? The very thought seemed right. But of which army?

The horse seemed a bit nervous as he prepared to mount. It nickered and danced about. Stroking the side of its face, he said gently, "It's all right, boy. I'm friendly, even if I'm a Yankee."

The soothing strokes and the low tone of voice settled the animal down. The amnesiac put his left foot in the stirrup, and with effort, swung into the McClellan saddle. This, too, felt natural.

A sudden wash of dizziness came over him, and his stomach experienced waves of nausea. Bending low, he waited for the nausea to pass, then with his head still spinning slightly, he nudged the horse forward. Soon they were out of the trees and moving across the body-strewn field. By the position of the moon in the low western sky, he knew he was headed south.

He kept the animal to a walk because of the pain in his head. He'd ridden but a short distance when he felt a warm trickle of blood down the side of his face. Drawing rein, he removed the bandanna, wrung the blood out of it, and tied it around his head tighter than before. Though his body welcomed the warmth of the captain's uniform and overcoat, he knew he must find help. Now that he was in a Confederate uniform, he could at least approach a farmhouse. Surely they would help a man they believed to be one of their own.

"Thank You, Lord, for letting me find a gray uniform. Since I'm in Tennessee, I'd be in grave danger in a blue one."

Dizzy spells came and went as horse and rider moved across the fields southward. It struck him that he had used his voice several times since finding himself on the frozen battlefield, but even it did not sound familiar. "Lord," he said in a half-whisper, "how could the loss of my memory serve any good purpose?"

Suddenly his mind was filled with a verse of Scripture. *And we know that all things work together for good to them that love God, to them who are the called according to his purpose.*

"Romans 8:28," he heard himself say. "I do love You, Lord. Bad as my memory is, I know that. All things work together for good, You say. All right. I'll accept that. It's in Your Word, so I believe it. But I sure don't understand this situation. Why can I remember some things but not others? As soon as that poor man back there identified the fort as Donelson, I knew it was on the Cumberland River, and that I was in Tennessee. But why can't I remember my own name, or where I'm from...or which army I belong to?"

He stayed on a southern course, unaware that the town of Dover was less than two miles off to his right behind a low line of hills. Between dizzy spells and intermittent waves of nausea, he racked his brain, trying to stimulate his memory.

Many names came to mind, all military or political. He recalled Richmond and Washington and knew they were the Confederate and Federal capitals, but frustration came over him because he could not remember where his own home was or the name he had lived with all his life.

All his life? How old was he? By the looks of his hands, he guessed himself to be somewhere in his late twenties or early thirties. Maybe. Why would he remember that hands change with age, but not remember his own age? Still, he was sure he was yet a young man. His body seemed strong and firm. In spite of his wound and the freezing cold, he had been able to lift the wounded Yankee and carry him in his arms.

Soon the moon dropped out of sight in the west, and was replaced by the breaking dawn. The early gray light showed that he was passing by a cemetery. He knew there would be names and dates on the grave markers. Strange. He knew he was in the Civil War, but could not recall what year it was, or even the decade.

Turning into the cemetery, he dismounted and studied the names on the tombstones, thinking that looking at some names might possibly jar his memory and tell him his own. He noted that the stone of a fresh grave indicated the deceased had died on February 3, 1862. He estimated the grave to be two, not more than three weeks old.

So it was February 1862.

He tried to recall the year he was born, but there was nothing. Nothing but that horrendous blank wall in his brain.

Once again, he was aware of blood trickling down the side of his face. A dizzy spell came over him. He leaned against the horse and clung to the saddle until it began to pass. He was about to mount up when the faint sound of water met his ears. He looked over the horse's back, through the trees, and saw a small ice-edged brook on the far side of the cemetery.

He led the horse around the cemetery's perimeter to the gurgling stream. He removed his hat and the blood-stained bandanna, knelt on the bank, and tossed the icy water into his face. It refreshed him and helped clear the thin fog that remained in his brain.

He washed the bandanna in the stream, squeezing out the blood, then broke off a piece of ice along the bank. Pressing the ice to his wound, he held it there with the bandanna for several minutes, hoping to stay the flow of blood. When he checked it, the bleeding had slowed. He broke off another piece and held it there until it appeared the bleeding had stopped. Soaking the bandanna in the stream and wringing it out, he tied it around his head once again and replaced the hat.

He was just rising to his feet when he heard his horse nicker, and a cold voice from behind him snapped, "Get your hands up, Reb!"

OTHER COMPELLING STORIES BY
AL LACY

Books in the Battles of Destiny series:

☛ *A Promise Unbroken*

Two couples battle jealousy and racial hatred amidst a war that would cripple America. From a prosperous Virginia plantation to a grim jail cell outside Lynchburg, follow the dramatic story of a love that could not be destroyed.

☛ *A Heart Divided*

Ryan McGraw—leader of the Confederate Sharpshooters—is nursed back to health by beautiful army nurse Dixie Quade. Their romance would survive the perils of war, but can it withstand the reappearance of a past love?

☛ *Beloved Enemy*

Young Jenny Jordan covers for her father's Confederate spy missions. But as she grows closer to Union soldier Buck Brownell, Jenny finds herself torn between devotion to the South and her feelings for the man she is forbidden to love.

☛ *Shadowed Memories*

Critically wounded on the field of battle and haunted by amnesia, one man struggles to regain his strength and the memories that have slipped away from him.

Books in the Journeys of the Stranger series:

☞ *Legacy*

Can John Stranger, a mysterious hero who brings truth, honor, and justice to the Old West, bring Clay Austin back to the right side of the law...and restore the code of honor shared by the woman he loves?

☞ *Silent Abduction*

The mysterious man in black fights to defend a small town targeted by cattle rustlers and to rescue a young woman and child held captive by a local Indian tribe.

Available at your local Christian bookstore